The
Orchard
Girls

Praise for *My Mother's Shadow*

'A well-written, intriguing read full of family secrets . Brilliant.' *Fabulous*

'An emotional and involving story.' *Woman & Home*

'An intriguing, twisting story . . . I loved it.' Dinah Jefferies, author of *The Tuscan Contessa*

'Thoughtful, sad and beautifully written.' *Daily Mail*

'A delightful debut about family and secrets.' *Prima*

'A compelling family story . . . Beautifully written.' Sheila O'Flanagan, author of *Her Husband's Mistake*

'Absolutely captivating.' Jo, Jo's Book Blog

'A gripping family mystery told in lush, evocative prose.' Erin Kelly, author of *We Know, You Know*

'Had me gripped from the start . . . I cannot recommend this novel enough.' Abby, Anne Bonny Book Reviews

'A delightful family mystery . . . Beautifully written and hugely enjoyable.' *The People*

'A charming and beautifully written story.' Nicola, Short Book and Scribes

'An intriguing family drama, with a little bit of mystery . . . A perfect read.' Karen, My Reading Corner

'A beautiful, heart-warming and at times gut-wrenching story.' Melisa, Broadbean's Books

'An emotional rollercoaster . . . I wanted to keep reading and reading.' Trish, Between My Lines

Praise for *Summer of Secrets*

'I was completely enthralled.' Kathryn Hughes, author of *Her Last Promise*

'I loved this touching exploration of love and its capacity for consolation and destruction.' Judith Lennox, author of *The Secrets Between Us*

'The perfect summer read.' Liz Trenow, author of *Under a Wartime Sky*

'An atmospheric and gripping read.' *My Weekly*

'Wonderful characters and a very moving storyline.' *Sun*

'Sumptuous, atmospheric fiction . . . Like having a cup of tea with your oldest friend.' Beth, Bibliobeth

'Characters that will capture your heart. Compelling and emotional.' Linda, Books of all Kinds

'I adored this wonderfully evocative book . . . Highly, highly recommended.' Karen, Hair Past a Freckle

'Rich in detail and beautifully told. Five stars from me!' Rachel, Rae Reads

'Powerful storylines steeped in poignancy and emotion . . . Utterly compelling, brilliant writing. Highly recommended!' *Hot Brands Cool Places*

'If you love dual timeline stories you will absolutely love *Summer of Secrets*.' Jo, Bookmad Jo

'Highly recommended.' Karen, Books and Me

'An emotionally charged, harrowing and majestic novel.' Kaisha, The Writing Garnet

'Go and buy your copy now. I finished it last night with tears streaming down my face and it's all I can think about since. Heartbreaking and beautiful.' Kirsty, Novel Delights

Nikola Scott started her career in book publishing before she became a writer herself a decade later. Her acclaimed debut novel, *My Mother's Shadow*, was translated into over thirteen languages and was a long-running bestseller in Norway. Her second novel, *Summer of Secrets*, was also published widely around the world. Nikola lives in Frankfurt with her husband and two sons.

By Nikola Scott

My Mother's Shadow
Summer of Secrets
The Orchard Girls

The
Orchard
Girls

NIKOLA SCOTT

REVIEW

First published in Great Britain in 2021 by
HEADLINE REVIEW
An imprint of HEADLINE PUBLISHING GROUP

1

Cataloguing in Publication Data is available from the British Library

ISBN 978 1 4722 6079 6

Signature design on page 470 by Tea + Honey Studio

Typeset in 12.25/14pt Garamond MT Std by Jouve (UK), Milton Keynes

Printed and bound in Great Britain by Clays Ltd, Elcograf S.p.A.

HEADLINE PUBLISHING GROUP
An Hachette UK Company
Carmelite House
50 Victoria Embankment
London EC4Y 0DZ

www.headline.co.uk
www.hachette.co.uk

For Sam & Jacob

Violet

September 1940

One

Fight or flight.

Violet had overheard Barker talking about it with another chauffeur a few nights ago, when she and her mother had come out of Sally Vaughn's tea party. Violet had coughed loudly to warn Barker of their approach, because Lady Etherington didn't like her staff being literate on odd subjects, and she certainly didn't like them hanging across the bonnet of a car, gossiping. Which was vastly unfair because Barker was the most loyal of souls and if Mother didn't watch out, she'd be making *him* fight or flight, *flight* right to the western front, most likely, and then what would she do?

Fight or flight was the body's response to danger, Barker had said, when it had to choose between self-protection and escape. Uncannily, it gave words to exactly how Violet felt much of the time herself. Whether she was trooping down to the air raid shelter, practising her debutante curtsey or sitting in the drawing room at night, a piece of needlework slowly turning to felt between her hands, there was a buzzing restlessness inside her, something imprisoned that wanted to burst out and be free.

The fight part was difficult, with Mother breathing down her neck all the hours of the day, but the flight part – oh, to do exactly that, to kick off her stupid satin dance shoes and run without stopping until she'd reached the end of the world and could live in a cottage by the sea where no one cared if she didn't appear promptly at nine o'clock for kippers and eggs.

She chuckled softly to herself.

'Ooh, what?' her cousin Romy said next to her, eager for diversion. St Mary's Church was hot and packed on this beautiful September afternoon, the pews jammed with London's upper class waiting for Harry McGregor, society scion and crusher of debutante dreams, to walk up the aisle with Lavinia Cooper, who had always seemed to Violet very nice, and entirely undeserving to be chained for life to someone like Harry McGregor.

'Just thinking.' Violet fanned herself vigorously with her hymnal and looked back to see if there was any sign of the bride. 'About weddings and prisons.'

Romy giggled appreciatively. 'Most girls would give their right arm to be Lavinia today. Your mother first in line.'

Violet glanced at her mother, who was clasping her gloved hands and gazing up at the torment of Job on the stained-glass window with an expression as close to dreamy as Violet had ever seen on her rather hard face.

'Well, hope springs eternal, doesn't it?' She leaned back, tugging her gas mask bag into her lap. It had been a trying day already. Her mother had spent some of the morning arguing Cook out of signing up for the Women's Voluntary Services – the butler and kitchen maid had joined the war already, lucky things – then mercilessly chivvied their one remaining maid, Daisy, to do something, *anything*, with Violet's appearance. Violet had felt very badly when, after an hour's ministrations, she looked exactly the way she had before: small and skinny, nose dusted with freckles, brown eyes round and hopeful under hair that refused to stay one colour but changed with the light, a shimmering mass of tawny browns shot through with gold. Romy always said Violet's hair was her best feature, but Lady Etherington seemed to consider it her personal foe, which was why it was now pinned back so tightly that it had frozen Violet's face in an expression of surprised pain.

'Sit up straight,' her mother snapped as Violet surreptitiously tried to extract a few of the worst hairpins. 'And try not to wave your arms about too much.'

She surveyed Violet's pale pink satin gown with displeasure. In the dim light of Violet's bedroom, it had seemed the least worn out from the last few months of social gatherings, but in the

4

daylight, the maid's late-night stitching-on of beads to cover the worst patches was all too obvious. Being impoverished and trying to hide the fact from her cronies took up almost as much of Lady Etherington's time as trying to launch her daughter into society.

'You look nice, Vi,' Romy supplied helpfully.

'And the reception is at the Wentworth Hotel.' Violet didn't care at all what she looked like and was only trying not to get Daisy into trouble. 'It'll be dark inside; no one will notice. It's just a party, Mother.'

'Nothing is *ever* just a party,' Eleanor Etherington said cuttingly. 'Most especially this one.'

She paused, unusually dramatically, and Violet was filled with a dreadful sense of foreboding. There were only a few things in life that made her mother look this animated. Surely not . . . surely . . .

'Edward will be there.'

'No!' Violet turned, as much as the cramped space in the pew allowed, and stared at her mother in horror.

The first year of the war had much curtailed London's social season, with balls and court presentations cancelled and a lot of the eligible young men disappearing to fight the Germans. But somehow – and Violet wasn't at all clear how this had happened, because she had certainly tried her best to avoid it – by the time the social circuit had wound down, she had found herself saddled with Edward Forester.

'He's away training,' she said urgently. 'He told me himself.'

She distinctly remembered their last bone-achingly dull conversation, which had taken her through Edward's naval training in such detail she thought she was going to faint clear off her chair. She'd distracted herself by thinking of the new horse Romy was going to get, and whether her mother might ever let her go to a theatre production that Romy's half-brother Duffy had invited them to, perking up only when Edward finally announced that he would be gone for a long time.

'A very long time, Violet.' Dolefully fixing his washed-out

blue eyes on hers, he had clasped her hand, and Violet had nailed a commiserating smile on her face and resisted the urge to wipe her palms on her skirt.

'I wish you'd calm down, Violet.' The effort of infusing a discreet murmur with stridency was making a muscle jump in her mother's cheek. 'Anyone would kill to be in your shoes, *anyone*.'

'I certainly know whom I'd kill first,' Violet said darkly, and Romy vibrated with suppressed mirth.

'It's a big wedding, Vi,' she said soothingly. 'And the Wentworth's rooms are cavernous, especially if we have to go down to their shelter. Chances are you might not even see him.'

'Oh, she will,' Eleanor Etherington said.

'I'll keep you company,' Romy promised. 'It'll be fine.'

It was easy for her to say. Romy was only two years older than Violet, but she somehow managed to be everything Lady Etherington thought suitable in a young lady and yet had everything that Violet wanted, too, including freedom to go out and about in London, often spending whole days running errands like a grown-up. She was engaged already, but to a nice, normal man called William, who didn't bore you stiff with vapid conversation about torpedo destroyers or promised to be gone for a very long time and then turned up out of the blue just when one felt let off the hook a bit.

Growing up, Vi had been desperate to have an older sister like Romy and to live in York Square. Her aunt and uncle weren't much better off financially than Violet's own parents, but they weren't quite as dedicated to keeping up appearances. Consequently, their house was cheerfully shabby, noisy and . . . Violet was never quite sure how to put it . . . warm, she would settle on eventually. Comfortable. Free. The moment you stepped into the hall, it let you be the way you were.

Meanwhile, in her own house, Violet couldn't even go up the stairs without being accosted in some way by her mother, and with coal doled out carefully and most paintings and extraneous furnishings in the upper floors sold off over the years, Cavendish

Place was cold and dark and echoey. It had become even worse since Violet's father had rejoined his old regiment six months ago. He had last been heard from ordering people about somewhere in the African desert, where Violet enviously imagined him striding around in his boots with a cup of tea, barking commands at people and generally having the time of his life.

Her father. Violet seized upon him with relief. 'Papa doesn't like Edward,' she said to her mother's profile. 'He said, please never leave me alone with that fellow again, remember?'

'Don't be absurd,' her mother snapped. 'I've cabled your father already – just on the off chance that tonight's the night, you know; we couldn't possibly leave your happiness at the mercy of unreliable communication to Africa – and he sent back his consent.'

'Consent?' Violet said, truly alarmed now at how fast things had progressed in such a short time. 'But *I* haven't given my consent, Mother. I don't want to marry *anyone* at the moment.'

'Keep your voice down, Violet,' her mother said icily when a woman in purple brocade turned to survey them interestedly. 'Things are not always about what you want.'

'But they *never* are,' Violet wailed.

'Choice will be a lot less plentiful when this war is in full swing,' Eleanor Etherington continued. 'I got married right out of the season – for heaven's sake, Violet, do stop making that face. Ah, we're starting, finally . . .'

At the back of the church, the wooden doors creaked. A slant of sunlight fell straight down the middle of the aisle, as if God himself had planned on making an entrance, then was extinguished when the doors clanged shut. The organ launched into a wheezy chord and whispering heads turned towards the bride, hanging off her father's arm.

Fight or flight. Violet prayed desperately as she watched them shuffle up the aisle. Please God, let me be strong enough to do one of those, or else I'm going to wake up tomorrow engaged to Edward Forester.

Two

'It really is too sunny a day to be holed up inside a ballroom all afternoon,' Romy sighed as they walked towards the grand glass doors of the hotel, criss-crossed with brown tape, sandbags piled up on both sides of the entrance. She looked at the cloudless blue sky longingly. 'This would have been a perfect outdoor wedding. Blasted Germans.'

Daytime raids on London had been sporadic so far, just enough to numb the population into complacency. Still, Lavinia's parents had deemed it wise to hold the reception at the Wentworth, which, with its steel and concrete structure, was said to be one of the safest places in London. Should air raid sirens interrupt the festivities, the guests would be able to wait it out in one of the vast cellar shelters expressly opened for the purpose.

The foyer – grand and glittering, with sweeping staircases leading to the upper floors – was heaving with people. Eleanor Etherington was almost immediately roped into a conversation, and Romy pulled Violet over to one of the big mirrors. Setting her gas mask case on the mantelpiece, she smoothed down her hair and settled the straps of her gown more securely across her shoulders. They stood next to each other, Romy slender and perfect, her hair gleaming sleekly in the low light, Violet slight and currently scowling, tawny curls straining against the pins.

'I forgot to put on my pearls.' Violet tapped her collarbone and gave mirror-Romy a mocking, shock-eyed gasp. 'I think I'll just have to nip back home for them and take a long time returning, long enough for Edward to find a nice, sweet girl to be his true love.'

'You'll be doing all of London a huge service by taking him off the market,' Romy laughed, then she turned to Violet, more serious. 'You know, Vi, you might just get used to the idea in time.'

'Not you too,' Violet said, aghast. 'First Papa, and now you're taking their side?'

Romy carefully tugged loose a few of Violet's hairpins, then tucked a stray lock behind her ear, her fingers cool against Violet's temple.

'Here, take my necklace for tonight. It's not pearls, but it'll fill the space.'

She settled the silver disc against Violet's clavicle. Violet touched the ring of diamonds set into the silver, still warm from Romy's skin.

'I'm always on your side, you know that.' Romy nudged her gently. 'But trust me, it's a lot easier when you're in charge of your own household and,' she grimaced, 'when you have a bit of money for a change. As Mrs Forester, *rich* Mrs Forester, you can do so much more than now. And it would get your mother off your back for a bit.'

'Edward seems a steep price to pay.' Violet shook her head.

'He's just your ticket there.' Romy shrugged. 'That's how it works, a ticket, nothing more. You can't fight the whole system *and* your mother single-handedly. Something will have to give—'

'Ladies!' A mop of tousled blond hair and a familiar grin loomed in the mirror behind them.

'Duffy!' Violet said joyfully. 'I didn't know you were coming! You said you were done with simpering debutantes.'

Duffy rubbed his hand ruefully across the top of his head, making his hair stand up even more. 'Couldn't miss Harry's wedding, though, could I? Mate of mine. Got me out of an awful pickle a while back. We let a goat loose at the club and they thought it was an intruder. Constable chased me all the way down Hanbury Lane.'

9

'Duffy!' Romy said, shocked, but Violet grinned. Duffy was Romy's half-brother from Amanda Etherington's first marriage, which had left her widowed shortly after he was born, and Violet had practically grown up with him. Duffy was cheerfully entitled, always on the verge of doing something fun and full of stories of past capers.

'Don't go all prissy on me, you two. If you ask me, Harry just wanted an excuse for a last good party before he leaves. I'll have to stay out of the limelight, though. Nothing like a wedding to get all the mothers worrying about who's left on the plate. But the good thing is, it's an early do – God bless wartime shaking things up a bit, eh? – so there's plenty of time to nip over to the 400 later. Now, what have I missed?' He rubbed his hands, looking around. 'Why are we hanging about in the front hall?'

'We're hiding from Edward,' Violet craned her neck to look around the lobby, then snatched up her gas mask case. 'You haven't seen him, have you?'

'Not if I can help it. Shocking bore. But never you fear, Duffy is here. Things'll be all right now.' He offered each of them an arm and started towing them to the open doors of the ballroom. 'With any luck, this will be a night to remember.'

'You always say that,' Romy reminded him.

'But who's to say that it won't finally be true tonight?' With a flourish, he stood aside and let them pass.

The ballroom was thick with perfume, cigarette smoke and the heavy scent of lilies. People were talking at the top of their voices; girls moved hopefully through the throng. Wallflowers skulked along walls and chaperones surveyed their charges with gimlet eyes. It seemed the same as every other party Violet had been to this year, and yet uniformed guests reminded everyone that there was a war on. Even the band couldn't dispel the odd, slightly restless feeling in the air, which increased when the air raid sirens suddenly sounded at mid afternoon. Staff came in to move proceedings downstairs, where it got more crowded and louder by the time the last stragglers were inside.

Nerves mounted at the booming and crashing noises above them, seemingly more intense than usual, but Violet was only relieved that, for the moment, Edward was nowhere to be seen, even after the all-clear had sounded and they'd trooped back upstairs. She had just begun to cautiously exhale when Duffy materialised next to her.

'Duck, Vi, I just saw him.'

Instantly Violet sagged down behind Duffy's broad back.

'Violet, whatever are you doing?' Eleanor Etherington barked from behind her. 'And Dudley,' she fixed him with a suspicious stare, 'how nice to see you.'

'Wouldn't have missed it for the world, Aunt.' Duffy loomed over Lady Etherington's hand, giving Violet a cheeky wink, then reached for his cigarette packet. Across the room, Edward Forester's pale blue eyes had now homed in on their target.

'Oh no,' Violet moaned when he started moving, dipping his head with a polite smile here, a neat bow there.

'God, he's good at this,' Duffy muttered. 'There's no way that man was born the way we all were, you know, with all the screaming and the blood—'

'For heaven's sake, Duff!' Romy slipped her arm through Violet's. 'Remember, he's your ticket,' she whispered.

But watching his approach, Violet couldn't remember why that was a good thing at all. Her future was right there, in the excited sheen on her mother's face, the determined set of Edward's pale features. They would dance, her mother nodding her benevolence in time with the music. There would be glasses of lemonade pressed into her hand, dances stood out if Violet appeared tired. And more. A wedding, much like this one. Exiting the church through a tunnel flanked by Edward's naval chums. Children raised by Nanny, who'd already raised Violet and her father, and who would probably pass into nanny heaven while reaching for a stack of nappies from the airing cupboard. And then, twenty years from now, Violet would be standing exactly where Eleanor Etherington stood now, watching her own daughter do the whole thing all over again, if, God willing, they survived the war.

'Violet, how very nice to see you.' Edward bobbed a perfect bow.

'Yes, lovely,' she said dully. 'I thought you were due for training . . .'

'I was going to be, but we've had to relocate – oh, don't press me, Hitler wants to know, wink wink, but it afforded me a few days' stay in London. Would you like to dance?'

One of Edward's more redeeming qualities was that he didn't require her to say too much as they shunted in time with all the other couples crammed onto the smoky dance floor.

As a child, she'd had a music box with small ice-skating figures turning under a glass dome, white paper dots flurrying around them in make-believe snow. She had loved watching them, the tiny skirted figures with their hands in a muff, the men in long black coats, their feet stretched out behind, hands linked as they turned, always the same route, the small red gashes of their mouths open in endless silent merriment. Now, among the crowd of people jostling around her, she remembered the way the glass dome had distorted the garish putty faces and had to blink hard to dispel the sense of being trapped inside that globe herself, unfit for ever doing anything but stretching one leg behind her, holding hands with her putty man and turning on the blue-painted lake for all eternity.

She searched for Romy, saw her dancing, spotted Duffy by the door.

The door . . .

'Actually,' Edward said, 'there is something I'd like to talk to you about, Violet.' He dropped his voice to a throaty murmur and grasped her hand. 'Maybe later, if we had a minute, we could slip away. And don't worry, your mother knows you're safe with me.'

Abruptly, she stopped, pulled her hand out of his.

'Will you excuse me?' she said. 'Need to ... powder my nose ... the cloakroom ...' And without another word, she turned and pushed through the throng towards the door.

'It's not working, that ticket-to-freedom speech, Romy. It's just not.' Violet tugged at the bodice of her dress to give herself more room to breathe, tossing her gas mask on the ground. 'Have a look and see if Mother's coming.'

Romy obediently stuck her head outside the little nook Violet had dragged her into, but the lower floors of the hotel were vast, and people were rushing and agitated, talking in anxious voices. No one paid them the least attention. 'The coast is clear,' she said. 'Oh no, wait, there's Duffy.'

'Hiding, are we?' Duffy slid into their small space and expertly rearranged the folds of the drapes. 'Can't say I blame you. All that air of expectation, and Edward mooning about like a love-sick calf.'

'You're no help, Duffy,' Romy said impatiently.

'I'm not going back,' Violet said wildly. 'He's asked me to *talk*.'

'Can't stay in here,' Duffy said reasonably. 'Bit of a tight squeeze, to be honest.'

Music drifted into their little nook. '"I Hadn't Anyone Till You" is my favourite tune,' Edward had said just before. 'What is yours, Violet?' She saw herself sitting at a polished cherry-wood dining table with a greying Edward across from her. *Charles Dickens is my favourite author. What is yours, Violet?* And her mother, who'd got her into all this, who never listened, who would even now be disapprovingly scanning the room; her father, who'd abandoned her, along with all his promises ...

Fight or flight.

'Let's go out,' she said wildly. 'Dancing. Drinking.'

Romy gaped. 'Are you mad? Aunt would *kill* you. And where on earth would you even go? It's only just gone half seven. I think—'

'The 400, of course,' Duffy said approvingly. 'A drink first at the Colonial Bar. Make a night of it. I'll take you.'

'You would?' Violet flung herself onto Duffy, who shrank back in alarm. 'Thank you, oh thank you.'

'Duffy, no,' Romy said. 'What if there's another air raid? It's all right for you, you can just pop into any shelter along the way, but Violet is barely seventeen.'

'I'm sure there isn't going to be another one. They've only just left,' Violet said bracingly. 'If anything, it's safest now. Oh Romy, please? If you're with me, Mother won't be quite so cross.'

'The 400 is totally safe, sissy, like here,' Duffy threw in helpfully. 'Underground, steel girders and all. Just think of it as a bomb shelter, only with music and dancing.'

Romy bit her lip. Her hair had lost some of its sleekness and her lovely brown eyes were troubled.

'Come on, Romy,' Violet urged. 'Together for ever, you and me, remember?'

'And Duffy, apparently.' Romy sighed. 'All right. Because I love you and I want you to be happy. But if we get into any trouble, I'm blaming it all on you. And Duffy, of course.'

Three

Petrol had been rationed for a good year, but Duffy, who worked in the Foreign Office – to Violet, a nebulous occupation, with his main value being that he knew everyone and anyone – was still able to drive and had parked his small car a few paces down the road. Heart beating wildly, Violet hurtled towards it without looking left or right and dived inside.

'Is she there? Has she followed us?'

'No,' Romy said uneasily, peering through the window as Duffy started the car. 'But something strange is going on. I wish you hadn't hustled me out so fast, Vi, they were all talking so worriedly when we left. And what is that glow over there, all that smoke?'

'Maybe from the air raid. Or the last of the sunset.' Violet gave a cursory glance out into the darkening street, then ducked out of sight again. 'All it means is that we have plenty of time for you to teach me everything. Champagne drinking, dancing, and that thing you do with your eyelashes.'

Romy had to laugh, and settled back against the seat. 'All in one night?'

The two girls were thrown around a lot, even though Duffy drove slowly through Kensington, his headlights thin strips beneath their slotted cover. Violet was busy imitating Edward's horror, making Duffy double over with laughter at the steering wheel, but even though Romy laughed and threw in an occasional comment, her expression remained troubled.

Outside the car window, darkness had begun to settle on houses and trees. Except Romy had been right, it wasn't really dark, was it? The sky to the east, whenever Violet caught a glimpse of it above the streetscape or between two houses, was a strange, smudgy orange. Cloud-like, blooming upwards and oscillating, the orange glow roiled amidst changing hues and levels of brightness.

'Fire,' she said involuntarily. 'From the air raid this afternoon probably, but it's all the way over to the east.'

'You know, I think we should turn back, Duffy,' Romy said, craning her neck to keep track of the glow. 'With how bright that is, the fire must be enormous—'

A vehicle loomed out of the darkness, forcing Duffy to screech to a halt. Violet was thrown to the ground and Romy fell on top of her.

'Goodness,' Violet said breathlessly, as they settled back into their seats.

'To Vi's house.' Romy's voice was urgent now. 'That way, Duffy.'

'Oh Romy, we've come this far,' Violet begged.

'Let's just try to get to the West End,' Duffy said. But he soon fell silent, his eyes fixed on the eastern horizon whenever he stopped to let ambulances and lorries manoeuvre past in the near-darkness. There were a lot of them out and about. And even though Violet valiantly carried on the conversation, she eventually ran out of things to say, and without the sound of her voice, the inside of Duffy's car shrank. She suppressed a sudden shiver as blacked-out windows, papered-over gas lights and closed doors stared back at her impassively.

No. She shook herself. This was her night, her one night of freedom. It was just unnerving going so slowly and not really being able to see or know what had happened. The moment they got to the Colonial Bar, there'd be a band, Duffy had said, with a black person singing, and champagne. Look, other people were out, walking. She tracked the progress of a couple holding bundles, gas mask cases dangling at their sides, and in between houses saw a man handing his family into an Anderson shelter.

'Almost there,' she said emphatically, although they were barely through Knightsbridge. 'We'll have so much fun.'

But suddenly, as if someone had turned on the sound, there was the long, rolling swell of the air raid sirens.

'Again?' Romy said, horrified.

Inside the Wentworth, Violet had been distracted by the thrum of voices and music and dodging Edward, but now the sound was very close. Rising in a wave-like crescendo that fell and rose, echoes thrown back from afar in different pitches, a strange, haunting harmony that pushed and pulled you with the urge to burrow deep underground . . .

'It'll be all right, Violet,' Romy said as Duffy made an abrupt turn. 'It'll be fine.' She kept repeating those words over and over again, breaking off abruptly when the car stopped at the next corner and a warden knocked sharply on the window.

'Nearest shelter is the church crypt down at the end of the street,' he barked when Duffy wound down the window. 'Hurry now.'

'What's happening?' Romy asked.

'Where on earth have you been these last few hours? The Germans have finally done it. Hundreds of them. Thousands. The entire East End is on fire!' Without another word, he hurried away.

Duffy inched around a bus, tapping his fingers impatiently when he was forced to stop to let two people across the street. In a window of a ground-floor flat, a dog was peering out forlornly.

The sirens had stopped wailing, but now, horrifyingly, there was something else.

The drone of aircraft. A puckering, rattling rat-tat-tat, terrifying in its relentless monotone, far away at first, but close at the same time too, splintering the insides of the car where Romy was chanting under her breath again and Duffy cursed in the front. Up ahead was the church the warden had indicated, but progress was agonisingly slow as the puckering above them grew louder, punctuated by ear-splitting cracks and booms.

'Duffy, leave the car,' Romy shouted. 'We'll have to run for it.'

Suddenly, a deafening boom on top of them, and then the front end of the car lifted, and they were thrown up and forward, riding a roaring wave of noise.

Violet had lost her bearings, the noise filling her up entirely. They had come to a crashing halt and yet it felt like they were still moving, upwards, towards the facade opposite them. Her eyes were wide open and she saw the church tower above, a spire, a cross – but no, she wasn't moving, the tower was coming towards *her*, falling, almost in one piece, bricks and rubble flying away from it as it came straight at the car, the spike of the weathervane directed at her, about to run her through at any moment . . .

A hand reached across her and pushed open the door, and they fell out of the car, and then she was wrenched up hard and pulled forward into a stumbling run. As they ran, she looked back over her shoulder, once, twice, and each time her mind took a snapshot. The tower turning sideways. Snap. The beautiful swirly window at the bottom crashing into the nave of the church. Snap. Walls collapsing in a shower of bricks and glass. Rubble raining, a strange pattering sound amidst the cacophony. The car – Duffy's car – crushed by an enormous stone pillar. Duffy's round face next to her, his eyes wide and terrified. Romy a flash of silver at her side, her hand still clamped around Violet's wrist. Violet scrabbled at the air, which seemed to solidify, become a wall of dust and grit she had to push against, and then Romy's hand was ripped out of hers.

'Romy!' she screamed. She groped blindly into the dusty air, coughing and sobbing until she stumbled across something soft. Duffy loomed out of the dust and together they half carried, half dragged Romy away from the street.

'In here,' Duffy shouted, and the three of them fell into a doorway, clawed at the paving stones to crawl into the farthest corner. They pushed themselves against the wall, a heap of limbs and satin and evening dress. Violet's face was smeared with tears and dust, her dress torn up to her thigh, her ears . . . something was wrong with her ears, she couldn't hear, she couldn't see. She dragged her dress across her eyes until her vision cleared, then fell onto Romy, who had sunk against the side of the doorway. A flash of light briefly illuminated the doorway, and she saw that her cousin's mouth was moving, her eyes wide and glassy, before darkness fell again. She brought her ear right up close, but she couldn't hear anything through the ringing inside her skull, just felt her cousin's breath on her cheek. And then another flash of light, and Violet's eyes dipped down to the dark stain across Romy's stomach. Horror started pulsing; she heard a noise, a keening, and it took her a moment to realise that it was coming from her, was working its way through a throat raw with screaming.

She slipped her arm around her cousin's shoulders and tried to heave her upright. In the orange bloom outside the doorway, they saw the stain across Romy's belly glisten wetly, grow bigger . . .

'Romy, no,' Violet croaked, horrified.

Duffy was crouched, trying to see, but Romy slowly turned her face towards Violet, her eyes flickering, her face smeared with dust. She opened her mouth, her breath warm on Violet's cheeks. And Violet was back in her aunt's house, in the nursery with Romy, narrow beds pushed together to whisper secrets until Nanny appeared like a vengeful ghoul. They were galloping across Richmond Park on a dew-sparkling morning. She was practising her curtsey, Romy falling about laughing. *Vi, you're not even* trying.

'Duffy,' Violet sobbed, 'we have to get her to the shelter.'

'That *is* the shelter!' Duffy shouted hoarsely, pointing back at where the church had been.

'Romy, you'll be all right.' Violet found her cousin's hands and squeezed them tightly. If you just looked at her hair, her eyes, her face, she was fine, she'd be all right, wouldn't she, she'd be fine. But Romy shook her head and smiled, just a quirk of the lips, and then her face went slack, her hand fell away from the dark stain across her stomach, the other one going limp in Violet's grip.

'No!' Violet screamed. She brought her face close, forced herself to be still, willing her cousin's breath to flutter against her cheek again. The moment stretched into an eternity of terror, then Duffy reached for Romy's neck, felt for her pulse, turned horror-stricken eyes upon Violet. She heard herself screaming again, her nails digging into Romy's arms, and the doorway narrowed to fire and smoke, cracking bombs and the incessant, relentless drone of the planes that burrowed into her insides like nails, until she was a part of it all, was inside the noise and the dust and the cacophony of sounds that had borne Romy away for ever.

Frankie

September 2004

Four

'You could have chosen a bit more of a festive place, Frankie.' Conrad looked around the café doubtfully. People were jostling each other in a disorderly queue by the counter, the enormous metal tea urn hissed and spat dark brown tea into thick white mugs, and from the kitchen came sizzling, shouting and smells of frying bacon. 'You only turn twenty-eight once, you know.'

'I love it.' Frankie beamed as Beatrice set down the tray with plates of eggs, beans and toast. 'There's even cake.' She pointed to a flapjack, the kind that was tightly wrapped in cling film and had most likely been in the glass display case for a few days. 'And Bea's brought a candle.'

'You can't light that here,' Con said worriedly as Beatrice gouged a hole into the solid mass of the flapjack and stuck the candle in. 'We'll probably get kicked out for playing with fire.'

Just at that moment, there was a bellow from the fry station and the flash of a flame. A great cheer went up from a group of workmen, and the fry cook stuck his head through the hatch and took a bow.

'Jesus.' Con tucked his beautiful tweed jacket tightly around him and made sure his leather bag wasn't touching the floor. 'I'll have you know, Frankie, that I wanted to celebrate your birthday in style.'

Frankie looked down at the flame that Beatrice had coaxed out of the cheap mini candle and remembered other birthdays celebrated in style.

'Times of change and revolution birthdays are,' her dad used to say when she was a little girl. 'Go on, Francesca, sniff the air

23

for all that possibility and newness.' He'd lean forward with a dramatic flourish – her dad was a musician, and thus prone to dramatic flourishes – and little Frankie would lean with him, sniffing hopefully at the air.

'I th-th-think I f-f-feel it,' she'd say quickly when she saw the expectant light in his eyes, and he'd happily lead his band mates in a special rendition of 'Happy Birthday', followed by a prolonged rehearsal in her honour.

'But when we're done here,' he'd add, 'let's make a day of it, Francesca, get a takeaway, watch the sunset up on the heath. And no, I'm not letting *her* within ten feet of you today. I put you into this world and I have first dibs on celebrating with you. You tell her that from me, Francesca. You tell her.'

Her – Frankie's grandmother – was great at celebrating birthdays too, though. 'I thought we could have a party with your school friends, or an outing to the zoo. We'll make a day of it, Frankie love, I won't take no for an answer. Tell him I'm picking you up at ten.'

No matter how hard Frankie tried to do it all, sniff the air for change and go to the zoo, listen to her dad's band and celebrate with her grandmother, she could never make a day of it with both of them at the same time. Over time, her birthday became fraught with tension, joining the long list of issues her dad and her grandmother had wrangled over for as long as she could remember. Frankie's living situation. Frankie's crippling stammer, which her dad swore would sort itself out on its own and her grandmother insisted on fixing with endless recitals of famous ballads and speeches. Frankie's schooling and who would be there for parent-teacher evenings. Where she would spend the holidays and for how long, who would organise her school uniform for when she went back, would it be be second-hand or new, who would take her on her first day . . .

One of the first things Frankie had done when she'd started living on her own was to stop celebrating her birthday in style.

There was another loud whoosh from the fry station, and customers hastily surged away from the counter as a small cloud of smoke billowed.

'It's perfect,' she said happily.

'See?' Beatrice nudged Con. 'Stop being difficult and give Frankie her present.' She snatched a parcel out of Con's hand. 'It's from both of us. I know you said you didn't need anything, but you're always scribbling away in those exercise books like the proverbial penniless journalist, and Con noticed you were running out, so we thought you might like something properly grown-up . . .'

It was a leather-bound notebook. Just the right size for her satchel, with thick, creamy pages and a leather ribbon to tie around. It was sumptuous and classy, something she would never have contemplated buying for herself, but now that she had it, she knew she couldn't live without it.

'It's . . . it's b-b-b . . .' Out of nowhere, Frankie felt the letters start to bristle in her mouth. She broke off, tried to breathe out the words on a long, slow swell of air the way her grandmother had taught her back then. She'd learned to manage her stammer over the years, but every now and then, it jumped back into her throat as if it had never left.

'It's b-beautif-f-ful,' she finally got out. She wanted to say a lot more, how touched she was, how glad that they were here for her birthday, but instead she smiled and stroked the gilded edges of the notebook.

'And now,' Con said in a dramatic whisper, 'for the biggest birthday present of all.'

Slowly, ceremoniously, the three of them turned towards the window, where a big, rather impressive office building sat across the road, three words clearly visible above the entrance.

The London Post.

Never mind her birthday, those three words were the real reason the day had a special glow. Today, they were joining the

London Post, Frankie and Con as staff writers and Bea in the marketing department.

'I guess it's good that you're a fast birthday celebrator, Frankie, because we have to be there in exactly thirty minutes.' Con flicked back his cuff to check the time, as he'd been doing every five minutes since they'd got here. 'God, I can't believe it. Finally I'll be knee-deep in London society gossip, and I'm sure you'll get your fill of human interest love-fests, Frankie.'

'And I'll market the hell out of you both,' Beatrice promised. 'It'll be brilliant. Oh, your candle's gone out, Frankie. Here.' She lit the tiny stub again. 'Make a wish, quick, before it's melted away.'

'Wish for us to have a great first day,' Con said encouragingly.

'I'd like a corner office,' Beatrice urged her.

And Frankie leaned into the tiny teardrop-shaped flame, smelled the honey sweetness from the flapjack, and wished for times of revolution and change.

In the vast marble-clad foyer, the receptionist curtly informed them that someone called Felicity would come down to fetch them shortly and could they please wait over there so as not to be in the way.

Frankie was studying the framed editions of the *London Post* lining the wall, all the way back to 1929, with its old-fashioned yellowing masthead, and thinking about her dad. She hadn't talked to him in a while and she missed him. He was a good person to share exciting news with; he always said it reaffirmed the fact that the universe was at its core a friendly sort of place, which she hoped was particularly true today.

'They all seem to be in a great big rush,' Beatrice whispered as behind them the revolving doors spewed yet more people into the lobby. 'And it's a lot bigger than the *Phoenix*.'

'Anything would have been bigger than the *Phoenix*, Bea.' Frankie grinned. 'Considering that we were working out of Lydia's flat.'

While certainly a lot smaller than the *London Post*, *Phoenix Magazine*, where the three of them had worked until a few days ago, hadn't been a poky set-up by any means. On the contrary, in the five years that Frankie had worked for Lydia Marquart, former TV chef turned editor, the *Phoenix* had become a slick, glossy monthly covering news, in-depth stories and celebrity features across south-west London and northern Surrey. The biggest feather in Lydia's cap, however, and the reason they were here, had been the *Phoenix*'s hugely successful online edition. It had won the coveted Digital Media Award earlier in the year and subsequently caught the eye of General Media International, a media conglomerate that owned a range of newspapers and magazines. After lengthy negotiations, Lydia had let her beloved *Phoenix* become part of the *London Post*, along with its entire online marketing team and any editorial staff who wanted to stay on. She herself had gracefully retired, no doubt thinking up more ambitious projects from the luxury of her new country home.

Frankie would miss Lydia, of course, but she couldn't understand why anyone wouldn't want to stay on. Among journalists, the *London Post* was one of the talked-about-in-hushed-voices holy grails, and everyone, not just those in the newspaper world, knew its editor-in-chief, Hugo Ramsey. Hugo was a legend. A journalistic luminary. A force of nature. He had started out modestly – just like she had, Frankie sometimes secretly thought – but his instinct for news and single-minded pursuit of a story had made for a meteoric rise, which had led him to take over the editorship of the *London Post* not too long ago, prompting a flurry of acquisitions of smaller news outlets.

'Well, we're not in Kansas any more, that much is clear.' Con seemed nervous all of a sudden, fiddling with his portfolio, inside which, Frankie knew, each of his stories was mounted on white paper. 'Please tell me your birthday wish was that Hugo Ramsey loves us.'

'He will.' She patted his arm. 'Before you know it, we'll be sauntering up the Brompton Road every morning like we've never done anything else.'

'Yeah.' Con made a face, then straightened his shoulders determinedly. 'Okay, change of subject, please. How come I never knew you were from London, Frankie? Did you know, Bea?'

But Beatrice was watching the receptionist. 'How can she talk into two phones at once?'

'I'm only half from here,' Frankie said. 'I've moved around quite a bit with my parents. My dad was in a band.'

'The world is our oyster,' Harry O'Brien was fond of saying, 'even if you have to crack a lot of them to get what you want.' Record scouts always hung around pubs and small venues, everyone knew that, so every performance could be that one lucky oyster. A long weekend playing a gig here, travelling as an opening band for two weeks there, Frankie and her mum always along for the ride. Sometimes Stella had gently objected when he let Frankie stay up late to listen to the band playing, talking about music and how you had to make sure the establishment didn't take the art out of the artist. 'Let the girl have a bit of fun, Stella,' Harry would say, grabbing his wife around the middle and swinging her up and around to make her laugh. And it *had* been fun; it had been carefree and thrillingly grown-up to be part of things like that. Only every now and then, Frankie thought she wouldn't have minded not moving quite so often, hitting the road with the band, hanging round the edges of a world in flux where people were constantly packing and unpacking. But it made her anxious to dim the excited light in her dad's eyes, and whenever she was anxious, she started stammering so badly she couldn't say anything at all.

'My dad had a bit of a wandering heart,' she added when a slightly more precise answer seemed to be required, but she stopped there. There was no need to tell them that Harry

O'Brien's heart was not in a place where it could wander all that much these days.

'And the other half?' Con asked interestedly. Frankie rarely talked about herself.

There was a small pause, then she said reluctantly, 'In between, I lived with my grandparents.' Some of the glow seeped out of the morning. 'Down the road from here, actually. Shall we ask the receptionist to call up for us again?'

'Don't hustle them on our first day,' Con said, shocked. 'They'll come for us when they're ready.'

Frankie nodded and kept her eyes fixed on the receptionist as if she was the most important thing in the world. In her mind, though, she saw herself pushing back out of the revolving doors, winding her way through the familiar streets towards the house she knew so well. The stucco facade with its faded grandeur under the peeling plaster, the ornamental boxwood trees standing sentry by the door, which her grandfather used to cut and cut until they were lopsided and vaguely sausage-shaped.

She still had the key her grandmother had given her all those years ago. 'Come and go any time, Frankie,' she had said. 'You don't need to ring the bell. This is your other home.' The heavy door would swing open, slowly and a little grudgingly, then close with a reassuring *thwack* behind her. Above, the vast chandelier broke the light into a thousand shiny shards that danced around the room; below, the black-and-white tiles were smooth and cool on bare feet running across them in summer. The zingy sweetness from the freesias on the hallway table mingled with the fusty scent of the enormous embroidered family tree. Her grandmother had tried for years to sell it, but it refused to find a taker. 'Haunted, most likely by my mother,' she'd always grumbled. 'Better use it to hide this big damp spot here.' And on the door frame into the drawing room, a straggly line of pencil marks had been drawn, starting at *4 ft 2 in*, and the words *Frankie, six* next to it. 'Another three quarters of an inch,' she heard her grandfather's voice chime in. 'At this rate you'll be roughly the size of a ladybird by Christmas, Frankie love.'

Involuntarily she felt her lips curve into a smile at the memory. But then she remembered, with a sharp squeeze of her chest and a familiar ache at the back of her throat, the day those pencil lines had stopped and her life behind that black door had come to an end, abruptly, devastatingly, because of what her grandmother had done . . .

'There's our guide,' Con suddenly hissed. 'Let's go.'

Five

A young woman had swept through the turnstile, clocked them by the pillar, waved them forward and turned again without even breaking her stride. She was dressed entirely in black, except her shoes, which were all purple straps and see-through heels.

'I'm Felicity,' she said over her shoulder. 'Sometimes people call me Fliss.' The last bit was delivered somewhat threateningly, as if they certainly wouldn't be enjoying the privilege. 'You'll be the Phoenixies?'

'Yes.' Frankie thrust her foot into the lift door before it closed.

'Bit chaotic this morning,' Felicity announced importantly as they went up. 'Trouble with the online edition, plus lots of newbies arriving.' She threw them a lofty glance. 'And June Seymour isn't here; she runs Society & Culture, you know.'

'Of course we do,' Con said eagerly. 'I loved her series on celebrity husbands—'

'Save your fawning, she's away all week. Hugo's just called a general staff meeting, with editorial meetings right after.' Felicity started tapping at the screen of what looked like a little personal computer. 'And he doesn't like people to be late, by the way, so you'd better hustle.'

'*Late?*' Frankie bit back the rest of what she wanted to say. It wouldn't be wise to get on the wrong side of this hard, shiny girl on their first day.

'Nice shoes,' Con said instead. Bea rolled her eyes.

'Yeah.' Felicity smugly folded one slim leg over the other. 'Okay, *you*,' she fixed Beatrice with a stare as the lift doors opened, 'are down there, head left for Marketing. Your online colleagues have been here since last week, working hard. You two come with me.'

'Good luck, guys,' Bea whispered, and Felicity smirked slightly, as if they'd need it.

They followed her through desks piled high with everything from computer monitors to newspapers, notepads and jumbles of cable. Someone's phone was ringing and she snapped it up, barked something into it, scratched a number onto a Post-it and stuck it on the monitor, all in one fluid motion. The moment she'd slammed down the receiver it started ringing again, and when the caller finally gave up, another phone chimed in.

'Should we . . .' Frankie pointed towards a phone that was both flashing and buzzing. Lydia Marquart had drummed it into them never to let a phone go unanswered. *Grab it, love, it could be the prime minister.*

'Don't pick up someone else's line,' Felicity said dismissively, even though she'd just done the very same. 'People don't like sharing around here. And never Hugo's. Only I answer that.'

'But we can pick up our own phone, yeah?' Con asked, winking at Frankie, then clearly wishing he hadn't when Felicity turned and fixed him with a withering stare.

'Well you don't have a secretary waiting to take down your shorthand, if that's what you're asking. I'm not sure what ancient set-up you had at the *Phoenix*, but this is the *Post*.'

'I . . . Of course . . . er, I mean, of course not,' Con muttered as Felicity swung ahead of them in a fluid, shark-like undulation and flung open a door

Noise hit them first, chatter, laughing, shouting, solid like a wall, and then they saw that the room was crammed with people. Some were wedged around a table and the rest stood behind the chairs or against the narrow windowsills. Up front, a small group of people faced the crowd, looking awkward and ill at ease.

'Go on, up to the front,' Felicity barked, and Con and Frankie started pushing after her. Frankie had to keep her head from swivelling excitedly as she clocked John Sievers, who covered

Parliament; Miles Harvey, the finance editor; Xavier Merrell, whose stories about the housing crisis had recently made waves. Her heart was jumping inside her chest and her skin was fizzing all over with a thrill of wild joy. She had finally made it. Shy, stammering Frankie O'Brien, who'd gone to a bog-standard C of E secondary, who had never set foot inside journalism school, who'd been paying her own way since she was eighteen and had clawed herself up the ladder, had arrived where she'd always wanted to be.

She sped up impatiently to follow Con, but unbelievably, just before she reached the front, something caught between her ankles. Unable to brace herself in the narrow space, she pitched forward, flailing furiously. Really? This was going to be the first impression she made on Hugo Ramsey? At the last moment, a pair of jeans-clad legs hove into view, and a hand gripped her arm, hoisting her back to her feet. She saw blue eyes in a face made entirely of cheekbones and jawlines, blinked, almost lost her balance again. The hand pushed her forward.

'It's that way.' A low, growly voice snaked through the general hubbub, sounding infuriatingly amused.

Furious with embarrassment, she ripped her arm out of his grip and hurried to catch up with the others. And then, finally, she found herself face to face with Hugo Ramsey.

She had met Hugo before, when Lydia Marquart had first brought him into the *Phoenix* office to introduce her star writers to him: a narrow, slim-shouldered man with a shock of white hair framing a fine-boned face. Everything about him was sharp and crisp, from his clever eyes and narrow nose down to the razor-edge crease of his trousers and the citrusy zing of his aftershave.

'Francesca O'Brien?' He nodded as Frankie stepped up.

'Yes.' She strove for her most suave tone. 'I'm so looking forward t-t-to . . .' She pushed back determinedly at her stammer.

'You're late, angel,' he said crisply. 'Go on, join your fellow newcomers.' He gestured to the people lined up next to him. 'Well, now that we're complete – and make no mistake,' he wagged a finger in Frankie's direction, 'tardiness is one of my pet peeves; I have many, so do try to keep track – we can make a start on our first ever general staff meeting. Don't worry, it won't be a regular thing. I know you all have many other important things to do.'

Chatter flared briefly, punctuated by the discordant shrill of telephones and voices from the TV monitors as a few last stragglers squeezed in.

'But I wanted to introduce all the latest editions to the *London Post* family. *The Daily Beat*, the lovely Glamorous Travel Gals website, the *Phoenix* . . .'

As he jabbed his thumb along the line-up facing the crowd, Frankie breathed in the warm, used-up air in the meeting room and hitched a determined smile on her face.

'. . . a terrific chance for growth and success for the *London Post*. The new digital age – stop groaning, people – is firmly upon us and we *must* keep our online edition on a strong course . . .'

At the back, Frankie spotted the jeans man again. Among the restless crowd, he alone seemed at ease, lounging against the wall, one long leg folded casually over the other. While apparently listening closely to Hugo, she realised that he was actually engrossed in the newspaper discreetly folded into the crook of his elbow. When Hugo gave a particularly theatrical flourish, the man started, and before Frankie could look away, he had caught her eyes. She gave a tiny shrug, which he acknowledged with a quirk of his eyebrows before returning to his article.

'Frankie, *listen*.' Con gave her a nudge and she snapped to attention, but not before noticing that the jeans man was smiling to himself as he read on.

'. . . With the addition of all this wonderful new journalistic talent, however, it is inevitable that there will be some restructuring across the department to accommodate the new folk – yes,

yes, I understand . . .' Hugo held up his hands at the swell of voices, some disbelieving, others angry. 'I under*stand*. I know none of us can bear the thought of losing esteemed colleagues. But it's an opportunity for us to sharpen our pencils. Remember, everyone, it's about the paper and it's about the reader, but most of all,' he paused dramatically, 'it's about the stories. All of us, egos or wallflowers, will have to take a big step back and let those stories shine. Now, what this means,' he raised his voice, 'is that everyone will undergo an evaluation process as of today. *Everyone*. It's only fair, really, to give you all the opportunity to show your mettle. Fliss is circulating a memo with the details as we speak, with a lot of legal mumbo-jumbo for all you union-lovers out there, but I, personally, look forward to a healthy competitive spirit.'

The angry muttering rose.

'What about those of us who've been here for years?' shouted an older man with a salt-and-pepper beard.

'If they continue doing their excellent work, they'll be fine,' Hugo said bracingly. 'And now, without further ado,' he executed a dramatic hand-sweep, and Frankie got the sudden and very strange sense that he was enjoying this, 'I give you your new *London Post* colleagues. And yes,' he added, turning his sharp eyes towards the newcomers, 'the evaluation process will include you too, I'm afraid.'

This couldn't be happening. Surely, *surely*, her job wasn't already on the line before she had even been here a full day?

Journalists whose bylines she'd read a million times and whose job security she was, apparently, partly responsible for surged towards Hugo. By sheer force of will, Frankie kept the smile on her face, focusing on a spot near the door, where the man with the cheekbones was surveying the melee.

Eventually Hugo gave a sharp whistle. 'Enough chuntering,' he barked. 'Of the newbies, you and you will be with Helen over there. All of you' − one of the newcomers, looking terrified, started scurrying even before he pointed at her − 'will be going with Sievers. You lot, find Xavier Merrell. Go, go, move those pretty legs . . .'

Relieved to escape the aggressive undercurrent in the meeting room, Frankie turned and started following Xavier's group, but Hugo waved her back impatiently. 'Society & Culture stays here.'

'But Mr Ramsey, wouldn't I be more suited to politics or local news? That's what I did at the *Phoenix*.' Frankie was tracking Xavier Merrell's disappearing back closely. She'd been late once already; she certainly wasn't going to repeat the offence.

'Hugo'll do. And I want you here, so kindly do as I say.'

'Okay.' Frankie sat down on the nearest chair.

'Listen up.' Hugo clapped his hands at the now reduced group in the meeting room. 'Since June Seymour is away this week, I'm stepping in for her. Gives me a chance to get up close and personal with everyone for the evaluation.'

'June isn't ill, is she?' asked a woman with a razor-sharp bob. Frankie thought she recognised her as Victoria Freewell, who worked part of the society beat.

'We're certainly all wishing her the very best,' Hugo said, slightly ominously.

'I have a question,' a younger man with longish hair said mulishly.

'And I have many for you, Mallory, most of which concern your utter rubbish of a piece on the opening of the National Ballet season.'

There were about six or seven people left, including the jeans-clad man, who was still leaning against the wall, now paying very close attention to Hugo, Frankie noted, and Felicity, who was tapping away on her tiny screen.

'All right, people, let's hear what you're working on. Mallory you're first, although I'm not entirely sure why June's been dragging you along for such ages . . .'

Six

Frankie thought she'd had her fair share of eccentric bosses and office drama over the years. She'd done a maternity cover at a weekly once where the deputy editor had a penchant for throwing office supplies; she'd had a drink upended in her face by an angry interviewee a couple of years ago; and Lydia herself had been fairly pushy, albeit in a jolly-school-matron kind of way.

But nothing in her eight years as a journalist had prepared her for the next thirty minutes of Hugo Ramsey's editorial meeting.

His finger jabbed the air again and again, and story pitches were rattled off so fast that at some points Frankie wasn't even sure whether they were speaking English.

'Fifteen words,' he'd bark the moment someone went on for more than a breath, and not infrequently he cut them off altogether and moved on. With growing dread as the finger jabs went around faster Frankie realised she would obviously be expected to do the same – she'd be asked to speak in front of all these people – but she'd assumed she'd be going into local news, current affairs, politics; she had prepped nothing at all for Society & Culture.

'Francesca.'

She summoned a random idea because she'd have to say something, but when she opened her mouth, her tongue suddenly and horrifyingly locked up and refused to move.

'U-u-u . . .'

Oh God, please not now. Breathe, Frankie, just bloody breathe out the words . . .

'Silence doesn't fill the paper, dearie,' Hugo said mockingly. 'Even if you pitch it in fifteen words.'

Somehow she managed to form words that sounded like 'U-u-underfunding of the f-f-fine arts programmes in sch-sch-schools.'

'Public or state,' he said.

'St-st-state. I'll have more s-s-soon.' She shut her mouth on the lump of spiky, uncooperative letters. This wasn't happening, this could *not* be happening . . .

'No you won't, because it's utterly dull. You're in the big league now, dearie. Conrad—'

'Interview Celeste McIntyre at the Starlight Gala tonight,' Con fired before Hugo had even finished.

'Celeste McIntyre hasn't been seen in public in more than two weeks.' Hugo pointed to jeans man. 'Max, go—'

'My contact says her PR doesn't want her to but she's absolutely set on going, to make up for the nanny debacle,' Con gabbled, holding up a brightly coloured flyer with *Starlight Children's Trust* emblazoned across the front.

Vaguely Frankie remembered something the press had termed 'Nannygate' in which a film star called Celeste McIntyre had got married to great fanfare just two months ago, only for her new husband to be caught in flagrante with his children's nanny, who then promptly sold a tell-all story to a tabloid.

Grudgingly, Hugo turned. 'I'm listening,' he said. 'At the very least it's an improvement over *f-f-fine arts at sch-sch-schools.*'

Frankie flushed a deep, angry red and twisted her fingers together so tightly that pain shot up her arm. God, how she hated that stammer, hated with every fibre of her being that it always showed up when she least expected or needed it.

'Your stammer doesn't own you, Frankie,' she heard her grandmother say in her mind. 'You have your own voice.'

For a moment, the meeting room and Hugo's mocking voice faded and she was ten again, back in her grandmother's flat, the two of them standing across from each other, red-faced and breathing hard, fists balled as if in battle.

Now this is the Law of the Jungle – as old and as true as the sky—
'Louder, Frankie, like you mean it!'
And the Wolf that shall keep it may prosper, but the
Wolf that shall break it must die.

They had chanted the famous words back and forth, over and over again, until Frankie could say them all, loud and clear, until she had a voice.

She untangled her fingers one by one, laid her palms flat against her thighs. Only a few more minutes and then this meeting would be over. She'd crack open her new notebook and put together a list of kick-ass ideas. She'd email them to Hugo and it would be fine. All would be fine.

'Hugo, *I* am covering the Gala,' Victoria bristled. 'You can't just—'

'I can do anything I want,' Hugo said, 'and now that Conrad has mentioned it, I want the McIntyre interview. What else, Conrad?'

'Apparently Celeste McIntyre thinks the Starlight Children's Trust is the best opportunity to get back out there, wants to do right by the charity; she's even one of the prizes. But it's totally on the hush-hush because she doesn't want to implode the event with paparazzi to distract from the cause. The Gala is well stocked with celebrities this time around, actually, so I'm wondering if we don't need *two* people covering it' – he smiled at the scowling Victoria – 'because apparently Celeste McIntyre is not the only recent recluse making an appearance tonight. She'll be accompanied by none other than . . .' he paused, clearly hoping to eke things out for maximum drama, 'Violet Etherington.'

Frankie's head snapped up, and for a second she stared at Con, her eyes wide. He was scanning Hugo's face for a reaction and didn't notice, and Frankie quickly looked away again, carefully smoothed out her face.

'Now *that*,' Hugo said slowly, 'would be a coup.'

'Yes,' Con said, eagerly. 'They're very friendly, have teamed up occasionally for some of the illiteracy and early learning stuff.'

Frankie looked down at her lap, willing the conversation to move on.

'Is your contact actually at the Gala, Conrad?' Victoria asked icily.

'Well . . .' Out of the corner of her eye, Frankie saw Con flush. 'No. But I've been in contact with Etherington's assistant already, and she's confirmed her attendance. I think I can easily—'

'I've got an interview with Charles Trewethan lined up, and I know Billy Simms, the celebrity chef, via a friend of a friend,' Victoria said triumphantly.

'I don't want any half-bit celebrities,' Hugo cut across her. 'Not when I can have McIntyre *and* Etherington.'

God, Frankie wished they'd stop saying that name. As if he had heard her, Hugo suddenly did stop; in fact, everyone had fallen silent altogether, and when Frankie finally glanced up, she found Hugo looking straight at her, head cocked expectantly to the side.

'Welcome to the conversation, angel,' he said softly. He plucked the flyer out of Con's hand and slid it neatly down the table towards her. 'I want Francesca to do the Gala.'

There was a split second of stunned silence.

'What on earth do you mean?' Victoria's voice squeaked in horrified disbelief and Frankie's hackles rose. Why shouldn't she be going to the bloody Gala? For the briefest moment, she flashed back to two voices ringing across a drawing room.

*When Pack meets with Pack in the Jungle, and neither will
go from the trail,
Lie down till the leaders have spoken – it may be fair words shall
prevail.*

'What Hugo means,' she said coolly, 'is that Violet Etherington is my grandmother.'

Silence fell, utter and absolute. Then mutters and whispers struck up and reverberated around the room, Con and Victoria, for the first time, a united front of open-mouthed confusion. Hugo must have done background research on them all, Frankie realised. She had always kept her connection with Violet very quiet, but it wasn't hard to find if you were looking, and Hugo clearly had. He was still smiling down at Frankie, but even as she looked at him, something else crept into his smile, something shrewd and calculating, and a shiver flurried down her back.

'Get Granny to introduce you,' he said, oblivious to Victoria's enraged hissing. 'Cosy up to McIntyre. I want to know what she's been up to, what the nanny's doing now. Get a good soundbite from your grandmother too, while you're at it.'

She could just say no.

'Miss O'Brien?' Hugo raised his eyebrows.

Tell him, Frankie, just say it . . .

'Okay, fine,' she said.

'June would never do that to me,' Victoria muttered angrily.

'June's not here, though, is she?' Hugo flicked his cuff back to check his watch. 'And maybe that's a good thing. Time to shake things up around here, tighten the reins a bit – yes, Mallory, I mean you: "bathroom renovations at the National Theatre", are you joking? Never fear, before this whole restructuring business is over, we'll have you working like a well-oiled machine.'

He dismissed a furiously mouthing Victoria and a glowering Mallory, pointed at jeans man.

'Max, you're good to go on that Hidden London profile, catch me up on it tomorrow. Fliss, give Conrad the round-up of indie theatre costume design June's been dragging her heels on. Might be nice to go with the Globe renovations. Oh, and Francesca?'

Hugo had been prowling the room, firing orders, but now he came to a stop right behind her, making her crane her neck awkwardly.

'Just as interesting as McIntyre, perhaps even more so, is the fact that your dear grandmother hasn't been seen out and about much at all in the last few months. Is there anything in particular you want to fill us in on?'

He was so close that she smelled lemon and mint and freshly laundered shirt and had to resist the urge to lean away.

'No,' she said quickly. 'Actually, we haven't really been in touch . . .' She saw his eyes sharpen with sudden interest and broke off quickly, shrugging in as non-committal a way as she could. 'I don't know what it's about.'

'Well,' he pursed his lips thoughtfully, 'one thing at a time, eh?'

And he was gone before Frankie could tell him there was no way she could possibly wangle an introduction to Celeste or use her grandmother to cosy up to anyone. That Violet hated this kind of salacious gossip, hated any personal intrusion into her life and wasn't particularly fond of journalists to begin with.

But most of all, what she should have said right away, so there wasn't a shadow of doubt about the exact parameters of the situation, was that she hadn't spoken to her grandmother in ten years.

'Well, well, well,' Felicity said to no one in particular. 'I guess it really is all about fancy connections. I'll ring them to change the name on the list, Vicky, shall I?'

Victoria snatched up her notepad so violently that a sheaf of papers slipped through her fingers, and when Frankie bent down to help, she all but slapped her hand.

'Don't. Touch. My. Stuff.'

The others had already filed out, including Mallory, who seemed to hold Frankie personally responsible for Hugo's final digs at his piece and had muttered something about nepotism and *all being well for some*, leaving Frankie alone with Con. He was closing his portfolio with exaggerated care and turned to leave without looking at her.

'Con,' she stepped in his way, 'I obviously didn't *mean* for this to happen.'

'Yeah. Sure.' Beneath his flair, his confident stride and his obsession with celebrity gossip, Con was the most good-natured, generous person she knew. Now there was a distinct edge in his voice. 'So how come, in all the years we've known each other, you never once mentioned that your grandmother was Violet Etherington? That's huge.'

'It's not that huge,' Frankie said, mutinously if somewhat lamely, because yes, of course it was huge. Violet was huge. She was always involved in one fight or another; had, for as long as Frankie had known her, been waging a very public battle against social injustice. Her voice was on the radio, her picture in the newspapers, she knew everyone and anyone. She was on at least three national charity boards, was speaking out on women's issues, against illiteracy, the glass ceiling. Twenty years ago, she'd started a small safe house to shelter women suffering from domestic abuse, and under her guidance it had grown from one flat housing four women to a chain of houses financed by its own charity called Safe Haven.

But what made her so unique was that she had always managed to court maximum publicity for her causes without ever glamorising her philanthropy, and she absolutely, resolutely refused to ever expose her personal life. A blessing for a teenage Frankie, who couldn't have imagined anything worse than to have to play any part in Violet's limelight.

'Lydia can't have known, can she?' Con said, still in that same edgy voice. 'She wouldn't have let you get away without using that connection for *something*.'

'No, she didn't know.' Frankie regarded him levelly. 'And I'd like to think I can hold down a job on my own, thank you very much.'

'Is she the reason you know London so well? That story you gave us earlier, about your dad and his wandering heart . . .'

'Stop making out like it's a big conspiracy.' Frankie was getting annoyed now. 'My parents and I travelled a lot with his band, yes. And, not that it's any of your business, but my mum died when I was six and Violet insisted I live with them during Dad's gigs and things, so I could keep going to the same school and have some structure. I haven't been in touch with her in a while, which is why I don't go on and on about her. That's it.'

There was more to it, quite a bit more, actually, but she wasn't going to go into all *that*.

They regarded each other, Frankie angry and flushed, Con stony-faced, with his arms crossed in front of him. He was the first to relent. 'I'm sorry about your mum.'

'And I'm sorry about the story.' Frankie sighed. 'I don't know anything about the Gala. Where is it even being held?'

'At the Wentworth Hotel,' Con said reverently. 'You know that fancy Knightsbridge hotel where they always film those period TV series? It'll be all lit up and beautiful – and just think of the gowns and the shoes.' He shook his head. 'I can't believe that two hours ago we thought we were at the top of our game and now we're being "evaluated".'

Frankie couldn't bear the defeated note in his voice. 'The moment Hugo sees you in action, all your amazing contacts, he'll know the *Post* can't do without you.'

'Listen to you, "the *Post*",' he mimicked her. 'You sound like one of them already.'

'He promised Lydia he'd keep us on, remember?' Frankie motioned him towards the door.

'Get your head out of the clouds and into survival of the fittest, Frankie. I could read Ramsey's notebook over his shoulder during that speech of his. There was a list of names and some were already crossed out, even before the evaluation has officially begun.'

'Then we'll just have to work hard and show him,' Frankie said firmly. 'We're in this together, Con.'

'I'm not sure Darwin was a great one for group projects,' Con said moodily. 'But we can always go down fighting, I suppose.'

44

Seven

By midday, everyone in the newsroom knew that Violet Etherington's granddaughter had joined June Seymour's team and was going to the Gala instead of Victoria. Not many of them cared as much as Victoria and Con, but enough eyes were on Frankie that she felt slightly itchy with the exposure of it all.

Her desk turned out to be a narrow half-table in a dark corner by the back doors, just big enough to hold a computer and a phone. Judging by Victoria's tight-lipped sneer and head-toss, this was a direct expression of Frankie's true role in the pecking order, but, grateful to finally be out of the limelight, she sank down behind the monitor.

'And before you ask, no, you can't have any of my contacts at the Gala,' Victoria said venomously. 'Here's a brochure, though.' She tossed a glossy press pack in Frankie's direction, throwing deliberately short so the floor around her was showered with papers and leaflets. 'Have fun with Granny.'

'Thanks a lot,' Frankie said wearily. She might not cherish great expectations for her birthdays these days, but this had certainly exceeded all of them. She started shuffling the press pack together and tried to imagine seeing Violet at the Gala, just like that, in front of hundreds of party guests, after all this time.

She spent the rest of the morning trawling the internet and the paper's database to brush up on Celeste McIntyre, and didn't get up again until the newsroom had emptied around lunchtime and she went to retrieve some copies from the printer.

'Come on, you stupid thing,' she hissed at the printer when it started clicking ominously and ground to a halt. She knelt down and tugged out the paper tray, peering into the dark space behind it.

'You seem to be spending a considerable amount of time on the floor today.' A gruff voice came from above and the familiar sight of jeans-clad legs hove into view. 'Is that a magazine thing or a first-day thing?'

When Frankie looked up, she saw the same irritatingly amused expression as that morning.

'Neither,' she said in what she hoped was a forbidding tone. 'Now if you d-d-don't mind . . .'

'I don't mind at all,' the man assured her and settled himself against the printer. 'Max Sefton.' He extended his hand downwards. 'Hugo forgot to introduce any of us at the ed meeting earlier. Which was much more eventful than June's usually are, so thank you for brightening things up a bit.'

Looking at the paper tray, Frankie braced herself for the inevitable mention of her grandmother. But all he said was, 'Such a hoo-ha over a silly party.'

He was still holding out his hand, unhurried and so enviably un-awkward that Frankie finally grasped it. He pulled her up, not hoisting her like he had this morning, but more gently, and when she looked into his eyes, crinkling around the edges, something inside her unclenched a little. Up close, she saw a narrow silvery scar running down his right cheek and a matching one on the back of his hand, as if he'd got into more than a few fights with the neighbourhood boys in his day and was well able to stand up for himself. There was a fluid grace beneath the worn fabric of his Oxford shirt, which was so soft it cried out to be touched. Alarmed, Frankie took a small step backwards. She had absolutely no intention of touching anything or anyone, blue eyes or not.

'Now. Lesson One. A swift kick goes a long way around here. Goes for technology as well as people, probably.' He kicked the bottom of the printer, twice. Nothing happened.

'It clearly needs a woman's touch.' He shook his head sorrowfully.

'A misanthropic printer?' Frankie grinned. 'It's just the paper tray.' She unclasped the top half of the printer and wrenched the entire thing upward.

Max Sefton gasped. 'I've never seen it do that before,' he said, deeply impressed.

'Wait until you've seen *this*.' Frankie reached inside and pulled out a wad of crumpled papers topped by the ink-smeared face of Celeste McIntyre, then replaced the paper tray and slammed the printer closed. It gave a series of condescending beeps and reluctantly spewed out the second half of the Celeste round-up, followed by something from the London Transport Museum on abandoned Tube stations.

'Wow.' Max gave a small theatrical bow before plucking the Tube station papers from the pile. 'The newsroom's printer whisperer. You'll be run off your feet.'

'Yes, well.' Her smile faded a little when she saw that outside the printer nook, people had drifted back after their lunch break, including the still glowering Mallory, who was hanging across his desk for a hissed exchange with Victoria Freewell. 'I'd better get back.'

Max Sefton followed her gaze and nodded thoughtfully. 'Can I interest you in the scenic tour?' He pointed to a narrow door next to them, which, Frankie discovered, deposited them at one end of a long, narrow corridor.

'Some sort of fire escape route. Up there's the lift up from the lobby and those are the main newsroom doors, but this then runs all the way towards the back stairs. Perfect for clandestine conversations or leaning heavily on a source. Or for trying to dodge a furious Victoria.'

There was just enough space for two people to walk side by side, and for a few moments Frankie was so preoccupied with trying not to bump into Max, who seemed all height and limbs in the narrow corridor, that she almost missed his next comment.

'Everyone's just edgy about the evaluation. It'll get better, I promise.'

'I wasn't worried,' Frankie said curtly, hoping very much that she hadn't appeared in need of propping up.

'You'd be stupid not to be.' The soft, growly voice was suddenly serious. 'I've known Hugo a long time. He's very good at what he does, but he's not messing around.'

'Hugo is just doing what he's told,' Frankie said briskly, 'and I'm going to do the same, because I certainly don't want to lose my job on my first day here. Now, if you'll excuse me . . .' She reached past him for the door handle and saw her workspace only a few paces beyond the door. All snappishness forgotten, she flashed Max a grateful smile. 'Thanks for the tour.'

'Good luck, Frankie O'Brien,' he said, his eyes bluer than ever.

Max's words hung in the air after they'd parted, laced with some unspoken warning. Frankie thought of what Hugo had said when he'd asked about Violet's recent reclusiveness: *one thing at a time*. She'd been preoccupied with everything else, but looking back now, there was something slightly ominous about those words.

She pursed her lips and scanned the printouts, looking at the pictures of people in evening dress and elaborate fascinators. She wondered whether there really was a reason Violet hadn't been seen lately. Maybe she was busy working on a project; she often got so absorbed by things that she couldn't bear frivolous distractions. Frankie imagined her at Cavendish Place now, pulling one of her trusty evening gowns out of its wrapper, reaching for the clothes brush to spruce it up a bit.

Chin in hand, Frankie stared down at the printout, remembering the first time she had sat on Violet's bed, warm and flushed from her bath, watching her get ready for an evening function.

Being in Violet's room, being together anywhere in a close, familiar way, had felt awkward when Frankie first started spending time with her grandparents after her mum had died. Her dad was young, more like a big brother than a dad, while Violet was unbending and outspoken. She had a lot of rules about everything, and Frankie had spent the first few visits to Cavendish Place shadowing her in an attempt to figure out what they were.

'Oh, come on in, then, and sit on the bed,' her grandmother had said when she saw Frankie hovering yet again, shyly peering in through the bedroom door.

Frankie's dad always spent ages before a concert choosing what worn-out T-shirt would go best with his black jeans, and he sometimes did boxing exercises to *boost his mojo*. Her grandmother didn't seem all that bothered what she looked like, even though she was properly famous, not like her dad, who was always waiting for his big break. Violet got most of her dresses through her close friend Jools, who ran a very popular vintage consignment shop three streets away and was an easy-going white-haired woman with big swooshed spectacles and a flurry of colourful scarves. One of Frankie's favourite things about dividing her time between Violet and her dad was visiting Jools and sitting hidden from view behind the counter of her overstuffed shop, sorting buttons into Jools's button box.

'You can help me with my speech,' Violet told her as she turned back to the mirror and settled the capped sleeves of a severe-looking, slightly old-fashioned Chanel dress. She set her hair, then did her face, and Frankie watched as bit by bit she transformed into someone very different: evening Violet, society Violet, who told the mirror that *we cannot be complacent* and *it's our responsibility*, looking fierce and formidable and ready to do battle. Violet always sounded a bit cross, but Frankie didn't think she actually was, it was just the way she spoke, crisply biting words out of the air in a way Frankie had never been able to. She and her grandfather had watched her on TV together the previous week, and Frankie had been in awe of the fluid, sure way her grandmother had sparred with the moustached interviewer.

'It's just a masquerade,' Violet said when she caught Frankie's solemn look, and unexpectedly, she spread her arms and did a wide, funny sweep with her leg. It caught Frankie by surprise and made her giggle. 'You look b-b-beautiful,' she said shyly.

'I wouldn't go that far,' her grandmother chuckled. 'But I still know how to curtsey.'

She plucked an ancient woollen throw from the armchair and tucked it around Frankie's legs. 'This place is just as damp and chilly as it was when I was little.' She hesitated, then reached and touched Frankie's cheek. Violet didn't hug people much, Frankie had noticed, not like Dad, who was always embracing and squeezing hands and dropping kisses. You could tell Violet was a bit out of practice; her touch was awkward as she slowly, carefully smoothed back Frankie's fine blonde hair. 'But we won't buckle, will we?'

'We w-w-won't,' Frankie had no clue whatsoever what 'buckle' meant, but the sound of that 'we' mingled with the warmth of her grandmother's hand cradling the back of her head and the pressure in her chest eased slightly. The lamp made the room feel small, like a bubble that held only her and Violet, and rain pattered on the window. Frankie was wearing an old bathrobe of her mum's, which she had found on a hook behind the door and which was slightly too big, so that she could pull all her limbs into it and imagine her mum inside it with her.

Violet looked down at her for so long that Frankie wondered if maybe she knew about the bubble and the bathrobe, then she smiled, not fierce or formidable at all, but softer, sadder.

'We'll get along, you and I,' she said. 'I know we will.'

Frankie sat on that bed many times after that to watch her grandmother get ready. At the very end, Violet always picked up her little beaded evening bag, checked that her speech notes were inside, and clicked it shut. Frankie didn't like this last moment, the finality of that mother-of-pearl clasp snapping together, just like she hated the sound of her dad's guitar case closing before he went off for an evening gig. It meant that she would be left behind in a dark, quiet flat, lying in bed, counting cars passing by outside and waiting.

It had taken two years for her to stop dreading that moment, two years to really and truly believe that Violet would always come back, would always be there for her. That Violet would never let her down.

Violet

September 1940

Eight

'Violet, how *could* you?' Eleanor Etherington's voice was harsh and ragged. 'Leaving the wedding, no word to anyone, what on earth were you *thinking*? Oh poor Amanda, it's unbearable, and all because . . .'

Violet hadn't been able to stop shivering ever since they'd emerged from the doorway, she and Duffy carrying Romy's body, both of them screaming through a fog of dust and smoke. At some point someone came and took Romy from them. Violet dimly remembered fighting against that, because after all their cries for help, she found she couldn't let go of her cousin after all. They'd prised her off and pushed her into a lorry, and after that a lot was hazy and floating, and by the time she looked at the tired face of a doctor, it was as if her body had separated from her mind and her limbs were moving of their own accord. She spoke in a horrible, grating monotone that sounded nothing like her voice, as her hands twitched uncontrollably against her sides. She had deep cuts on the backs of her arms and was covered in blood, but after establishing that it was mostly Romy's and tending to the rest, the doctor had left her to sit on a chair in a curtained-off corner of the corridor to await her mother.

Violet had risen quickly when she saw Eleanor coming, had reached out for her, expecting her to . . . what, she wasn't sure, maybe to be held, told it was all right. Instead, her mother started snarling, and Violet's arms fell back by her sides, and she'd stood letting the wrath wash over her.

'Of all the things, of all the stupid, unforgivable things. Romily, oh, the poor child . . .'

Observing her mother's red eyes, the lines of exhaustion and fear etched into her forehead, Violet strained to focus, because it seemed of paramount importance that she heard them, all the things she was responsible for, all the horrors she had caused.

'Violet, are you listening? Violet!'

'I'm sorry,' she heard herself say, because something seemed to be required of her. 'It was my fault. I'm sorry, Mother.'

'Well, sorry isn't enough.' Her mother broke off. 'Sorry isn't enough at all. And Dudley . . . and us searching for you everywhere, the sirens and the Germans up above, and Edward had no idea where you were, *powdering your nose*.' She imitated him in a scathing squeak. 'Violet, you could have been *dead*! And Romy *is* dead and all because of you, your obstinacy, your stupid . . . Just you wait until your father hears this. Romy is dead because of *you*.'

She clapped her hand in front of her mouth, then thrust a dress at her daughter and snapped together the curtain panels so hard one of them ripped off and she was forced to stand there holding up the fabric to hide Violet from prying eyes.

Black spots were dancing at the edge of Violet's vision as she tried to breathe past the swollen insides of her mouth, push air down into the nausea and rage and shame roiling at the bottom of her stomach. Her fingers caught in the chain of Romy's necklace, the silver disc cold against her skin. She closed her hand around the necklace, tried to will herself to go back in time, back in front of the mirror when she still had the power to change what would happen . . .

'Get dressed!' her mother snapped.

Violet took a step, and then the floor came to meet her and she fell into a void of black velvet, where all was dark and quiet and she didn't need to feel anything at all.

Somehow her body got her through the days leading up to Romy's funeral. When her mother had tracked down the tired doctor and made him have another look at Violet, he was impatient.

'She's fine,' he said as behind him noise from more casualties swelled. 'She's had a nasty shock. Keep her warm, have her rest, get out of London. All I can tell you, ma'am.'

But Violet didn't want to be warm and drink tea, and she dreaded resting because what little sleep she got was there solely to support a melee of nightmares in which she was running, carrying a heavy burden, in a world that was deafeningly loud and orangey bright, and from which she awoke drained and hollow-eyed.

After their sporadic attacks throughout the summer, the Germans were now battering London in earnest. Night after night Violet lay in the cellar room at Cavendish Place, feeling every boom, every crash in the very marrow of her bones, the noise of the planes filling her with a nameless, paralysing dread. In the mornings, she dressed haphazardly, wouldn't leave the house, and refused point-blank to take Edward Forester's calls. The only person she was desperate to talk to, who might make the weight that had settled on her chest lessen in some way, was her father. Cheerful and larger than life, quick to be riled but unable to stay cross for any length of time, he seemed like the only thing that was warm and real in her life. Once or twice she had asked if she could ring him, only to be told that he'd been cabled the news and there was a war on. Part of her wondered if her mother did it on purpose, to keep them apart as a punishment, as if Violet didn't deserve whatever absolution Henry Etherington could have possibly offered, what love he might have extended.

Whenever she came to that, however, Violet bowed her head and accepted it. The fuzzy blur of the world at the hospital had sprung back into focus, a biting, sharp-clawed clarity that illuminated every corner of her insides, slowly peeling away the layers of shock and fear, hardening around the one thing that sat inside her, the thing she didn't need her mother's grating voice to tell her, because it was already there, branded on her insides.

Come on, Romy. Together for ever, you and me, remember?

Heat flooded over her, instantly replaced by an icy cold, and when she wasn't whispering those words back to herself in a rosary of shame and guilt and self-loathing, she felt her cousin all around her, her breath on her face, the faint whisper as she died. That moment of Romy's death, the orange glow, the incessant burrowing noise of the planes above them, the booming and crashes, Romy's long, slow hiss of air . . . Violet couldn't unfeel that moment, she couldn't unsee Romy's face going slack in acceptance of death. It was the first thing she saw when she rose, the last thing she thought about at night.

Come on, Romy. The words had started echoing in her mind, were getting louder and louder, gathering in force until she thought she would burst right open, would start screaming and never stop until her mother had her committed to a mental asylum. She worried about it, this scream inside her, the way her body would be gripped by a tremor she couldn't control, that left her weak and shivery.

'Violet, go and change, Cook's rung the bell twice already. Violet, are you listening?'

'Coming, Mother.'

But her fingers threaded themselves through Romy's necklace or worried against the side of her skirt as she cradled her shame and her grief and the abject horror at what she'd done, and she didn't know how she could go on with it all.

And then it was the day of Romy's funeral.

'We're a bit early.' Her mother reached to straighten the collar of Violet's coat, then frowned. 'You really should return Romy's necklace to Amanda.'

Violet stepped out of her reach, her hand finding the circle of diamonds. She couldn't give it away; she needed to touch it constantly, to remind her of what she'd done.

Maybe it was her daughter's silence, maybe it was her white

face, but something prompted her mother to say, 'You *must* get a grip, Violet. We have to look to the future now.'

Her tone was gruff and Violet realised dully that this was the closest she would come to forgiveness. Her mother seemed to be waiting for something from her, something other than 'I'm sorry', which she'd been repeating over and over again until it had become entirely meaningless, but Violet only moved her boots a fraction, felt the damp September morning and the leafy cemetery close around her.

'And there's something else . . .' Eleanor Etherington paused, and Violet forced herself to lift her head, to bring her mother's face into focus. 'I've finally had an answer from your great-uncle Gareth. I'm going to take Amanda; we're shutting down both our houses and moving to Yorkshire for the duration of the war.'

'What?' Violet said hoarsely.

'Surely you remember Gareth.' Her mother lifted her old-fashioned parasol. 'He lives in West Yorkshire, near Skipton.'

Violet dimly recalled an enormous house that felt cold even in June, the long journey they'd had to undertake to get there, the rolling hills and misty fields. She forced herself to marshal her thoughts.

'But I . . . I don't want to go,' she said.

'Of course you do. Clearly we're not safe here, and Amanda . . .' Eleanor Etherington swallowed, and for the first time, Violet saw an expression cross her mother's eyes that was not anger or rage or disappointment, but genuine sorrow. The two Etherington brothers were not nearly as close as their wives had become over the years, and her sister-in-law was the closest friend Eleanor had. 'Amanda can't possibly stay here, where everything reminds her of Romy, most of the servants gone, the nights such terror. It's best that we remove ourselves from the situation altogether and sit out the rest of this godforsaken war somewhere we can at least leave the house without fearing for our lives.'

She looked away and dug her parasol into the gravel with small, angry jabs, and Violet tried to imagine the coming winter, a white, blank, cold world where her mind would have nowhere to go but back to the doorway and Romy, where she'd be sitting alongside her aunt day in, day out, her lovely, smiley, round-faced aunt, who had aged before her eyes, whose daughter Violet had taken away . . .

'Mother, please,' she said, her voice more urgent. 'Please don't make me go. I promise I won't do anything bad, I'll be so good, I'll listen to you on everything . . .'

Her mother regarded her. 'My mind's made up,' she said flatly.

'But Father,' Violet said. 'He'll be back on leave and want to see us, and he won't be able to come all the way up to Yorkshire. Please, Mother.'

'Sea travel is dangerous, the Continent is in turmoil. He won't be coming back any time soon.' Her mother straightened at the sound of an approaching car. 'And anyway,' she added, 'he knows we won't be here, because he rang two days ago.'

'He rang? You said . . . Africa . . . he wouldn't be able to . . .' Violet scrabbled to find a memory of hearing a phone ring, a conversation. 'Why didn't you fetch me, Mother?'

She imagined her father, the phone clamped to his ear, drumming his fingers on a rickety table in a field tent, or an embassy maybe, and a wave of longing washed over her so fierce that she thought she might be sick. 'I wanted to talk to him, Mother, I *asked* you, it was the only thing I ever *asked*.' Her voice was getting louder, her ears were ringing, and she pushed her knuckles against her teeth to stop herself.

'It wasn't an official call; Duffy arranged it on the side. We had just a few minutes, a terrible line.' Her mother's tone was curt.

'Did you . . . Romy, I mean . . . I wanted to be the one to tell him how . . .' Violet couldn't get the words out.

'Violet, he's in the middle of the desert fighting the fascists. Hardly the time for a long heart-to-heart,' her mother snapped.

'You two, always yammering away about things. There's a war on, you know.'

Violet stared at her, and whatever tiny seed of shared grief had been between them a minute ago died.

'You did it on purpose,' she said in a low, even voice. 'I asked you – I *told* you I accept full responsibility, I *said* it was my fault. How can you possibly keep punishing me when I spend every minute of every day punishing myself? I wanted to talk to Father, and I don't want to go to Yorkshire.'

Her mother seemed slightly taken aback that Violet was saying more words than she'd spoken all week, but she rallied quickly. 'Well, it's not about what you want any more. There's been enough of what *you* want, don't you think, Violet?'

Up ahead, as if through a haze, Violet saw Duffy coming towards them, walking slowly to support the bowed figure of his mother. She had only exchanged a few words with him since the night Romy died, horrible, stilted words of comfort with their mothers close by.

'It doesn't look like William was able to get back in time for the funeral,' Eleanor said. 'Amanda said he was devastated.'

Without another word, she pushed herself off her parasol and walked to join them, leaving Violet standing alone, waiting to bury her cousin and hating her mother more than she could ever have imagined.

Nine

Hatred pushed Violet through the rushed days that followed the funeral, days of list-making and shopping, ears and eyes towards the sky in case of more raids, while Daisy dragged down the old trunks and hastily started filling them with all the things Eleanor Etherington deemed necessary for their evacuation. A futile, impotent fury was constantly churning up her stomach. Rage at Cook, who cemented her mother's Yorkshire plans by announcing that she was leaving them for the Auxiliary Territorial Service. At Barker, who procured enough petrol to get them to Halifax, where he was joining the Territorial Army. At herself when she succumbed to her mother's orders and accompanied her on a shopping trip to Oxford Street shortly after the funeral. But most of all, an overpowering, suffocating rage at her mother. If her mother hadn't pushed and prodded her towards Edward – who, she informed her daughter with barely concealed satisfaction, was very happy to wait for Violet until she felt 'more like herself', as if Romy's death was an illness she had to recover from – Violet would never have felt the urge to break free at Harry McGregor's wedding, would never have made Romy— No. She stopped herself, dug her fingernails into the deep, barely healed cuts on her arms until she was blinded by the pain. No, it was Violet's fault, hers alone, she accepted it. But acceptance was no longer enough, not in the face of this new-found loathing, which filled her up with a restless, furious energy, made her pace around her bedroom, unable to stand being anywhere close to her mother and wondering if she was finally losing her mind.

*

'We'll take three each of those woollen skirts. And where are your jumpers?'

Lady Etherington had sold a diamond bracelet and matching earrings and lost no time getting ready. Her ever-growing packing list included things like new mackintoshes, warm winter jackets, woollen stockings, masses of undergarments and enough tea to feed most of Yorkshire, and for some reason, that list, together with her mother's sanctimonious needs-must expression, made Violet angrier than ever.

'That style would suit you, miss,' a shop girl said encouragingly, holding out a worsted skirt. Violet took it without really looking at it, felt the fabric snag at her fingers and imagined herself parading her rage around Yorkshire.

'There won't be much to shop for up north,' her mother said, because obviously England turned into barbaric hinterlands somewhere north of Bath. 'Clothing rationing won't be far off. I lived through the previous war, don't forget,' she added importantly. 'You'll be glad to have these sturdy cardigans. That's one good thing about this whole mess,' she added to Violet in an undertone. 'No more worrying about expensive ballroom finery. Pick a colour, Violet, please.'

She moved on and Violet snatched up a black cardigan and thrust it at the second shop girl, who was hovering by her side, then abruptly turned away and walked across to the sweeping stairwell, looking down into the floors below. God, what she wouldn't give to be twenty-five right now, and a shop girl like the one still holding the cardigans, to be free of all of this . . .

Suddenly her eyes locked on something a level further down. Familiar round shoulders, flushed countenance, shock of untidy blond hair.

'Duffy!' she said loudly, and a few women inspecting fringed shawls on a nearby table looked up. Violet moved quickly, skirting her mother discussing the merits of wool over cotton, until she reached Duffy, stooped over some leather gloves.

'Vi.' He looked up, surprised.

'I saw you from up there,' she said breathlessly. 'I . . .' She broke off, because now that she was here, she wasn't quite sure what she wanted. 'How are you?' she said instead, an inane question when the last times she'd seen him he'd been holding his dying half-sister and then standing at the side of a grave containing her casket. She swallowed. He'd lost weight; his skin was mottled and grey, his bright button eyes sober.

'I was in the area; not my usual thing, to be honest.' He looked around the department store. 'But I thought I'd pick up something for my mother. She's . . . well, you know.' He gestured slightly helplessly towards the boxes of gloves that the sales assistant had set out, and Violet swallowed again.

'I tried to call, you know,' he said softly. 'I wanted to make sure you were all right. But Aunt Eleanor . . .' He rolled his eyes comically, and for a moment the old Duffy was back. 'She said you weren't seeing anyone.'

'I wasn't,' Violet said, 'but not you, *you* I'd have seen.' She cast around for something else to say, something that breached the great big horror lying between them. 'I can't quite bring myself to talk to people,' she said.

Duffy looked down at his hands. 'It's the shock,' he said. 'I've only been back in the office this week, but I can't seem to focus on anything for very long. Or stay still.'

Violet nodded frantically, and then to her dismay, she felt her eyes fill with tears.

'It's my fault, Duffy,' she choked out, and the tears dripped down onto the floor.

'Violet,' he said softly. 'Don't do this to yourself.' And even though he always said he couldn't abide females carrying on, he put his arm around her shoulders. Not awkwardly, and certainly not romantically, just two people drawing solace from proximity, and Violet realised that no one had touched her since they'd left the harried doctor at the hospital. She hadn't sought it out either, couldn't really bear the feeling of flesh close to hers, not after Romy . . .

'Shh,' he said. 'Hush now, Vi . . .'

There was a sharp intake of breath next to her, and Duffy dropped his arm instantly.

'Violet Philomena Etherington!' Her mother stood with the shop girl hovering. 'Here you are, too torn apart to help me do the most basic things, and I find you . . .' she bit back the next word with some difficulty, clearly becoming aware of the ogling eyes of the floor staff, *'here,'* she finished in a hiss. 'And poor Dudley, too, as if it's not enough that—'

But an all-too-familiar sound cut across her final words: the undulating rise and fall of air raid sirens. Violet involuntarily gripped Duffy's arm, crowded right up close to him, heart beating so loudly it made black spots dance in front of her eyes. Her mother huffed impatiently and pulled her away. Across the floor, a thin, elegant woman clapped her hands briskly. 'If you'll all make your way down to the cellars, please,' she ordered. 'There's no need to agitate.' This was directed at two younger women who had dropped their parcels and were diving for the stairs. 'There's enough space for everyone.'

In the cellars, the walls still bore signs of previous shelving, and between the rugs scattered on the floor you could see naked concrete. Despite the pretty chairs dotted along walls and the tea served by shop girls circling with little hawkers' trays of pastry and magazines, the atmosphere was tense. Many shoppers sat clutching their gas masks, faces upturned to follow the sound above, while others tried to distract themselves with conversations about how many stockings one should purchase before clothes were rationed, and whether one should take the children for a prolonged stay in the country.

'We all have to do our bit, don't we,' Eleanor Etherington told the woman sitting next to her.

Violet snatched up her gas mask. 'I need some water,' she said, and before her mother could find a reason to hold her back, she'd disappeared into the corridor. She poked her head into the other storage rooms until she found Duffy sitting by himself in a corner.

He smiled when he saw her. 'Bad luck, eh? The one time I venture out shopping on Oxford Street, I'm stuck down here with a bunch of jabbering housewives.'

'I'm sorry about Mother,' she said quickly.

'Oh, don't worry on my account.' Duffy folded his fingers round his cup of tea and moved to the side to make room for her on the bench.

'But she's so . . .' Violet sat down and groped for words to explain her mother's readiness to blame her without sounding as if she didn't fully deserve it. She shook her head mutely, watching two uniformed young women lounging against the wall, pert blue skirts and crisp white shirts under smart jackets, caps jauntily perched on their hair. Wrens, she thought. Earlier in the summer, Romy's friend Cecily Rankling had gone on and on about how gorgeous their uniforms were until Romy had, unusually severely, said that it wasn't meant to be a fashion show. Romy had toyed with the thought of joining up too, Violet remembered.

Covertly she watched one of the Wrens, a snub-nosed blonde, laughing as the other one shook her head in mock exasperation. They couldn't have been much older than Violet herself, but like Romy often had, they seemed to belong to a different world entirely: self-possessed, relaxed, completely and utterly sure of their space in the world. Violet found she couldn't look away, then blushed when the blonde girl, sagging back against the wall and tapping her fingers impatiently on her crossed arms, looked up and caught her staring.

Quickly Violet flicked her eyes down to her hands, fingers fluttering against the sides of her skirt, worrying at the fabric. It had become a tic of sorts, which she couldn't seem to make herself stop. She felt the blonde's eyes on her and her insides squirmed. What would they see? A weak, spoilt society girl, with plenty of time on her hands to go shopping and wait for a husband? While they were out there making a difference. With enormous difficulty, she turned away.

'So?' she said to Duffy. 'You're back at work?'

'Yes.' He sighed. 'There is a lot to do, actually, what with Hitler's gimlet eye on us.'

Violet stared at him in astonishment. In all the years she'd known Duffy, he had never once mentioned work in anything but tones of exasperation, as if it was an imposition endured for the briefest time possible before moving on to what was really important.

'And I'm spending a lot of time with my mother before she leaves,' he added. 'Just . . . keeping her company. It's difficult, with my stepfather away. And I walk. A lot. Especially since my car . . .' He broke off, and Violet tried not to think about the last time she'd seen his car, pinned to the street by a piece of church.

'Where do you walk?' she asked in a slightly strangled voice.

'The park mainly. And just around London.'

'I wish I could do that,' she said fiercely. 'Just leave and go walking. But my mother, she's always . . . there.'

'There's a lot of room to walk in Yorkshire,' he pointed out.

She made a derisive noise and he chuckled. 'I had a feeling you weren't going to be keen. Aunt Eleanor is moving heaven and earth to go quickly. It'll be good for Mother, though, and it'll keep you all out of harm's way.'

'But where will *you* be?' she asked. 'Are you joining up?'

'I'll be here,' he said. 'Working. And walking,' he added with a wry shrug.

'You're so lucky,' she said longingly. 'So, so lucky.'

He looked at her for a long moment, then gave her a small smile. 'If you call the Blitz lucky, I suppose.'

Flushing at her own stupidity, Violet was precluded from answering by a shop girl bobbing up in front of her.

'Will you knit for the troops?' She was holding out a skein of wool and a set of wooden needles. 'You just knit squares,' she added helpfully when she saw Violet's look of incomprehension. 'And we'll stitch them together for blankets.'

Violet flushed a bright red. 'I'm not good at knitting.' Two sensible-looking women whose needles were already clicking away glanced over, and Violet felt the heat spread.

'Oh all right,' she said crossly, snatching the wool and the needles out of the girl's hands. She looped the wool around her fingers, cast on clumsily, then swapped the needles over and began to knit.

Duffy watched her. 'Goodness, Vi, at this rate, our troops'll be freezing to death,' he remarked.

'You try it then,' she said angrily. Her hands started trembling, and however she aimed the needle, she kept missing the loop, until she dropped the whole thing into her lap and balled it up. When the girl passed by, Violet thrust it back without looking at her, praying that the Wrens hadn't noticed the exchange.

'I can't bear it, Duffy,' she said in a low, hard voice. 'Not just Romy, but *all* of it.' She made an angry sweeping motion with her hand to encompass everything from Yorkshire to the shop girl, now discreetly unpicking her stitches; her mother sitting two rooms along; the German planes above. 'I feel like it's all closing in on me,' she said more quietly. 'I have to do something to make it go away – that night.'

'Just join the Red Cross in Yorkshire,' Duffy said soothingly. 'There must be women rolling bandages and collecting clothes and—'

'I won't,' she said savagely. 'I'd rather run away.'

Alarmed, he fumbled for his handkerchief, but she waved it away. He sighed. 'Can't say I blame you.'

Violet ran her finger around the edges of Romy's necklace. She was watching the Wrens again, picturing Romy among them, willowy and capable in that uniform. 'I can't wait for you to join us, Vi,' she would have said. 'William says it's important work, you know, not all fun and socialising.'

The blonde flicked back her cuff with an expert gesture, said something to her companion. And then it came to her.

'Duffy,' she said, quietly at first, then a little louder. 'That's it, Duffy! I'm not running away. I'm going to enlist.'

Ten

Duffy's head snapped up.

'Your mother would *die*,' he said, awed. 'And please, if heaven has any mercy on my poor battered soul, don't let me be anywhere close by when it happens.'

'She's cross anyway, regardless of what I do,' Violet said breathlessly. 'Romy talked about it, she said she was going to join up.'

'All right. The WRNS, then,' Duffy said cautiously. 'Serving officers breakfast and helping at parties and such.'

'Parties?' Violet said incredulously. 'I'm never going to a party again in my entire life. I want to get *away* from all that, not do *more* of it.'

'I'm pretty sure you have to be of age for the Wrens anyway. I suppose there's always factory work.' Duffy shook his head. 'Or intelligence – but that would involve lengthy background checks; you'd be in Yorkshire long before then. Have to be good at chess, crossword puzzles, that sort of thing. You could be a WAAF – ooh, you could be a searchlight operator.' He warmed to the subject. 'And there's the Land Army and the Timber Corps, although you might be a little on the skinny side for the Timber Corps, and . . . What?'

Violet was staring at him and for the first time in three weeks, the fat, foggy shreds of misery and anger lifted.

'The Land Army,' she said slowly. 'Duffy, that's it.'

She had seen posters, cheerfully red-cheeked women perched atop tractors or bent over rows of plant life on fields, looking healthy in their breeches. Breeches. She held her breath. She'd never worn breeches in her life. Common, Eleanor Etherington would call them. But: *We could do with thousands more like you*, the posters said. *For a healthy job.* Yes, that was what she would do. She would work hard, day in and day out. There would be trees and fields and sky. And maybe, bit by bit, she might work off all that rage, that loathing, she'd stop being filled with shame and guilt, she would finally sleep, she would be able to breathe again.

'I'm going to be a land girl.'

'Vi, honestly,' Duffy said urgently. 'Working in all weathers, hoeing turnips and draining fields and all sorts of ghastly things to do with bulls and cows.' He flushed but recovered quickly to add, 'Never mind that now. All a girl like you needs to know is that it's dark and back-breaking and thankless. Clearly you've never been to the country. It's nothing like London at all; things are still practically medieval out there. Farmers taking all sorts of licence, dangerous prisoners of war, possibly . . . Violet, are you even listening?'

'How do I go about becoming one?' Violet said impatiently. 'I'd need to sign up under a different name, otherwise Mother would immediately find me and drag me home. But how to take my rationing card under a false name, and also—'

'Violet,' Duffy leaned forward, 'really not. They say all sorts of things about land girls that I can't possibly repeat in female company, but rest assured, they're saying them, and I can't think of anything more unsuitable—'

'Duffy, stop fussing,' she cut in impatiently. 'My mind's made up. I just somehow need to get through the process quickly and be assigned before we leave for Yorkshire. Question is . . .' She frowned, pursed her lips and then slowly turned towards Duffy, who, seeing her face, leaned back as far as he could go.

'Oh no!' he said. 'Under no circumstances will I be a part of this, Vi. Aunt would kill me.'

'How would she ever suspect you?' Violet said beseechingly. 'You're so good at this kind of thing, Duff, you always know how everything's done, and you know *everyone.* If anyone can help me, it's you.'

His face softened slightly. 'Well, I suppose at least you'd be out of London and safe.' He cleared his throat and looked away. 'It is a bit difficult to be worrying about one's friends in the thick of everything. Won't have all too many people left at this rate,' he added awkwardly, and Violet flushed, her fingers twitching against her skirt.

'Duffy . . .'

But he shrugged her off. 'Time's of the essence, though, if you're really set on this. You're meant to be leaving for Yorkshire in two weeks.'

'Yes,' she said eagerly. 'Exactly.'

'We'd get you to sign up somewhere across London, so you won't run into anyone.' He tapped his chin thoughtfully. 'I know what, I'll talk to Lady Bellingdon; good pal of mine, runs some part of it if I remember correctly, was going on and on about it. Tell her you're one of our maids who needs to be sorted immediately because we're closing down the house. She'll understand. Medical, easy, I know someone who'll just tick the box; mightn't even have to attend, difficult anyway, what with Aunt breathing down your neck. Training, well, let's see what we can swing. Now, your rationing card, that's the tricky bit; I'll have to think about it.'

Violet pressed his hands. 'Oh thank you, Duffy, thank you,' she said fervently.

He waved her off, red with embarrassment.

'Thing to remember is that the WLA isn't a military set. Belongs to the Ministry of Agriculture, if I'm not mistaken. You'll be employed by wherever you're going. So if Aunt did find you, you'd be out of there in a jiffy. Although it would be shockingly unpatriotic of her to kick up a fuss when everyone's supposed to be pitching in. And the other thing is, will they need you at such short notice? Sometimes you're all agog to sign up and then nothing happens. Lucinda Roy signed up for the WAAF on day one, couldn't wait to get stuck in, and now they're keeping her hanging. Well,' he flashed her a smile, 'let's just hope there's a field out there with your name on it, Vi.'

Once he'd shed his misgivings, Duffy took to 'Operation Turnip', as he kept referring to it, with dogged determination, moving heaven and earth for an application in the name of Lily Burns to be processed quickly and for a position to be found. Leaning heavily on a variety of chums, he settled Violet in a place that wouldn't involve bulls, prison labourers or any of the truly unspeakable farm work.

'Apple orchards in Somerset, Vi,' he said. 'No training, they need someone now. Part of a big country estate, Winterbourne, owned by a family called Crowden. I knew one of the sons, Oliver. Died in France, poor chap, but there were more siblings, so things must be ticking along if they need land girls to bring in the harvest. Nice and peaceful and out of the way. Apples to eat if you're hungry.'

In the busy, frantic days that followed, Violet sometimes wondered whether Duffy needed something to latch onto as much as she did; whether he too was desperate to take his mind off what their life had become without Romy. At night, paralysed with fear as the bombers flew over, she thought about the sky stretching endlessly above fields and orchards, about a place where she wouldn't have to be Violet any more, but Lily, who was hard-working and steadfast and had never done anything wrong. But then she'd dig her fingertips deep into the raw scars on her arms until the pain made her gasp, because it wasn't right to be looking forward to leaving the memory of Romy behind. She didn't deserve to be free of her guilt and her responsibility and simply become someone new.

'Once more, you are . . .'

'Lily Burns,' Violet said. 'I was a housemaid, but you've closed up the house and evacuated and I wanted to do my bit.'

'Bi-it,' he corrected her. 'Keep your accent nice and neutral. I will say, though, Vi, you might not have many other talents, but you're awfully good at sounding common.'

'Thanks a lot.' Violet stroked the green jumper that was part of her new uniform, then slipped it deep into her handbag to join the rest of the things she'd been sneaking into the house little by little: the cord trousers and white shirts, the brown socks and the Land Army badge pinned onto her hat. With only a few more days to go and almost no staff left, her mother had been forced to divide her efforts between her own packing and that of her sister-in-law, which meant that Violet could move freely between the two houses to meet Duffy. During a few hours of unusual freedom, she was able to slip away for her interview, a surprisingly perfunctory affair with little opportunity for 'Lily' to profess her deep love for the country and her willingness to work hard.

'But it's not enough to talk like her, you have to *be* Lily,' Duffy said urgently. 'Don't take anything for granted, don't act all prissy when you have to eat rats for dinner.'

'I will *not* have to eat rats for dinner,' she said. 'It's an apple orchard. There's bound to be pie. And anyway, in here it's all about doorstep sandwiches and turnip paste and hot tea in flasks.' She held up a magazine called *The Land Girl*, which, while a tad overly romantic in places perhaps, had become her main point of reference.

'If you're lucky,' he said darkly. 'Or you might just be eating turnips.' He raised his eyebrows. 'Raw.'

'So the food might be a bit plain,' she said impatiently.

'Bi-it,' he corrected, but then he laughed, a proper laugh that reminded Violet of the old Duffy. It seemed to startle him as much as her, because he broke off almost immediately and looked away.

Violet touched Romy's necklace, then leaned forward and said quietly, 'I really appreciate you doing this, Duffy.'

There was a pause, and then he said, 'Anything's better than sitting here and thinking about things.'

'You'll be safe here, though, won't you?' She was suddenly gripped by the terrible fear that she might not see him again. 'You won't get yourself killed?'

He looked at her. 'I'll try not to,' he said with a wry grin. 'And you, well, once you're there, just try your best, and for heaven's sake, *stay* there. I've waved through the paperwork, but there's no telling how long this little charade will hold up, and it certainly won't if you try to move elsewhere. That rationing card was a piece of work . . . Violet, are you listening? Once you're on that train, there's not much I can do for you.'

'Look.' Violet waved *The Land Girl* under his nose. 'It says we all have to band together against the enemy. Surely that's more important than little old me not having a proper rationing card?'

Duffy squinted at the picture.

'Girls on tractors,' he said heavily. 'God help us.'

The last day flew by in a whirl of furniture draped with sheets and curtains closed tightly in all but their small sitting room, where her mother was writing last-minute notes to acquaintances brazening things out in London. They would be leaving first thing in the morning, her mother with Aunt Amanda to Yorkshire, and unbeknownst to everyone but Duffy, who had organised a car to take her to the station, Violet on a train from Paddington to the West Country. She had squirrelled away some of the warm clothes meant for her Yorkshire wardrobe, packed up her uniform, hidden her small case in an alcove off the front hall and bundled up her new Land Army overall coat on top, silently thanking the heavens that the butler had gone a few months back. The goodbye note to her mother crackled in her pocket. It had taken her a long time to come up with suitable wording, what with Duffy vetoing most of her bolder suggestions, ranging from 'went to join Father in the desert' to, slightly more menacingly, 'you will never find me so don't even try', until he had finally sighed that there was no way to sugar-coat Violet's madness.

Dear Mother,

I'm leaving to join the war effort. Please don't try to come after me. By the time you read this, it'll be too late anyway. I'll get in touch with you at Uncle Gareth's if I need help. But I won't, I promise.
See you after the war.

Your loving daughter,
Violet

Duffy's eyebrows had disappeared all the way up into his shaggy blond hair. Then he shook his head resignedly. 'Just remember that you might not see her again. Who knows what's going to happen to any of us? She loves you, even if she doesn't show it very often. Take proper leave of her, Violet, or else you might regret it.'

'Of course I will,' she said impatiently. 'It'll be fine, you'll see.'

But now, standing in the front hall and listening to her mother's pen scratching across paper in the sitting room, quiet after the furious pace of the last two weeks, Violet felt weak and weary and not at all fine. She thought of her father, somewhere in the desert. Her mother had asked Duffy to sort out another telephone call, but it hadn't been possible, and in the end she had simply cabled their departure date. Violet tried to imagine what he might be doing right now, whether he was thinking of his daughter, but she couldn't even summon up a proper image of him. Romy was gone, and the two houses they'd grown up in together would be shuttered and dark maybe for years to come. Duffy would be walking the streets of London restlessly between his rooms and the office. There would be no more parties, no more glamorous dresses and music. She shivered, imagining them all as tiny dots, flung apart, unable to communicate, and she didn't think she'd ever felt this alone.

Lily was going too, though, she reminded herself firmly, to pick apples at Winterbourne. She straightened Romy's necklace, letting her fingers rest on the silver disc, before she turned and went to bid her mother goodnight.

Frankie

September 2004

Eleven

It was mid afternoon and Frankie was no nearer a plan for how to approach Violet at the Gala tonight. Should she ring her now and just get it over with? Cross paths with her casually at the venue, use the element of surprise to finagle an introduction to Celeste? There was usually a press area, though, and Violet might be besieged by other reporters and charity people, especially if she hadn't been out and about for a while. Unusually indecisive, Frankie couldn't bring herself to do one or the other, mainly because she simply couldn't imagine that in just a few hours she'd be seeing her grandmother, she'd be *talking* to her. And not only that – she swallowed uneasily – she was supposed to be interviewing her for a soundbite on Nannygate. Unless things had changed dramatically, hell would freeze over before Violet would comment on another woman's scandal.

She pushed into the loos and almost fell over Felicity and Victoria, standing in front of a long white garment bag hanging off the back of the door, zipped open to show a red satin gown.

'It's such a shame you can't wear it,' Felicity said commiseratingly.

'What now?' Victoria rounded on Frankie. 'Are you spying on us?'

'Sure, what else could I possibly be doing in the loos?' Frankie rolled her eyes.

'Don't let us keep you.' Victoria reached to zip up the garment bag.

'Are we … I mean, do I actually need a proper evening gown?' Frankie didn't really want to ask advice from Victoria, but she had hoped to get away with going to the Gala in the smart black trousers and blazer she always wore for work.

'June likes us looking the part,' Victoria said icily. 'Says we get more out of people if they think we're one of them.' She looked pointedly at Frankie's face and hair, which, a quick check in the mirror showed, were nowhere near black-tie presentable. Where the hell would she get an evening gown from at such short notice?

Victoria lifted down the garment bag. 'Come on, Fliss, some of us have actual work to do.' At the door, she stopped and turned. 'What size are you anyway?'

Frankie briefly thought about ignoring her, but Victoria's voice had thawed a fraction and she gave herself a push. 'If you were to be able to help me out with the dress, Victoria, I'd owe you so much, honestly,' she said. 'And again, I'm really sorry about the Gala piece. I'm an eight.'

Victoria regarded her for a long moment, then hoisted up the dress more securely in her arms. 'So am I.' And she swept from the room, the metal brace of the hanger clanking against the door frame.

Left in the loo, Frankie blinked furiously at her reflection, then snapped on the tap and washed her hands for several minutes until she felt marginally calmer. Before she could change her mind, she pulled out her mobile and punched in a number.

As it rang through, she imagined the gowns bursting out of the old wardrobe in the overstuffed shop, pictured the black rotary phone next to the till, the drawer where the button box had lived.

'Jools's Quality Vintage, London's finest vintage consignment shop,' a cheerful voice sang.

Frankie took a deep breath.

'Hello, Jools, it's me.'

*

'I'll come to you,' Jools had offered. 'The *London Post* is the big building with the shiny front? There's a Costa Coffee a little way down the road. You can change in the loo.'

'Oh please, Frankie, can I come, too?' begged Con, his earlier coolness forgotten. 'If I don't meet the woman who just happens to have a vintage ball gown on her rail and is able to sew you into it in a Costa, I don't think I will survive this hell of an afternoon.'

'Rough day, darling?' Jools said as Frankie and Con hurried into the café.

'You have no idea,' Frankie sighed. 'Jools, this is my friend Con. He works with me at the *London Post*. Con, this is . . .' Her eyes fell on the dress Jools had brought, along with a selection of evening bags and a pair of torturous-looking heels. 'Jools, the *Jacqmar*?'

The Jacqmar had been on a mannequin for years, lovingly tended under its dust protector, the little gems on the bodice polished by hand, because even though she'd had plenty of offers, no one was ever quite good enough to go to a ball in Jools's Jacqmar.

'Consider it your fatted calf, my lovely.' Jools's eyes were too bright suddenly and Frankie felt a lump in her throat, because when she had walked out of Violet's life, she had also lost Jools too. 'One call a year for my birthday, ha. Did you forget where my shop was? Last time I saw you was at your grandpa's funeral, and then you vanished before I could even say hello.' She pulled back, her gaze sharp.

It wasn't a memory Frankie cherished. Hiding in the back of the church, cheeks wet with tears, then slipping out before the last hymn had faded, turning her back on the hunched figure of her grandmother alone in the front pew.

'It was a bit d-d-diff . . .' Frankie could feel Con's eyes on her, and with a furious hiss, she broke off. 'It's b-b-been . . .' she tried again, but to no avail.

'Easy does it,' Jools said gently. 'We have all the time in the world.' She always did have all the time in the world, Jools. 'Remember all that Darwinistic chanting you and Violet did for your stammer?' She settled back against her chair comfortably. 'Violet favoured Rudyard Kipling, which is morally a little tricky these days if you ask me,' she told Con, who looked startled. 'Old imperialist that he is. Listen, Conrad, is it? Would you get an old woman a glass of water?'

Con, who looked like he'd much rather be listening to more morally tricky stories about Frankie and Violet, got up with extreme reluctance. Frankie watched him hurry over to the counter and lean across it, urgently trying to catch the barista's eye.

The moment he was out of earshot, Jools turned to her.

'Quickly, before he comes back. I'm so glad you called. I would have started tracking you down myself before too long. Something strange is going on with that grandmother of yours and I'm at my wits' end.'

'Strange?' Frankie said slowly. 'I heard she's not been seen out much, actually, but . . .'

'Well I cannot for the life of me figure it out. She doesn't come and see me any more, and whenever I stop by, I seem to constantly be hovering at the door. Says she's busy, lots on, but then I have Mrs Harefield in my shop – she's on the Safe Haven committee with Vi, you know. Bought the most gorgeous vintage Dior dress, bit boxy on her maybe, but there's few figures a Dior can't improve – anyway, she's telling me they haven't seen Violet in a while and is she all right? Thing is,' she paused worriedly, 'it's not just me. People are starting to notice, papers are sniffing around.'

'They always do.' Frankie shrugged. 'Until they get bored, because there's never anything of interest there.'

Over by the counter, Con had finally managed to get three glasses of water and was rushing back to their corner.

'But the point is, this . . . this absence *has* piqued their interest,' Jools said urgently. 'Twice already I've caught someone lurking with a camera in front of her place. You know what Violet's like. And what the press is like.'

'Given that I'm one of them, yes, I do. We're not all jackals, you know,' Frankie said icily just as Con set down the glasses, sloshing water on the table.

'Thank you,' Jools said. 'Go put on the dress, Frankie, while I talk with your friend. But,' she grabbed Frankie's arm and held her back, 'think about what I said, please. And call me tomorrow, all right? I want a proper catch-up. Now that you're back, I'm not letting you go again.'

She lowered the Jacqmar into Frankie's arms and gave her a shove in the direction of the loo before Frankie could tell her that she wasn't back. Not like that. Not even one little bit.

Twelve

The Starlight Children's Trust had been around for years, fighting children's illiteracy and campaigning for early education, and the Starlight Gala was one of its biggest money-raisers. Accordingly, the organisers had pulled out all the stops. The courtyard outside the entrance to the Wentworth Hotel was filled with trees in large wooden tubs and strung with fairy lights; the facade was lit up like a Hollywood set. Cars spilled out glamorous-looking guests, who smiled and waved for the cameras before they were funnelled towards the enormous glass doors by unsmiling young men and women dressed in black and wearing badges emblazoned with *SCT*.

Everywhere, photographers jostled among fireworks of flashes and shouting, and hints of Celeste's attendance must have spread after all, because paparazzi had gathered on the street opposite, adding to the noise level in front of the hotel.

'Ava, over here,' a photographer was calling to a beautiful black-haired woman in a poufy dress whom Frankie vaguely recognised.

'This way, darlin'!'

A glamorous couple turned and waved regally.

Frankie had decided to stay out here and wait for Violet to arrive, but now, trapped in a throng of bodies and clutching sweaty handfuls of Jacqmar, she was starting to regret her plan. A photographer's elbow connected sharply with the side of her mouth, leaving her lips bare and a blood-like smear of lipstick on his woollen sleeve. Maybe it would be better to get inside the hotel after all.

But just as she had started to push her way towards the

entrance, a familiar sputtering noise came from behind, and all thoughts of a plan of action vanished. She turned on her heel, her eyes searching the street, and there it was. Violet's ancient Hillman Hunter.

Memories chased each other, faster and faster. The creaking of the handle to wind down the window as she waved goodbye to her dad, feeling her heart thud with homesickness. The cracked criss-cross pattern etched into the back of the seat in front. The way the leather had stuck to her bare legs in summer. How often had she sat in that very car right there? A hundred times? A thousand?

The first time Violet had come to fetch her to stay at Cavendish Place was a few months after her mother had died, for a long weekend. Frankie hadn't wanted to leave her dad, who'd been in a bad way since then, and her dad hadn't wanted her to go, because he didn't like much of anything those days, least of all Violet. 'Rich hag,' he'd grumble. 'Never left us in peace, always calling Stella and stirring up trouble with her posh ways. Nothing's ever good enough for her, least of all yours truly. Don't need any charity, do we, Francesca?'

But Violet had arrived one Friday, and after a lot of shouting about how he could possibly think that taking a six-year-old girl to gigs with him was a good thing, she'd swept into Frankie's room and shoved some clothes into a bag. Terrified of this angry, rigid-backed woman who moved fast and spoke loudly, Frankie had clung to her dad, begging him to be allowed to stay. But ignoring them both, her grandmother had taken her hand, and an hour later, Frankie found herself at Cavendish Place. The weekend was a disaster. Awkward and strained, pervaded by her grandparents' visceral grief over the loss of their daughter, Frankie's own crippling shyness, her homesickness for her dad, and, of course, her stammer, which precluded any conversation longer than a few words.

One thing she had never forgotten, though.

When she'd climbed into the Hillman that very first time, a lunch box was sitting on the back seat. Things had become a little difficult at home, with her dad needing so long in the mornings to get himself out of bed, spending evenings and afternoons plucking away at his guitar, his cheeks wet with tears. Simple things, like Frankie's clothes and how she got to school, weren't really something you'd mention in the face of so much despair. She knew how to make herself a cheese sandwich, and where her mum had kept what she'd called *household spendies*, in the old chipped teapot hidden on a kitchen shelf. But the teapot was slowly emptying and there didn't seem to be much money elsewhere in the flat, and Frankie had started to be concerned.

The first lunch box held a sandwich filled with proper big slices of ham, a Penguin bar, an apple and a small packet of crisps. The second time, it was a cheese sandwich, a little green chocolate in a triangle shape and a banana. That time, a piece of tape was stuck to the top. There was writing on it: F-R-A-N-K-I-E. Frankie spelled out the letters to herself.

'I thought we'd try something,' Violet had turned around in her seat and regarded her. 'If you like, that is. You could call me Violet – "Grandmother" makes me feel about a hundred – and you could be Frankie. Your mum had a two-syllable name, and so do I, see? Vio-let, Ste-lla and now – ta-daaa – Fran-kie. Has a nice ring to it, doesn't it? Short and bouncy.'

Frankie had nodded, wordless with gratitude. Violet had noticed, then, how difficult Frankie found the spiky mouthful of her own name whenever she was asked to introduce herself. How her dad, from some beautiful, patina-coloured memory of bussing around Italy on his honeymoon, insisted on rolling his r's spectacularly when Frankie could often barely get past the 'tsch'. *Frankie*, though, *Frankie* was different. Full of soft, gooey letters that slid out from between her lips, and bouncy was something to aspire to when you were a thin, sad, pale girl who flushed with nervy embarrassment the moment anyone so much as noticed her.

It was so silly that she never mentioned it to anyone, that thrill she got when she saw her new name on that lunch box, the day 'Frankie' was born. She imagined her grandmother finding an old ice cream carton, then getting tape and a marker and carefully spelling it out. It felt to Frankie like Violet was labelling her, giving her her very own place in time and space the way no one else had done since Mum had died. Not the teachers, who frowned when she was late or missed school; not Dad, who played his songs and talked to her about his art and where they would go next, more restless and wandering-hearted than ever.

It took a good while for Frankie's visits at Cavendish Place to be less intimidating. It wasn't like a story in the books, where the grandmother was all bubbly hugs and Victoria sponges. Violet had an opinion on everything and took a great many things very seriously, things that Frankie didn't enjoy and her dad usually let slide, like dentist's visits and vaccinations and parent-teacher meetings at school. She was meticulously organised in ways that Frankie's dad never aspired to be, that he mocked even. But it also meant that she was always there when she said she would be. She'd given Frankie a small calendar in which they marked down her visits, and, rain or shine, Violet would be parked in the no-parking zone opposite the newsagent's, reading the paper with her glasses perched at the end of her nose, Frankie's lunch box sitting on the back seat.

After that first time, she never came up into their flat – Dad refused to ask her in – and she rarely gave Frankie anything to take back with her. But bit by bit, more things appeared in Frankie's orbit. A warmer jacket on an owl-shaped hook at Cavendish Place, her own towel hanging over the ancient heater in the bathroom, a pair of thick socks, PJs and shirts and jeans in the empty drawers in her mum's old childhood room.

'You don't need to bring that,' Violet said eventually, a little impatient, when Frankie came to the car clutching her small, threadbare bag. 'You have everything you need back with us.'

'Okay,' Frankie would say. But she didn't stop bringing her bag, even when it was mostly empty, because she didn't want her dad to feel slighted. 'Back so soon, Francesca?' he'd ask sourly. 'Was it all Harrods hampers and tea with the Queen?'

Frankie loved her dad too much to talk about her visits with Violet in great detail. But she sometimes wished she could have shown him that behind the grand address, there wasn't much richness at all. There weren't any fancy toys or meals or high-end outings; just a sandwich lunch with her name on it, a plate set out for her breakfast, and someone to look up from a cup of tea and smile when she came into the kitchen. She wanted to reassure him that she would never leave him, that he was her family just as much as Violet. But most of all she wished that it could somehow be okay for her to have both. That her grandmother wouldn't use that strained voice when talking about Frankie's 'other life', like it was a life lived in shadow, not worth it. That her dad wouldn't get that hard, displeased look around his eyes, making Frankie coax him out of a shell of disapproval and injury whenever she returned. That she wouldn't be stretched thin between the two people she loved most in the world, never quite enough for one or the other.

Feeling the ghost of an empty overnight bag in her hand, Frankie pushed towards the car, was almost there now, had drawn level with the back door . . .

'Excuse me, may I help you with your ticket?'

One of the Children's Trust employees had materialised next to her, showing an entire set of very white, very even teeth.

'I'm with the press,' she said, her eyes still on the car. A young woman was driving, which was odd – Violet always drove herself, fast and slightly recklessly – but there was a flash of grey hair, a dark red gown in the passenger seat. She was here.

'Oh?' He sounded unconvinced. 'Then let's just get you checked in over here, shall we?'

She fumbled for her temporary press pass, a piece of cardboard with her name and a crooked *London Post* stamp that Felicity had given her. Earlier, Frankie had felt a stab of pride, but now it looked rather makeshift in the man's hand.

'No O'Brien on the list, I'm afraid,' he announced.

Bloody Felicity, Frankie thought savagely as behind them, people surged towards the Hillman Hunter. But just as the young man started shunting Frankie away, a voice came from behind them.

'She's with me.'

Thirteen

The same, was Frankie's first, wild thought. She was just the same. Violet in her *masquerade*, that straight back, the clipped tone. And yet altogether different too, more stooped, her face criss-crossed with a new web of lines that had deepened around her eyes and mouth, her skin almost too heavily made up below a feather fascinator clinging to the front of her wavy grey hair. There was something else as well, which Frankie couldn't immediately put her finger on. A strange, vaguely disassembled air, or maybe it was that her face had drained to an almost grotesque white, her eyes huge and hungry, burning across Frankie's face, her arms, her dress, her face again.

'You're here,' she said hoarsely. 'You . . .'

'I'm ever so sorry, Mrs Etherington,' the young man wrung his hands, 'but she's not on the list.'

Without taking her eyes off Frankie, Violet plucked the press pass from his hands. 'We'll go in together.'

Now here was the Violet she remembered. Frankie felt a small zing of irritation as her grandmother took her elbow and steered her towards the hotel, leaving the young man to rush alongside them and create a path amidst camera flashes and shouts for Violet's attention.

'I can't believe you're here.' She walked faster now, her eyes fixed on the grand vaulted entrance into the Wentworth Hotel, dragging Frankie along like a recalcitrant child.

Just get the interview, Frankie thought, then she could deal with the rest of all . . . *this*.

'I moved back to London a few days ago, I work at the *London Post* now. Which brings me to a favour I wanted to ask . . .' She stumbled a little, felt her heel turning. 'Violet, could you slow down?'

But just then, among a hailstorm of clicks and flashes, a woman appeared behind them. 'Thank *God*, you're here, Vi! Quick, inside.'

An enormous mass of hair surged around a cheerful face, its signature gap-toothed grin beaming, and Frankie gasped.

'Celeste McIntyre!' It came out a lot more enthusiastic than she had meant it to, but maybe she wouldn't even have to ask Violet for the introduction, could just get on with things on her own, which she would vastly prefer.

'The very same,' the woman grinned. 'New assistant, Vi? Violet?'

But Violet had moved away a few paces and was standing in the middle of the hotel's entrance hall, taking in the staircase sweeping upwards on both sides, the elaborate cornicing, the enormous age-darkened paintings lining the wall, until her eyes came to rest on a gilded mirror above a fireplace to the left. She was gently buffeted by the crowd and entirely heedless of people calling her name, someone thrusting a microphone in her face. She started violently when Celeste tapped her arm, and it seemed to take her a moment to focus, but then she smiled.

'Oh, Celeste. How nice to see you.'

'Well.' Celeste seemed taken aback. 'We did agree to meet here, remember?' She frowned at Violet. 'I say, though, I thought I was going to be the only one feeling a bit queasy tonight, but are you all right? You're looking a little grey around the gills.'

Frankie had taken out her notepad and flicked through to her interview questions, found the pencil stub she'd stashed in her evening bag. Now she glanced up sharply. Celeste was right. Beneath the mask-like sheen of powder, Violet was sweating, and a mottled flush had crept across her ghostly cheeks.

'Celeste, how is the nanny?' A reporter, flanked by one of the

SCT minions, thrust a recorder in their midst. 'Will you and hubby be splitting up?'

'Tonight is about the fact that one in five children cannot read properly by the age of eleven. Surely in a technologically advanced country famous for its education, this must be rectified?' Celeste said in a dignified way, shaking back her mass of hair. 'I'm not going to comment on personal matters.'

Undaunted, the journalist turned to Violet. 'Mrs Etherington, what's your take on the situation?'

Frankie had just deftly inserted herself in front of two journalists angling for Celeste's attention, so she almost missed the strange flicker crossing her grandmother's face, something restless and vague and – yes – a little bit panicked? She frowned and twisted sideways to get another look, but already it was gone, replaced by Violet's usual pleasant if slightly steely expression.

'That we must help our children learn and grow, to become good citizens, good people?' Violet asked back. 'I think that's not a situation, it's a basic human right.'

'I meant about—'

'I know what you meant, Laurence,' Violet said pleasantly. 'Let's just take your picture, shall we?'

Laurence held up his hands in good-natured defeat and waved the photographer forward. 'Celeste and you together, if you'd be so kind,' he said. 'And who is your pretty friend? Great dress,' he added appreciatively.

Frankie opened her mouth to clarify that she was with the press, but Violet spoke before she could get a chance. 'This is my granddaughter, Frankie.'

'Goodness,' Laurence said, looking startled. 'A granddaughter – who'd have . . . Of *course* she'll be in the photo.'

'No she won't,' Frankie said firmly. 'I'm here to get an interview with Celeste. I'm with the *London Post*,' she told Celeste, 'so if you don't mind . . .'

'Of course,' Celeste said. 'How fab for you to have some company, Vi. Here, let's get the photo out of the way, though.'

She threaded her arm through Frankie's on one side and Violet's on the other.

'Actually, I really would rather not be in it.' Frankie tried to pull her arm out of Celeste's. 'Violet . . .'

But all she managed to do was attract more attention. Laurence was scribbling away in a businesslike manner, raking his eyes across Frankie to get every detail as the photographer moved into position, while behind him, obviously scenting something interesting and finding the elusive Violet Etherington at the centre of it all, more reporters were now crowding in. It was absurd, Frankie thought furiously. *She* was supposed to be on that side, with her notepad and questions, doing her job, for heaven's sake. Out of the corner of her eye she saw the *London Post* photographer, a girl called Jade, lift her camera.

'Frankie short for Francesca, yes?' Laurence asked briskly. 'Francesca Etherington, is it?'

Violet opened her mouth, but Frankie had finally had enough. It was what Violet had done back then, labelling things the way she wanted them, and now, a decade after she and Frankie had exchanged their last shouted words, she was doing it again, as if no time at all had passed. But Frankie didn't *need* Violet to label her any more, didn't her grandmother *get* that? That she had done enough, had taken enough from her . . .

More flashes of light, but Frankie didn't care; she pulled away, and in the small kerfuffle that ensued around Celeste, brought her face very close to her grandmother's ear.

'My name is Francesca O'Brien and I'm here to get an interview with Celeste. Nothing more, nothing less.'

Her voice was low and hard, and for a moment she wondered if Violet had even heard her, because her eyes were curiously blank under their heavy make-up. Then, suddenly and without warning, Violet sagged at the knees and slithered to the ground at Celeste and Frankie's feet.

Frankie was sure her heart had stopped beating for a full minute before she fell to her knees next to her grandmother's body. Above her, Celeste was shouting for the charity staff and a medic while trying to shield Violet from the reporters at the same time.

Things were a bit of a blur after that. All Frankie was conscious of was Violet's face as she was shuffled into a large, empty room and sat on a gilded chair. The Children's Trust staff hovered anxiously, the medic eventually pronounced her shaken but fine, and Violet kept telling people to stop making such an ungodly fuss just because an old woman was stupid enough to stumble in her heels.

'I don't know.' Celeste looked after the departing medic doubtfully. 'Shall I call my limo back and whiz you over to the hospital?' Her lipstick had smudged and her enormous eyes were concerned behind the double layer of fake lashes, one side of which was threatening to slide down towards her cheek. Her hair surged around her like a stormy sea. 'It's too big for me really, pitches you all over the place,' she confided to Frankie. 'Next time I'll roll up in my stepdaughter's Mini. Although – well, who knows if I have that option much longer. It's all been very tense at home.'

Frankie tried to say something, but the adrenaline had drained in a great big gush, squeezing her chest tightly and trapping any response, should Celeste even have required it.

'Celeste,' Violet finally said, faintly but firmly. 'I'm fine. I didn't eat very much is all. My assistant is coming around to pick me up in a moment, and I'll go and see my doctor tomorrow. But you need to be out there, showing your face. We talked about it, remember?'

Celeste got up reluctantly, fingering her skirt, which had

ripped up the side when she had crouched over Violet. 'Do you have a safety pin, Frankie? Ah, never mind, they'll just have to take me as I am.'

'Will you stay for a bit, though, Frankie?' Violet asked quickly.

Frankie looked at Celeste and opened her mouth. She had to do the story. But the anxious, panicked look was back on her grandmother's face and Celeste was grumbling that she wanted to stay in here, 'where no one's asking me any stupid questions about that nanny rubbish', and Frankie, who'd once dragged a crooked landlord into the most disgusting tenement block she'd ever seen, who'd dug in her heels on a councillor's guilt when everyone else told her she was mad, knew she couldn't possibly do an interview right now. Not with her throat impossibly tight, with Violet's hand hectically flicking her thigh and Celeste huffing irritatedly at the minion who stuck his head in and asked was Mrs McIntyre going to be much longer because people were waiting.

'Oh, I forgot, you wanted me too, right, Frankie? Come find me later.' Celeste bent to give Violet a kiss on the cheek, rubbing a bit of lipstick away with her thumb. 'And Vi, call me tomorrow, yeah?'

After the flurry of activity, Violet was sitting very still now. Only her right hand was still moving, worrying at the small silvery sequins of her gown. In the mirrored panels on the walls, a sea of empty tables and chairs was reflected back to them, a crowd of Frankies and Violets.

'So many of us.' Violet's whisper was far away and shivery, as if she wasn't just seeing them, but more faces, a whole ballroom full of people. 'Just like back then, a beautiful Saturday in September. The Wentworth, so grand, supposedly the safest place in London.' She had left the sequins, was scrabbling at the skin on her arms now, dragging her nails across an old web of scars on her arm. Frankie moved closer, frowning, because

Violet seemed to have forgotten she was even there. 'Romy and I, we're always together. She's so pretty, Romy, so full of life still. And then, just hours later, dead in my arms – blood everywhere, over her dress, mine, my hands – dead at nineteen. There were three hundred German bombers above us, London was burning, Black Saturday, that's what they called it later, but I didn't know it was going to happen, I didn't *know* . . .'

Her nails had dug deep grooves into the soft skin of her scars, and she was scratching, pushing in deeper; any moment now she was going to draw blood.

'V-V-Violet, st-st-stop.' The words were tangled and spiky with fear as Frankie snatched at her grandmother's fingers and gripped hard.

Violet started at her touch, then sank back on her chair, looking at the red grooves in her arm, the scratched skin exposed and ugly beneath Frankie's fingers.

'I'm g-g-going to take you to the doctor,' Frankie said, furious with panic. 'I shouldn't have—'

'No!' Violet quickly smoothed out the grooves with her fingertips. 'No. I'm just remembering. In all these years, I've always managed to avoid the Wentworth, ever since I attended a wedding reception here sixty-four years ago.' Her lips were white, but her voice sounded a little more normal.

After a moment, Frankie nodded cautiously. 'You told me about Romy but I still sometimes forget that you were in London during the Blitz. I can't even imagine what that must have been like, all those nights in the shelter . . .'

An odd expression flitted across Violet's face, then her features tightened. 'I was only here for the first few weeks. I spent the remainder of the war in Yorkshire, with a distant relative.'

Frankie opened her mouth but Violet tapped the skirt of Frankie's dress. 'I can't believe Jools let you have this. Although,' she tried to smile, 'I can't think of anything more fitting for your return.'

After all the tension and awkwardness earlier, Frankie felt an odd rush of release. Finally it was out there.

'Happy birthday, darling,' Violet said.

'Yeah.' Frankie exhaled carefully.

'Just tell me what I can do to make things right,' Violet said quickly, urgently. She was close enough for Frankie to smell talcum powder and a flowery perfume. 'I'll do anything, I just want for us to be good again.'

'You could introduce me as Frankie O'Brien, for a start,' Frankie said quietly.

The air between them had been soft with relief and regret and the sweet, sharp twang of nostalgia. But the moment the words left her mouth, Frankie saw her grandmother's expression change. The tightening of her lips she knew so well, the barely-there frown, the irritated, disapproving tilt of her chin.

Violet had always disliked Harry O'Brien. She didn't say in so many words, not the way Harry called her horrible names, like *rich hag, battleaxe, entitled bourgeoisie*. But Frankie could see it in her frown when Frankie and Harry did their special goodbye handshake. It was there in the huff when she saw Frankie's too-small, holey blouse, her disapproval when they were waiting to tour the C of E secondary school Violet and Harry had finally managed to agree on and Harry rocked up twenty minutes late.

'It's nothing to be ashamed of, to be an Etherington.' Even Violet's tone was exactly the same as it had been back then: that slightly strained effort of ostentatiously holding back all the things she really, truly wanted to say about what it meant to be an O'Brien. 'You're also your mother's daughter, you know, and my Stella was special, you have no idea how very special she was . . .'

'*Your Stella* married him and took his name,' Frankie said coldly. 'You can't change that, no matter how hard you always tried. Do you know what it was like to be pulled between the two of you, trying to love both of you equally with you hating

99

each other above my head? And then you . . . you . . .' She pushed at the things she'd nursed and resented for so many years, but somehow, now that she was here with Violet, she couldn't find the words.

'If you had *any* idea, if you *knew* what he was really like,' Violet said hotly, 'what he did to Stella. It was his fault, *all* of it.'

'I l-l-lost both my mother and my father by the time I was eighteen.' Frankie wrestled furiously with her stammer. 'And that was *your* f-f-fault. You, who were meant to love me, who were meant to be on my side, always.'

She got up so quickly that the chair toppled over behind her with a loud clatter.

'Don't, please, Frankie,' Violet pleaded. 'I'm sorry about the thing with the name . . .'

She probably didn't mean to make Frankie's complaint sound petulant and childish, but when Frankie looked back at her, she saw her grandmother sitting very straight, her eyes hard, and realised she had meant it, of course she had, along with all the things she'd said and done ten years ago.

'Whatever,' Frankie said coldly. 'You know, I don't think you really want to patch things up. How can you, when you clearly regret nothing at all? You put Dad in prison ten years ago, and you'd still do it all over again.'

Fourteen

Before Violet could say anything else, the door opened and a young, dark-haired woman appeared. If she'd heard the shouting or was in any way surprised to find Violet and Frankie glowering at each other, she gave no indication, just nodded the briefest of greetings.

'I've made a small statement to the press, so that's all taken care of, and if you're ready, Mrs Etherington, I've brought the car back round. I'll wait outside.'

'I'm leaving anyway,' Frankie said angrily, and the young woman nodded as if that made complete sense and disappeared again.

Violet opened her mouth, but Frankie cut across her. 'What happened ten years ago doesn't matter any more,' she said coldly. 'Because Dad's coming out, did you know? He's being released in four weeks. Finally, he'll be free.'

Mercifully, Con and Bea were in bed by the time Frankie got back to the tiny flat they shared – a hovel, Con said grumpily, that shuddered every time the Northern Line thundered by below. They'd left a note on the table. *Hope your birthday went okay*, Bea had written, and *Can't wait to hear about the Gala*, Con had scrawled below.

Frankie crumpled up the piece of paper and threw it across the kitchen, then sat down with her head in her hands for a long time, trying to figure out how to write a story without actually having a story.

It was absurd. There she had been, right up close with Celeste McIntyre – she'd *talked* to her – but when she'd finally rushed back into the crowd, Celeste had been up on stage for a speech and was whisked away by charity people before Frankie could get to her again.

Just write, Frankie, write *something*. Writing was her thing, it was what she did best. During those years when her stammer had kept her silent, she had filled exercise books and diaries with all the words she couldn't say out loud, turning them into something sleek and elegant and biddable.

So she wrote. Drinking one cup of tea after another and feeling the occasional rumble of the Tube below, she sat over her beautiful grown-up birthday notebook and wrote her way through the absurd tussle on the red carpet, the shock at her grandmother's fall, and then the memory of Violet sitting in the ballroom looking so . . . so bloody *lost* – the cheek of her looking *lost* after all the things *she* had done; she wrote through Harry O'Brien being released from prison in just over four weeks' time and how on earth she would support him on a job that was turning out to be precarious at best. She wrote it all out of her system until she finally had a piece that didn't include the kind of dirt Hugo clearly expected but which, she felt, might quite possibly pass muster.

'What on earth is this?' Hugo swept through the editorial department like a tempest the following day. 'Your jobs are hanging on by a thread and this is what you give me? I've never seen more rubbish about Corfu than this sorry excuse for a travel piece. Sina! Where are you, woman? Jesus on this good earth, stop crying, will you? Waddington, you have an hour to produce more on the minister than this. Rooney, I have no words.'

Slightly bewildered, Frankie watched Rooney catch a two-pager drowning in red ink and exclamation marks. She had filed her own copy electronically, had been expecting edits back through the system, brisk and unemotional and certainly not like this, in front of *everyone*, like something out of a movie.

Hugo reared up next to her workspace, his citrusy scent sharp and shrill. 'Broom cupboard not available?' he said amiably, taking in her makeshift desk covered with piles of newspapers and cuttings. 'Felicity, what have I told you about editorial synergy?' he shouted across the newsroom. 'Organise a proper desk close to the others, for heaven's sake.'

'There isn't space,' Felicity shouted back, phone clamped in the crook of her shoulder.

'That large one,' Hugo snarled, pointing.

'It's Mallory's,' Victoria was finally forced to interject. 'He has a breakfast meeting, and . . .' She was stuttering a little and it was clear she had no idea where Mallory was.

'Well, once he graces us with his presence, he'll find that sharing is caring,' Hugo snapped. 'Felicity, make it happen. Victoria, go help; what is this, nursery school? Goodness, June has been pampering you.'

'I'm fine here, honestly,' said Frankie, who didn't remotely want to sit next to Mallory.

'Of course you are, angel, especially after your glorious night full of beauty and grace and worthy causes.'

Hugo prowled around her workspace, picked up her lucky pen, straightened a pile of photos showing Celeste's face, and Frankie was forced to swivel on her chair to keep up with him, trying to make out the amount of red ink on the paper in his hand. Her heart lifted slightly when she couldn't see all that much. Maybe it had been enough, maybe . . .

'I should have let Crawley go in your stead, or Victoria. Even Mallory would have been better.' Hugo slammed the paper onto her desk. It wasn't her piece at all; just a single paragraph of text. But then she caught a few words, recognised more, until she realised that the entire paragraph was made up of half-sentences and parts of expressions that she had laboured over for hours yesterday, now chopped up and pieced together.

'Look, Hugo, I'm sorry about not getting enough on Celeste,' she said quickly. 'It was all a b-b-bit chaotic, to be honest. I'll do better next—'

'First things first. Where are the details of Violet Etherington's fall? Jade said they whisked her away too quickly for anyone to get the scoop, and the official statement was some bland one-liner. But apparently you were right there next to her and bound to have some good material.'

'I had to take her into the b-b-back room and wait with her there, make sure sh-sh-she was all right.' Frankie breathed slowly, willing her stammer to calm down.

'Is she?'

'Yes, although—'

'Did the fainting have anything to do with her recent winding-down of events?' Hugo cut across her.

'No . . . well, that is I'm not—'

'Well excuse me for thinking that you were at the Gala to work,' he said sharply. 'What else could you possibly be doing but focusing solely and entirely on your job. Step up your game, dearie, or you'll find yourself out of it. Now. I'll give you the chance to amend the Gala portion of the piece yourself, but only because you've gifted us that rather surprising photo. You look a tad disgruntled, but the *sujet* more than makes up for it. You, Mrs E *and* Celeste McIntyre. There might be some hope for you after all.'

Lost for words, Frankie stared at the photo. They'd been caught in mid movement, but Celeste still managed to sport her signature grin, while Violet looked a little like a deer in the headlights, clutching a scowling Frankie, who was very obviously straining away.

'Good God,' she said faintly, trying not to think what Victoria would say when she saw that Frankie had not only stolen her story but was actually *in* it.

'Have it on my desk by one,' Hugo said crisply. 'Now, for McIntyre.' He held out another piece of paper, on which Frankie recognised two, maybe three of her original bits, liberally supplemented with a lot of new text.

Tough times for Celeste McIntyre ahead? the caption read. *Nannygate seems to have left its mark on McIntyre, who attended the Starlight Gala last night looking wan and worried, waving off all questions and disappearing to her table as soon as she was able . . .*

'She looked beautiful,' Frankie objected. 'And she talked to a lot of people.'

'And yet not to you,' he pointed out icily.

'Well,' Frankie started. 'She said she felt a bit queasy, but that was just before Violet fell – and that things were tense at home.'

'Queasy, all right, queasy is good. Tense, too. What else?'

'You can't use that, Hugo, it was obviously not on the record. She was just chatting.'

'No one is ever "just chatting". I expected an interview, Miss O'Brien. What's the official definition of an interview – yes?' He pointed Frankie's lucky pen at Con like a schoolmaster.

Throwing Frankie a stricken look, Con quickly rattled off 'A meeting to obtain information, writing up said information in question-and-answer form.'

'Since we don't have that,' Hugo said icily, '*queasy*'ll have to do. Goes well with this.'

He slapped another picture on her desk. Celeste's lipstick was smeared, her skirt ripped, her hands held out in supplication. Frankie looked up incredulously. 'Hugo, my grandmother had just *collapsed*, she was right *there*.' She jabbed the space outside the frame of the picture. 'Look, I'm sorry about the interview, I truly am, but by the time Violet left, Celeste was out of my reach. It won't happen again, I p-p-pro . . .' She would have given anything at this moment, a little finger if need be, to be able to get the words out properly.

'Our readers want news,' Hugo said impatiently. 'If they want a load of tosh about how beautiful the cause is, and how gracious the Starlight Trust is for hosting, they can read the brochure.'

He extracted her original piece from his back pocket and, in a voice both treacly smooth and devastatingly penetrating, proceeded to read it out loud.

'*An evening to remember* blah blah, *such an important cause* blah blah, *one in five children leave primary school unable to read or write properly*, fine, that really is quite unfortunate, but there's no reason to go on and on about it . . . *cannot continue on this trajectory, time for a change . . .*'

Frankie tried to drown it all out, the whispered exchange between Felicity and Victoria clearing half of Mallory's desk, Hugo's relentless recital, the blare from the TV screens, a door slamming. She fixed her eyes on Hugo's white skin, the careless tilt of his collar, the way his fingers folded around the edge of the paper. He had small hands, like a child, dainty almost. Out of the corner of her eye she caught Bea's anguished face as she sidled across to Con's desk for a whispered update. Con's mouth was moving – excitedly, Frankie thought, suddenly savage with rage, eagerly, smugly; he hadn't got to do his story on Celeste, and now he was bloody *smug* about her dressing-down?

She jumped when Hugo's recital stopped.

'You can count yourself lucky that Mr Crawley was able to lean on his contact in a way you clearly weren't able to on yours and added some substance. Here.'

Sources close to the McIntyre family finally confirm many of the issues revealed in Maria Convoy's shocking tell-all, describing the slow but corrosive disintegration of a marriage that had surely been doomed from the outset, given the ease with which McIntyre inserted his paramour into the new household. However, friends question why Celeste put up with it, given that she not only knew about Charles's purchase of a small flat for Convoy, where they would escape for hours at a time, but that her salary indirectly paid for it as well, making her humiliation complete.

There was more lurid detail of trysts and betrayal, some quite graphic and a lot of it carefully worded conjecture. Frankie looked up at Hugo. 'That is *not* my piece,' she said levelly, all trace of her stammer gone.

'It is now.' Hugo handed her back her lucky pen with a flourish. 'Conrad seems to have realised that a promise I made to my old friend Lydia Marquart constitutes in no way a get-out-of-jail-free card, regardless of one's illustrious relations. Now, I like you, little Francesca O'Brien. But do yourself a favour and pull it together.'

Fifteen

Frankie waited until the noise had risen to normal levels again, then, holding herself very straight and avoiding looking at anyone at all, she walked over to her new workspace. Victoria must have got out a ruler, because Mallory's mess stopped exactly two thirds of the way across, giving Frankie fifty centimetres of his desk together with a half-table wedged against the end, so close to the wall that no chair would fit.

'How do I go about getting my computer set up over here?' she asked Felicity when she saw her passing by with an armful of newspapers.

'Call IT,' came the curt answer.

'And a stool or something?'

'Do I look like Habitat?'

Sighing, Frankie reached across to use Mallory's phone.

Victoria's eyebrows shot up. 'Not sure where you worked before, but in such a cramped environment, the unwritten etiquette is to respect each other's space. Get your own phone.'

'I need a phone to *ask* for my ph-ph-phone.' Frankie pushed out the last word with some effort. God, if she wasn't careful, she'd be back to full-time stammering before too long.

Victoria regarded her coolly, then pointedly flicked her gaze to Frankie's hand on Mallory's phone. Without another word, Frankie turned, walked all the way down to IT and found a woman who promised she'd get her computer set up in the next twenty minutes.

'You don't happen to have a stool as well, do you?' Frankie asked.

'Wow,' the woman said. 'I've heard that everyone's in a tizzy up there, but things must be really bad if you've run out of chairs. Here, take that one if you like.'

Frankie carried her stool up the back stairs slowly, delaying the moment when she'd have to enter the newsroom with its wash of impatience and tension and noise, sitting behind that joke of a desk on her stupid stool.

Just before she reached the back door, Beatrice and Con came out.

'There you are,' Bea said, relieved. 'Are you all right? Don't take it to heart, Frankie. You write so well and—'

'Really, Bea, I'm fine.' Frankie didn't mean to cut her off, but she couldn't bear the look of concern and pity on her friend's face. 'It was just a teaching moment, all right? I'm lucky June's out and I have the opportunity to work with Hugo directly. I'll just have to try harder to make it work, is all.'

Beatrice gaped at her. 'Have they brainwashed you in some way? He was a total bastard just now – we even heard him from Marketing.'

'Well, he did send her to write a story on Celeste McIntyre,' Con pointed out.

'And how brilliant of you to save the day,' Frankie snapped.

'After you stole my story from me.' Con stopped himself immediately, looking contrite. 'I'm sorry, Frankie, that came out wrong. But what on earth *happened* at that Gala?'

'It's a bit of a long story.' Frankie shifted her stool onto her hip.

Con waited for her to say more, then shrugged. 'Well, shall we put it behind us and be excited to see our names up there together on our third day here? *Francesca O'Brien and Conrad Crawley*,' he wrote in the air with a flourish just as the door opened and Max Sefton appeared.

'Conrad, you're needed.'

'This place is so crazy,' Beatrice muttered into Frankie's ear, giving Max a sidelong glance. 'I spent the morning putting this entire slideshow together for the online edition, only to find out it was already up there. They're all off their rocker about that evaluation thing. You hang in there, you hear me?' Giving her a quick hug, she disappeared back down the stairs.

'You have a phone and a computer now,' Max said, 'so you can write more things for Hugo to tear down.'

'Th-th-thank you.' Frankie gritted her teeth. For some reason the thought of Max listening to Hugo's reading of her piece was especially unbearable.

'Don't worry, I only caught a sentence or two,' he said soothingly.

'Are you a mind-reader now?' Frankie snapped.

He gave her a long look. 'It's your face,' he said, very seriously and to her irritation not remotely put out by her snappish tone. 'It's so fine and pale and always a bit suspicious, like you expect the world to get right up in your business if you aren't ready to bite. But every now and then there's a stricken look in your eyes, all stormy and distressed.'

'What?' Forgetting to be irritated, Frankie gaped at him, heat creeping into her cheeks as she imagined him looking at her long enough to notice her eyes, stormy or otherwise.

He wasn't remotely self-conscious, however, an enviable quality, she thought grudgingly, and his assessment was surprisingly accurate. She did stay well away from anyone being up in her business, and at this moment she was resolving most especially to stay away from easy-going blue-eyed men in faded jeans.

'Anyway,' he went on, 'the silver lining is that if you survive Hugo's rather old-fashioned way of editing – he does it purely for psychological terror, because elsewhere he's all about digital and online and *must go with the times* – you can work anywhere.'

'I'd be fine if I could make it here for a bit. It's kind of my dream job, you know.' She gave an awkward shrug, because confessing things was not nearly as easy for her as it clearly was for him. 'How long have you been here?'

'Two years, if you can believe it.' Max shook his head. 'Most of that trying and failing to be assigned to politics. A crowded beat, fine, I understand, but Hugo loves picking up on what you don't want to be doing and sticking his fingers in deep. Says it keeps you on your toes.'

'You could try reverse psychology.' Frankie gave a wry grin. 'Pretend to be really interested in . . . abandoned Tube stations. Or whatever you're working on.'

'I'm doing a big series on the decline of Britain's stately homes,' Max said. 'The *just* decline of Britain's stately homes, because according to Hugo they're a superfluous remnant from a former gilded age chock-full of wrongly distributed wealth and ill-used resources.'

'Goodness,' Frankie said faintly. 'But didn't he go to Whittington school? And he's on the board of the National Portrait Gallery.'

'Someone's done their homework.' Max raised his eyebrows. 'If you want a tip, hero-worship in private. The mood is a tad tense at the moment.'

His smile took the sting out of his words, however, and she smiled back. 'Well, he looks the part anyway.' She shrugged. 'All dapper and rugged up, like he'd spend most of his time at the Havisham Club.'

'What would you know about the Havisham?' Max said, surprised, then, 'Of course. The famous Violet Etherington.'

'Forget it, I don't even know why I mentioned it,' Frankie said quickly. 'I haven't spoken to her in ten years, and all of a sudden her name's like a broken record around here.'

'Well, she's a bit of an enigma, I guess. What celebrity out there hasn't given a personal interview, ever? Why haven't you spoken in ten years?'

Max's face hadn't changed, showed the same casual, careless amusement as before, but she very much regretted having let that bit slip. God only knew what would happen if anyone here – and Hugo in particular – realised just how much there was to dig for once you scratched the surface of the Etherington–O'Brien family set-up. Back then, Violet had used her considerable social might to keep her son-in-law's prison sentence out of the limelight, or at least away from her, but information about it wasn't difficult to find if you were prompted to look. Frankie suppressed a sudden shiver at the thought of a conversation at the editorial meeting addressing her father's criminal charges.

'Oh, you know, boring family stuff,' she said lightly.

'Sounds like I need a bit of liquid cheer to coax it out of you.' He nodded. 'Anyway, just pretend you don't care about Hugo capitalising on your connection with your grandmother.'

'I do, I care very much,' she snapped. 'But,' she grinned, 'I'll try, if you'll pretend to care massively about the decline of Britain's elite housing.'

He nodded appreciatively. 'That's the way to bounce back. Trust me, you'll be an expert at that before too long.'

Her determination to bounce back was severely tested, however, when she exited Hugo's office after lunch, having battled with him over every word pertaining to Violet's fall and Celeste's interview. To her surprise, he did finally agree to a wording that Frankie felt even Violet couldn't really object to. The final version of the McIntyre piece, however, was shockingly slanted and heavy with implication due to Con's amendments, and had Frankie itching with shame every time she thought about it.

'I really liked Celeste. All I can hope is that Legal will take out the more glaring lies,' she told Max when she ran into him in the little kitchen later.

'Ah, she'll be fine,' he said. 'McIntyre's always coming apart at the seams and then putting herself back together. She'll understand that you're just doing your job.'

'What I can't get over is how I fell into this helpless trance in

Hugo's office.' Frankie shook her head. 'Nodding at things I would never have contemplated writing at the *Phoenix*. And somehow I still admire him. The way he sees the heart of something, can cut apart a sentence to get to the essence, even if I hate the actual story.'

'That's his speciality, screwing with your head. Come on, I'll buy you a coffee downstairs. Or a brown dishwater beverage anyhow,' Max offered.

'Francesca!' Hugo stuck his head out of his office as they passed and held out a folder. 'Cabals and power play at the board of the New Line Theatre Group; they want to tear down the old Guildhall. Worthy enough for you? Don't let me down again, my lovely.'

'I won't,' she said eagerly. But he'd already closed the door again.

'Let's run away before he can think of more cruelties,' Max muttered but just then, a voice shouted from the newsroom. 'Francesca, telephone!'

'Where *have* you been?' Felicity said accusingly when Frankie came through the door.

'Talking to Hugo,' she said dismissively. 'Just tell them I'll ring back.'

'Are you sure? You might want to take this one.' Felicity's expression was positively wolfish as she held up the phone. 'It's the police.'

Sixteen

It was her father, she knew it. She *knew* it. He'd messed things up just weeks before he was going to be released, he'd been assaulted, he'd harmed himself somehow . . .

No one around her even pretended not to eavesdrop, and Frankie couldn't stop her hands from shaking as she fumbled for the receiver, making Felicity raise her eyebrows and trill under her breath, 'Someone's guil-ty!'

Max told her to shut the hell up and put the call through to the conference room, which Frankie could have kissed him for, and then again for the fact that he didn't follow her inside but hovered by the door to keep people out.

'Ma'am,' an exasperated voice shrilled out of the phone. 'Anyone there?'

'I-I-I,' Frankie took several deep breaths. 'S-s-sorry,' she said hoarsely. 'At work,' she added on a long, slow air swell.

'We have your grandmother here,' the woman said, then quickly, because Frankie had gasped out loud, 'There's no cause for immediate concern; in fact, she seems in fine fettle.' She paused and Frankie could hear an annoyed hubbub of voices. 'It's just . . . well, we'd like you to pick her up, is all.'

'Pick her up?' Frankie's voice rose, relief making her sound a lot sharper than she'd meant to. 'Why?'

'Well, we can't be sure. She was sitting on a bench at the top end of the Serpentine. A jogger had circled several times and was a little worried that she hadn't moved in a while, and then she seemed . . . not herself?'

Frankie felt a rush of relief. 'That's not my grandmother,

then. Violet was born in London, she's lived here all her life. She's been in that park a million times.'

'Says so in her purse,' the policewoman said.

'Someone's stolen it, clearly,' Frankie said dismissively. 'And how did you even find me here?'

'Card in her wallet, some kind of ID; says *London Post* on it, your name.'

Frankie flashed back to Violet plucking the press pass out of the minion's hand. 'I'll be right there.'

There certainly didn't seem to be anything wrong with Violet's voice. Frankie could hear her the moment she set foot in the police station.

'I'm perfectly fine to walk home from here; there's no need to call *anyone* on my behalf.'

'Ma'am, your granddaughter is on her way,' came a soothing reply. 'You can leave the moment she gets here.'

'Why did you have to go and bother her? Frankie, honestly, I didn't *ask* them to.' Violet was loud and looked a little wild, but otherwise she seemed all right.

'Well I'm here now,' Frankie said gruffly. 'So what happened?'

'Nothing,' Violet said vehemently. 'There I was, walking in the park and minding my own business, and next thing I know I'm being spirited away, having to wait here for you. There'd better not have been any journalists witnessing my arrest. You're holding me wrongfully, you know, young woman. I could have your head for this. In fact, I *will*,' she snarled suddenly. 'I'm going to write a letter to the superintendent, the commissioner . . .'

'Violet,' Frankie said, slightly alarmed at her savage expression. 'You're not under arrest. They were just being cautious.'

'I'm fine.' Violet thrust her face forward, her voice so sharp that both Frankie and the woman, who surely had to be used to a whole lot more aggression from actual criminals, flinched backwards.

'Okay.' Frankie held out her hands, slowly, like you did when you didn't want to startle a cornered animal. 'I understand that you're fine. I'm fine, and she' – she threw a glance at the policewoman, who nodded – 'is also fine.'

Violet's face was working; her body seemed braced for something, muscles tensed. Was she going to come flying at them? The thought darted through Frankie's head and, instinctively, she brought her fists up, at the same time wondering wildly, incoherently, how on earth this could possibly be Violet, her *grandmother*.

But just as quickly as it had come, the snarling rage on Violet's face vanished. 'Well, we'll be going then,' she said. 'Thanks very much for your help.'

Frankie's mouth fell open and she looked at the policewoman, who was holding out Violet's coat.

'You don't need to come with me, Frankie.' Violet squinted at the coat as if deciding whether it was truly hers, then shrugged herself into the arms, waving away the woman's help.

'Violet . . .' Frankie started, but, still fumbling with the coat, her grandmother had turned towards the door and was walking into the corridor, briskly and with a hint of impatience, as if she couldn't understand what the hold-up was, let alone all the fuss. 'You've got your coat on inside out,' Frankie said to her disappearing back.

She looked at the policewoman and found that she was studying her thoughtfully.

'Has this ever happened before?' she asked.

'The arguing? Yes. The walking, definitely. Sitting on a park bench, yeah, I'm sure she occasionally sits down.' Frankie rubbed her face with her hand. 'Look, thank you so much for ringing me. I'd better go and catch up with her. Nobody saw her, right? No one was taking pictures or anything?'

'No, not that I was aware of.' The woman took a small breath, as if she wanted to say something else, but then she just nodded and extracted a small piece of paper from a folder. 'Here,' she said. 'This was the woman who found her; she left her number in case we had any questions.'

'Questions?' Frankie was confused. 'I mean, it's nice of her to be so concerned, but . . .'

'Yes, well, by the time we got there, Mrs Etherington seemed all right, but the woman absolutely insisted we had to get her picked up by someone. I think she might be in social work or something. Certainly seemed knowledgeable.'

Knowledgeable about *what*?

'Frankie?' came Violet's impatient voice from the front.

'Okay,' Frankie said wearily, taking the piece of paper. 'Thank you.'

After all the noise and belligerence at the police station, Violet seemed very quiet in the taxi home, sagging tiredly against the back of the seat and staring out of the window.

'Violet, what happened at the park?' Frankie felt a bit awkward, given that the last time they spoke she'd been shouting at her.

'Just a misunderstanding,' Violet said, vaguely but a little strained, and Frankie was reminded of the moment she'd first seen her on the red carpet the night before, with that odd, disassembled air around her, the brief panicked flare in her eyes when the journalist asked her a question.

'Here we are, ladies,' the driver said jovially. 'That'll be ten pound fifty, then.'

Violet slid along the seat towards the door.

'Wait,' Frankie said, but her grandmother was already out on the footpath.

'Granny doing a runner?' The cabbie cheerfully but pointedly stuck his hand through the window as Violet strode up the steps to her flat.

'Keep the change, thank you.' Frankie shoved some money at

him, before taking the steps two at a time. 'Violet, wait, let me make you some tea or—'

'You know, I'm really tired all of a sudden. I think I'll close my eyes for a bit,' Violet cut in. 'You must have a lot of things to do.'

'Don't be like this.' Frankie was stung. 'They called me to help; I'm here to help, I—'

But there was a soft click and the door closed in her face.

'For heaven's sake,' she said angrily, the flaky black paint of the door swimming a little in front of her eyes.

She marched back down the steps, past the tree sausages and across the road, furious and at the same time strangely shaken. She stopped, looked back. The day had turned murky and grey, and she squinted through the gloom, waiting for lights to come on in the kitchen, evidence of Violet making herself a cup of tea, taking it through to the sitting room. While partial to a lie-in in the morning, Violet firmly opposed any kind of proper daytime nap, claiming that the moment you were horizontal between 9 a.m. and 9 p.m., you were either fatally ill or ready for the infirmary. This didn't include closing her eyes in her big armchair for a bit, though, and she had certainly *looked* tired. Maybe she was coming down with something. The flu, maybe. It came on quickly, people said, and it could make you dizzy, too, which would explain why she'd fallen the day before. Or – God – a heart attack. Maybe she was in there right now, splayed on the ground and unable to get up; maybe she was throwing up, and would lie in a puddle of her own vomit until tomorrow, choking . . .

Frankie had crossed the road in three big jumps and was up the stairs, fumbling for the small, square key on her key ring.

'Violet,' she whisper-shouted, 'where are you?'

The front hall was dark and deserted. No Violet lying on the ground in the throes of a heart attack, but no homely sound of her rustling the newspaper in the drawing room either. Silence.

Frankie kicked off her shoes, conditioned by years of being told that shoes inside were for the country, and set them next to the hallway bench, where they'd always had their place. She frowned at the umbrella stand, which was lying on its side and had pinned a piece of paper to the floor. She straightened the stand, picked up the paper and peered beyond the bench into the dark, silent drawing room. She was strangely reluctant to turn on the light; she wasn't entirely sure whether this visit fell under *come and go any time* or was just plain creepy. What if Violet was in the bathroom and half dressed? But at the end of the corridor, the bathroom was dark, too. All right, she'd just have one look in Violet's bedroom, then she'd go. All that New Line Theatre stuff was burning a hole in her bag; she was going to be up all night anyway, so if Violet was all right, she'd be on her way—

In the door to Violet's room, Frankie froze. Lying on the bed, very much horizontal, her grandmother was fast asleep, fully clothed and, Frankie had to blink twice, still wearing her shoes, firmly laced and crusted with dried mud.

Violet didn't stir, not even when Frankie tripped over that stubborn edge of the carpet that always curled up, and banged her shin against the edge of the bed.

For a long time, she stared down at her grandmother in the gloomy half-light of the bedroom, willing her to move, to sigh in her sleep, to do something, *anything* that a normal sleeper would do, let alone someone as violently opposed to naps as Violet; but she slept on, unmoving, arms folded over her chest, fingers interlinked.

Utterly at a loss, Frankie squinted at the piece of paper she was still holding. It was thick and a little grainy to the touch. *Shoes*, it said in big letters, above – Frankie frowned, brought the paper closer to her eyes – a series of drawings, rather crudely done but very clearly showing a shoe with six holes, a snaky line as shoelaces. It was repeated four times, one below the other, and in each picture, the snaky line took on shape, looped itself through the other end, until it was finally fully tied in a crooked bow.

Frankie frowned, looking from the paper to the shoes on Violet's feet. The shoelaces were thick and a slightly different colour from the shoes, the loops big and childlike, secured with a double knot. She backed away, her eyes on the paper as she pulled the door closed – and stopped dead. A second piece of paper, stuck on the door at eye height. *My room*, it said in the same big felt-tip letters.

Slowly, very slowly, Frankie reached for the light switch, and in the yellowish light of the overhead lamp she saw a third sign: *Bathroom*.

Seventeen

It was like a horrific, torturous treasure hunt. Half running, half stumbling, Frankie was back in the hall, crouched down next to the umbrella stand to understand where that first paper had come from, when she spotted another, attached to a basket under the table. *Shoes in here.* Somewhere far away, her mind strayed to seven letters on an old ice cream carton, the childhood relief of being assigned a place, replaced by irritation at the high-handedness of it last night. But this . . . Her heart started beating faster and faster as realisation dawned, unwillingly, agonisingly slowly, because she didn't want to take in the full implication of this – *please God, no, please God* . . . She pressed her lips together when she saw the word *Keys* scrawled above a nail that had been pounded crookedly next to the front door at Violet's eye height. Hands shaking, she turned on every light she could find, as if that would help her understand.

Coat in cupboard
Wear socks
Tie shoes
Key goes into lock
Close door behind you
Lock door

It went on and on, the red letters on creamy white swimming before Frankie's eyes, gathering force, turning into long wavy lines across her vision as she spun around.

Please, no, please . . .

She fumbled for her phone, found the little piece of paper the policewoman had given her earlier – could it really only have been a few hours ago? – misdialled twice before finally getting a ringtone.

'Karen Ellmore.' It was a bright, chirpy voice, young enough to be a jogger coming across an old woman sitting on a park bench.

'I . . .' For a moment Frankie fought a whole mouthful of letters, wasn't sure if she could get any words out at all. She took a few deep breaths, tried to open her throat. 'Th-th-this is Frankie O'Brien . . . I mean Etherington . . . You were kind enough to take care of my grandmother earlier. The p-p-police . . .'

'Ah, yes,' the voice said, immediately interested. 'Is she all right? She was arguing so much I was worried the police would just let her go. Or that she was alone.'

'I t-t-took her home,' Frankie said.

Silence fell. Frankie couldn't bring herself to ask, the voice at the back of her mind still begging *please, no.*

'I don't mean to be intrusive, but has this ever happened before?' the woman asked.

'I . . . I don't really know.' Frankie felt her tongue twist around the consonants. 'W-we . . .' she breathed out slowly, 'haven't been in contact lately.'

'Ah.'

She heard the woman – Karen – rustling on the other end. 'You need to get her checked out. Dementia can take many different forms, and if you get it diagnosed early, you can get help . . .'

She said a great many more things, woolly, bloated bits of sentences about brain scans and care facilities and tests, but Frankie's brain had snagged on the word. The one that had a lot of consonants in it, difficult, gnarly letters that made saying it out loud impossible, even if she had wanted to. Which she didn't.

'She doesn't have *that*,' she cut in breathlessly. 'She's just . . .'

Bright and funny. Infuriating and overbearing. Stubborn.

She could imitate any voice perfectly but she sang in the shower so badly her grandfather had once turned off the water at the mains to get her to stop. She drove too fast, she cared too much about too many things too deeply. Violet was a lot of things, but there was no way she was *that*. On the contrary, she was utterly, amazingly *sane*.

'. . . she isn't,' Frankie finished loudly.

There was a pause.

'I'm really sorry,' Karen said quietly. 'Maybe I got it wrong, but I work in a special care facility, you see, and come across a lot of things. I think you need to talk to your doctor to really understand what this could mean for you, for your family. What she needs in terms of care . . .'

If she had argued or discussed or tried harder to convince her, Frankie would have stood her ground. Instead, the gentle tone, the knowing undercurrent in Karen's voice, as if she already knew what Frankie was trying so very hard not to, made her blood run cold.

'I have to go,' she finally got out, and then she hung up and shoved her phone back into her bag, all the way down to the bottom.

Somehow she made it down to the kitchen, vague thoughts of spooning sugar into something hot to jolt her back to reality, to fix whatever *this* was.

Keep milk in fridge
Butter away from Aga
Windows closed
Hob off
Milk bottles outside
Put tea bag in mug
You hate *sugar*
Use one tea bag only

Just in time, Frankie reached the back door, which had been

left unlocked despite a large sign taped to it that said *Lock door*, before throwing up onto the bottom end of the steep, narrow stairs leading up to the street. Gripping the banister, she heaved and heaved as if trying to rid herself of all those bright red letters, the phone conversation, the muddy shoes. Finally she went back into the kitchen, numbly thinking of a bucket or newspaper to clean up the mess before giving up and sitting down right there on the floor next to the rubbish bin. Maybe there was an explanation, she tried to tell herself. But, rubbing her face and trying to swallow down the acid taste in her mouth, she saw, on top of the overflowing bin, a whole wodge of used tea bags. There were ten of them at least, all squeezed together in one big ball, the imprint of a hand still clearly visible across the gauzy brown surface.

Use one tea bag only.

She closed her eyes.

'What on *earth* are you doing here?'

Frankie looked up to see her grandmother in the kitchen door, up and awake and looking strangely, blessedly normal. Pale and tired, yes, with smudged half-moon shadows beneath her eyes and a small imprint from a pillow tassel at the base of her jaw. But the way her ancient dressing gown was tied tightly around her middle, her hair brushed back behind her ears, it could have been fifteen years ago, when she would walk into the kitchen in the mornings grumbling about how the authorities could possibly think it humane to force children to school this early. Only now it was eight at night and Violet had slept on her bed in her shoes.

'What's going on?' she said, looking around her and frowning.

She looked fine, Frankie thought as she got to her feet, she *looked* normal, didn't she – but then Violet's eyes flicked to the pieces of paper tacked up around the kitchen, and a dark flush crept up her cheeks. She bit her lip nervously, her fingers fluttering against the seam of her cardigan, worrying at a stray thread in that new way Frankie had already noticed at the Gala. More things fell into place: the strange see-saw of intensity and vagueness, the flickering expressions, the fainting, the odd present-tense talk about Romy and the Blitz.

And Frankie knew, right then and there, that *fine* wasn't even on the same planet as what was happening here, and that there was, quite possibly, no *normal* any more. Fear unspooled when she saw her grandmother's expression, resigned and panicked and afraid all at the same time.

'So.' She cleared her throat. 'This is . . . new.'

It was completely inadequate, but Violet nodded and then, horribly, her eyes were very bright, her mouth working, and she pressed her hand in front of her mouth.

'I don't know what to do,' she pushed out between her fingers. 'Oh Frankie, I don't *know*.'

Abruptly she sat down at the kitchen table, put her head in her hands and started talking, a gush of fear about all the things she knew she must have forgotten but couldn't *remember* forgetting: money miscounted, names and faces mismatched, things misplaced and then found in strange corners of the flat.

'How long has this been happening?' Frankie whispered. 'Why didn't . . . ?'

'Why didn't I get in touch?' Violet asked wryly, and Frankie flushed when she thought back to Violet's many attempts to repair the rift between them over the last ten years. Letters Frankie hadn't answered, phone calls she'd ignored, because Violet still refused to concede that she'd done anything wrong that day when Harry O'Brien went to prison.

'Okay, but Jools. Violet, she thought you'd gone *off* her. Is this why?' She gestured at the signs. 'She said you don't even let her into the flat any more.'

'You know Jools, always right up in your face,' Violet said

belligerently, then she sank down. 'I couldn't, Frankie,' she said, more quietly. 'I just couldn't face it. And I don't really know *what* to say, either, because I try to reconstruct what happened afterwards and I don't understand it. Mrs Langley at the corner shop gave me back money I apparently paid extra, a hundred *pounds*, Frankie. Mrs Bellfour doesn't return my greetings because apparently I've slighted her on the street. But I can't tell you what I did; there's this dark grey fog, an absence, a hole in my time, there's a hole in *me*.' Her voice had risen again and she pushed her fist against her mouth. 'So I try to remind myself of everything that's important,' she jerked her thumb at the signs, 'because then maybe I can go on as before.'

'But Mrs Potter, where's Mrs P?' Frankie forced her voice to be calm. 'Surely she'd have noticed all this . . .'

But when she looked around the kitchen, she realised just how dirty it was, with food crusted to the hob, the surfaces sticky with rings and dried-up puddles. The floor hadn't been swept in days, weeks even, and the windows would have had Mrs Potter quit on the spot.

'I let her go.' Violet hung her head. 'She was getting on a bit anyway, and the kitchen stairs were hard for her, and I . . .' She broke off. 'I was so ashamed,' she whispered. 'The other day, I must have missed the toilet, went all over the floor, but I didn't realise until I went back in a few hours later. I can't let Mrs Potter be in a hovel like this, I can't bear the thought of her seeing me like this, or Jools, or *anyone*.'

'She would never judge you.' Frankie tried to keep the shock out of her voice. 'We love Mrs P, remember? She's so nice.'

'I don't care. I can't bear it.' Violet's voice was flat and final.

'But you need help, Violet. And today, what happened in the park?'

'I don't know.' Violet frowned, traced the pattern on the sticky plastic tablecloth. 'It's like my legs are possessed, I just find myself walking and walking, all the time, long stretches, too. Usually it's totally fine, but sometimes I get lost, or I think I do anyway, because I end up in places I didn't mean to go.'

'And what's happening with your work? The charity boards, the speaking engagements, Safe Haven?'

Violet looked away. 'I'm worried that something will happen at an event or that I'll start talking rubbish. I keep trying to support things in some way, not to leave Safe Haven in the lurch. Mia has been a huge help. And she doesn't ask any questions at all. I just told her the doctor said I was to take things easy, bit of a dickey heart. She's been smoothing things over, discreetly cancelling what she can. I was hoping no one would notice if I gradually disappeared. Fat chance of that!' she said bitterly. 'She's fielding more press enquiries about my absences now than about women whose lives are in danger. That's partly why I came to the Gala yesterday. She drove me there and was going to pick me back up right after I'd made an appearance. I was hoping to quell the rumours for a bit, and of course I wanted to support Celeste. And then, of all the things, I had to go and faint in the most public way possible.'

Frankie swallowed uneasily when she pictured Violet reading the *London Post* tomorrow.

'Do you think the fainting is connected in some way with . . . you know?' she asked quickly.

'Not sure.' Violet said. 'Maybe it's because I don't eat all that much. I'm often so tired, and it's tough to make food for myself without . . . well . . .' She thrust her thumb at the sign above the cooker without looking at it. *Turn off hob.*

Frankie couldn't remember when she'd felt more helpless. 'Your GP . . .' She seized upon that idea with some relief. 'You were meant to get yourself checked out today. Dr Morrissey, what did he—'

'I haven't been,' Violet said firmly. 'And I won't, I can't bear anyone knowing, I just can't, Frankie.'

*

They went back and forth over the same ground for a long time. Frankie, averting her eyes from the half-eaten bowl of baked beans on the countertop and the five pieces of toast next to it, each with a single bite taken out of them, had heated a can of soup from the cupboard, made tea. But throughout, Violet clung stubbornly to the need for discretion and the refusal of any kind of exposure, the mention of which made her obstinate and shivery with some nameless fear that Frankie couldn't quite put her finger on.

'Violet, what do you want me to do?' she said finally, not even trying to keep the exasperation out of her voice. 'You don't want Mrs Potter, you don't want me to tell Jools, you don't want to see a doctor. I get that you don't like people knowing your business, I understand that pulling back from work is hard. That you're ashamed about all of this.' She waved her hand at the filthy kitchen. 'But you need to figure this out. And just think, it might still turn out to be something else altogether, something harmless. A virus. A bug. But for that, you need to go and see someone. Maybe we need to check you into a hospital for a full physical or something and then a—'

'No!' Violet sat up straight. 'No, please, Frankie, I beg you, please don't put me in a home. I'm *trying*, I swear, I'm trying so hard . . .' Her voice had risen hysterically, and even when Frankie tried to interject, Violet talked over her, louder and louder, until her voice was ringing in Frankie's ears and she didn't think she could bear it. It wasn't supposed to *be* this way; Violet was supposed to be the strong one, the opinionated, independent woman who ran roughshod over Frankie's life. '. . . I'll be better, I promise—'

'Violet, stop!' Frankie shouted. 'I said *hospital*, not a *home*. For *tests*.'

Violet broke off abruptly, sank back onto her chair, breathing heavily. And then no one said anything for a long time. Tentatively Frankie reached out, even when Violet looked like she wanted to shrug her off, then scooted all the way forward with her chair and awkwardly put her arms around her grandmother. Shivers were running down Violet's back and arms, travelling across their embrace, until Frankie too was shaking, her cheeks wet with tears, her hand patting her grandmother's back, a tiny, useless gesture compared to the magnitude of this. Neither of them, she realised, had yet been able to say the word out loud, had referred to it in any other terms than *it* and *this*. Because it could still be something else, couldn't it? Wasn't Violet's skin warm and didn't her ribcage lift up and down with each breath? Wasn't it all still working? Blood pulsing through her veins, her muscles tightening to clutch at Frankie, tears welling up in her eyes, air pushing through her lungs, all functioning the way it should. Frankie closed her eyes and breathed in her grandmother's scent, so achingly normal, so exactly the same that it simply didn't seem possible that Violet wouldn't, any moment now, straighten and clap her hands together briskly, reach up into the cupboard next to the Aga for the special biscuits. *What a gloomy day. Let's treat ourselves, shall we?*

Instead, they sat in a kitchen that smelled of burnt food and vomit and sour milk.

'Then there's only one option,' Frankie said finally into Violet's hair. 'I'm going to move in with you.'

Violet

October 1940

Eighteen

For so many days, Violet had been anticipating the adventure of catching a train and all else that lay ahead; the relief of extricating herself, chrysalis-like, from her old self and burrowing beneath the layers of Lily Burns. Lily, she'd decided would be a quiet, no-nonsense girl, eminently capable and brave, with a sense of humour.

Instead, she'd found herself pushed into the corner of a carriage stuffed to the gills with servicemen and civilians fleeing London, where she crouched for hours, racked with anxiety, as raucous conversation flew back and forth around her. And then there was the fact that she was wearing breeches. *Breeches*. Whatever rebellious impulse she'd had, creeping up from the coal cellar early that morning and putting on her uniform, had vanished the moment she walked down the platform, mortifyingly aware of the sight of her legs for all to see.

Now, her face hot and flushed, her arms pressing her suitcase hard against her chest in case someone ripped it from her, she didn't dare move lest even more of her was touching the man sitting next to her, a tired-looking soldier whose head kept drooping closer and closer to her shoulder. Surreptitiously she fumbled for her papers and, chin pulled deep into her overcoat, wearing her hat with its gold Land Army badge pinned to the front, read through them again. *Lily Burns*, she whispered to herself. Lily Burns would stop flushing this very minute; she'd shove the soldier back upright and icily ignore the two men eyeing her from behind a large woman with a basket. Lily Burns wasn't going to be a pushover; she was going to stand her ground. And then someone sent by her employer, a Mr Hardwick, would pick her up and tell her what to do.

Excitement reared its head again, gave her another nudge. She, spoilt, good-for-nothing Violet, actually had an employer, was going to *work*. All she needed to do was to get through this journey. *Lily Burns* and *Mr Hardwick*, she murmured to herself one last time as the man next to her slowly settled his head on her shoulder. She tucked the papers away and pressed her hand against her chest, where she felt Romy's necklace a small hard presence against her skin. She didn't look up again, not even when a whole group of uniformed men got on and gathered everyone into singing 'There'll Always Be An England'.

The sun was low in the sky when, after many interminable delays, the bus driver finally called, 'Barleigh!' down the bus and came to a halt in a village square. One after another the passengers dispersed, until Violet finally had to face up to the dreadful truth that the bus, which had been supposed to be here in the early afternoon, had arrived too late for anyone to wait around for her. It took her a good ten minutes of hovering by the bus stop and imagining her mother around every corner before she finally worked up the courage to ask two women gossiping across a fence about Mr Hardwick.

'At chapel, most likely,' one of them said. 'That's where he can usually be found. Evensong,' she added at Violet's questioning face. 'What heathen parts are you from, then?'

'Er, London.' Violet had never given London's religious standards a single thought, or indeed been in the habit of attending service more than propriety required.

'Ah,' the woman said, as if that clarified everything. 'You'll be one of them *girls*, then?' She managed to sound both disparaging and guiltily thrilled.

'A land girl, yes.' Violet seized gratefully on the one constant in this confusing conversation and smiled at the women. She hadn't expected a pat on the back, certainly, but neither was she prepared for the distinctly snide way the woman looked her up and down.

'It's thataway,' she said finally, and as Violet walked away, she could feel the women's eyes on her back until she'd turned the corner.

She must have misread the situation, Violet tried to tell herself; she'd just got them at a bad moment. But the women's abruptness had done nothing to dispel the growing sense that her endeavour was doomed. Night was coming, and if she didn't find Mr Hardwick, she would have no idea what to do.

She walked slowly, face still flushed with embarrassment after the exchange with the women, eyes fixed on her feet marching along the village lane. Dust settled on the tight, hard-leathered shoes that had pinched her toes raw all day, her coat hung suffocatingly heavy on her shoulders, her gas mask banging against her side with each step. She thought of the small amount of money Duffy had pressed on her. 'To cable home if things get dire,' he'd said, raising his eyebrows as if he already knew that she wouldn't be able to see this through. *You're so useless, Violet,* she heard her mother's voice chime in. *Women aren't meant to be on their own.* She shrugged off her coat angrily, flung it on her case, pulled at her tie and unbuttoned her shirt at the top. For a few moments she looked back in the direction of the village and fanned herself with the end of her tie. It smelled different out here, she thought after a little while. Crisp, a bit smoky. Loamy and earthy, like they said autumn smelled in the books, and above it all, a sweet, fizzy scent, carried across on a breeze that stirred Violet's hair and cooled her cheeks. Apples, of course. Winterbourne was apple country. She turned away from the village to look across the valley for the first time – and forgot her mother and Duffy, forgot about being afraid and alone.

The lane curved in a long, lazy arc all the way around the

valley, disappearing at the far end in a haze of foliage that blazed orange, purple and red in the sun. A patchwork of fields and orchards fell away to her right; woolly contours of hedges bordered meadows and trees moved gently in the early-evening breeze. Birds were wheeling across a vast blue canopy shot through with streaks of pink, lavender and orange, and below it, nestled amidst knots of trees and hedges, was Winterbourne House.

Built from the same golden stone she'd seen in the village, the house rose three storeys high, two wings neatly tucked behind. The low-hanging sun turned it a rich honey colour, lingered on the white window frames, picked out the splash of late roses climbing around the front door. The house wasn't far from the lane as the crow flew, but the road meandered around the edges of the valley for a while before connecting up with a long, tree-lined drive sweeping up to it. On one side of it, outbuildings and sheds were scattered around what looked like a large stable yard, shielded from sight of the house by small patches of trees.

It was beautiful, Winterbourne. Graceful and yet entirely at ease, as if it had always been there, rising from the countryside along with the trees and meadowland and glowing its muted gold through the centuries. Something seared through Violet at the beauty of it all. Pain and joy and longing. And then a sound drifted up the lane, and when she blinked again, she saw, through the trees and bushes ahead, the small steeple of a church.

Unexpectedly, the little church was rather full, and the door squeaked so loudly that Violet froze in mid step across the threshold as every head swivelled to the back. Up front, the clergyman turned in surprise and the man reading aloud at the lectern abruptly broke off. He stared at Violet, took in her red, sweating face, the bedraggled-looking hat sitting on hair rising hectically around her head. He opened his mouth, then, gripping the side of the lectern, started reading again. Violet stood against the back wall, her eyes on the floor, until, judging by the asthmatic swell of the organ – and after what sounded to her untrained religious sensibilities like an undue amount of talking about sin and redemption – things seemed to be winding up. Relief gave way to dread, however, when she realised that she had to find Mr Hardwick among the people filing out of the church past her. She should ask someone. *Do it now, Violet, just ask . . .*

'How dare you come in here in the middle of service?' A low voice was suddenly right next to her, so close that she nearly jumped out of her skin.

It was the reader. The first thing she thought – stupidly, really, because why would it matter in the face of his obvious anger – was that he wasn't nearly as tall as he'd appeared up on the raised dais of the lectern. And the second thing was that he had to be aware of that fact, because he was holding himself almost unnaturally straight, the severity of the posture accentuated by his stark black suit and white shirt, sharply pressed and immaculate against Violet's own rumpled, creased appearance.

'And looking like that, too.' He averted his eyes from her body and she frowned down at her uniform in confusion. 'Button up your shirt this instant. Wait for me outside. You will not speak to anyone nor elicit attention of any kind.'

She fought an overwhelming sense of disorientation.

'Are you Mr Hardwick?' She formed the words carefully. Honouring Duffy's advice, she had decided not to affect a working-class accent, knowing that it would trip her up sooner rather than later, but instead kept her voice as neutral as she possibly could.

'Name?' He extracted a small black book and a pencil stub from the inside of his coat.

'Vi . . . er Lily. Lily Burns.'

'You're too small.' He made a note in the book. 'We need someone to drive a tractor.'

'I'll do my best, I won't be a bother,' she said, trying to sound firm.

'You certainly won't be if you know what's good for yourself. Go.'

He stood aside, but the church entrance was too narrow for them both, and in an effort to stay out of his way, she stumbled against the doorway.

'Walk properly,' his voice barked from behind. 'And where's your coat?'

'I took it off . . . the sun . . .' she mumbled.

'Coats are to be worn outside at all times.'

Dusk had settled in the shadows of the church windows and across the lane outside, smudging the vivid autumn colours. With the same slate-coloured roof and upward steeple as Winterbourne House, the church jutted out above the valley like a figurehead on a ship. Squinting, Violet could make out some activity in the stable yard, but it was difficult to see in the fading light. It would be blackout soon, she realised, automatically looking up to scour the darkening sky, straining to listen for the telltale thrum of aircraft engines. All was quiet, though, just a breeze playing through the trees around the chapel. A few parishioners stood in the forecourt, heads together, one of them nudging the others at her approach. Snapping back his shoulders, Hardwick motioned Violet towards a horse and cart off to the side, apparently eager to get her out of sight. But not quickly enough. One of the group had broken away, a man with razor-short hair and a small moustache.

'Ah, Hardwick. Corralled your wayward charge, have you?' He leaned closer and took in Violet's breeches and white shirt, still flapping open at the neck, with heavily lidded eyes above cheeks puffy with the miasma of red veins. Violet fought the urge to step back. Always in the shadow of her mother, on the arm of a polite youth or in the company of Edward, she'd never been so openly *looked* at by anyone. If the moustached man noticed her itchy embarrassment, it seemed only to make him smile more broadly. 'My, my, they do breed them well in the army,' he said cosily. 'Must revise my opinion on women joining up. Welcome to the valley, my dear.' But before his hand – white-skinned, puffy and sweaty-looking – could connect with hers, Hardwick pushed her the last few yards towards the cart.

'For heaven's sake, put your coat on, girl.'

'No wonder you keep them all tucked away in the orchards, Hardwick,' Violet heard the man say, and when she chanced a backwards glance, she saw him wink in a conspiratorial way that seemed to set Hardwick's teeth even more on edge, making his jawbones jut out sharply. Quickly she fumbled her coat out of the handle of the suitcase and shrugged it on, then sagged against the side of the wagon, limp with exhaustion.

Hardwick had walked over to the little group to say his farewells. He moved among them easily, clearly well known, but at the same time, there was something ever so slightly cautious about the way he held himself as he nodded deferentially at the clergyman and bowed stiffly to a heavyset woman before taking his leave. He hadn't managed to shake off the moustached man, however, who was keeping pace, still smiling in the oily way that made Violet double-check the buttons on her coat.

'Up,' Hardwick snarled, and reflexively Violet jumped. Rolling herself awkwardly onto the wooden perch, she saw the moustached man watching her flailing legs and quickly pulled herself up to sitting, looking straight ahead.

'Well I'll let you go, Hardwick, you'll need to get home safely before the blackout,' the man said grudgingly. 'But I might have to come for a little inspection soon. See all this glorious female workforce in the flesh, eh?' His hand slipped forward, patted her ankle. Revolted, she whipped her leg out of reach, but he just laughed and waggled his finger at her. 'I'm Mr Manson, the local magistrate, and I sometimes fill in for the ARP warden. So you have to be nice to me. We've only had the odd visit by the Germans so far, but over by the coast, they've had several air raids already. Never fear, though, I'm here to protect all pretty girls.'

Hardwick snapped the whip so hard that the horse practically jumped forward. Violet winced at the streak across its neck but she didn't dare look back at Mr Manson, nor at Hardwick, whose body was ramrod straight next to hers.

Nineteen

Hardwick drove fast, clearly wanting to make the most of the fading light, which had brought with it a chill that made Violet's teeth chatter slightly. The road curved around the valley and they turned into a driveway marked by a set of enormous iron-hinged pillars. The gates had obviously been removed, most likely in one of the metal drives earlier in the year.

'No smoking.' Hardwick finally spoke. His voice was brisk, more confident now, as if, away from church and village, he was back on his own territory and it was clear who was in charge.

'Yes,' she said nervously.

'Yes what?'

It took her a moment to realise what he wanted.

'Yes, er, Mr Hardwick,' she mumbled.

'Your uniform is to be in order at all times. I know other places let you supplement liberally, but not here. No rolling-up of trouser legs or shirtsleeves, no matter what the temperature. You must be decent at all times.'

Violet noticed that his emphasis on 'decent' bore an uncanny resemblance to the way the women had spoken about the 'girls': a mixture of derision and condescension that made her flush with its pointed implication.

They drove under a vaulted stone archway, then the horse was clopping across the stable yard, stopping in front of one of the doors. A groom peered out, clearly having anticipated their arrival, because he immediately scurried forward to take the bridle.

'Evening, Mr Hardwick. Will that be all?'

Hardwick tossed him the reins without a word, jumped down and stalked towards a building adjoining the large archway they'd just come through.

'Wait here,' he threw over his shoulder at Violet.

She set down her case, slumping in exhaustion the moment he disappeared into the building. She kept her eyes fixed on the door, ready to snap back upright at his reappearance. But the minutes ticked away, the stable yard almost fully dark now, and still she stood, her legs aching unbearably as she tried to recall his exact words. Could she have misunderstood? Was she supposed to go somewhere? She'd just sunk to her knees, trying to control the trembling in her thighs, when a shadow reared out of the darkness.

'Curfew's at nine, no exception.' Hardwick strode ahead, moving sure-footed through the darkness, as she scrambled to follow. 'Blackout is, obviously, strictly observed.' She felt more than saw him gesture around the dark stable yard.

'Yes, Mr Hardwick.' Violet tried to penetrate the darkness around her as he made his way between what seemed to be the wooden buildings she'd seen from the road. This had to be her accommodation, and please God let there be a bed, a doorstep sandwich and a friendly face in there *somewhere*.

'No leaving the grounds unless it's your day off, and days off will only be granted when all work is done and behaviour has been exemplary. No talking to the villagers or orchard workers if you cross paths in the fields. No socialising of *any* kind. You lot will keep to yourselves.'

He came to an abrupt stop at a door and opened it with a sharp snap of his hand. It was even darker inside, a fathomless, velvety blackness. Involuntarily, Violet shrank back.

'Are you waiting for a written invitation?' he asked brusquely.

'Will you, I mean, won't you come in and show me around?' she stammered.

He looked at her as if she'd lost her mind.

'No male visitors inside the barn, *ever*,' he said, his voice hard on the last word. 'My daughter will check on the curfew later. Make sure to tell the others that breakfast is half an hour earlier than usual tomorrow. The way the weather's been going, we're up against it now. And one last thing.' He gripped her arm so hard that she winced. 'You will not be filthy or improper or any of the other things you might be used to. Females have no place in my orchards except to do exactly as they're told, work hard and keep their mouths shut the rest of the time.'

She gasped, at the coarseness of his words, the unspeakable meaning behind them, the unwanted touch. A spiral of anger rose, bristled.

'I will work hard,' she said through gritted teeth.

'I will work hard, what?'

'I will work hard, Mr Hardwick,' she hissed, but before she'd even got the last word out, he had thrust her across the threshold and closed the door so she pitched forward into the black emptiness.

Trembling, she groped for her suitcase, which, she discovered, had sprung open, scattering clothes across the dusty floor. All the way at the other end, there was a lit rectangle with a ladder leading up towards the sound of voices.

'Hello?' Her voice was thin and, to her horror, suddenly choked with tears. 'I'm down here,' she tried again, now managing a hoarse bellow.

'Hello?' A moment later, an old-fashioned oil lamp dangled down the hatch, then two figures slid down the ladder.

The young woman holding up the lamp was tall and a little older than Violet. Her legs were long and rangy in her trousers, her jumper snug around her upper body. An armlet with the letter F embroidered on it was wrapped around her arm. She had to be the forewoman then, in charge of the girls. Violet remembered reading about it in the pamphlets.

'You're the new girl?' She held the lamp closer to Violet.

'I'm Lily Burns.' Violet remembered just in time to even out her accent. In the lamplight, she picked up a stray shirt and closed her suitcase.

'Goodness, are they sending us *children* now?' the other girl asked. Her jumper didn't fit her quite as well and her hair was blowsy above a round, kind face as she squinted at Violet. 'You look barely older than my little sister. Didn't Hardwick want someone who can drive a tractor, Kit? Can you drive a tractor?' she asked Violet hopefully.

Violet tried to stand taller, but it only seemed to highlight her shortcomings, because the girl called Kit closed her eyes seemingly in agony, prompting Violet to say, with some spirit, 'I can most certainly try.'

Kit, eyes still closed, shook her head as if reality was too painful to contemplate.

'Ah, Kitty, no use agonising,' the other girl said soothingly. 'We'll make it work. I'm afraid you've long missed tea, though,' she told Violet. 'Come and meet the others.' She gestured ahead of her.

'Er, here?' In the small yellow circle of lamplight, Violet looked around the barn, which, except for a few pieces of rusty machinery and tools, was empty.

'Upstairs.' Kit gestured towards the ladder. 'Joan, I think she means you to carry her suitcase.' She gave a mocking laugh at the blowsy girl's retreating back, and Violet flushed and turned back to pick up her case.

Tucked under the eaves, the attic stretched the whole length of the barn below. It was surprisingly comfortable, with rush matting on the floor, a row of neat bedsteads, and a curtained-off area in the back, presumably for washing. Oil lamps dangled off nails and threw shadows on walls and beds, and two windows on either end of the gabled roof were blacked out with leather hide tacked into place. A gaggle of young women in various outfits – most of them bulky with sweaters and coats, Violet noticed – were grouped around a stove, which radiated warmth into the rather chilly air.

'Everyone, this is Lily,' Kit said. 'Lily, this is everyone.'

There was a dip in the hum of voices as Violet stepped forward, feeling dusty and dishevelled, a shirt sleeve dangling out of the side of her suitcase.

'Red and Kate. Linda. Ellen. Mary. Lucy.' Kit rattled off the names.

Violet moved closer to the warmth of the stove and nodded cautiously. 'It's nice to meet you all. Where do I . . .'

An ear-splitting whistle shrilled from behind them. 'She's early!'

The attic became a mass of moving shadows as quickly, efficiently, the group scrambled for their beds. There was a grating noise as someone slid a cover of sorts around the stove, a series of small *phtt* noises as the lamps were extinguished, and then darkness.

'. . . put my things?' Violet finished, stunned.

'Lie down,' someone hissed.

Below them, the barn door creaked open. Violet turned wildly towards the sound. She felt a hand on her leg and, remembering Manson, recoiled, but it simply pushed her in the direction of the bed closest to the hatch.

Below, light drew near. Violet fell onto the bed, still in her boots. A muted glow filled the hatch and she held her breath, waited for someone to climb up the ladder. But the light remained where it was and her skin prickled as she imagined someone standing there, silent and listening. Minutes passed until, finally, there was the rustle of footsteps and the barn door opened again. And then, unbelievably, she heard another sound. A metallic grinding as a key was inserted into the lock, a loud click as it turned. They were locked in? What kind of a place was this where they were *locked in*? The door was rattled briefly as though to answer her question, and then all was silent.

Bewildered, Violet strained for sounds of the other girls, for someone to tell her what on earth was going on. But except for one or two suppressed whispers, most of the others seemed to have fallen asleep, judging by the even breathing and snuffly snores drifting down the line. Violet tried to sit up. The straw mattress rustled loudly, someone gave a tired *shh* and she sank back down. What would happen if there was an air raid? No one had told her where the shelter was. At Cavendish Place, Cook tucked warming pans down their mattresses to ward off the damp chill of the cellar shelter, and then made them all cups of Horlicks before they went down, sometimes with a plate of ginger snaps, which were Barker's favourite . . .

She ripped off her boots and shook off her coat, then pulled the blanket over herself and pushed her feet all the way to the freezing bottom of the bed. Outside, the wind had picked up, making the eaves creak and moan as if she was in a ship tossed about in a bottomless black void. Churning up her belly, it burrowed beneath the thin exterior of Lily Burns to where there was just Violet, gripping Romy's necklace and feeling lonelier than ever before.

Twenty

Violet didn't think she'd slept at all, but she must have drifted off at some point just before dawn, because the next thing she knew, someone was shaking her shoulders. Dragging open her eyelids, she saw Kit's face swimming above.

'Come on,' she said impatiently.

Violet struggled upright and staggered out of bed, just in time to see a mass of green wool and beige cord disappearing down the hatch.

'Wait for me!' She pulled her coat from underneath the blanket, where she'd dragged it halfway through the night, convinced she'd be frozen solid by morning, then pushed her feet into her boots and hastened towards the ladder.

Running her fingers through her hair and trying to unflatten her hat, she caught up with the girls outside. The day was only just dawning, with slim fingers of light tentatively touching tree crowns and shed roofs. In the stable yard, figures were trundling back and forth; someone was packing a wagon with crates and farm implements. A whinny drifted over and a sudden sharp pang of homesickness cut through the tired haze in Violet's mind. Early mornings just like these; Romy and Violet at the nearby stables in Hyde Park, feeding Romy's pony Desdemona carrots, giggling over silly girl things. Pushing the memories away, she pulled her coat tightly around herself and tried to draw strength from the way her legs and arms melted into a sea of identical beige.

They were heading across the stable yard now, back towards the archway Violet had come through the previous night. A small bell tower rose above the arch with – Violet blinked – the broad face of a sun painted across a large sundial. The arch was flanked by two wide buildings, not wooden, like the sheds and stables, but built of stone. The one Hardwick had disappeared into the night before was perhaps an office building; from the other, with smoke coming out of its chimney, emanated delicious smells of something fried. A workers' canteen of some kind, Violet thought, catching a glimpse of long tables and benches inside. She had last eaten sometime around noon the previous day, when she'd wolfed down the sandwiches Duffy had pressed on her: two slivers of thin white bread with cucumber in between. God, what she wouldn't give for Cook's crumpets now, drenched in pre-rationing amounts of butter and honey, and eggs and kippers and—

'Oof.' She'd run straight into the back of the girl in front of her. 'Sorry.' She smiled at the girl – Lucy? Ellen? – but she didn't pay her any heed.

'Kit, it looks like they're *finished* already,' she breathed in horror.

Below the sundial, horse-drawn carts were filling up with workers, one already pulling away. No one was paying them much attention; if anything, Violet thought, they avoided looking at the girls altogether.

'What on earth . . . ?' Kit pushed to the front of the group just as two women hurried past them, empty baskets bobbing up and down on their backs. 'We're *never* late.'

Something flickered at the edge of Violet's mind, something urgent and, given the girls' horrified expressions, quite terrible. *Make sure to tell the others . . . half an hour earlier than usual . . .* She opened her mouth, then immediately shut it again, deciding that honesty would not be the best way forward right now.

'There he is.' Joan quickly checked her uniform, held back another girl, whose coat was flapping open.

'I'll do the talking,' Kit said in a low tone, and all around Violet the girls nodded, moving reluctantly towards one of the horse-drawn wagons, where Violet spotted Mr Hardwick supervising the loading of equipment.

At some point last night, she had started thinking that maybe she'd mistaken the scene at the church: his revulsion at her supposed impropriety, the way he'd tried to hide her from the villagers' sight, pushed her into the barn like a farm animal. But seeing him now, feet planted apart and pushed into the ground, as rigid and unbending in his work clothes as he'd been in his churchgoing suit, unease slowly pooled at the bottom of her stomach and she knew she hadn't imagined it at all.

'Good morning, Mr Hardwick.' Kit sounded confident enough, but Violet saw her hands clench into the back of her jacket.

'You'll be clearing fields on Thistle Hill today.' Hardwick didn't turn around. 'Jones will take you. You have three days to finish.'

'We only need a moment to fetch some breakfast and our lunch, but we can eat it on the go.' Kit quickly motioned three girls towards the canteen.

'Breakfast is over.' Hardwick's voice was curt. 'And your lunch went elsewhere.'

'Elsewhere?' Kit repeated faintly.

'Should have been on time.' He turned, seemingly oblivious to the furtive groan that went up from the group, Violet's ringing out long past the others. She was so hungry she'd gladly have eaten raw turnips at this point.

'We weren't aware that we're late,' Kit tried, just as a young woman emerged from the canteen pulling a trolley loaded high with dishes and plates, a cast-iron urn. She navigated the stoop, starting slightly when she noticed the small assembly below the sundial. Her clothes were rough and of indeterminate colour, a sack-like dress around her thin figure, black hair tied back under a kerchief.

Hardwick turned. 'What on earth are you gawping at?' He narrowed his eyes at the girl. 'The pigs need feeding and Mrs

Dawson has asked for five chickens to be plucked and gutted. And you lot, gather yourselves this instant.'

Violet had no idea what that meant, but it had to be a well-practised command, because within seconds, the knots of girls huddling close together had re-formed into three lines, with even spaces between them, leaving a stunned Violet standing alone. The young woman pushed at the trolley again, and as it came closer, something caught Violet's attention. There was bread in a basket, and a slab of cheese carefully wrapped in waxed paper, a bowl of apples. The porridge urn was partially full; she could hear its contents slopping up lazily against the insides. For a moment, she forgot everything: her exhaustion, the silent land girl formation next to her, Hardwick standing up front. All she knew was that she would die, right here on the spot, if she didn't have a piece of that cheese wedged between two thick slabs of bread, an apple, a portion of thick, hot porridge, studded with raisins, perhaps . . .

'But there's still food on there.' Her voice rang across the yard. A shocked murmur travelled through the group, and she regretted it instantly.

'Move,' Hardwick barked, and the young woman walked faster, staring straight at Violet, her strange amber-coloured eyes flashing something indeterminate. At the last moment, Violet jumped aside and the trolley rattled past.

'New girl.'

Violet's insides plummeted. Too late, she remembered that she was supposed to keep her mouth shut, and that it was, in fact, her fault the others had been denied their breakfast. She moved past two tired, bleary-eyed girls, past Kit, who, unable to openly glower at Hardwick, was fuming at Violet instead, and stepped out in front of the formation.

'Look at me.'

Reluctantly Violet lifted her head, saw his clean-shaven jaw, the meticulous way he'd buttoned his shirt under a waistcoat, the carefully mended hole below his collar. His expression was flat, his eyes as hard as they'd been the night before. But behind his dispassionate gaze, she saw something new, something that made her, for the very first time, truly grasp the meaning of *fight or flight*. She felt her body strain away from him and towards the relative safety of the other girls, wanting to burrow in between them and hide behind Kit's broad back. It couldn't have been more than a small twitch, but Hardwick noticed, and it seemed to please him. He came closer, now openly inspecting her, and Violet, knowing only not to keep her back to him, turned with him in an ungainly pirouette. He fixed his eyes on her, almost as if daring her to do something – as if he would welcome it even, because it would give him an excuse to . . . What? Violet thought wildly. What on earth was he going to do to her, here, in front of everyone?

Across his shoulder, she suddenly saw Kit's face. The older girl still looked distressed, perhaps at their helplessness, perhaps at the inescapability of their situation, but she seemed angry, too, and had braced herself, shoulders leaning forward, fingers curled into fists. Something in Violet responded to Kit's stance, and she pushed her feet into the ground and straightened, so suddenly that she caught Hardwick's shoulder. And somehow – she wasn't sure how, she certainly hadn't *meant* to – she caused him to brush clear across her front. She flushed immediately, embarrassment choking her, but a strange expression flitted across Hardwick's face: a thrill of excitement, a sudden hunger. And then, unbelievably, he came closer. *Fight*, something inside Violet roared, and before she could check herself, she'd flung out her hands and pushed him away, so hard that he lurched backwards, arms wheeling comically, and crashed to the ground, where he lay for a stunned second, winded into immobility.

The girls gasped. Kit's face was a mask of horror, Joan clapped her hands in front of her mouth as he jumped to his feet again. But then another noise popped up, which Violet didn't have to work very hard to identify as . . . a giggle.

Twenty-One

The girl's hair was a dark red, tied in two cheerful bunches, and she'd done something to her hat, had moulded it into a jauntier shape, a scarf tied to the top. Like Violet, she'd clearly been in a rush, because the tails of her blouse flapped out of the dungarees she was wearing under her short jacket, giving her a messy if cheerfully carefree appearance.

'You think it's funny?' Hardwick jabbed his finger in the direction of the girl's breastbone, his voice hoarse. 'And looking like *that*, too.' The second time the jab was more of a punch, and the girl yelped in pain, fell backwards. Something pinged away from her, hit Violet's knee. Keeping her eyes on Hardwick, she bent and groped along the ground until her hand closed around the oval shape of the girl's Land Army badge.

'Gather yourselves,' Hardwick snarled, and everyone snapped upright. This time, Violet knew what to do, and stood straight-backed and blank-faced next to the red-haired girl, keeping her eyes locked on the golden wand above the sundial. *From Darkness, Light* was etched below the exaggerated sweep of the sun's rays. She kept her eyes on the words, the outline of the badge digging into her fist, repeating them in her mind over and over again, like a prayer. *Darkness. Light. Light. Darkness.*

'I will not tolerate insubordinate females.' Hardwick was still breathing heavily and a strand of his carefully combed hair fell across his forehead. 'You will do as I say. All. The. *Time*.'

'Please, Mr Hardwick.' Kit took a step forward. 'They didn't mean any disrespect.'

Hardwick looked at her, and then, as suddenly as his rage had erupted, it was gone. His features tucked themselves back behind his cold, haughty face, a sweep of his hand settled his hair, a pull on the waistcoat restored his former crispness, and when he looked at Violet, took in her slight figure, saw the red-haired girl's flattened hat and flushed face, he seemed amused almost at the thought that someone like them could possibly leave any impression on someone like him.

'One, you can thank Burns there for you missing your breakfast and your lunch.' He flicked his hand in Violet's direction. 'She was supposed to pass on the message last night. Two, let's settle the score before you go, shall we?' He extracted a small black book from inside his jacket. 'One demerit each for tardiness, two each additionally for Simpson and Burns.' He looked at Violet, who didn't understand anything except that it wasn't good. 'An additional demerit each if I don't see you moving within the next sixty seconds, *and* I will most likely forget to pick you up, thus making you miss dinner as well. Go.'

There was a scramble as the girls surged towards the back of the wagon, lifting each other up with practised movements until Violet was the last one standing. Above her, Kit's face loomed, angry and upset.

'See what you did?' she hissed down. 'Thirteen bloody demerits when we didn't have one all week. Get up here at once.'

Joan looked tired and annoyed, and the other girls were eyeing Violet and the red-haired girl with open dislike, muttering amongst themselves. The cart moved, and at the last moment, Violet pulled herself onto the back ledge, where she knelt until an arm dragged her all the way in.

'Come and sit with me,' the girl with the red hair whispered.

Violet wedged herself onto the wooden board hammered into the side of the wagon, her hands shaking with delayed fear.

'Did you not bring your gloves?' Kit glowered at Violet's bare hands.

'I didn't get any,' Violet said defiantly when she saw that most of the girls were wearing brown workman's gloves or had wrapped cloths around their palms.

'Suit yourself,' Kit snapped, jolting forward as the driver stopped to let someone pass. 'But don't slow us down. And do *not*, I repeat, do not give *him* any other reason for more demerits. We were doing so well until you came. And I swear, if we miss out on tea, too, because of either of you mouthing off to Hardwick or being gormless idiots, I'm going to kill someone, and it will very likely be one of you.' She lapsed into a furious silence.

The early morning had flooded paths and outbuildings in a pale wash of light, and, looking back, Violet spotted the young woman in the sack-like dress leaning against the trolley watching them leave.

'She always does that,' the red-haired girl whispered into her ear. 'His daughter, you know; her name is Myra.'

'That's his daughter?' Violet turned.

'Meant to be our chaperone, too,' the girl said, 'even though, look at her, she's barely older than Kit. Rarely says much, either, she's just *there*. It's like she enjoys us being put down, maybe because it means she gets less of it at home.'

Violet digested this. 'But why is everyone so . . .' she fished for a word that would accurately describe Hardwick's open loathing, the village women's disdain, the land girls' fear, 'so tense?' she finally settled on, even though it wasn't remotely adequate to describe what it felt like.

'It's this whole system he's set up for us.' The girl shrugged. 'It's all in that little black book of his, all his poison. I haven't been here long enough to understand it completely, although I doubt I ever will; he keeps it deliberately confusing if you ask me. Makes up rules on the spot and changes them around so that it's impossible for you not to break one if he decides you need to be punished. Then he doesn't sign our time sheets, delays wages, cancels any holiday we might have. Or, the worst, engineers it so we miss our meals. It's meant to be our night off at the end of this week, not anything special, eighteen hours basically, but she,' she jabbed her head at Kit, 'has been on at us all week not to get into trouble. I shouldn't have laughed, I reckon, but it was so funny, him lying there like a stranded bug.

'He's got a wicked temper, I tell you. I had an uncle like that, choler eating him up from the inside. He almost threw my little sister under the bus when she ran off one time. Died of the French pox. My uncle, not my sister.' She grinned and tossed her head, nearly sending her hat flying. 'He's ridiculously devout, too, Hardwick is. Constantly beetling off to chapel, working off whatever's stained his soul. He doesn't let us go, though, oh no; not that I would – I'm an atheist, y'know – but I do object to him thinking we're too dirty for church. Doesn't like women, I think, particularly women doing men's work. If you ask me, we make him uncomfortable.'

She tucked in her shirt serenely and Violet nodded, thinking about the gleam of excitement in Hardwick's eyes, the revulsion that had instantly replaced it.

'And good thing too,' the other girl said savagely. 'The world's riddled with injustice as it is, womenfolk underpaid and over-worked. It's only my third week here; I was on sugar beets over by the coast before. Things aren't too bad here really: a warm bath once a week, laundry done in the big house, and the food's good – if you get it, that is – plus you're obviously safe from air raids. Although you do have to put up with Hardwick in exchange for all that . . .'

Violet watched Myra get smaller until she was just a dot in the distance.

'She doesn't look anything like him.'

'I agree.' The girl slid her gloves on. 'Takes after his wife, the kitchen maid told me. There's some mystery there, I could sense it, but I couldn't get any more out of her before the cook came to bustle her away. Hardwick's got them all terrified, the whole estate over. Small man lording it over his kingdom, that's what it is. Well, looks like we're here.'

They were clattering along the edge of a wooded copse towards an enormous mass of spiky branches and foliage stretching away across a field.

'I'm Red, by the way.' She pointed at her hair underneath the hat. 'Because of that, and also I'm a socialist.'

'Lily,' Violet said. 'Oh, and I still have your badge.' She turned her fist and opened it, her palm creased where the edge had dug into her skin.

Red looked at it thoughtfully. 'You'd think it protects you somehow, being part of the services.' She plucked the badge from Violet's hand. 'I guess at the end of the day it's just a piece of metal.'

She slid the pin into her hat, but it caught on the wool and hung crooked.

'You'll get in trouble again,' Violet said quickly. 'Here, let me.' She pinned the badge straight, pausing to run her thumb over it. 'It's still something to live up to, I suppose,' she said, almost inaudibly. She handed the hat back. 'What are we going to be doing exactly, do you think?'

'Clearing the fields of blackberry brambles.' Red sighed, and Violet gaped at the thorny mass before her. The brambles she knew yielded pretty baskets of plump fruit drenched in cream or eaten in a pie. Nothing like this enormous thicket rearing up at least twice her height in some places.

'It's brutal. You'll see,' Red added, flicking a pitying look at Violet's bare hands.

Twenty-Two

Kit, when she stopped being angry, proved to be quite a good leader, efficiently organising teams for the various jobs, supplying them with tools from rusty buckets left behind by a farmhand. 'You know he'll be back to check the ground with a magnifying glass. Do not leave anything behind. Freedom comes our way on Saturday night,' Kit shouted, raising her fist, 'as long as we Do. Not. Fail.'

Amidst cheers and *hear hears*, Kit raised her eyebrows at Violet, who looked back stonily, hands clenched around her tool, a wooden handle with a curved blade. How hard could it be to do a bit of weeding?

An hour later, she knew. Sweat trawled dust and bugs into her eyes as she hacked at the soil, fought brambles and ripped away tangled branches, and she couldn't hear anything other than her breath gasping in her ears and the pounding of her heart. The sun travelled slowly across the sky, eventually dipping back down to tinge the wispy clouds a fierce orange. Her stomach gnawed with hunger, a dull, aching emptiness that made the brown-green of the blackberry tangle oscillate in front of her eyes. Thorns found their way through the burlap fabric Kit had tossed her for protection, piercing her skin, while the handle of the billhook slowly rubbed the inside of her hand raw.

That night, she had no energy left for anything at all, not for being afraid of Hardwick – mercifully absent from the canteen – not for dinner itself, which, after all the anticipation, she shovelled down without even noticing what it was, not for Kit's various pep talks about working smarter not harder, nor for any other possible displays of confidence. The arch between her thumb and pointer finger had been worn down to what seemed to Violet like actual flesh. Even the grating screech of the key locking them in at night didn't penetrate her fog of exhaustion. Maybe that was what they did in the country, she thought numbly. At least she would sleep, wouldn't she? For the first time since Romy's death, her body would be forced by sheer physical exhaustion to drop into a bottomless well. But the pulsing pain in her hand kept her locked in a strange half-consciousness, shot through with nightmares of smoke and screams and death, until she found herself back atop the cart the following morning, her swollen red hand carefully laid across her lap as if it didn't even belong to her.

She tried, she really did. She tried to throw herself into the fray around the buckets for a different tool. She tried to make friends with Red, who looked rather exhausted herself after two days of clearing brambles. She tried to dodge Kit's barked commands and somehow wrestle back some control over this strange hell. But inside that blackberry thicket, where the outside world narrowed down to the end of her blade, the pain – from her hand, her shoulders, her body permanently in a half-crouch – became a living, breathing thing that drowned out everything else. At first she fought it, but gradually she gave in, because when it came down to it, she deserved this, didn't she? For even thinking she could work off her shame and guilt; that she could run away from what she had done to Romy, from who she really was: this useless, weak girl, fit for nothing but curtseying and dancing, like putty figures turning under a glass dome.

Sometimes she imagined writing to Duffy, asking for his help to move elsewhere. But how would she send off a letter if she wasn't allowed to leave the estate? Where was there a post office and how would she get a stamp? At Cavendish Place she would have left the letter on the hallway table and it would be gone that day, an answer appearing magically in the same silver bowl a day or so later, a letter opener next to it. Could she get herself reassigned on her own? But her paperwork and fake rationing card were precarious at best, she knew, and Duffy had said not to rock the boat unless she was ready to give herself up to her mother.

She thought about her mother a lot. What small scraps of news had filtered through – of nightly bombings, rubble-strewn streets and casualties – made her sure that Eleanor had left for Yorkshire, was perhaps even now shivering in Uncle Gareth's unheated drawing room, cursing her wayward daughter for dragging down the family name. It was thoughts of her mother that made her go on. Rattling back to the stable yard at night, she looked out across the dusky valley and knew she couldn't return to her. It was as simple as that. However weak she might be, however useless, she wasn't giving up, not now, not soon, not ever.

But at night, when the sound of the girls' breathing and creatures skittering across the roof made it feel as if the attic was slowly closing in around her, Violet indulged in hazy, angry dreams about running away from it all once more. To vanish into the cool autumn dawn, walk beneath trees, across meadows and along streams. She would live on fruit and nuts, she'd walk until she reached the sea and live there by herself, new and clean and away from it all. Away from her mother's claustrophobic life – her mother, who'd never taught her anything that mattered; away from the memories of Romy dying. But whenever the night took her back to Romy, Violet raked her nails across the scars on her arm and the raw flesh on her hand, until the pain brought her back to where she was and kept her there for good.

Kit's voice became hoarse from shouting, and still the brambles continued to rear up defiantly. Sometimes Violet wondered if

Hardwick came back here at night and made them magically regrow just to spite them.

'We have to get cracking, girls,' Kit croaked breathlessly on Saturday morning. 'Come on, give it your all, just another few hours. Tonight is the night and then exactly eighteen hours of freedom awaits. Come *on*.'

Because it had been so long in coming, and especially because the girls hadn't had any letters in a few weeks, the eighteen hours had taken on near-mythical proportions. Plans were ambitious and transportation arrangements rivalled a military operation, from what Violet had gleaned through her fog of exhaustion. Some were trying to visit family or friends, others wanted to catch a dance on the other side of the valley, and all of them would have to be back by late morning tomorrow. Violet, who struggled to survive one hour at a time, had no plans whatsoever.

'Give it up, Kit.' Joan rubbed a hand over her sweaty forehead. 'We'll never get it done.'

'No. The dairy van leaves at five p.m. and I'm going to be on it,' Kit said furiously. 'We're getting this done if it kills us.'

'Easy, Kit.' Red looked glassy-eyed and queasy with tiredness as she grimaced at Violet. Unfortunately, when Kit caught the grimace, it unravelled the last shreds of her sanity, and she broke into a hysterical rant.

'If we're not done by nightfall, I'm holding you personally responsible. You're not bloody trying hard enough.'

A small spray of spittle hit Red's cheek, but she didn't even flinch, just turned in the direction of Kit's frantically jabbing finger, and something inside Violet finally snapped.

'What on earth is wrong with you?' she hissed at Kit. 'We've *been* trying, everyone's been *trying*.'

'It's girls like you who give all of us a bad name,' Kit spat out, incoherent with rage. 'City girls who swan in thinking this is all a big adventure. For us,' she motioned to the line of girls moving in and out of the hedges, 'this is actually important. We need the money, we want to do a good job, be proud of what we do.'

'Spare me the lecture,' Violet said, now even more angry at Kit unknowingly echoing her own ruminations about her uselessness. 'Look at her.' She pointed at Red, straggly-haired and dishevelled, then thrust her own raw hand into Kit's face. 'Do we look like we're *swanning*?' She dropped her hand and gave Kit a look of disgust. 'You sound just like *him*, do you know that?' She gripped her billhook, managing not to wince at the stab of pain shooting up her arm, and stalked down to the far end of the blackberry thicket.

'Kitty, do lighten up a little,' she heard Joan say. 'We might still make it.'

'Yes, well.' Kit stomped off angrily to fetch a rake.

'Good on you.' Red popped up next to Violet. 'Hey, I saw some horsetail down by the stream.' She nodded at Violet's hands. 'I'll gather some before we leave. If we mix it with water and put it on your hand, it should help.'

To her great horror, Violet felt a sudden prick of tears. With an enormous effort, she swallowed it back. 'That would be wonderful,' she said.

Violet wanted to show Kit up for her dismissive attitude, she wanted to rage through the thicket until she'd single-handedly cleared it, but as the day wore on, she felt like she was moving through syrup. All around her, the land girls cut and pulled and tore at the blackberry vines, but despite working through lunch, and Kit's voice leaving her altogether somewhere around two o'clock, there was a last clump of hedge left by the time Hardwick rode by to inspect their progress at half past three.

'Well, well,' he said, sounding sickeningly pleased. 'Nothing for it, you'll have to stay late today.'

'Please, Mr Hardwick, it's just this last little bit left; another hour's worth of work at the most.' Kit pushed whatever was left of her voice through clenched teeth. 'We could come back tomorrow afternoon and finish it. You won't even have to take us; we'll walk both ways, I promise, it wouldn't put you out.'

'Walk,' he repeated thoughtfully.

'We haven't had a day's holiday in so long, Mr Hardwick, we're all worked off our feet. We really are due time off,' Kit insisted, and Violet couldn't help but admire the other girl's gutsiness.

'You are free to leave when your chores are done, that was the agreement.' Hardwick turned to go.

'But we've had lifts and things organised, for which we have to leave *now* if we want to make them.' Kit had to jog a little to keep up with him.

'You won't,' he said. 'Because don't forget the time you'll need to walk back too. I hadn't realised how easy you've had it, Miss Pritchard, being taken here and back every day on the cart, which we can ill spare during harvest time, as you know.'

Whatever tiny triumph Violet might have felt at Kit's public dressing-down flickered and died when she saw the older girl's face. Her throat moved hard to swallow back any further retort, her eyes glittered brightly and her hands shook as she fumbled for her cigarette pack.

'Tsk, tsk, Miss Pritchard. You know the rules.' Hardwick calmly took the pack out of her hands and dropped it; ground it deep into the loamy soil with his foot.

Kit was finally defeated. Her shoulders slumped and all the tension left her body.

'All right,' she said tonelessly. 'Fine. We'll finish here, and then we'll walk back.'

When he'd gone, Kit knelt down and dug out her cigarette pack, tried to flatten it, but her hands were shaking so hard, Joan took it from her. Inside, most of the cigarettes were broken in half, tobacco crumbling into Joan's palm.

'I'm sorry, Kit,' she said miserably. 'You'll see her another time, I'm sure.'

Kit nodded mutely and walked back to the hedge.

'Her?' Violet looked at the girl called Lucy.

'Her mother.' Lucy picked up her bucket. 'It's too far, really, unless you can go overnight. The last time we were meant to have time off, Hardwick came up with an emergency cleaning of machinery needed the next day, and the time before that, we'd all apparently got so many demerits we couldn't leave either. We've been extra, *extra* careful this time around, but it's no use. For some reason he doesn't want us leaving the estate. I think he's ashamed of us, or maybe he's afraid we'll talk about all *this*.' She waved her hand at Hardwick on his horse barely visible along the village road.

'He's just plain evil,' another girl said darkly.

'Come on, then,' Kit threw back at them over her shoulder, but listlessly, her face so drawn and tired that Violet suddenly heard herself say:

'I'll stay and finish up here. Then you can go.'

It was hard to say who was more surprised, the others or Violet herself. Kit frowned.

'Is this some sort of joke?' she said. 'Are you trying to get us in trouble with Hardwick?'

'Oh, come on,' Violet said exasperatedly. 'More likely I'm getting myself in trouble.'

'But why would you do that?' Kit hadn't moved. 'It's not as if we – I – have been all that welcoming.' She had the grace to look abashed. 'And *he* said we couldn't, so we can't.'

'Actually, what he said was that you could go when the chores are done,' Violet corrected her. 'They'll be done *while* you're going. As you said, it's just a matter of an hour's overlap, maybe a little more if I'm on my own. But I'll be back in plenty of time before curfew.'

A faint tinge of hope flitted across Kit's face. 'And we'd just come back tomorrow, bold as brass?' She shook her head. 'I don't think so. He'll come down on us so hard, we can forget about ever leaving again.'

'But at least you'll have gone. Who knows what he'll do to keep you from leaving next time,' Violet pointed out. 'And he never said you can't go at all; he was too busy being triumphant that circumstances are preventing you.' She'd been good at keeping her voice neutral so far, mainly because she'd been too exhausted to speak much, but now she heard herself sounding too sophisticated, so she added a vague 'Anyhow.'

'He seems to be able to do what he wants,' Kit said darkly. 'We haven't left the estate in yonks.'

'He thinks we're filthy,' said a girl Violet thought was called Ellen.

'But he brushes past us too closely sometimes.' Lucy shuddered. 'I think,' she flushed, 'he enjoys it, even though he hates it at the same time, y'know.'

'He says horrid stuff under his breath sometimes,' a freckled girl said.

'We asked for a set of bicycles, two girls to a bike even, to save the farmhands having to take us around the estate in the mornings and so we could go into the village and pick up our post—'

'But he said hell would freeze over before he would have us careering around the valley like . . . *whores*.' Joan whispered the last word delicately.

'Doesn't want us mobile,' Red said sagely. 'He has more control this way.'

Violet stared at the group. 'But the Ministry . . . and other jobs – why haven't you all moved to different *jobs*?' she said incredulously. 'Surely, with the war on and everything . . .'

'Bit difficult,' Kit said wearily. 'Winter is coming and no one wants extra mouths to feed, let alone a land girl hanging around and needing wages. Kate joined two weeks ago from further down south, and she said the farms in her area were letting girls go. They're not supposed to really, but I guess some can't afford to keep them. And since they actually need us here to bring in the harvest, packing and grading the fruit and all the rest of it, we'd be frowned on if we left for sure.'

'But have you lodged a complaint?' Violet asked. 'Aren't there Land Army women meant to look after us?'

'Two girls left here in July – I replaced one of them – and apparently one of them wrote to the Land Army and someone came to check on things,' Joan said.

'And?' Violet prompted.

'Well it all *looks* fine, doesn't it?' Ellen said. 'Because the orchards always had migrant workers before the war, the barns are all set up, better and cleaner than in some other places. It's all the things you don't see on the surface: the rules, the not socialising, *him*. He was told to make sure we get enough time off and are allowed to go into the village. But he's quite well respected, so no one gave him too hard a time in the end. Those girls, though, got a bit of an earful from the county secretary about not sticking it out.'

'Right, well.' Violet pursed her lips uneasily. But then she remembered Hardwick's triumphant sneer and looked around at the girls' eager faces, and it felt so good to fit in and push back at being useless that she said, more firmly, 'My offer stands. I hate that barn anyway. It'll be nice to be out here for a little while longer.'

'Bit of fresh air, eh?' Red snorted with laughter. 'I'll stay with you. I was going to a workers' rally on the other side of the valley, but I can give that a miss. That way there's two of us if he does roar up screaming bloody murder.'

Violet was wordless with gratitude.

'But cough up a few snacks, ladies,' Red added briskly. 'Or else we might just faint with hunger and give the game away.'

This broke the tension. There was laughter and chatter and Violet's arm was pressed. Someone unearthed a piece of bread, another a couple of apples.

Kit still stood rooted to the spot, wavering between obvious longing and fear. 'I don't know, girls.'

'We're women, Kit, *wo-men*. How many times do I have to tell you?' Red said exasperatedly.

For the first time that day, Kit smiled. 'It's our job title, you twit. Regardless, though, we can't just leave you two behind.'

'If we're careful, he'll never know that we went or that they stayed,' Joan said. 'He's not coming back here tonight, he said that. And he'll be at chapel anyway. And Myra's not coming to lock the doors until nine. She only ever just listens, and there'll be enough of us up there to make breathing noises. So whoever has plans around the area will just have to avoid Barleigh and sneak back into the barn before nine. And the rest of us visiting folks elsewhere will slip in tomorrow.'

'Why did we never think of this before?' Ellen clapped her hands excitedly before scrabbling through the lined-up gas masks for her cardboard case.

'Because it's madness,' Kit said gruffly, stuffing her broken cigarette pack deep into her pocket. 'Complete and utter madness.'

But then she looked at Violet and squared her shoulders. 'But I really appreciate it.' It had clearly cost her some effort.

'I know.' Violet turned before she could lose her resolve. 'Hurry and go or you'll miss your lift.'

Twenty-Three

The thought of Hardwick coming to check on them after all spurred the two of them on, and they didn't talk again until they'd finally dragged the last armful of brambles over to the fire, added the remaining bits of dry brush and branches, then stoked and poked it so it would burn down to embers well before the blackout. Bending over, the coals suddenly wavered in front of Violet's eyes and she felt her legs give. Pushing back just enough to keep the soles of her boots from catching a spark, she sat down and slumped over her knees, her throbbing right hand in her lap. Red had disappeared down to the little stream behind the trees, and returned with a long iron poker, which they'd used to loosen the soil, and a bucket.

'For Hardwick.' She held up the poker. Violet grinned until she realised that Red wasn't joking. 'For your hand.' She held up the bucket.

'Do you think the fire's all right like this?' Violet asked. 'Or is it too bright?'

'I think as long as it's just the coals, yeah. And we're leaving before too long.'

'But not yet.' Violet took a deep breath of smoky, crisp autumn air. 'I really don't like that barn.'

Red settled down next to her and started pulling apart strands of a green, reedy plant and mashing them up with a rock, mixing in small drops of water until she had a paste. She slid a piece of tin across Violet's lap, gestured for her to lay out her hands. Violet flinched in anticipation, but the sodden mixture was soothing and cool on her raw hand, and little by little, the throbbing lessened. Red pushed the coals together, making the embers spark, then sat back and held a small piece of bread in front of Violet's mouth. Violet nodded.

'Did you ever think you'd be this hungry?' She crunched down on the dry bread, thinking she'd never tasted anything more delicious.

'You spoilt city folk.' Smiling, Red heaped a bit more horse-tail slush on Violet's hand, then pushed another piece of bread between her lips.

'Thanks for staying,' Violet mumbled through her mouthful. 'Feels good to thumb our nose at Hardwick, doesn't it?'

'I'd rather sort him out in the open.' Red ran a finger along the poker in a businesslike fashion, weighed it in her hand. 'He's just going to keep on if all we do is tiptoe around him.' She sighed. 'What made you join the Land Army?'

Violet didn't want to talk about what had happened before she came here, not tonight, when her toes were warm and the night was comforting, her mind pleasantly hazy. 'Just . . . it was something different, I suppose.' She watched the air above the coals oscillate with heat. Shadows had begun smudging the outline of the tree trunks and gathering in the little hollow by the stream.

'Same for me.' Red nodded vigorously. 'No way was I going to be stuck in Chelmston with the women and babies while out there people are fighting like mad and dying in air raids. I'd have been a pilot if my dad had let me.'

Violet poked her finger into the sludgy paste and tried not to think about people dying in air raids.

'Our village is only fifteen miles from Birmingham.' Red grimaced. 'Prime target, what with all the factories and things.' She gave Violet a pained half-grin. 'Da only agreed to let me come here because it's out of harm's way. His version of evacuating, I suppose.'

As Red talked on, Violet studied her out of the corner of her eye: the mischievous face and determined set of her chin, tousled hair stuffed into bunches. It occurred to her that even with all the teas and parties and dancing lessons, she'd never had a proper, real friend. Except Romy.

'He should see Hardwick in his rage, though.' Red was rolling her eyes comically, and Violet wondered what it would be like to talk to her, really talk. She opened her mouth, the urge overwhelming, then closed it again because she didn't think she could bear Red's expression changing as she realised what the real Violet was like, what she had done.

'Being out here is definitely better than being stuck at home,' she said instead, her heart heavy.

The coals had died down to a warm faint glow now, and the breeze blew small clouds of smoke away from them into the darkly pinkening sky. Red's breathing was slowing, and behind them the little wood rustled and sighed in the darkness, a lone robin still singing in the trees. Violet felt her eyes close and wished they could just go to sleep right here, curled around the fire like people did in the olden days. Bit by bit, her mind emptied, and finally, with a rush of release, she gave in to the warmth, floated, reached towards the stars, the night endless around her, free . . .

'Watch out!'

The clearing was suddenly loud with hoofbeats and a sharp voice, and then a shadow loomed out of the darkness, holding a burning torch. Violet screamed and jumped up so fast that she sent Red sprawling sideways. She squinted through the wavering torchlight. Not Hardwick, was her first thought, followed quickly by the realisation that meeting strangers at night wasn't necessarily a good thing either.

'Get away from us.' She wrenched the poker out of Red's hand and waved it threateningly. 'Leave us alone!'

'For heaven's sake, stop making that awful ruckus,' a male voice snapped. 'Anyone would think I'm about to commit murder.'

Holding the torch higher, he advanced, raising his eyebrows at the poker. Dressed soberly in a quilted jacket and riding breeches, he seemed to list slightly sideways, and Violet frowned at the way he held his right leg, until she saw the bulky outline of what looked like a leg brace beneath the trousers.

'What?' the man asked roughly when he saw her staring, and the flame of his torch twitched above his hand. 'Don't think I'd have it in me to save damsels in distress?'

Violet flushed, lowered her poker. 'No, of course. I'm sorry.'

The man glowered, then abruptly said, 'And who might *you* be then?'

'Women's Land Army.' Violet pulled herself up straight, tacking on a 'sir' at the end that sounded a fraction more defiant than necessary. 'We're from the big house down the valley.'

He took in her muddy trousers and jumper, her scratched and stained arms, Red's scowl, the tin lid held up like a shield in front of them, dripping horsetail paste onto their shoes. He gave a brief laugh and shook his head. 'Two land girls, sitting by the fire. How very poetic. How come you're not with the rest of your herd?'

'They left us to finish up,' Violet replied in a dignified voice. 'And we're *not* a herd.'

'Finish yourselves off is more like it.' He jabbed his torch at the bed of coals glowing softly. 'You were about to fall in when I came up.'

'We were not,' Violet said indignantly. 'We're capable of taking care of ourselves. And we were just about to douse the coals anyway,' she added hurriedly, realising how dark it had got. 'Quickly now, Red, the blackout – in fact, er, sir,' she gave a meaningful glance at the man's brightly burning torch, 'maybe you shouldn't be . . .'

'I'm looking for my sister.' He turned, shining the torch around the clearing. 'Have you seen anyone out here? A girl?'

'Just us.' Red picked up the bucket and disappeared in the direction of the stream. The man pushed his hand through his hair impatiently, then thrust the torch upright into another of the farm buckets. The flame twitched violently. 'I swear, the time I spend looking for that tearaway. Well, she knows the valley like the back of her hand. No doubt she'll find her way back. Come on then, I'll escort you home.'

'You go and look for her, we're perfectly fine.' Violet picked up a stray tool and laid it with the rest.

'I'm aware of that.' The man gave her a sardonic smile. 'I just thought I'd offer, since it's so dark and all. Merry over there insists on chivalry at all times, and I have to do what he says or else he sulks for days.'

Violet twitched around, flushed with embarrassment at the thought that someone had been watching them all this time.

'My horse, land girl.' He gave a snort of amusement. 'Bit jumpy, aren't you?'

He whistled softly under his breath and a horse trotted out of the darkness, magnificent with his powerful chest and an elegant, muscular build, a white lightning bolt zigzagging down his nose. 'Keep your distance, though, he's been in a foul temper all d— Hey!'

Violet had disappeared beneath the enormous brown face, holding out her hand for the horse to sniff.

'Aren't you gorgeous,' she crooned, stretching all the way on her toes to run her hand along the horse's neck, smoothing down the fringe above its eyes. It laid its head on her shoulder and closed its large, liquid eyes in apparent bliss.

The man gave a growl that ranged somewhere between irritation and grudging appreciation. 'I should have known. He terrifies every groom the war has left to us, but the moment a pretty girl comes along, he's soft as butter.' He observed Violet, now hanging off the horse's neck and whispering into its twitching ears, then shook his head in defeat, patting the animal's rump affectionately. 'You're a wicked devil, and greedy to boot.' He rummaged around in the saddlebag and offered Violet an apple. 'Here, give him this and he'll remember not to bite you next time.'

'Oh, he wouldn't,' she said adoringly. 'He's just a softie under all that majesty, isn't he? But as they say, whatever shall befall us, we must keep up appearances, isn't that right?'

'Says who, the prime minister?' The man raised his eyebrows.

'My mother.' Violet felt a sudden, uncontrollable laugh bubble up. What would her mother say if she could see her daughter like this, shredded hands covered in remnants of green sludge, talking to a stranger at night? With a start, she realised that it was the first time she'd laughed out loud since the night of Romy's death, and she broke off instantly. But the man was smiling back, an unexpectedly sweet smile, and behind the tense, angry set of his jaw, the ruffled hair, the rumpled clothes, she could see that he was probably only a few years older than she was. The burning torch softened the shadows on his face, picked out the generous curve of his mouth in glowing gold, shimmered in his eyes. Something strange tugged at her insides. She wanted to look away, to check on Red, who could be heard splashing down by the stream, but she found that she couldn't move, not when wild and exciting and unspeakable things were stirring between them.

'Your apple,' she heard him say. The round, nubbly shape rolled gently into her palm. Fizzy, sweet apple scent drifted up when the horse took it from her palm, and still she looked at the man and he back at her.

'Merry is a good name,' she stammered, feeling desperately wrong-footed and strange and yet bubbling to the brim with all those things that were slowly filling the dark, hollow places inside her. The horse snuffled gently against her cheek, rooting in her hand for another apple.

'You're hungry, aren't you?' she said breathlessly, running her fingers through its mane in an attempt to regain control. 'Your master keeping you out late, is he? I know, it's so demoralising to be overworked.'

'Starting a revolution, land girl? You'll be—' He broke off with a gasp, leaned closer. 'What in heaven's name happened to your hand?' he asked incredulously. 'Are you donating your *skin* to the Ministry of Agriculture?'

'I didn't get any gloves.' The horsetail paste had rubbed off when she'd stroked Merry, and the patches on her hand were dark in the torchlight.

'Good God. Wrap it up or you'll frighten people.' He extracted a handkerchief from his pocket and handed it to her, watching her fumble with it, then made an impatient noise. 'Here, I'll do it.'

'No, really,' she said quickly. She bunched the piece of fabric around her hand and retreated a little along the horse's back.

'Some help would be nice,' Red's disgruntled voice rang from behind, and she appeared, cross and wet. 'I lost my footing, almost fell in.'

'I should get on,' the man said. 'Keep it.' He nodded at the handkerchief, then looped the reins over Merry's head and hovered by the saddle to get his good leg into position, knuckles standing out sharply in preparation for the upward pull. Involuntarily, Violet moved towards him but, seeing his forbiddingly straight back, decided against it.

'Here, Red, let me.' She turned Red away from the horse and made a show of splashing water over the embers until she saw out of the corner of her eye that the man had pulled himself up onto the horse, lips pressed tightly together as he straightened.

'Well, goodbye,' she said awkwardly over her shoulder, realising for the first time that she didn't know his name.

'Fare thee well, land girls.' He tapped the side of his head, held out his hand for the torch. She handed it up to him. He didn't smile at her again, but his eyes lingered on her face. Then Red threw the rest of the water across the coals and a cloud of wet smoke billowed across the clearing, and when Violet turned back, the man and his torch had gone.

Frankie

September 2004

Twenty-Four

Violet fought Frankie all the way. It was ridiculous, she couldn't possibly impose on her time like that, it was utterly absurd. 'Remember that we're not on speaking terms. And, anyway,' she snapped, 'won't you be looking after your dad soon?'

She was clearly striving for, but didn't quite manage, a neutral voice, and Frankie felt the familiar spike of anger. Maybe Violet was right. Maybe this was a really, really bad idea. She had spent ten years making things work without relying on anyone at all, had learnt to live without her dad, had cut herself off from Violet, Jools, her old world. Could she possibly forget about those ten years and come back to live here, just like that?

But then she saw the trapped, frightened look in her grandmother's eyes and realised that beneath the spikiness and the stubborn insistence on discretion, fear loomed, vast and seemingly insurmountable. Of what was happening to her, the many small indignities and humiliations to come, the helplessness, the loss of the independence she had worked for all her life.

'I'm staying,' Frankie said curtly. She got up and held out a hand. 'Whether you like it or not.'

Violet's bedroom was reassuringly familiar, with its stacks of books and a towel tossed across the chair. A tarnished silver-backed hairbrush was in a small tray, a handful of hairpins scattered on the dresser, small, homely, normal things. Violet disappeared into the bathroom and Frankie stood by the bedroom window, looking out into the dark garden. A breeze had come up, whispering through the trees outside, branches clicking and tapping on the window. As she opened it, feeling cooped up inside the old flat, she heard a small exclamation from the bathroom.

'Vi, are you all right?' She poked her head out into the corridor.

'Yes, yes.' Violet's voice sounded high and strained.

Frankie frowned. 'Sure?'

'Oh, absolutely fine. I'm . . .' There was a small thump, as if someone had hit the inside of the door.

'I'm coming in,' Frankie said.

Violet had somehow got herself tangled up in a knot of tights and skirt. Half perched, half sliding off the edge of the bath, she was red-faced and furious and randomly pulling at whatever fabric edges she could find, succeeding only in getting her legs further wedged together.

'Violet, stop.' Frankie grabbed hold of her just as she was about to pitch backwards into the tub.

'This stupid skirt won't come off,' Violet shouted. 'This stupid, stupid skirt.'

'Wait, I'll help you.' But she couldn't get any traction, not with Violet thrashing around; there was a loud ripping sound, and Violet tore and kicked at the skirt until it finally lay at her feet.

'Stupid effing bloody thing.' She was sweating and breathing hard, her hair a tangle of grey around her angry face, and then, without warning, she put her hands over her eyes and started crying. *Ugly crying* she'd have called it back then. Great big heaving sobs, her cardigan lying in a heap on the floor, the waistband of her tights cutting into the white skin halfway down her thighs. Horrified, Frankie put her hands on Violet's arms, hating herself for her stab of revulsion at the quavering body, and the sudden desperate wish to be anywhere else but here.

'Leave me, just go.' Violet tried to dodge Frankie's grip, scarlet with what was quite obviously excruciating embarrassment,

'Please, I'm fine.' She managed to hit Frankie in the face with a flying elbow.

'I won't.' Frankie gripped Violet's upper arms, averting her eyes from where her fingers were digging into soft flesh, then scuttled her along the side of the bath, kicked the toilet lid closed, flung a towel on it and pushed her down. 'I'm – going – to – help you – if – it – kills me. Or you.'

She gripped the waistband of the tights and tugged it down Violet's legs. Her face flamed when she inadvertently touched skin, grazed the crêpey flesh on her grandmother's thighs, less revulsion now and just a feeling of wrongness: like nails down a blackboard, like stroking fur against the grain, this strange parody of the many times Violet had helped Frankie into the bath, had spun her round to wrap her in a big towel, when now, twenty years later, it was Violet who had to be undressed like an angry, mewling child.

'We're – going – to – get – through – this.' Frankie felt sick with rage. She made her breath shallow so she couldn't smell Violet's body as she unbuttoned her blouse, focusing on one button at a time. At some point, Violet stopped struggling and entreating Frankie to leave her alone, and just sat there, lifting and lowering her arms, her face level with Frankie's. She closed her eyes as if it helped her not to be here, in the chilly, narrow bathroom with the ancient water heater rattling slightly behind her, her granddaughter touching her in places she shouldn't ever have to.

'Would you like a bath?' Frankie asked tentatively. Violet opened her eyes, regarded Frankie kneeling in front of her.

'I would, really,' she said quietly. 'But I don't think I can bear any more of *this*,' she gestured at the skirt, the blouse in Frankie's hand, 'tonight.'

'I don't mind,' Frankie said, flushing because she did mind, but she didn't *want* to mind, she *hated* herself for minding.

'You do, and that's fine, because *I* mind,' Violet said hoarsely. 'God, I mind so bloody much.'

179

'Yeah.' Frankie pulled herself up on the edge of the bath and sat there rubbing her hand over her face. 'I would too,' she said. 'I'm so sorry, Violet.'

She snagged the bathrobe off the hook and leaned forward to settle it around Violet's shoulders. 'Why don't we compromise: I'll leave you to wash in here and get you a hot-water bottle for your bed.'

Things recovered slightly when Violet got into bed, hair brushed and looking marginally more like herself, although she still seemed jittery. She arranged her pillows, groped across the surface of her nightstand looking for something, then slid it under her pillow. 'Turn on that night light over there, it's less bright. And will you sit for a bit?'

'Okay.' Curled up in the armchair, Frankie pulled out her mobile to send Con a quick text: *Staying at my grandmother's.* She paused, deleted the last word, then retyped it, deleted it again, flicking a glance at Violet, who had sunk back against the pillow, her face etched with deep lines. This was Con, for heaven's sake, just tell him. But then she remembered how curious he'd been at the Costa, their spiky conversation on the back stairs, his slightly desperate keenness to get a foothold at the *London Post*. Better to explain it in person, properly. *Staying at a friend's house*, she typed instead. *Meet me in the lobby first thing tomorrow?*

'Can you smell the trees?' Violet's eyes glittered against the pale oval of her face, the rest of her body a vague mass of shadows. 'Apples have such a sweet, gentle scent at this stage. Later, when they're ripe, it's stronger, more robust, then they rot, become effervescent and a little bitter. At this time of year, the smell of autumn, fires burning, fruit, it makes me think of the war. Of picking apples.'

'In Yorkshire, you mean?' Frankie suppressed a yawn. Tiredness was starting to seep into her legs, making her shiver in the cold breeze that stirred the curtains.

Violet shifted, and something gleamed in her hand. 'Do you sometimes have the feeling that time slides? That something that happened in the past is suddenly right here, part of the present? After your mum died, I didn't think I'd survive. I would go through the day and then, like a glass door sliding, I'd be back in the moment again when your dad rang us to say that she was gone. Do you know that he waited a whole *day* to tell us about the car accident? She had already been dead for all those hours, and I still pictured her in your little flat, with you.'

'He was in pieces, d-d-devastated.' Frankie automatically jumped to his defence, but Violet just went on.

'And Romy's death, too. I couldn't stop reliving it, the moment she died and the days after; it was so real, like I could *feel* it happening over and over again. And now it's back, that sliding-time feeling, only it's stronger, so much stronger. One moment I'm walking down a street and all is fine, then I blink and the street is rubble-strewn and filled with smoke. I smell blackberry brambles smouldering wetly on a bonfire, and then it's only Mrs Billingsworth's gardener burning a pile of leaves. I'm up a ladder amidst apple trees, rows and rows of them in the orchards, I'm young and strong; and then I'm old and creaky, and it's just the one little apple tree your grandfather planted for me. All is melding into one, as if time has become fluid and I don't really know where I am, what I am. Have you ever felt that? Or is it all part of – well, whatever is happening to me? Am I really and truly going mad?' She delivered the last word defiantly and yet so obviously afraid to hear the answer that Frankie took her time thinking about it.

'Maybe it's the way the year unfolds,' she said eventually. 'All the little traditions and milestones lining up so that smells and sounds become linked to them. Always at this time, we'd go for our first ice cream. Today we would have gone shopping for new shoes. I smell Shalimar and there's Mum, clear as day, getting ready for work. I hear that plinky-planky guitar sound, you know when they tune it, and I turn, expecting Dad to be there . . .'

She caught herself and broke off, not wanting to have to defend her father in front of Violet. But her grandmother's eyes were fixed on the shadowy trees moving outside.

'Maybe,' she said. 'Whatever it is, it's getting stronger, like time itself is unravelling, the past pushing into the present, and I don't know where one ends and the other begins. The Gala at the Wentworth – it was like it was calling me back to where it all began, the beginning of a thread starting to unspool all over again. And I'm afraid where that thread leads, Frankie. I'm so afraid.'

She whispered the last couple of sentences furtively, as if something was right there, waiting for her, and for an irrational moment, Frankie fought a surge of fear, too, a feeling of monsters in the dark.

'Calling you back where, Violet? Romy? Yorkshire?'

But her grandmother's breathing had become even. She'd fallen asleep.

Quietly Frankie eased her cramped legs from underneath her, closed the window, then tucked the blanket more securely around Violet's shoulders. Violet's hand had been resting on the edge of the pillow, fingers curled around something, but just as Frankie was about to straighten, they relaxed, let the object slide onto the sheet, where, with a slight clunk, it hit a small book tucked halfway beneath the pillow.

The lights of a car passing outside cut a sharp, bright swathe through the bedroom. Violet stirred, the book slid and Frankie reached out to catch it. A sudden sting made her hiss, and before the headlamps had fully died away, she saw that she was holding a brooch, and the pin, gaping open, had embedded itself in her finger.

Quickly, cradling her hand before it could drip blood over a sleeping Violet, Frankie tiptoed outside, found a plaster in the ancient bathroom. She wasn't generally squeamish, but the evening suddenly caught up with her and she sank down on the closed loo. Violet's tights were lying in a twisted knot on the floor, and Frankie tried not to imagine what other things the next few weeks and months might bring. Instead, she worked the pin back into its little eyelet, straining to remember when she'd had her last tetanus jab.

The words *Women's Land Army* ran around the edge of the badge, a sheaf of grain in the middle. On her lap, the little black book had fallen open and there was a strange indentation in its middle. It took her a moment to realise that the Land Army badge must have been kept in there for a long time, because the book had moulded itself around it. A very long time, she thought, startled, when she picked out a date: *10 October 1940*.

It seemed to be a ledger, albeit a very small one. Columns ran down the page with dates and names next to them, and – she squinted more closely – tiny lines, four in a row with one across. A tally of some kind. She turned to the previous page, then the one before that; they had been glued together and she had to carefully detach them. There was a cluster of names that appeared together, changed a little, with a core group remaining the same all the way back to spring 1940. Occasionally a note had been scratched next to the marks. *Late*, several said. *Improper*, one or two. *Unruly. Blackout.* The entries had all been made by one person in small, cramped, old-fashioned longhand, although the execution changed a little: sometimes almost painfully exact, other times a little slanted and rushed-looking.

Frankie shivered. She couldn't put a finger on it, but there was something unpleasant about it: the relentless repetition of the tallies, the deep grooves left behind by the pen, the fact that the book contained nothing else, no to-do lists, no notes, no appointments and certainly no praise. Just a long, endless list of wrongdoings that built and built until it finally culminated in a double line beneath which the tallies started anew. She squinted at a particularly emphatic double line, with the words *blackout fine* and *time sheets* scratched in the margins, and wondered what fate had befallen Burns, Pritchard, Simpson and their comrades on what seemed, judging by the way the pen had torn the page, a particularly disastrous day.

She flicked all the way to the beginning of the book, where the ink from a large oval stamp had bled out and faded into the grain of the endpapers. The words *Winterbourne Orchards* ran along the top, there was a bit of curlicuing and leafy plants, which had become indistinguishable with age, and another few words at the bottom. *From Darkness, Light,* it said in old-fashioned serif letters, reminding Frankie of an old school letterhead or a university seal.

'Frankie?' A tired voice came from the bedroom, and Frankie quickly got up, fumbled the badge back into its hollowed-out space, the pages closing obligingly around it. Holding it behind her back, she walked into the bedroom.

'Do you think you could close the curtains?' Violet said drowsily, curled up on her side now. 'I seem to be waking every time a car passes.'

'Sure,' Frankie whispered, setting the book on the bedside table. She pulled the curtains shut and Violet was asleep again before she had even closed the door.

Twenty-Five

'Ah, Miss O'Brien has decided to make an appearance after all, welcome, welcome.'

Hugo Ramsey popped up next to Frankie's desk so suddenly that her eyes flew open, giving her a more alert appearance than she would otherwise have been able to muster.

She had spent so long cleaning the kitchen the previous night, then sitting over her New Line Theatre Group piece with a cup of very strong coffee and a tumbler full of cooking sherry she'd found in the cupboard, that she'd fallen asleep right at the kitchen table. She'd been woken by the clatter of milk bottles out on the street, a slow spiral of dread unfurling before she was fully awake. Mercifully – given the circumstances – her grandmother seemed a little under the weather and said she wouldn't mind staying in bed for a bit. After some negotiation, she agreed to Frankie asking Dr Morrissey to pop over to check on her and for Jools to sit with her for a few hours until Frankie returned, if and only if Frankie took down the signs around the hallway and kitchen and put them back up later. But if she so much as breathed a word of anything else to either of them, Violet would never talk to her again for the rest of her life. 'And I'll come back and haunt you, even after that,' she threatened, sounding so much like her old self that Frankie had left Cavendish Place marginally cheered.

'You missed the editorial meeting.' Hugo now perched delicately on the edge of Frankie's workspace.

'We were told it was every other day.' She coughed to sound more awake.

'That was June Seymour's modus operandi, dear heart. Mine

is every day, short, snappy. Crawley was there.' Hugo jabbed his chin in the direction of Con's desk, and Frankie felt a flicker of annoyance. She'd waited for Con in the lobby this morning but he hadn't showed – obviously because he'd been too busy arriving nice and early for an ed meeting he might have mentioned to her.

'I'm sorry,' she said. 'I'll know for the future.' Her desk phone shrilled but she was loath to pick it up with Hugo still standing there, taking in her somewhat rumpled appearance. She'd let it go to voicemail.

'Francesca's phone.' She heard Felicity's exasperated voice from somewhere. 'Oi, a Dr Morrissey for you. I'll tell him you're busy, shall I?'

'No, I'll t-t-t . . .' Frankie's arm shot forward when her stammer precluded her from actually saying it, but Felicity had already hung up. Frankie glowered at her. So much for not answering each other's phones.

'It's not your lovely grandmother who's in need of medical attention, is it?' Hugo was closer now, seemingly without moving, and Frankie pressed her back into the wall behind her. 'Is that the reason she's been housebound lately? Why she fainted? Is she ill?'

His foot tapped against the steel drawer below her desk with each question, and Mallory, who'd been flicking industriously through a pile of papers while clearly hanging on every one of Hugo's words, cringed theatrically at the last one, sweeping his stuff away from Frankie's side of the desk.

'No one is ill,' Frankie said angrily.

Hugo gave her a piercing look, then held up the paper. 'Have you seen your piece?'

It was big, too big, really, given that she had not done her job particularly well. Headlines and text flowed around the photo of the three of them and two pictures of Celeste looking – Frankie flushed with shame – discombobulated and hectic.

'Your very own byline in the *Post* and it's only your third day here. Not bad, not bad at all.' He tossed the paper onto the desk.

Helping Children Reach for the Stars. By Francesca Etherington, with contribution from Conrad Crawley. Out of nowhere, joy flared, wild and triumphant. A byline in the *London Post*! But it vanished almost immediately.

'Hugo,' she said loudly. 'Con wrote most of that Celeste stuff; he should have been credited first, and definitely not just for contribution. And my byline is Francesca *O'Brien*. How did this—'

'Don't you think this has a grander ring?' Hugo looked at the byline admiringly. 'It could be your pen name, you know, your alter ego. Which reminds me, I did notice there was no actual soundbite in it from your grandmother, my lovely. Now, do tell, is really all as it should be with the Etherington ladies?'

It was one of Hugo's particular conversational gambits, to change direction so suddenly that the other person couldn't but trip up.

'It's f-f-f-f . . .' Frankie cleared her throat several times, then choked out a 'Sorry,' exaggeratedly miming a frog in her throat. God, she hated that stammer, but even more she hated that it appeared to be back for good.

'Well,' Hugo continued, seemingly oblivious to her stuttering, 'then it wouldn't be a huge undertaking to see if your grandmother might be amenable to an interview, to mark your start here at the *London Post*. Nothing elaborate, just the two of you chatting cosily of an evening. No, no need to say anything, wouldn't want you to properly choke. Just think about it, angel, will you?'

'Congrats on the story,' Con said coolly when he stopped by Frankie's desk a little later. At least he had waited until Victoria and Mallory were gone.

'At the risk of sounding like a broken record,' Frankie sighed, 'surely, *surely* you know I didn't ask him to do the byline like that? In fact I asked him to take my name *off* that story altogether.'

'Of course. And it looks like you had an absolutely terrible time, too.'

He tapped the picture of Frankie next to Violet on the red carpet. The Jacqmar was glamorous in an understated way, her hair glowed beautifully and the make-up Jools had insisted on helping her with made her look so different she almost didn't recognise herself.

'So you're working on the New Line board scandal?' Con gestured at the website on her screen.

'Yeah, you?' Her mobile gave a small buzz and she snatched it up quickly. She had left another message for Dr Morrissey, asking him to call her as a matter of life and death, which had made Felicity's eyes positively bug out of her head, and she didn't want to miss his call again. But it was just a text from Beatrice asking about lunch.

'Opening of a new wing at the National Museum,' Con was saying next to her. 'Can it get any duller?'

'That's nice.' Frankie kept her eyes on the mobile screen, willing it to ring, and she didn't notice at first that Con had fallen silent. 'I'm sorry, Con,' she said quickly. 'I obviously don't mean *nice*. I haven't had a lot of sleep; can't quite think straight today.'

'Sure,' he shrugged. 'I'll talk to you later. Bea's meeting us at one downstairs.'

'You know, Con, I'm sorry, but I can't. I just . . . I have too much going on. And there's something I wanted to talk to you about. This morning, when I was waiting in the lobby,' she added pointedly.

'Yeah, sorry, I ran into Felicity and she told me about the ed meeting. What's up?'

'It's the flat.' She took a deep breath, because suddenly she didn't want to say it. Saying it out loud would make it all too real, when right now she would have given anything to slope off to a fry-up at the greasy spoon with Bea, and later go home, share a bottle of wine and watch telly together. 'The *hovel*,' she added in an effort to inject a note of humour. 'The thing is, and I'm really sorry, Con, but I'm going to have to move out.'

'What?' He stared at her incredulously. 'Why?'

'My grandmother . . . It's . . .' she swallowed, flicked a glance at Felicity's desk. 'Something's come up and I'm staying with her for a bit.'

Realisation dawned on his face. 'Is that where you were last night? When you said you were with a friend, I thought maybe you meant Jools.'

'I'm sorry.' She hesitated. 'I wanted to explain in person. That I was really sorry and of course I'll pay my share of the rent until you can find someone else.'

'I thought you said you weren't in touch with her?' he said incredulously.

'Shh,' she said hastily. 'We weren't.' For a moment she debated whether to tell him the real reason she was moving in with Violet, to talk it through until it didn't feel quite so heavy, until it became part of the world, real and thus somehow manageable. But something else had crept into Con's expression, something curious and keen and faintly unpleasant.

'Well,' he said slowly. 'Didn't take you long to conveniently realign yourself with your fancy relations. So much for your much-lauded integrity, Francesca *Etherington*. You do realise that Hugo's just using you for that byline, right? Because being Violet Etherington's granddaughter lends his society page so much more gravitas? It's probably why he didn't let you go with Xavier Merrell; he wanted you here. But you don't have to move in with her, you're already the favour—'

'It's not like that,' Frankie hissed.

'Well then, tell me what it *is* like.' He threw up his hands. 'I thought we were in this together, that we were friends.'

'We *are* friends.'

'Friends talk to each other.'

'It's a long—'

'—story, of course. That's all you ever say about everything,' Con said flatly.

Just then, Frankie's mobile rang. Dr Morrissey. She snatched it up. 'Thank you *so* much for ringing back,' she whispered, turning her back on Con.

'Harder than Fort Knox to get through to you,' Dr Morrissey grumbled. 'I'm a busy man, you know. Any dried peas stuck up anyone's nose?'

Hysterical laughter pushed up. 'That was t-t-twenty years ago,' she croaked, horrified to hear a small sob in her voice. 'And it was a Lego brick.'

'Of course. A blue one. What can I do for you, my dear?'

Con was still hovering and Felicity was listening with every fibre of her being; without looking at either of them, Frankie sidled around her desk and stepped out the back doors.

'She seemed fine when I last saw her, about, hmm, six months ago, maybe? In fighting form.' Dr Morrissey sounded admiring, as always when talking about Violet, for whom he harboured a long-standing and not very secret *tendresse*. Then his voice turned brisk, businesslike. 'She'll need to come in, Frankie.'

'Well the thing is, she doesn't exactly want to.' Frankie pursed her lips. 'I was wondering, is there any chance at all that you might be able to pop by today and diagnose something that would then bring her into hospital for tests, and you could start running those . . . other ones without her knowing?'

Dr Morrissey smothered a hoot of incredulous laughter when he realised that Frankie was serious. 'I'm not necessarily the one who'll be doing most of the tests. I'm the starting point, and then depending on what we find, there're several routes to take. You'll have to wait for specialist appointments for some of them, possibly quite a while. In the meantime, there'd be the day-to-day situation to consider, supervision, cognitive treatments, care . . .'

'I'm going to move in with her.' Frankie tried to sound as confident and pleased by this choice as she could.

There was a pause, then Dr Morrissey said, very carefully, 'Frankie, are you sure? It might look doable at the moment, but it can get very un-doable very quickly. However, there's no arguing that a familiar environment and loved ones around is the best thing, especially in the early stages. Although,' he coughed delicately, 'she did mention that you weren't, well, around much in the last years. That all sorted out?'

Frankie opened her mouth, closed it again. No, it wasn't, not at all. She hadn't stood still long enough for it to be sorted out. The moment she paused, she could feel it bubbling beneath the surface, a decade of resentment and betrayal, let down by someone she'd loved and trusted completely. And when her dad was released, she would be back exactly where she'd been on the day she'd walked out, suspended between them, stretched ever thinner as she absorbed their hatred of each other.

'It'll have to do. And anyway, it might all turn out okay, mightn't it?' Frankie said this last bit very fast. 'Maybe you'll see right away that it's something else altogether, high blood pressure or she needs vitamins, or thyroid stuff. Something that can be fixed. If you could just come and have a look at her . . .'

'You Etherington girls, one more stubborn than the next,' he said. 'All right, I'll pop in as soon as I can and contrive a way to get her into the practice.'

'Thank you,' Frankie said fervently, 'you're a life-saver, honestly.'

Dr Morrissey paused. 'There might not be much to save here,' he said seriously. 'You have to know that going in, Frankie. The best you can hope for is to make it as comfortable for her as you can. But there's no going back; there never is.'

Twenty-Six

Maybe there *was* a way of going back, though, something that Dr Morrissey, nice as he was, couldn't see from the pedestal of the medical profession. She'd had it before, Violet had said last night, this feeling of losing time, and it had passed then. So what if Frankie could help it disappear now by bringing to the surface whatever had caused it?

Leaning against the wall next to the back stairs, she opened her notebook. Last night, she had written down everything she could remember from the last few days, a jumble of notes and questions, underlined, crossed out, linked with arrows. Structure didn't matter, really. It was the writing-down that was important, that turned worries into words and imposed order, made her heart slow, her mind less fragmented. She flicked past bits from the Starlight Gala and the police station, the shoes, the tea bag clump, until she came to the little black book, the Land Army badge. She had noted what she remembered from the pages, drawn the circle, the Winterbourne Orchards stamp, from memory.

It's calling me back to where it all began. And I'm so afraid.

Afraid. It was all across the page, that word. Afraid of her own state of mind and of bringing it out into the open. But most of all, Violet seemed afraid of the past.

Lost in thought, Frankie circled the words *where it all began* – Romy at the Wentworth and her horrific death. Violet had talked about Romy very rarely, had only told a teenage Frankie about the air raid once and Frankie had never forgotten the expression on her grandmother's face. She drew an arrow from Romy's name across to *Women's Land Army* and the date from the book, *October 1940*. If Violet had been in London for the first few weeks of the Blitz, like she'd said, then she might well have been in Yorkshire in early October. Frankie pursed her lips, wishing she had looked more closely at the pages, but her grandmother's name would have jumped out at her, she was sure. Maybe her behaviour had been exemplary? Unlikely, knowing Violet.

She grimaced, rubbed her aching eyes. Maybe she'd ask her tonight, if her mood was right. And in the meantime, there wouldn't be any harm in doing a bit of research on the WLA in 1940s Yorkshire, trawling the internet for any mention of Winterbourne Orchards.

She traced the word 'afraid' again. Somehow, in that fluid time between then and now, young Violet was transferring some old fear onto old Violet, something that weighed so heavy on her mind that it was slowly giving beneath the pressure. Or was it the other way around: had her unravelling mind somehow opened a chink in her armour, letting in unwanted memories and fear?

'I thought I heard someone back here.' Noise from the newsroom flooded the corridor as Max Sefton stuck his head through the back door. 'They were talking about the Guildhall business at the ed meeting this morning.' He closed the door behind him. 'Hugo update you? You know, I met Allan Petworth from New Line last year, I could give you a few tips for your piece if you like.'

Hugo's just using you for that byline.

'Thanks, but I don't need any help,' Frankie said coolly, wrapping the leather thongs around her notebook.

'Never doubted it for a minute,' Max shrugged, 'but if you want me to have a look, one colleague to another, you know where to find me.'

His smile was genuine, not hungry, not derisive, just friendly.

One colleague to another. Frankie gave herself a hard mental shake, because that was exactly what she was. She'd been working for eight years, for heaven's sake; she wasn't going to let a few spiteful comments derail her.

Suddenly feeling bold with resolve, she fished out her mobile. 'Hey, do you mind if I give you my number? That way, if Hugo has any more meetings I don't know about, you could message me?'

He grinned appreciatively. 'You haven't lived until you've been propositioned on the back stairs of a top-tier newspaper. Course I don't mind.'

'I'm not propositioning you.' Frankie flushed. 'I was merely—'

'Just a joke. You'll have to programme it in for me, though.' He held up his phone. 'It's new and I have no clue how to use it. And call yourself with it, so you have mine. Just in case.'

A minute later, hidden behind her monitor, she made a face. Proposition him, ha. She'd never propositioned anyone in her life. The men she usually dated were serious types, rather non-propositionable, if she was honest. Bookish mostly, and overly earnest, perhaps, now that she looked back on them, but she liked things to be predictable. Not that she was in any way putting Max in a pool of 'men to date'. They were nothing more than colleagues. And yet he somehow brought out something very different in her, a strange, stroppy boldness, a reckless daring that was distinctly un-Frankie-like.

It was that loose-limbed confidence, she thought as she covertly watched him fall into conversation with John Sievers, making the usually rather stern John throw back his head and laugh. The way he was able to turn anything into a joke, didn't seem to care about office politics but just went for what he wanted, entirely oblivious to what anyone thought of him or how he'd improve their view.

Just then, Max glanced over and winked at her across the rows of desks. She looked down quickly, fighting whatever was making the back of her neck prickle, her face flush. Maybe she'd be okay with being just a teeny, tiny bit more than colleagues.

Research into Winterbourne Orchards proved unproductive, with only a smattering of mentions across the internet; a list of apple varieties in a Fruit Growers' Association almanac, a bit about the family who'd owned the estate and a local history waxing lyrical about the beauty of Winterbourne House and the graceful surrounds of the Barleigh valley. This last bit was the most interesting – if ultimately the most disappointing – because Barleigh, and by extension Winterbourne, wasn't in Yorkshire at all, but in Somerset.

So nothing to do with Violet, Frankie thought. Maybe the book belonged to a friend, someone she'd known across the network of the Women's Land Army? She scrolled through old, grainy images on her screen. Land girls had been a particularly cheerful bunch, all huge smiles, wind-tousled hair and healthily glowing cheeks.

I'm up a ladder, young and strong, Violet had said. Frankie pictured her grandmother looking like these women, brimming with vitality and comradeship. They could certainly do with a bit of female comradeship around here, she thought as she studied a picture of four women proudly brandishing their rakes.

'Are you deaf? Hugo needs a word.' A voice cut into her thoughts and Frankie almost jumped out of her skin when she realised that Felicity was standing right behind her, hands on her hips as she leaned towards her monitor. Quickly Frankie tried to close the window but missed the little button twice before the picture of the land girls disappeared.

'Is it too much to ask for you to see your boss, Francesca, or are you looking to take up farming?' Felicity exchanged a look with Mallory, who'd been watching Frankie's fumbling with some interest.

'Is it too much to ask that you don't tell me what to do, Felicity?' Frankie said angrily.

'Then don't make me your messenger,' Felicity threw over her shoulder as she huffed off.

'I didn't *ask* you to take my message,' Frankie shouted after her, words she bitterly regretted later, when she trekked halfway across London for a lunch with Allan Petworth only to find that it had been cancelled while she was in Hugo's office.

'You specifically said I shouldn't take down *any* messages for you,' Felicity said in an injured tone when she got back. 'Make up your mind, will you?'

The day went further downhill when a press release Frankie was sure had been on her desk that morning disappeared. She narrowed her eyes at Mallory, who was typing away innocently. He and Victoria had conducted a pointedly audible conversation about the Gala piece, discussing the photo of Frankie in such minute detail that Frankie thought she was either going to staple their mouths shut or hang herself with the computer cable, and after that, the press release was gone.

With a sigh, she rang to have the information faxed over again. On the way to the fax machine, determined not to let the press release out of her sight this time, she passed Felicity, perched against Con's desk. Frankie had been too rushed off her feet to talk to him again – and, to be honest, hadn't been all that keen for more of his views on her inadequacies – but any last impulse to patch things up died immediately when she heard him say, 'Yeah, it's a flat share for a year, if you hear of anyone looking. We're left in a bit of a bind and you seem to know everyone.' He had his hands clasped behind his head in a faux-casual scribe-with-suspenders pose that set Frankie's teeth on edge.

'You're not in a b-b-bloody bind. I *s-s-aid* I was going to cover my share until you found someone.' She fought hard to get the words out.

196

'He just wanted to help,' Felicity said censoriously. 'London housing is a huge issue, you know, although obviously not for *some*,' she added pointedly. 'So you and Granny are going to be flatmates, eh? Will you have us over for a house-warming? I always wanted to have a little nose around those grand houses in Belgravia.'

Frankie slowly turned towards Con, who had the grace to flush. 'I don't know what the hell your p-p-problem is,' she said angrily, 'but I'd very much appreciate it if you didn't air every piece of my b-b-business in public.'

'We were just chatting. Fliss had some ideas.'

Fliss was it now?

'Francesca, calm down.' Felicity shook her head. 'But now that I think of it, maybe you *should* suggest doing an inside piece on Etherington's house. Hugo would jump at it, I'm sure. Quite the opportunity for you, isn't it, especially now. Wasn't that what you were just saying, Conrad?'

Frankie couldn't even look at Con, who didn't say anything to refute the comment and she was so angry, she knew she wouldn't be able to get past the first syllable of whatever pithy retort she might think up. She turned on her heel and stalked over to the fax machine, where, shaking with rage, she waited for the press release to come through. But as if that wasn't enough, walking back to her desk, she found Felicity rootling through some of her papers.

'Wh-wh-what are you doing?' She all but pushed the other woman away.

'I'm looking for that folder I gave you earlier.' Felicity held up a red file folder, which she had tugged out from under – Frankie's blood ran cold – her leather-bound notebook.

'F-f-fine,' she said, inserting herself between Felicity and her notebook.

Felicity threw her a quick appraising glance over her shoulder as she went, and Frankie sank down at her desk, gripping the notebook, which, mercifully, still had the leather thongs wrapped tightly around it. How could she have left her notes on Violet lying around in a place like this? What would Felicity do with that kind of information? Never mind Felicity, what would *Hugo* do?

All of a sudden, Violet's insistence on discretion made a whole lot more sense. Celeste was one thing, but the thought of Violet being part of some salacious gossip machinery was unbearable; to be discussing her current situation at the editor- ial meeting, with Hugo, with everyone agog – no.

She watched Felicity gabbing into her phone, saw Con staring fixedly at his screen, and slid her notebook deep into her bag, piling other papers on top. Violet didn't want to tell anyone? Well, that was just fine by Frankie. In fact, not just for Violet's sake, but for purely selfish reasons, Frankie would prefer for her grandmother's name to come up as little as humanly possible around here. She'd show Con, she'd show Hugo. She'd show all of them.

Twenty-Seven

'I can't believe this, I really and truly cannot believe it.'

Violet had flung open the door before Frankie had even come up the front steps, her face set in an enraged scowl. Frankie quickened her pace, fumbled for her mobile. Was Violet having a seizure of some kind?

'I'll ring the doctor,' she panted.

'He was already here, thank you very much,' Violet snapped. 'And I don't need a doctor, *you* need your head examined. What are they doing to you over at that blasted paper, brainwashing you?' She thrust today's edition of the *London Post* in Frankie's direction.

'I'm sorry, Violet, I couldn't keep them from printing *something* on your fall,' Frankie said urgently. 'But I tried to make it sound okay.'

'Not that,' Violet said angrily, 'although *also* that, the day I live to see my own granddaughter writing about me, but *this . . .*' Violet shook the paper, making Celeste McIntyre's photo balloon out grotesquely. 'Such utter drivel. Celeste is the wronged party here, and you're making her sound like a train wreck.'

'It's not my fault,' Frankie hissed. 'Hugo sent me to do that interview. I didn't get it done because . . . well, I stayed in the back room with *you*, didn't I, so a colleague had to add information for the piece to run. And Hugo has final say, he knows best what kinds of stories work for the paper, what people want to read.'

'Are you even listening to yourself?' Violet's voice dripped with disdain. 'When in the last ten years did you lose the ability to think for yourself? To *think* period?'

'I d-d-don't know.' Frankie's throat swelled with the effort of getting the words out. 'When I was having to sell Mum's jewellery to buy myself f-f-food? When I was visiting Dad in prison once a month? I can think for myself just fine. I'm just trying to do my job, I'm just bloody *trying*.'

'Well try harder,' Violet said coldly. 'Hugo Ramsey is a pathetic, tiny man, who had his head stuffed down the toilet one too many times at school and is still taking it out on the world.'

'He's a great journalist.' Frankie shouldered her bag. 'I'm lucky to be learning from him.'

'That's all the world needs, more bullies like Hugo Ramsey. Celeste is lovely, she's had a tough time and she's my friend. This hack job is beyond shabby – and using *my* name for it? For *this* you feel like being an Etherington is useful?'

'I don't want your name, I never have,' Frankie shouted. 'I don't *need* you.'

'Can I ask you kindly not to use it, then.' Violet looked at her dismissively. 'Stop letting people walk all over you, Frankie.'

Frankie was speechless. 'But it was fine for me to let *you* walk all over me for twelve years?' She ripped the newspaper out of Violet's hand. 'For you to tell me what to do, to make all my decisions for me? What clothes you thought I needed, what school you thought I should go to, where to live. You hated Dad's flat, Dad's band, Dad's music, *Dad*, my entire other life, so you barged right in there and didn't rest until it was all gone, until he was behind bars.'

'He put himself in prison; *I* wasn't the one who committed a crime.' Violet was dismissive. 'He was bad news, a no-hoper, and he took my Stella along for the ride. My beautiful, dreamy daughter, who'd never hurt a soul, he made her spend her days waiting for him in that hovel, cooking tea for his band mates—'

'He was a musician.' Frankie felt a roaring in her ears. 'He was following his passion. Surely you, who puts so much store by being true to yourself and following your path no matter what, surely you should *get* that.'

'True to yourself?' Violet sneered. 'None of us has the luxury of following our passions; someone always has to pay for it.'

'And who made you the great arbiter of good and evil?' Frankie wasn't shouting any more; she felt very tired. 'Who asked you to put your great big oar in?' She drew in a long, slow breath. 'Maybe I let people walk all over me. Maybe I'm a pleaser. After all, I did spend my entire childhood trying to be good so you and Dad wouldn't be constantly haggling over me. It was never enough that I spent time with you, never enough when I was with him. You always wanted more. But that's over and done with, and you don't – I repeat, you do *not* – have the right to barge in and take over any more. However, since clearly you're exactly the same as you always were, then you must be completely well now. So I'm leaving. Again. Congratulations.' She turned towards the door.

'Frankie, don't, please,' she heard Violet say behind her, 'I was just trying to—'

'Try harder,' Frankie said and walked out.

It had been her grandfather who had – entirely unwittingly – revealed to Frankie Violet's role in things, and not until some time into Harry O'Brien's arrest and subsequent trial. In fact, at first, Violet had seemed extraordinarily supportive. She didn't leave Frankie's side after the arrest, the circumstances of which remained somewhat hazy to an eighteen-year-old.

There had been a break-in, that much was clear, but her father said that he hadn't set foot in the house, or hadn't meant to any-way when he did, which wasn't until the very end, when he'd heard a commotion and rushed in to make sure that his friend Rudy wasn't going to do anything stupid. That was all he'd wanted to do, to make sure nothing stupid was done. Somehow, though, the gun – which Rudy had said he wasn't going to bring, truly he wasn't going to – had ended up in Harry's hand; some-how a shot was fired when the owner of the house suddenly appeared. Harry swore up and down that the owner had got hold of the weapon and then shoved it back at him – 'at me of all people, Francesca, when I'm a pacifist through and through' – just as the cops showed up at the scene.

'But what were you doing there anyway, Dad?' Frankie had asked him desperately during one of her few visits. 'And why was there a gun to begin with? That man's been in hospital for weeks, his leg might be permanently damaged. What if he'd been killed?'

'I wasn't *supposed* to be there, of course,' Harry had said urgently. 'I didn't know anything about the whole thing at first. But their driver was ill and Rudy asked me to cover for him, begged me, and then they were all relying on me, and by the time I realised what it was, I couldn't leave them in the lurch, could I?'

'But why didn't you just stay in the car?' she said helplessly.

'Rudy's my friend and he was in trouble, so I went in there to help. I never, on my life, meant for that man to be injured, you've got to believe me, Francesca. That's not who I am. I wasn't even supposed to *be* in the house, I was just there as a driver . . .'

They'd gone round and round and Frankie wanted to believe at least some of her dad's side of the story. But even if he'd been in the wrong place at the wrong time, things weren't looking good for Harry O'Brien in court.

'Please, Dad, let me ask Violet for help, get you another lawyer.'

'But that young chap they gave me is nice,' Harry said. 'He's a bit rushed off his feet, sure, but he'll do right by me.'

Frankie had no doubt that the harried young man was entirely capable, but he hadn't even had time to sit down when she'd first met him; how would he have time to find a new angle that would somehow lessen a sentence that looked increasingly like ten or fifteen years in prison?

'Violet knows so many people; she can find you someone who doesn't have a million other cases to go through,' she begged. 'Please let me ask her.'

But Harry refused to discuss it further. 'This is what my taxes pay for. I won't fork out a small family car's worth of money for a fancy lawyer.'

In her desperation, Frankie had turned to her grandmother anyway.

'Violet, I'm not for a minute saying that Dad should get off for this altogether, but maybe we could try to at least shorten his sentence a little. Can you ask one of your lawyer friends? I'd pay them back if it takes my entire life, I swear.'

'Harry doesn't want me to, love, I've offered,' Violet said.

'You have?' Frankie stared at her, gratitude and relief washing over her. 'Really?'

'I asked Frank Millworth to take it on, you know he's very good. But Harry said no. He won't consider it.'

Frankie had been so terrified about what would happen to her dad in prison that, as the days went by, she found herself racked with anxiety, unable to sleep for long stretches, stammering so badly she could barely string a sentence together. Finally Violet forced her to close up the flat and move in with them permanently.

'If you're lying there staring at the ceiling, you might as well do it here, where it's warm, there's food, and the electricity isn't constantly on the verge of being turned off,' she'd said matter-of-factly. 'I won't take no for an answer.'

And Frankie, who didn't have the energy to counter the low-grade dig at their flat, let alone stand up to her grandmother over her sleeping arrangements, packed their stuff into crates and bags, paid the last of the rent and made her way to Cavendish Place.

But Violet's final victory in the twelve-year battle over where Frankie was staying would be her ultimate downfall. Because it was during one of those sleepless nights that Frankie crept out of bed and down towards the kitchen, vaguely thinking of something hot to help her sleep, and overheard her grandparents talking in the next room.

'Violet, I'm telling you again, it's wrong,' she heard Gramps say. 'I know you have her best interests at heart, but it's not right, you know. He's still her father.'

'That man has never been a father to anyone.'

Frankie was used to Violet's dislike by now, but she'd never heard this cold, cutting tone in her grandmother's voice, so full of hatred that out in the hallway, she wrapped her arms around herself and shivered. 'He doesn't deserve her and this time he's gone too far. I'll be damned if I allow him to be let off lightly on this. Frankie's got to have a decent chance at making something of herself; I refuse to let her spend any more years following behind and being dragged down by that good-for-nothing. Frankie will not go under, not like Stella.'

Although Frankie had been taken aback by the venom in Violet's words, at its core the sentiment wasn't altogether new to her. But it wasn't until she went to see her father again that it all finally became clear.

'Francesca, love, I hate to put you in the middle of this, but could you possibly persuade your grandmother with this whole lawyer thing? I know I haven't been the best son-in-law, but it's getting down to the wire now; surely she can't refuse to help me? Not when I'm family?' He had become so nervy that he never stopped moving now, fidgeting, twitching, his hands strumming an imaginary guitar, his eyes darting every which way.

'What are you talking about?' Frankie said, confused. 'She said she offered to help you, wanted to ask Frank Millworth, but that you said no, which is what you told me.'

'Well, yes.' He flushed, clearly embarrassed. 'I know I said no at the beginning, but now – well, I suppose you could say I'm selling my values down the river. Truth is, I thought about what you said about all her contacts, and I got in touch with her.' He swallowed. 'Asked her if anyone she knew might be able to help me out of this mess, the young chap being a tad preoccupied and all.'

'Yes, so Frank Millworth, isn't that the man she suggested?' Frankie said, still confused.

'No, well . . . she . . . Apparently it wasn't possible.'

'But she said . . .' Frankie's voice was hoarse.

'She said there was nothing she could do.'

Curiously, when Frankie had confronted her, Violet hadn't hedged; in fact, she had seemed almost relieved to talk about it.

'Open your eyes, Frankie,' she'd said in that new cutting voice. 'Harry O'Brien is a killer. It wasn't enough that he . . . that Stella . . .' She took a deep breath, the way she often did when she talked about Stella's death. 'He tried to *kill* that man.'

'He was only the getaway driver,' Frankie said through gritted teeth. 'I would never presume for him to walk away from this, I'm not stupid, Violet, but ten years in prison, fifteen possibly? He's not a violent c-c-criminal, you know that as well as I do. He'd never even touched a gun before, he didn't mean to—'

'No one ever means to shoot anyone, do they?' Violet hissed. 'But you finally have the chance to be free, to be what you were meant to be.'

'To be what *you* meant me to be,' Frankie had said very quietly.

Something inside Frankie had broken that night, something that – ironically – Violet had been the one to build and nurture. The ability to trust implicitly, to let herself fall without fear. Unshaken faith in a place that never changed, was always there, without strings attached, without conditions.

She had pushed past Violet, packed her overnight bag for the last time and left.

Violet

October 1940

Twenty-Eight

Violet couldn't stop thinking about the afternoon on Thistle Hill and the evening at the clearing. The way she'd been part of the girls after days of hazy, exhausted isolation; how she'd sat there with Red, chatting just like any friends would do. And then the stranger on the horse. She couldn't quite remember him whole, just bits and pieces flowing together between shadow and torchlight. The side of his face, his mouth, the set of his shoulders, the amused gleam in his eyes. Lying on her straw pallet and staring into the darkness after the few girls remaining in the barn that night had done their best to breathe for the whole group and the sound of Myra's key had faded below, she reached for his handkerchief beneath her pillow, felt the embroidered edges and the letters GWC initialled into them as she called up his smile, his eyes seeking hers, intently but also reluctantly, as if he didn't want to but couldn't do anything about it. Over and over again she felt that sudden rush of warmth that had nothing whatsoever to do with the fire, the deep tug inside her, painful and searing and utterly lovely all at the same time. In the darkness, she smiled back at him, found herself languidly stretching towards his face, revelling in the warmth of this strange, delicious something.

God, she wished Duffy could have seen her inside that hedge, or Romy, who'd have laughed hysterically at the way she had swung her poker. Maybe she'd have been proud of her, too . . .

But Violet had barely acknowledged the thought when she felt the warmth change, become hard and tinged with bitterness. She wasn't supposed to be here to be befriended, to feel . . . well, whatever it was that she'd felt with the man. The mattress crackled as she turned away from the memories of last night and deliberately scraped the ravaged arch between thumb and finger along the rough fabric of her blanket. Pain throbbed and glowed, turning all the warm and lovely things acrid and sharp. She pushed her face into the pillow, and when she finally drifted into an uneasy sleep, pain and desolation followed her until she woke at dawn with the salty tang of tears on her cheeks.

'Are you all right?' she heard a voice whisper. Red, hair tousled and eyes heavy with sleep, was peering across the two empty beds separating them.

Eyes closed, Violet burrowed into the pillow and hoped the other girl might go back to sleep. She didn't want the ease of companionship, she didn't want the relief of unburdening. She just needed to focus on working and keeping her head down.

'Want to get out of here?' Red whispered. 'Walk around a bit without someone breathing down our necks all the time?'

The thought cut straight through the blackness in Violet's head. Yes. Oh God, yes, she wanted to barrel straight through that locked door and out into the clean, crisp dawn, feeling the sky rise above and lift some of this weight off her.

'But the door?' she breathed, turning her head.

'Just leave it to Auntie Red.'

They crept towards the ladder as quietly as they could. Many beds were empty; only a few girls had returned, lumpy, immobile shapes beneath their blankets further down the line of cots.

Red shook her head when Violet pointed at the door. 'I discovered something the other day when Hardwick sent me back to change my blouse,' she whispered, motioning for Violet to follow her into the small space behind the ladder. 'You can't really see it from the path, but I went behind the shed, thought I'd take a shortcut, and there it was.'

Handing Violet the lamp, she pulled aside a piece of sacking tacked at shoulder height. A hatch was hidden behind it.

'I couldn't do anything with it on my own,' Red breathed. 'And seeing as Kit has practically swallowed the rule book, I thought I'd leave it for a bit. But now that *you*'re here . . .' She raised her eyebrows meaningfully, and Violet had to bite back a grin at the thought that she, of all people, qualified as a revolutionary.

It wasn't difficult to detach the sacking, even if it meant Violet sacrificing the last few intact inches of skin on her hands. Conferring in nods and wordless gestures, they silently unhooked the hatch and lowered it against the outside wall. It had been almost too easy, and for a moment they hesitated, then Red extinguished the lamp with a small flourish and, half-climbing, half rolling, they went through the opening, landing in an ungainly sprawl in the long grass on the other side.

'Boo to you, Hardwick,' Red mouthed next to her, and Violet kicked her legs up high before scrambling to her feet, heart beating fast.

The hatch, which might have once been used to push feed from the inside through to animals outside, if the rusty trough half-buried in the grass was anything to go by, had hooks on the outside as well as the inside. 'We'll hook it back up now, and then later we'll just fasten it from the inside,' Red whispered. 'If we're careful coming round the side, no one will see us.'

They kept close to the walls at first, bracing themselves for discovery at every corner. Skirting the stable yard, they heard the occasional snort and stamp as they slipped down a lane to the left and through a wide gate into what looked like parkland. The thin white line on the horizon threw the trees into sharp relief, as if someone had snipped them out of the sky with scissors. Jumbles of trees, bushes and hedges stretched from the back of the stable buildings towards the road, where the more orderly of the orchards began.

'It's so quiet here,' Red breathed.

Like we're the only people in the world, Violet thought. A small breeze wove through the leaves; the tentative call of a bird cut through the still air. Fog hung in gossamer shreds below branches shrouded in shadow and frost crunched under their feet. There was no shouting from tradesmen, no cars stop-starting through the blackout, no clattering of dishes down in the kitchen as breakfast was prepared for nine o'clock sharp. And, more crucially, she realised, no air raid sirens, no distant booming and cracking sounds, no constantly scanning the horizon. This sky held nothing but colour as slowly, infinitely slowly, swathes of red and orange swallowed the fading scatter of stars and reached for the pale sickle of the moon before finally flattening into the light of dawn.

'It feels safe,' she said impulsively.

'I'm not sure safe is the word I'd use.' Red flashed her a half-grin. 'Given that most of the girls have left the estate without express permission and you and I have broken out of prison and are currently walking through someone's back garden. But I suppose it does a bit.'

She casually threaded her arm through Violet's, who tensed instantly, her skin prickling uncomfortably at the sudden intimacy. She'd noticed all the girls doing it, walking arm in arm, patting hands, squeezing a shoulder in comfort. A part of her envied them that ease of companionship, the way it seemed the most natural thing in the world to be close, but it was too much for her. Pretending to step around a grassy groove in the path, she let her arm slide free again.

'This is someone's back garden?' she asked to cover her awkwardness.

'Well, the privy and washing line are missing,' Red said, 'but there's the house it belongs to.'

As if conjured up by dawn itself, as if it had always been there and would outlive mankind altogether, Winterbourne House rose from the trees and parkland surrounding it. There were no gables and turrets, no fussy masonry details or unnecessary nooks and crannies. The stone gleamed coolly beneath the weathered slate-grey roof; two short wings on either side embraced a terrace from which wide steps led down to lawns. These too were unfussy and pragmatic, bordered by walnut trees and fruit hedges, making it clear that this wasn't an ornamental country retreat, but the hub of working orchards.

The sun had risen higher, beautiful and cold, as the white autumn morning hardened the hue of the stone, turning it almost blindingly sharp.

'"Winterbourne" suits it.' Violet shivered, and Red buried her chin deeper into her collar and nodded.

On the wide terrace, a few wrought-iron chairs were grouped around a table, all of them covered and pushed firmly together. No one had sat here in a while. Most of the windows were shuttered, and in the few that weren't, no one moved. No maid tugging down the blackout curtain or emerging from the big glass doors to start sweeping away the smattering of leaves that had collected in the corners. Thin streams of smoke from the chimneys were the only signs of human presence. One of the sons had died, wasn't that what Duffy had said?

'It's getting on a bit,' Red said. 'Let's head that way, loop round to the barn. The others should be back soon, too. What do you think, shall we tell them about our secret door?'

The ground rose steadily as they wove their way through trees and hedges, but it wasn't until they stopped and sat down next to a low stone wall to catch their breath that Violet realised their roundabout wanderings had brought them up to the village road. When she turned her head, however, all thoughts of the valley's geography vanished. Slowly she laid a hand on Red's arm, put an urgent finger to her lips.

In the clearing behind them, Myra Hardwick was kneeling under a tree, head bowed in prayer.

Her ugly brown coat was open to show a different dress than usual, something black and high-necked and severe-looking, and for the first time, Violet saw her hair loose: a mass of black waves tumbling down her back, wild and abandoned and startlingly beautiful. There was something very still, almost furtive about the way she held herself, as if she didn't want to be seen either.

Up on the incline, a sharp ping of light gleamed as the sun bounced off a weathervane. Of course, Violet realised with a start. The small church, where she'd first met Hardwick, only now they had come at it from below.

'Cemetery,' Red breathed into her ear, nodding at the weathered stone slabs and rusty crosses scattered up the hill. They sagged back behind the low wall, trying to tuck their heads down as far as they could.

'That way to the road,' Violet mouthed, 'or back down the hill?' But neither option – open and very visible in the brightening morning light – seemed at all appealing, and Red mimed a piece of rope and hanging herself with it. Violet motioned to the trees on the other side, but Red was sticking out her tongue, now in the last mock-throes of death. Then suddenly—

'What are you doing here?' Myra hissed. 'You're supposed to be in *bed*.'

After Violet's first encounter with the porridge urn, Hardwick's daughter had ignored her completely, slipping in and out of mealtimes so quietly that she'd barely left any impression. Not so now. Face set in a furious scowl, she advanced on the girls, who quickly scrambled to their feet. But Violet noticed that despite her fury, Myra was crouching slightly, and that although it clearly cost her some effort, she had pitched her voice low.

'The, er, the door was open,' she said, 'and we felt like going for a walk.'

'Liar,' Myra spat at her. 'I locked the doors myself last night.'

'It's our morning off,' Red said defiantly. 'And this is a church; you can't keep us from—'

'Lying, cheating scum,' Myra said murderously.

'Excuse me,' Violet began hotly. 'There's no need for insults.'

Just then, there was the sound of hooves and a carriage, and like an animal caught in a trap, Myra's head whipped up. A grating screech came from the church door, a sound Violet remembered well from her last excruciating visit there. Myra pulled her coat around herself, gathered her hair into a kerchief and dusted down her stockinged knees, as if to erase all trace of having been down here. She really was quite beautiful, Violet realised, with those cat-like amber eyes, her skin smooth, her full lips curving in a perfect heart-shaped Cupid's bow. Then she crowded right up close to them and said, very quietly but very clearly, 'If you breathe a single word about me being here, I will sneak out to the barn and kill you in your sleep.'

Before either of them could reply, she'd turned away, not back into the bushes where she'd come from, but up the hill, looking demure and collected, as if she'd just arrived from a contemplative morning stroll through the orchards.

Violet and Red stared at each other, dumbfounded.

'Is it just me, or did that make no sense whatsoever?' Red's voice was a whispered breath. Violet frowned, peered through the undergrowth to where Myra had been kneeling, then swivelled back in the opposite direction, towards where she had disappeared.

'You know,' she said slowly, 'we could have a quick look.'

'No, Lily,' Red whispered urgently, 'Hardwick is up there, literally yards from us. *Lily!*'

A narrow path had been trodden through the undergrowth, widening into a small clearing. There were no gravestones here; the cemetery simply petered out into the orchards.

'This is where she was.' Violet stopped.

Nestled into the roots of the tree was a small clutch of flowers, carefully arranged and bound with straw, and a rusty iron receptacle. Violet stooped to examine it closer and realised it was an old milk churn. The roots rose up from the soil a little here, creating a small overhang into which the churn had been wedged, shored up with soil and patches of moss, so that just the front part was visible. Pebbles, acorns and nuts had been set in a half-circle at the foot of the tree, an intricate pattern that must have taken hours and hours to complete.

'Beautiful,' Violet breathed in wonder.

'A grave?' Red's voice was hesitant.

It was and it wasn't; Violet couldn't quite make up her mind. The earthy tones of the pattern were interwoven with small clumps of wild grasses and evergreen, as if nature itself was embracing something much beloved, offering it a place of peace. Blinking hard, she saw the stark brown rectangle of Romy's grave, the thud of soil hitting her coffin, and fell to her knees. Sighing slightly, Red knelt next to her, gently straightened the small bouquet, retied the string that held it.

'We made her leave in a hurry,' she said to Violet. 'Look.'

The milk churn was open, the lid off to the side. 'Don't, Red,' Violet said roughly when Red reached inside and pulled out a scrunched-up cloth bundle.

'I'm just tidying it away; it'll get rained on otherwise.'

The cloth fell open across her palm and they looked down at the contents. A ring. A lock of sleek dark hair. A photo of a woman inside a frame, chin up, cat-like eyes gazing rebelliously out at the viewer.

'We shouldn't be looking at this.' Violet took the bundle out of Red's hand, refolded it along the well-worn creases and slid it back into the churn.

'The lid,' Red whispered. Violet picked it up. Laboriously scratched into its face in the neatest, tiniest letters were the words: *RIP Silvia Hardwick, b. 1896, d. 1931.*

Twenty-Nine

'Coming, Lily?' The others were climbing down the ladder, ready for lunch, but Kit hung back, stamping her feet against the damp chill hanging below the eaves. She seemed much happier after her visit and was clearly keen to make amends with Violet.

Violet and Red had walked back from the cemetery quickly and without talking much. They'd made sure to reinstate the hatch and remove all signs of their presence, then sat on Violet's bed until the rest of the group trickled in.

'Her mother,' Red said. 'Hardwick's wife.'

'It was kind of sad, wasn't it?' Violet's thumb arch throbbed painfully beneath the man's handkerchief, which she'd wound around it when Red said she couldn't face staring at Violet's raw flesh a minute longer.

'Sad and a bit spooky,' Red agreed. 'And what's this about us not telling on her?'

'I guess at least she won't give us away either.' Violet's mind was still on Myra's bowed head, so still, so small.

'A pact with the devil.' Red flung herself dramatically onto Violet's pillow and clapped her hands over her eyes. 'And all for a walk in the country? How stupid are we? Although it's his fault, you know; he just makes me want to go on the barricades by being so darn bloody-minded. But that stuff about her killing us in our beds . . . we'll have to start keeping watch at night.'

Violet swallowed, because almost as disturbing as Myra's wrath had been the way she had, so like her father, taken all her hatred and fury and grief and tucked it out of sight again, until she was back to being a pale, expressionless shadow. She shivered, imagining that darkness still in there, boiling and roiling, unseen and quiet.

'Goodness, it's got cold fast.' Teeth chattering slightly, Kit was rootling through a very small battered suitcase. Violet wondered if it was the only bag the other girl had brought. 'If I wear any more layers, I don't think I'll be able to move,' she muttered darkly.

Violet crouched down and quickly unwound her scarf, a cheerful red one that Duffy had insisted she take as a present. It still looked too new, she thought, the wool plump and shiny. Using the sharp edges of the bedstead, she snagged it in a couple of places, then dragged it through the dust beneath her bed until it looked a bit more worn.

'Here,' she said, careful to make her voice as casual as possible when she caught up with Kit at the top of the ladder. 'I'm not that cold; must be getting used to it. You can borrow it if you like.'

For a fleeting moment, she thought Kit would take it, but then the older girl pulled her coat more tightly around herself.

'No thank you,' she said brusquely.

'But I don't need it, honestly.' Violet tumbled down the ladder after her. 'And if you're cold, why don't you—'

'I said no thank you.'

Violet, red scarf wound defiantly back around her own neck, chose a seat as far away from Kit as possible and glowered down at her stew. Red had started inhaling her own portion so fast her spoon was a silver blur.

'Any gossip from last night?' she asked in between frantic swallows.

The other girls had come back with dramatic tales of creeping in under Hardwick's radar. They had pulled on their uniforms and inspected each other for stray shirt tails and buttons done up wrong, the mood congratulatory after a plan well executed.

'I took Joan home with me and she managed to snap up the only real talent around these parts,' Ellen grumbled. 'My sister was that cut up about it. Tom the postman,' she explained to Red and Violet with an eye roll. 'Serves almost the whole county, which is probably why it's taking such an age for us to get our letters.' She said the last bit a little louder and with a sidelong glance at Lucy, who, Violet remembered now, was waiting for word from her fiancé Matthew, who was with the navy somewhere in the Atlantic.

'Just think,' Lucy said determinedly. 'We'll be getting all our letters at the same time now; how lovely that will be.' But Violet noticed that her knuckles stood out as she gripped her spoon.

'I, however, was very restrained.' Ellen folded her hands sanctimoniously. 'I only danced with two servicemen. Not like *some* people I know . . .' She raised her eyebrows and waggled them comically at Linda, who promptly threw a piece of bread at her. Ellen caught it in mid-air and stuck it victoriously in her mouth.

'I hope you were all behaving with the propriety due your station, wherever you were,' Kit hushed them. 'Not disgracing yourselves . . . What?' She frowned at Joan, who was making discreet but frantic chopping motions across her neck.

Hardwick stood in the open door, back almost painfully straight; behind him, craning his neck to peer into the canteen, obviously delirious with excitement, was Mr Manson. Myra slipped into the room around them, her good black dress now covered with an apron so large it wrapped almost entirely around her. Red's spoon clattered onto the table and Violet's stomach lurched when she saw Hardwick's stony expression. Myra had told him then, there was no doubt. Violet would be dismissed, would have to leave, she wasn't ready, she didn't *want* to—

'Leave us,' Hardwick snapped at the other orchard workers. 'You lot, gather yourselves.'

'Executed in the prime of one's life,' Red whispered to Violet as they extricated themselves from the benches, but her humour sounded forced and her hands were shaking. A white-faced Kit stood up and moved into the small open space by the door, the rest of the girls straggling behind, each one looking more terrified than the next. Manson had sidled around Hardwick and was standing close enough to glance a hand off Kit's arm as she passed. Two more girls suffered similar fates, until Violet, who thought she could almost smell Manson's excitement, took a big sideways step and, thrusting out her own arm, managed to usher the rest of them past unscathed.

Hardwick had to call for order twice more as the land girls strained to keep together.

'Girls, girls.' Manson gave a wet-handed clap, to Hardwick's obvious fury. 'I wouldn't dream of bothering you on a Sunday, but when I mentioned to Mr Hardwick an issue I wanted to discuss with you, he kindly offered me a lift from church. Which, by the way, you should all be much more vigilant about attending.' He wagged his finger, letting his elbow graze Ellen's shoulder as he lowered his arm again.

'Now, Mr Hardwick told me you were working over at Thistle Hill yesterday. But such pretty little heads should know better than to have a fire burning past nightfall, shouldn't they?'

The stranger's torch. Could it really have been visible from the village? It must have burnt too brightly, and she had told him so too. Red flicked her a warning glance. There was no way of saying anything without giving the game away. Violet quirked up the corner of her mouth in agreement.

'Now, I really, *really* don't want to do this,' Manson paused regretfully, 'but I'm afraid I'm going to have to fine you. Hardwick, I'll leave it to you how you handle it, although I very much hope you'll send one of these pretty messengers to deliver the money. But see that it doesn't happen again,' he added, all trace of smiliness gone. 'We might not be in the line of fire all the way out here, but we do know our duty. You really need to have them under control, Hardwick.'

An embarrassed red flushed up Hardwick's neck and into the edges of his face, throwing his pallor into sharp relief, his eyes hard with dislike and rage. And yet when he spoke, his voice was so carefully polite that Violet, despite her own terror, couldn't help but wonder what exactly Manson had over him to make him this submissive.

'It won't happen again, Mr Manson,' he muttered.

'Oh, all right then,' Manson said, indulgent once more. 'It must be like herding kittens around here. Ooh, the stories I've heard tell this morning from over Redmond way – dearie me. Sounds like these girls were enjoying their night off, right, Mr Hardwick?'

'The hedge is done, you can check, honestly, Mr Hardwick, and you said we could go when it was done. It's done and all ready for planting, not a bramble in sight, and so we thought we could . . . since you had said it would be all right . . . I didn't think . . .' The words had come in a rush, as if Kit could stave off the moment of Hardwick's attack by continuing to talk.

'I *didn't* say you could go dancing, though, did I?' His voice was dangerously quiet, but Violet could see his fists bunching up the woollen folds of his jacket. 'I *didn't* say you could gallivant off across the valley.' The girls up front flinched as flecks of spittle gathered at the corners of his mouth and his eyes flashed. 'I *didn't* say leave a fire burning after nightfall.'

'It was just coals, honest. But there was a man.' Violet stepped forward, her voice breathless and panicked. 'On a horse. He had a torch burning, I told him not to, but he was looking for his sister.'

'A man? A *man*?' Hardwick's voice was high in disbelief, then he laughed, a horrible loud bellow. 'Of course there was a man. There's always a man where you sluts are concerned.' He had trouble getting the last few words out, and then a tide of unintelligible venom spewed forth as he grabbed hold of the nearest girl, Lucy, and shook her so hard that Violet could hear her teeth clatter. 'You're a disgrace, I'll report you, I will . . .'

'Mr Hardwick.' Kit moved forward. Frantically sobbing, Lucy tried to free herself, but he just shook her harder, her head snapping back and forth.

'You say you have a fiancé, but it doesn't keep you from throwing yourself out there. Sluts, all of you . . .' Eyes bulging above his spitting mouth, he was clawing at the top of Lucy's blouse, where her engagement ring was strung on a chain.

'Stop!' someone shouted – not Kit, who hovered helplessly, her mouth opening and closing, and not Violet, although she wished it had been, but Red. For a split second, Hardwick's grip loosened, and Violet leapt forward, caught Lucy around the middle and pulled her out of his reach.

The movement seemed to bring him to his senses. The mask of cold indifference snapped back into place, and he straightened until only the flush and the sweaty forehead gave any sign of what had just happened. And just like with Myra, this, to Violet, seemed the most terrifying thing of all, the thought of all that venom, all that hatred continuing to churn inside him, and what would happen when it finally erupted.

'You'll be paying the fine,' he said coolly. 'And just in case it wasn't spelled out clearly enough, you're expressly forbidden from ever attending social events, in the village here or anywhere else in the county. I run a tight ship and I will *not* have the estate besmirched by the goings-on of the likes of you, making free with the servicemen like army whores. If I catch any of you with your uniform less than standard, it'll be one demerit *each* from now on. And the same if a single one of you mouths off to me again – a demerit each.' He patted his coat, extracted the little black book from his inside pocket, licked the pencil in a businesslike manner and started writing. 'For those of you who didn't know, the rule has been that if one of you accumulates more than ten demerits, I won't sign that person's time sheet until they've had a chance to work them off. Given recent events, however, *no one*'s time sheet will be signed if any of one of you has ten demerits or more.'

A groan went up and Joan turned to Kit, who seemed rooted to the spot as she followed the line of Hardwick's pencil down the page. Without looking up, he pointed in Violet and Red's direction. 'You two are getting close.' Then he raised his eyebrows at Kit. 'And if you even think about running off and whining to anyone, I'll make sure the Land Army knows every single detail of your disgraceful behaviour. No one will touch you with a bargepole.'

'But we didn't *do* anything,' Violet said angrily before she could help herself. 'Tell him, Kit.'

A murmur travelled through the knots of girls, and Kit threw an angry glance around her before, unbelievably, lowering her head, leaving Violet to face Hardwick alone. He had watched the small exchange with a bemused, triumphant expression.

'The field is cleared, we're due to be paid,' she said, seething. 'The rules clearly state—'

'Did you not hear what I just said about your uniform?' Hardwick pointed at her red scarf peering out between the lapels of her coat. 'That'll be one more demerit for you, Burns, which . . . yes . . .' he tallied it up with exaggerated care, 'brings you to ten. I'll sign the time sheets next time, then, shall I?' He looked around at each of them in turn. 'Sloe hedges at the back of the house, and around the kitchen garden. Buckets and ladders are in the shed and don't come back until the entire lot's picked or I'll be giving you a whole load more than what *the rules state*.'

'Mr Hardwick,' Violet began hotly, but he was already gone.

Thirty

Violet stood by the door, her fists balled by her sides, as the girls slowly filed past her. Ellen was supporting Lucy, who was still sobbing quietly. One of the orchard workers, a woman with a red-spotted scarf tied around her head, started shepherding them towards a shed, but Violet, shaking with rage, waited until Kit came out.

'I can't believe you didn't say anything,' she said, not bothering to lower her voice.

'You have no idea what it's like,' Kit hissed, pushing the regulation hat down on her hair so hard that it dug into her forehead. 'He has all the power, don't you get it? He has *all the power*. I need to get paid and I need you to shut the hell up. I should never have gone for that stupid plan last night. I can't believe myself. It's easy for you to start a revolution; you look like you don't have much to lose. You'll just go back to wherever you came from and your biggest worry is if Mummy has enough butter for your toast in the morning.'

Violet flinched as if she'd been slapped. 'I was trying to look out for you,' she eventually managed. 'And them,' she threw after the girls trotting in the wake of the woman. She looked at Kit with disgust. 'Which is something *you* should be doing a lot more of.'

After that, she didn't look at any of them, refused to say anything else. Why on earth was she even fighting their battles, drawing Hardwick's attention onto her? She didn't need this exposure, she didn't need these girls. She didn't need anyone at all.

*

The hedges were groaning with sloes. Purple berries hung heavy between dark green leaves, readily dropping into the upturned umbrellas below at the poke of a stick. Violet had never seen berries picked this way – one girl hooking a walking stick around the branch, the other holding the umbrella to catch the raining berries – but she didn't give any outward sign of surprise, merely tried to stay out of the way of the needle-sharp thorns that brought unwelcome memories of the blackberry brambles. With Winterbourne House rearing cold and golden behind them, the land girls grimly picked their way along the sloe hedges stretching away from the kitchen garden along the wooded edges of the lawn. Around mid afternoon, a kind soul sent the little kitchen maid who occasionally helped in the canteen with a basket of sandwiches and tea. But in the face of Kit's angry scowl, no one dared take a break.

'Keep it going, keep it going.' She furiously kicked the food basket out of sight and elbowed Joan, who had stopped to pull off her glove and examine her palm, towards the hedge.

'Easy.' Joan's comfortable voice had a distinct edge to it. 'You don't have a monopoly on being angry, you know. We all left yesterday, we all keep getting demerits, and we *all* want our money.'

'So the less we can afford to be slacking,' Kit cut through her imperiously.

'Oh come off it.' Red dropped her bucket and folded her arms across her chest. 'You know full well that Lily is right, Kit. We should have stood up for ourselves, all of us.'

Violet barely had time to feel gratified before she heard murmurs of assent travel up and down the hedge. A couple of girls downed their sticks.

'Why were you even still at Thistle Hill after nightfall? And then to have a fire burning of all things,' Kit said angrily. 'You *know* that pig Manson makes Hardwick nervous.'

'We didn't! It was all the way down to coals, with no light

whatsoever. It was that man, like Lily said. He was careering across the countryside on horseback with a torch.'

'You should have told him to stuff his torch.'

'*That*'s when you want us to be brave? But then turn right around and cower to Hardwick?' Red laughed derisively. 'Can't have it both ways, Kit.'

'Get back to the sloes,' Kit hissed. 'That's all we have going for ourselves, to show him we can do it, that we're better than what he thinks we are.'

'But that's just stupid,' Red said, throwing her gloves into the bucket. 'We keep showing him and showing him and it doesn't do any good at all. No one would have cleared those brambles as fast as we did. We buckle under his injustice and then write it off as empowerment?'

'In case you've forgotten,' Kit snarled, 'I'm the forewoman and you're—'

'You're a coward,' Violet said quietly. 'You should be *protecting* us, not giving in to him. That's your job. We have rights.'

'He's got the longer end of the stick,' Kit shouted.

'Are you going to let him beat us up with it next?' Red shouted back.

'It's all my fault, I shouldn't have gone last night, I should have *known* he'd turn it on its head,' Kit shouted back, shaking her fist at no one in particular. Her hat had fallen off, hair standing on end as the girls crowded around in a babble of voices.

'We did all he asked us.'

'The field's cleared, isn't it?'

'Calm down, everyone.'

'Please, can we just get back to work?' Kit tried to cut through a few times, then, with a bellow, she finally threw her hands up in the air, ripped off her forewoman's armlet and tossed it onto the hedge. 'Someone else can be in the firing line for once. See how you get on.'

Somehow, the sight of the armlet on the hedge, frayed and

slightly grubby-looking, jolted them into silence. For a few moments they all stood breathing heavily, glaring at each other.

'Kitty, come on,' Joan said. 'Be reasonable.'

Red grimaced and rolled her eyes at Violet, but mercifully kept quiet.

'Well it's hard,' Kit said belligerently. 'I hate . . .' She paused, then burst out, 'I loathe him. He's such a bully. And you . . .' She whirled around and pointed an accusing finger at Violet. 'You take it back, this instant. I'm not a coward. I'm a *good* person.'

She shook her finger in Violet's face, a vein pulsing on the side of her neck, hair standing even more on end. She looked deranged and enraged and utterly magnificent, and suddenly, despite everything, Violet felt laughter rise in her throat. She clamped her lips shut, but still it fizzed up. Kit stared at her, crimson with outrage, and behind her she could hear Red give her infectious giggle, then she was nudging Violet, now roaring with laughter, and the others, too, began to laugh or smile with a mixture of relief and tension.

'I'm not laughing at you,' Violet gasped in between shouts of laughter. 'I promise. I'm sorry, I . . .'

Finally, even Kit cracked the hint of a smile. 'You'll all be sorry.' She shook her finger again, sending Red and Violet into more spasms.

At last the laughter died away and the girls collapsed onto the grass next to the hedge, Red wiping her cheeks, Joan shaking her head and closing her eyes in bliss. Even Lucy, who'd been picking in stony silence, was looking more cheerful.

'Tea time.' Without waiting for Kit's permission, she fetched the basket, started dispensing sandwiches, handing round apples and tin mugs.

Kit sat across from Violet, glowering at her gloves, her face flushed.

'All-right-I-reckon-I-should-have-said-something,' she finally said, pushing the words across her lips so fast they were more of a snarl than an apology.

Violet gave her a faint smile to acknowledge that nothing more was necessary. Kit looked up and, unexpectedly, smiled a proper smile. It transformed her face, drained the tension out of her eyes, softened the permanently clenched jaw.

'We should talk to our local representative,' Violet said thoughtfully, biting into her apple. 'Describe the state of things. That's what they're there for.'

'What is it with you and the rules?' Kit sighed. Then she jabbed her chin at Winterbourne House. 'She's our rep, actually, Lady Crowden.'

'Really?' Violet frowned. 'The one whose son died in France?'

'Across the valley, they're saying she can hardly rouse herself with grief,' Ellen whispered, looking behind her into the kitchen garden, where the maid had reappeared with a basket for cutting herbs, throwing them curious glances every now and then. 'Even if we wanted to see her . . .'

'Oh please, can I go if we do?' Red said longingly. 'I've never been inside a fancy house like that.'

'I thought you were a socialist,' Kit said scathingly.

'I am, but just think of the food,' Red moaned. She snatched up the last sandwich and almost swallowed it whole.

'We couldn't possibly disturb her when she's in mourning.' Joan sounded unsure. 'Anyway, it's one thing to write a letter to the WLA and another to lodge a complaint right here, with Hardwick breathing down our necks. I'm with Kit. You really don't know what he's like, Lily, *everyone* is afraid of him. The grooms, the other workers, the maids, even his own daughter.'

Violet caught Red's eye.

'Well,' she started, 'there *is* something we discovered . . .'

Thirty-One

'You shouldn't have been there.' Kit shifted uneasily when Violet had finished. 'What if he'd seen you?'

'I asked my mum about Hardwick.' Ellen leaned in again. 'She said that when the old lord died a few years ago, Hardwick was put in charge of the orchards until the oldest son was ready to take it on. But then *he* left for the front, and, well, didn't come back, and now Hardwick's back in charge again. He's well known across the valley, hard worker, disciplined, that sort of thing. Mum didn't really know anything about the wife . . .'

'Silvia,' Red threw in.

'. . . only that he raised the daughter alone at their home,' Ellen finished.

Violet bit her lip, felt those words – *raise, daughter, home* – bristle up against each other as she imagined Myra as a child, solemn and dark-haired, the softness of girlhood still lingering in her features and her smooth, rounded limbs, the tumble of curls down her back. A girl on the cusp of growing into a young woman and becoming her mother's daughter. What would it have been like to lie in your bed in the darkness, feeling the presence of Hardwick in the room next to you, all that grief and rage and shame . . .

She blinked, caught Red's eye; she was clearly thinking along similar lines.

'Why does Myra not want you saying she was visiting her mother's grave?' Joan frowned. 'It would be the most natural thing in the world.'

'It wasn't really a grave,' Red shook her head, 'because it wasn't in the upper area, with the rest of the dead people.'

'Oh Red,' Kit said wearily.

'Well that's what they are,' Red said absent-mindedly. 'You know, the more I think about it, I'm pretty sure it was . . . a shrine. A shrine *because* she's not buried in the cemetery.'

The moment she said it, Violet knew she was right. It explained the odd, almost pagan amalgamation of things, the feeling of secrecy, Myra's fury. But before she could open her mouth to say something, Joan peered down the side of the hedge.

'Girls, we have company.'

It was a little girl, maybe eight or nine. She was wearing a bulky-looking woollen dress and muddy shoes, a leather case slung around her shoulders. She was so intent on something wrapped in her skirt that she didn't see the land girls until she was practically stumbling over Lucy's foot.

Her head whipped up and she backed into the hedge, eyes narrowed.

'Don't be afraid,' Violet said quickly. 'We're just picking sloes.'

She pointed to the umbrella and buckets, and after a moment's hesitation, the girl gave a tiny up-and-down bob of her head, then sidled along the hedge, clearly keen to be on her way. She was slight of figure, with pale, downy hair and a small freckled face that was covered in dust and – Violet's stomach gave a small heave – a rust-coloured smudge. The same was smeared across her small hands.

'Are you hurt?' Violet got up deliberately slowly so as not to startle the girl, who clutched her skirt pouch more closely against her legs.

'Lily, it's just a gipsy girl,' Kit said dismissively. 'She's probably poached a duck. Go on, shoo!'

The girl dodged Kit's flapping hands easily, looking at her with a faintly puzzled but distinctly superior air. Stepping between her and Kit, Violet stooped down.

'Why don't you show us what you've got?' she suggested. 'And then wash your hands at the pump before you go home?'

The girl's thin shoulders slumped. Keeping a wary eye on Kit, she knelt and dropped the edges of her skirt towards the ground so that the contents rolled from between her hands.

'Good God in merciful heaven,' whispered Joan, and small noises of revulsion echoed around the group. Red muttered something that sounded like 'all yours' and scooted as far away from Violet as she could.

It was a rabbit, or it had been before a snare had torn off its leg and raked metal teeth all along its back, tearing off flesh and fur. Oblivious to Ellen's gagging, the girl lifted her face to Violet pleadingly, drawing her fine blonde eyebrows together as if in question, then reached – the land girls gasped as one – to stroke the rabbit's fur.

'Don't touch it, Lily,' Kit said warningly, even though nothing had been further from Violet's mind. 'It could be riddled with rabies.'

The girl looked at Violet and back at the rabbit. In the last light of the sun, the bones of her face were delicate, hair escaping in soft whispers from the grubby bow at the back. Her hand, gently touching the last intact pieces of fur, trembled slightly.

'He's not . . .' Violet groped for words. 'It's better that he's gone, see? He's lost a leg, he wouldn't have been able to run from the fox any more.'

The girl put a blood-encrusted hand on her arm, and it took everything Violet had not to flinch back in revulsion.

'What's your name?' she asked to buy herself some time.

The girl looked back down at the rabbit.

'Maybe she's deaf,' Red muttered. The girl flicked her an appraising look but still didn't say anything.

'Okay, no name. Shall we bury this fellow, then?' Violet suggested. 'You could make a headstone and plant flowers on the grave; you'd visit him and he wouldn't be alone.'

For the first time, the girl made a noise, a small exhale filled with both anguish and relief. Her entire body sagged back as she nodded. Avoiding catching anyone's eye, Violet extracted a handkerchief from her pocket, shook it out and let it float ceremoniously down across the rabbit. There was a collective sigh as the mangled body disappeared from sight.

'Basket.'

Joan handed her the basket that had held the sandwiches, and Violet, swallowing repeatedly, scooped up the bundle and laid it inside.

With a long-suffering air, Kit clapped her hands. 'Show's over, everyone, back to work. Come on, Kate, any slower and you'll be moving backwards. Gloves on, Ellen . . . And where do you think *you're* going?' She put her hands on her hips and glowered at Violet, who had just handed the girl the basket. 'We don't have time for babysitting!'

'But we have to bury him,' Violet said, and the girl looked up at Kit anxiously.

'Yes, Kit, have a heart.' Joan grinned, and small giggles ran around the group.

'Fine,' Kit said exasperatedly. 'But we pick first and bury later.'

The girl carefully set the basket down on a small mound of leaves before falling in step with Violet, who let her hold the umbrella as she poked at the sloe hedge.

The sun was streaming low across the lawns as the land girls followed the little girl into the woods. Some were carrying the full sloe baskets, others the picking tools, and Violet held the basket with the bundled-up rabbit. The girl seemed to barely touch the ground as she skipped ahead to a beautiful clearing, fair hair gleaming in the sun, the leather case bouncing on her back.

They stood in a respectful circle, Red every now and then emitting a stifled giggle, as Violet dug a shallow hole and the little girl tenderly lifted the bundle into it, adjusting the folds of the handkerchief. They scooped the soil back over it, set a rock on top and dusted off their hands.

'All right.' Kit's brisk clap made people twitch and clear their throats. 'Let's go, berries back to the shed, come on.'

'Ready?' Violet asked.

But the girl kept her eyes on the patch of soil, and Violet thought she could see tears glistening on her cheeks.

'Go on, I'll catch you up by the shed,' she told Kit, who rolled her eyes upwards but disappeared without another word.

The shadows had lengthened, and something moved in the undergrowth, but other than that, it was eerily still beneath the trees. The girl crept closer to Violet, who was looking at the small brown mound of the grave and remembering the demise of Romy's first pony, Filou. Romy had wanted to have a church service for Filou so desperately that her long-suffering mother had tried to persuade the vicar, to no avail. In the end, Duffy came to the rescue and organised a ceremony – a strange mixture of pagan rites and tea party – to send Filou across the rainbow bridge. Or really, he'd muttered to Violet, to the butcher.

She ground her teeth to hold back a choked noise, but the girl heard her and looked up questioningly.

'It's sad when someone dies,' Violet told her furiously. 'There's just no changing that. But it'll be all right.' She cleared her throat angrily. 'It'll be fine.'

The girl nodded and patted her arm.

'Now you're having to console *me*?' Violet said with a strangled half-laugh. 'We're a fine pair, aren't we?'

The girl wiped her face with her sleeve, leaving bright pink inroads in the dust. She offered her sleeve to Violet, who shook her head, held up her own sleeve.

'I'm Marigold,' the girl whispered. Her voice was hoarse, as if she wasn't in the habit of using it much at all.

'That's very pretty,' Violet said. 'I'm Lily.'

Marigold nodded, dragged her sleeve across her cheek again.

'Can I take you home anywhere, Marigold?'

The girl shook her head and pointed to the path ahead.

'All right then, let's get going or Kit will have my hide.'

Marigold slipped her hand into Violet's as she fell into step with her. Instinctively, Violet flinched at the touch, but then she forced herself to relax and grip the hand back.

'We're both flowers,' Marigold said shyly. She smiled a funny little half-smile and Violet felt the tightness around her chest ease a little.

'Yes,' she agreed. 'That we are.'

Thirty-Two

'Message for the land girls, if you please, Mr Hardwick, sir. No answer needed, they said.'

The kitchen maid thrust the envelope at Mr Hardwick and scurried back out again.

Kit held out her hand, but Hardwick had already ripped open the smart cream-coloured envelope and scanned the contents. Surprise flitted across his face, then his features tightened.

'You think you're very smart, don't you?' His expression hadn't changed, but for the first time since Violet had come here, she heard a note of uncertainty in his voice. And maybe he realised it, because he broke off before he could betray himself further and crumpled the heavy cardstock in his hand.

'Mr Hardwick? Sir?' Kit looked anxiously at the ball in Hardwick's palm. Hidden from view at the back, Red sidled around to retrieve the envelope from the floor and slipped it into the pocket of her dungarees.

'You're summoned to the big house,' Hardwick said through gritted teeth, biting off every word with effort. 'At three p.m. today.'

A murmur of excitement vibrated through the group, but Violet's heart dropped into her stomach, a hard, searing push all the way down. Could it . . . could it possibly be her mother? Had she somehow decided to sniff out Violet's whereabouts, when all this time Violet had assumed her safely in Yorkshire, dusting her hands of her wayward daughter? Was she sitting in Lady Crowden's guest room right now, her face hard, her smile forced?

Hardwick was rattling off instructions, and Violet worried at the edge of her sleeve, imagining the faces of the other girls when it was revealed who she was. Not Lily, not one of them, but a spoilt society girl. And even if they didn't dislike her as such, something would come down between them, because of their differences, because of her secrecy. She couldn't bear the thought of them whispering as she was driven away in her grand car, away from the first tendrils of friendship, of belonging, the first thing she'd ever done that actually felt real.

'You make up the time lost this evening, of course,' Hardwick droned on, 'and I don't have to tell you that you'll behave impeccably. Only those with clean uniforms will go, four at the very most. You'll enter and leave silently, as befits any worker on this estate. I am on excellent terms with the family and I will not have a horde of imbeciles drag down the reputation of the entire workforce . . .'

Violet stared ahead unseeingly, face turned in the direction of Hardwick's voice, nodding mechanically without taking in any of his words. For some reason, this seemed to annoy him, because when her eyes finally focused, she realised that he was looking directly at her. 'If I hear any tales of you running your mouths off, or any misdemeanour at all – and trust me, I *will* – then, so help me God, you won't like what happens.'

Still looking at Violet, he tossed the crumpled card to Kit, who caught it and whipped it behind her back in case he changed his mind. The girl just behind her took it and passed it on until it was out of Hardwick's reach.

'And you'd better be up with your work,' Hardwick snarled, 'or I'll have to let her ladyship know you'll be too busy.'

They filed out as fast as they dared, excited murmurs and whispered chatter breaking out before they were even through the door. As Violet reached the threshold, however, she heard her name being called.

'Did you have anything to do with this?' Hardwick was right behind her.

'The visit?' She managed to sound casual enough, but cursed herself when she flushed a bright red. 'No.'

'No what?'

'No, Mr Hardwick. Sir.' She tried to move away, but he gripped her arm, his breath on her face warm and moist.

'You'd better not have,' he said, even more softly, in his eyes that look of revulsion mixed with excitement – but at what? Her helplessness? Her physical proximity? She felt bile rise at the back of her throat, then he finally released her arm and pushed her away. Without paying any attention to the girls huddled around Kit, he strode down the path and disappeared into his office.

'Can I see the note?' Violet asked shakily.

It was brief and to the point. *Require the land girls' attendance. Monday afternoon, 3 p.m.*

She breathed out cautiously, squinted at the small, crabbed writing. It didn't *sound* like it necessarily had something to do with her specifically; it was just a bit odd. They had been talking about Lady Crowden only yesterday, and now here she was inviting them into the house. Red was guarding the envelope fiercely, and the girls marvelled over the embossing on the back: a large C against a printed background of trees and curlicued branches, from which a tiny apple dangled into the belly of the C.

'I wonder what she wants us for?' Violet swallowed.

'Never mind that. It's time to raise some issues, ladies,' Red said importantly. 'Missing uniform bits – two of us didn't even get a coat – bikes if she can swing them, time sheets signed, days off. Cruelty, bullying, humiliation. General ugliness.'

'Anything else?' Kit rolled her eyes at Joan.

'Please can we ask about our post?' Lucy pleaded.

'We can't just take over the conversation with a stream of demands,' Kit said doubtfully. 'Maybe she just wants us to do garden work or get to know us or something.'

'And he would be in such a rage if he found out we'd talked

about him behind his back.' Ellen shivered and looked over her shoulder. 'What he'd do to us would far outweigh anything good that might come of complaining.'

'But that's exactly what we'd complain *about*.' Red shook her head. 'The fact that we're so afraid of him we daren't complain.'

'And maybe *she* could tell him not to punish us,' Lucy said hopefully.

'Is she going to be here afterwards, every minute of every day?' Ellen shook her head. 'And she'll be that distracted, with being in mourning and all.'

They debated it for a little while, until Violet caught sight of a thin figure in a sack-like brown dress. Myra had been in the process of clearing away bowls and mugs, but, bent over a table by the door, her hand had stilled and she was clearly listening.

'We should go.' Violet cut across Joan and motioned them down the path.

'Yes, we've got the rest of the hedges to get through,' Kit said, immensely piqued that Violet had pre-empted her command. 'Hurry now. We can talk on the way.'

'Just knock, Kit,' Red said impatiently as they stood in front of the Winterbourne servants' entrance at three o'clock. 'Or we'll be late.'

'And that's officially the last word out of you,' Kit snapped at her.

After much back and forth, it had been decided that Kit as the forewoman would go, along with Joan, and also Violet, whose refusal was overruled, given her stand-off with Hardwick the day before. After much wheedling, Red was finally allowed to join as well, under the strict proviso that she was not to breathe a single word, communist-, complaint- or food-related.

'You can't boss me around,' she now started, outraged. But then her face took on a beatific expression. 'Pie,' she said reverently, 'apple pie – oh heavens . . .'

The kitchen maid had appeared, looking red-faced and cross and holding a dish in her hand.

'And what might you be wanting?' she said ungraciously, before setting the dish on an upturned barrel with a clatter.

'We have an appointment with Lady Crowden.' Kit pulled herself up.

'Someone'll come to fetch you, no doubt,' the maid said darkly. 'And yes, I burnt the pie,' she snapped when she saw Red staring at the dish. But Red closed her eyes and brought her face right down to the pie's surface. 'It smells divine,' she breathed. 'Come on, girls, have a whiff.'

A little while later – Kit hissing insults at Red all the way up the back stairs – they followed an imperious-looking footman through the green door into the hall. Violet kept to the back and hid behind Joan, more than ever convinced that her mother was going to burst out at any moment. Little by little, however, images of Lady Etherington faded as she took in the dust on picture frames and cornicing, saw a gauzy black shawl draped across a large hallway mirror, its edges lifting in the breeze from the back door. The land girls' footsteps echoed almost unnaturally loudly without any other sound to distract, and even in the rooms they passed – a pretty little turquoise sitting room, a cloakroom, a cubicle with a solid-looking telephone perched proudly on a small table – there was no sign of life. It was a house in mourning.

Violet's heart felt like a stone inside her chest as the girls walked silently into the drawing room, where the footman glowered at their trousers before pointing them towards one of the sofas. This – this sad, silent house – this was how Romy's house on York Square would be now too. Bowed down with grief and despair, empty of all the noise and the bustle that Violet had loved so much, when Duffy brought back school friends and Romy and Violet tore through the nursery until Uncle Rupert strode out into the hall and shouted, mock-despairingly, that children should be seen and not heard, and could Nanny please keep the racket down.

All this thinking about her mother, Violet thought angrily, had brought it close once more: how little she'd thought of Romy lately, too busy living this new life, making friends, being proud of standing up for herself. Her fingers dug deep into the ridged lines of her scars, raked down towards the raw flesh on her hand, searching for the pain that reminded her who she really was . . .

'Don't, Lily.' Someone pulled her fingers off the back of her hand. Red nudged her and smiled. 'That footman'll be ever so cross if you bleed all over his sofa,' she whispered. 'Not to mention her highness . . .' She jabbed her head in Kit's direction.

Grateful for the presence of Red's sturdy leg next to hers, Violet took a deep breath and looked around the drawing room, so similar to many others she'd seen, with their traditional oil paintings and heavy bookcases. Except someone here clearly liked photography, because a glass display case held a number of cameras ranging from antique to modern, and the walls were covered with a collection of large black-and-white photographs in black frames: a gleaming pile of apples, details sharp with focus; a scatter of dew drops across a spider web; frost captured on a pasture, each blade of grass perfect. A smaller photo hung next to the door as if in afterthought: a petite girl with wispy blonde hair.

'Look, it's her,' she hissed at Red.

'Gipsy girl, eh?' Red chuckled softly, and Violet smiled too, remembering Marigold's sprite-like demeanour, the inverted V of her delicate eyebrows, the small, wary face.

As if summoned by Violet's thoughts, there was a sound in the hallway and Marigold herself peeped around the corner. She didn't look much different from the day before, although her dress seemed a fraction cleaner, her face less dusty, her downy hair freshly washed, and she was still carrying the little leather purse slung across her back. She blinked when she saw the land girls, obviously surprised, smiled shyly, disappeared again. Violet heard footsteps and braced herself for Eleanor Etherington's sharp voice, wanted to simply get it over with now, but all thoughts of her mother vanished when a woman appeared in the doorway. Lank blonde hair in a bun, her body seemingly held upright only by a stiff black gown, she walked slowly, as if every step was an enormous effort. Marigold tripped ahead of her.

'Come, Mama,' she said. 'Sit over here.'

Lady Crowden took little notice of her daughter, who pushed a cushion behind her back and settled the stiff black folds of her dress before giving Violet a shy smile and slipping back out of the room.

'Good afternoon, your ladyship,' Violet said when it was clear that Lady Crowden's energy was taken up by perching on the edge of her seat and that Kit, overcome by the surroundings and the despair that hung like a cloud around their hostess, had lost her voice altogether. 'We're the land girls from the orchards.'

'I'm afraid I don't recall,' Lady Crowden said uncertainly. 'You're here because . . .'

Violet exhaled a long, slow breath, weak with relief. Not her mother, then, this wasn't about Violet at all. She was safe.

'You're our representative, my lady, you asked to see us?' She swallowed uncomfortably when she saw Lady Crowden look over her shoulder at the door, clearly desperate to escape.

'Maybe we should go,' Red said under her breath. 'I think there's been a misunderstanding.'

'Good afternoon.'

Violet froze, and next to her Red gave a small gasp, because leaning on the side of the door frame was the man from Thistle Hill.

Thirty-Three

'Lord Crowden,' the footman announced, slightly unnecessarily, because now that Violet saw him in the daylight, the family resemblance was very clear. He had the same fair hair as Marigold, although his was swept back imperiously; his grey eyes were bolder, his smile more confident.

'Oh Guy,' Lady Crowden said with evident relief. 'These girls are here and I'm afraid I don't quite know what . . .' She broke off, exhausted, and with a lurch, Violet realised that if Lady Crowden had lost her son, then this man had lost a brother and – she flicked her eyes to the little girl who had come back in with him – so had Marigold.

'It's quite all right, Mother,' Guy Crowden said. 'I asked them here.'

He took in Red, who grinned broadly, nodded casually at Joan and Kit, and finally, reluctantly almost, as if he didn't want to and yet wanted to most of all, he looked at Violet. She dug her nails into her thumb arch. Pain flared, the same exquisite teetering on the edge of something she couldn't control. Her cheeks glowed, her skin seemed paper thin, barely holding back the fizzy warmth inside. She was certain he could see right inside her, and wasn't sure if she loved or hated it.

'I see you've not managed to kill yourself yet. Nor your trusty sidekick.' He kept them seated with a casual flick of his hand as he sat down himself, slowly extending his leg.

Joan and Kit's heads slowly swivelled towards Violet and Red. Red leaned in to Kit and whispered, 'Torch man.'

'We didn't . . . well . . .' Violet flushed, then took a deep breath. 'You might have introduced yourself properly at Thistle

Hill, you know,' she said reproachfully. 'Or signed your note. We had no idea what to expect.'

His eyes flashed appreciative amusement, as if his wait for a belligerent retort had finally been gratified. Joan's expression of mortified shock, however, made Violet realise that it might be all very well for Violet Etherington to put someone in their place, but certainly not for Lily Burns, and she swallowed back any additional comment she would have liked to make, about violating the blackout and letting others take the blame and such. 'Pleasure to meet you now anyway,' she added lamely. 'Your lordship.'

'And you,' he said with amused politeness. 'Guy Crowden, at your service.'

Violet was suddenly reminded of the well-worn sequence of pleasantries that constituted these kinds of conversations. *Yes, our travel has been fine. What weather we're having.* And from there, just a short step to *Dickens is my favourite author. What is yours, Violet?*

She shook her head to dislodge the strange déjà vu, heard Kit and Joan murmur something unintelligible, but Red, undaunted, said, 'I'm Juliette Simpson, this is Lily Burns, Kit Pritchard and Joan Woods.'

He nodded in polite but casual acknowledgement, and Violet, with a stab of irritation, wondered if he would even remember their names. Her annoyance flared more brightly when he turned to scowl at Marigold.

'I thought I'd asked you to stay with Nanny. Please help Mother up to her rooms, then go back to the nursery, this instant.' He turned in time to catch Violet bristling. 'Yes?' he snapped, but she looked deliberately past him.

'Goodbye, Lady Crowden, it was lovely to meet you,' she said evenly as the woman got up, accompanied by Marigold. 'See you very soon, I hope, Marigold.' She threw Guy a superior look, which, to her fury, he ignored entirely.

'Would you care for some tea?' he enquired.

'Oh yes please,' Red breathed.

Kit rolled her eyes at the ceiling. 'I will never, ever take you anywhere again in the history of all mankind,' she muttered.

'Womankind,' Red hissed and lapsed into an injured silence.

Tea was an awkward affair, marked by Red's heroic but palpable restraint at taking only two scones, by Kit still rendered speechless and Joan nudging Violet to say something. Violet, meanwhile, was trying not to know so obviously how to have tea in a stately drawing room, not to mention tea with this impatient, restless man, whose grey eyes strayed to find hers when she was least prepared for it and had even less idea what to do when they did. Consequently, when she did manage a few platitudes, they were delivered in a strange, gruff voice, which, in the effort not to be overly elegant, bordered on rude and were met, in turn, with an infuriating look of amused appreciation.

With some relief she finally saw the footman arrive to clear the tea things, even though it clearly caused Red physical pain to let the last scone go.

'So,' Guy Crowden said, 'I asked you here because after I met you two the other evening, I realised that I was very much unaware of your presence, or the fact that my mother is responsible for you. You see, it was my brother who arranged for your employment earlier in the year, but with the change in circumstances . . .' for a second, his pleasant mask fell away, his face raw and pained, 'Mother has been somewhat preoccupied of late. I was only just released from hospital, and since it apparently now falls to me to see to things, I realise that there are a few issues that need addressing . . .'

'Oh yes, there are,' Red blurted out, relieved and heartfelt. 'Thank you!'

'. . . so I went to see Mr Hardwick just now, to catch up.'

Red froze. Kit stared at Guy, horror-struck, but he didn't seem to notice.

'He took me around your sleeping accommodation, which looks adequate – it was set up for the migrant workers years ago and we've never had any complaints – and he assured me that everything else was entirely in hand. Injuries, if reported to him, are treated promptly. There is plenty of food, baths and such; his daughter supervises all that. However,' he paused, 'there do seem to be some behaviour issues on your part. Punctuality, disrespect. Laziness.'

They gasped.

'We are *not* lazy or disrespectful,' Kit said, her face puce. 'We work just as hard if not harder than everyone else. *Sir.*' She tossed the last word at him, then closed her mouth, obviously horrified at herself.

Guy raised his eyebrows, as if her attitude corroborated Hardwick's accusations to the letter.

Violet felt a great weariness come over her. So Hardwick had found a way to pre-empt their visit. How could they put into words now the undercurrent of his loathing, the many injustices, the prison-like feeling, the embarrassment and humiliations, when he'd already skewed whatever complaints they might have dared to raise? Whatever they said now would sound petulant and childish, not to mention that Hardwick would be right there waiting for them upon their return.

'You've been fined for blackout violations; you've left the estate against his express orders; you weren't finished on time with your various, er, tasks. I'm not saying you *meant* to do all that,' Guy added hastily when Kit's face turned a dangerous shade of purple, 'but Mr Hardwick had all your paperwork there, your working times, results and infractions. His temper might be a touch on the . . . well, the dry side, but he's an excellent overseer, has been with us for years, pillar of the community, church elder, that kind of thing. My brother held him in high esteem, relied on him for everything.' He waited a moment, then looked at Violet. 'If you just *try* to be more compliant, I'm sure it can all be resolved.'

The amused gleam in his grey eyes was back, as if what he really wanted – more than to attend to their situation, more than to deal with Mr Hardwick – was to spar with Violet. She looked back evenly, made her voice as businesslike and devoid of emotion as she could.

'There are a few additional issues to discuss. We need missing uniform items – I have a list here – to be delivered as soon as possible, before the winter. We'd like to request an extra hour's heating in the evenings and five bicycles for when Mr Hardwick is too busy to take us places on *time*.' She emphasised the word with the faintest hint of mockery. 'And lastly, there is the small matter, possibly a misunderstanding on the worthy Mr Hardwick's part . . .'

'Not being cheeky at all.' Joan hastened to soften the dripping sarcasm.

'. . . we'd like to be paid.'

'Paid?' This Guy Crowden clearly had not expected, because he leaned back in his chair, not even noticing Marigold slipping back into the room and settling herself on the ground close to Violet, hidden from sight by the arm of the sofa. 'Aren't you paid by the Ministry?'

Violet looked at him incredulously. 'We're paid by *you*.' She stopped herself before she could tack on an *obviously* or something else to the effect of *how can you possibly know this little about your own estate?*, but it was very clear from her tone.

'Mr Hardwick is meant to sign our time sheets regularly and pay us on Fridays,' Joan said quickly, 'and since he's your overseer, well, technically . . .'

'We've done the work, we'd like to be paid for it,' Kit said.

Violet tipped up her chin and looked at Guy imperiously. The laughter slowly faded from his eyes as he stared back at her, transfixed, until Kit cleared her throat and he looked away, a faint flush blooming across his cheeks.

'Why only five bicycles? If there are nine of you?' he asked.

'We thought asking for nine might be a bit much,' Red confided. 'They're not technically having to be provided by the WLA. And we can ride two to a bike. The small ones go on the back, the big ones pedal.'

For a moment, Guy Crowden looked like he wanted to laugh. 'All right,' he said.

'What do you mean, all right?' Violet said.

'I'll look into it.' He reached behind him and pulled on a tasselled cord.

'Servants' bell,' Violet whispered when Red looked at her questioningly.

'Go on down to the kitchen,' Guy said. 'Mrs Dawson will have some leftovers from tea, I'm sure.' He winked at Red as the haughty footman reappeared.

Kit hesitated. 'But please, sir – when you speak to Mr Hardwick, maybe let him know there's no, er . . . ill will,' she finished reluctantly. 'None at all, yes?'

Red very much looked like she wanted to disagree about the exact amount of ill will there was, but in the end she just sighed and nudged Violet to get to her feet.

'You stay, Miss Burns.'

The land girls turned as one, drawing close together, and he said exasperatedly, 'I'm going to have someone bandage her hand, not sell her into slavery. Hawkins, send Miss Cox in, please. That is going to get infected, if it isn't already. I don't know why you don't ask Mr Hardwick for a doctor.'

Violet wanted to laugh. Ask Hardwick? And how was she going to pay for it?

'And you.' Guy pointed an accusing finger at the top of Marigold's head, peeking over the sofa arm. 'I'm getting quite tired of Nanny trying to hand in her notice because she's run off her feet looking everywhere for you.'

Violet opened her mouth to jump to the girl's defence, but Marigold clambered to her feet as if nothing was amiss.

'See you again soon?' Violet whispered as she passed. 'You're faster than Nanny, surely. Come and find us; we'll be over by the sloe shed, sorting berries.'

A smile flickered across Marigold's face and she jabbed her head briefly up and down before disappearing around the corner.

The room seemed unnaturally silent once the others had gone, and Violet threw Guy a covert glance. He wasn't tall, exactly, but lean and strong, his shoulders broad in his shirt, like someone most at home on the back of a horse, riding hell for leather into the sunset, rather than entertaining visitors in a fusty drawing room. In the light of day, however, his limp was more pronounced, and the last vestiges of her resentment at his careless, entitled attitude vanished when she saw the pain etched into the grim set of his jaw and the dark smudges below his eyes as he made his way slowly back to the sofa.

'Don't even think about it,' he snapped when he saw her offer a hand.

'I was just trying to help,' she said, indignant again.

'Well don't,' he advised, apparently deciding against sitting all the way back down and leaning against the back of the sofa instead. He stretched out his leg with a groan. 'I don't like people who are kind to me.'

'I'd be surprised if there are any left,' she said tartly, perching against the sofa next to him. 'Poor Marigold, the way you snap at her. What happened to your leg, then? Did you fall off a horse or something?'

She had added the last bit deliberately glibly, but regretted it instantly when he said, without looking at her, 'The war happened.'

She flushed even more deeply. 'Of course. I didn't mean to be flippant. And I'm sorry about your brother, I did actually hear from Duff . . . I mean, we heard. I was thoughtless. I'm ever so—'

'Sorry, yes, you said.' He bent over to run his hand down his leg, digging his thumb into a spot just above his knee, then frowned down at it. 'Everyone's feeling terribly sorry for me.'

She cast around for something neutral to say. 'It must be such a relief for your mother and Marigold to have you home,' was the safest she could come up with.

'Yes.' He shifted his weight. 'A huge relief for everyone.' But then he shook himself. 'I mean, thank you. You really are just being kind.'

She watched his mouth curve upwards in that smile that made her insides stir and whisper. Her body strained to close the distance between them; his eyes seemed to be reaching for her—

The door opened behind them and Violet snapped upright, inadvertently bumping into Guy. A woman entered, holding a basket. 'I didn't mean to startle you,' she said apologetically. 'You asked to see me, my lord?'

'Ah, Miss Cox.' Guy's voice was calm. 'If you could bandage this young lady's hand. She seems to have sustained some injuries while . . .'

'Clearing brambles,' Violet said. 'And picking sloes.'

'Quite,' he said.

She had hoped he would leave, but he didn't move as Miss Cox led her to a small table in the bay window where the light was better. She was lovely, Miss Cox, softly spoken and gentle, reminding Violet of one of her mother's lady's maids, Gerry, who had sometimes played Chinese chequers with her in the evenings.

The strangeness of her situation wasn't lost on Violet: who she really was and who she was pretending to be, her brown breeches coarse against the velvet seat of the dainty chair, the green of her jumper garish against the prettily patterned rosewood tabletop. Miss Cox bent over her hand with the iodine. 'Goodness,' she said when she saw the blisters and patches of raw skin. 'I'm sorry but this will sting.'

'S'all right,' Violet hissed, staring fixedly at a photograph of a single apple on a branch, so crisp it practically jumped out of the frame. 'Beautiful photos,' she said through teeth gritted against the pain.

Miss Cox's fingers tightened on the iodine bottle. 'Mr Oliver took them,' she said. 'He was very talented.'

'I . . .' Just in time, Violet swallowed back the words 'I'm so sorry'. 'He had a special eye,' she said instead. 'Much more accomplished than some I've seen in London.'

'Not a good place to be right now, all those air raids; you'd never feel a moment's peace.' Miss Cox gently dabbed a salve on Violet's hand. Her touch was so light, the smell of peppermint from the salve so crisp and fresh that Violet relaxed her fingers, one by one.

'Is it . . . I mean, what's been happening there?' she blurted out despite herself. 'We haven't had much news.'

'They're carefully keeping a lid on information,' Guy said. 'But from what I hear, they've been bombing London every single night.'

Miss Cox threw Violet a sympathetic glance. 'I'll keep your family in my prayers,' she said, and Violet nodded gratefully.

'Her ladyship is asking for Miss Cox.' Hawkins had reappeared in the door, radiating disapproval. 'And the others are waiting for *you* downstairs,' he added in a much less civil tone.

Miss Cox hastily finished tying the bandage, then gave Violet a small pot of salve and some bandages to take away with her before hurrying to the door. Hawkins was ostentatiously waiting for Violet, who, in the face of so much arrogance, took her time inspecting her bandage. When she'd made it abundantly clear that her actions were dictated by none other than herself, she rose.

'Well, goodbye. And thank you very much for your time,' she said to Guy Crowden, who, she realised, had observed her attempts at putting Hawkins in his place with some interest. She wavered, wondered about shaking his hand, then settled for a little bow, which made him smile.

'Don't mention it.'

Violet swallowed and wished with all her heart that he wouldn't smile at her like that with Hawkins watching.

'You'll think about our pay, the bikes and other things?' she said desperately.

'I'll consider it my patriotic duty.'

Thirty-Four

The three girls were waiting for her around the large scrubbed servants' table. Red looked positively drugged with food, Kit was anxiously peering towards the stairs.

'There you are,' she said, sounding relieved, then added, briskly, as if embarrassed by her concern, 'Let's get going, the others'll want to hear.'

The rest of the girls fell upon them the moment they came out of the kitchen garden. Red proved a good storyteller, acting out all the interesting bits, like Hawkins looking down his nose at them when really he should be out there fighting for England like the rest of them; Violet managing to be both polite and putting everyone in their place; and Kit very sensibly deciding not to say much at all, just glowering at everything in sight, which, of course, was incredibly useful too. Laughing, Kit pretended to take a swipe at Red, but then grew serious.

'Hardwick had got there before us,' she said soberly. 'Bad-mouthed us up and down. But Lily was very good at pushing at least some of our questions. And at least the lord now knows we're not getting paid.'

'I wouldn't be surprised if he comes through for us,' Red said, pretending to swoon, 'because he was ever so taken with our Lily here.'

'No he wasn't,' Violet protested hotly.

'I'll take it if it means we get paid,' Joan said.

'And bicycles. And a dishy lord to boot. Lily, you could do a lot worse.'

Lucy linked arms with her as Kit shepherded them down to the sloe shed to start sorting out the berries. They laughed and chatted, Kit and Red bickering good-naturedly, and Violet, buoyed by the camaraderie, secretly thought back to that last smile, which was still warm inside her . . .

A cry of dismay cut through her thoughts.

'Heavens,' Joan said in a choked whisper, looking through the open doors into the shed where they'd stored the sloes.

The buckets they'd picked today and the day before had all been overturned. Berries were scattered and mashed up amidst the nuts, glistening in the slanting light of the afternoon sun. Dark purple stains were smeared across walls and shelving boards, the clumps of berries oddly flesh-like. But it was the malevolence that made Violet's stomach turn more than anything else, the thought that someone had slipped in here and closed the door with the sole purpose of destroying their work.

She backed out and the others followed, leaving Kit still staring at the inside of the shed in horror.

'It was him.' Joan broke the silence. 'It had to be. He was angry about the summons, he wanted to teach us a lesson.'

'But he's responsible for the sloe gin.' Violet shook her head. 'Why on earth would he smash the output of his orchard? Kit, come away.' She held out her hand, and when the older girl didn't react, she grasped her elbow, pulled her out onto the path. 'We have to tell him.'

Kit wrenched herself free. 'He won't believe us.'

'He has to. No one in their right mind would do this.' She looked back over her shoulder, shivered slightly. 'No one,' she said, a little less convincingly. 'We're going to talk to him. You and me. The rest of you wait here, and don't let anyone see it.'

As far as human comforts were concerned, Hardwick's office was spartan to the point of ascetic. A desk lamp threw yellow light across a wooden table, another lamp dangled from the ceiling. The one straight-backed chair didn't invite visitors to hang about for cosy chats, and the rough jute fabric covering the window in lieu of curtains was firmly drawn. But nothing could disguise the sheer size of the operation behind Winterbourne Orchards. On the desk, stacks of paper, edges fastidiously squared, were weighed down with rusty old scale weights. Shelves held rows of narrow leather-bound ledgers and books. Maps covered exposed wall space, intricately drawn, some in simple wooden frames, and in pride of place behind Hardwick's desk was an enormous stitched sampler the size of a large flag. It was clearly old, brown in patches, the previously brightly coloured cross-stitches dark with age, and someone had put it behind glass to protect it. Vines and apples ranked the borders and *Winterbourne Orchards* was stitched along an oval outline at the top, mirrored by the words *From Darkness, Light* at the bottom. In between, a yellow house was painstakingly cross-stitched between two trees.

Once again Violet realised how little she was in the habit of questioning things, how naïvely she accepted what was right in front of her. She'd had no concept at all of what was involved in running an orchard, nor the fact that Hardwick, currently bent over an enormous volume with columns of figures down the page, was at the very hub of it all. She wished they could have met him at the shed or out in the open, rather than in this masculine place where he had all the weight and longevity of Winterbourne behind him and they – a small troop of roving workers, their position already precarious due to the approaching winter, now coming to report what would be registered as a loss in one of those ledgers – had little chance against the might of his imperium.

At the sound of their footsteps, he looked up. 'Back from his lordship so soon?' he asked, his face impassive.

'Something happened at the shed,' Kit burst out. 'It wasn't us, sir, honestly. The sloe berries, all of them, yesterday's and this morning's, they . . .' She broke off.

'Someone came in and upset all the buckets,' Violet finished quickly. 'Emptied them, tossed the contents on the ground, smashed them into pulp.'

Hardwick's jaw dropped. 'That would have been at least fifty bottles,' he said, incredulous. 'We opened the still especially for it; the bottles are ready, the gin purchased . . .'

He snapped his jacket down from the wooden hook and was gone without looking back.

'Well, you've done it now, haven't you?' Hardwick stared at the pulpy mess in the shed. 'How on earth did you manage this? I've never seen the like in all my life.'

'But we didn't do it,' Kit cried in anguish. 'How could we, and *why*?'

But Hardwick, clearly trying to channel his stunned outrage into something more scathing, rounded on her. 'See that it's cleaned up immediately. I have to see about the gin, but I'll be back, and then God help you all.'

He turned, almost colliding with the small figure of Marigold flattening herself against the entrance as he passed.

At first the little girl recoiled in horror at the wreckage, but seeing Violet amidst the girls, her expression cleared and she carefully picked her way around the edge. She looked at Violet questioningly.

'We don't know either.' Violet tried to smile.

Marigold nodded. She crouched to pick up a few intact berries, found a bucket and deposited them in it. Kit watched her for a long moment, then sighed. 'We'd better get this cleared up.'

They worked quickly and silently, using brooms and brushes to sweep together the worst of the mess while Marigold darted around them, weaving through their legs and picking up sloes as she went, quite enjoying, by the looks of it, the squashy pulp beneath her feet. By the time the shed looked less like a bloodbath – although it would take years for the purple stains to weather away – they had barely a bucket of berries to show for two days' worth of work. Wearily they washed up at the pump, still not talking, then trooped to the canteen. Word must have travelled already, because the other workers fell quiet as the girls passed by.

They sat close together, looking down at their plates.

'It's like we're outcasts,' Red whispered out of the side of her mouth.

'What else is new?' Lucy said bitterly.

Marigold had squeezed onto the bench next to Violet, dangling her legs, her funny little leather case strapped to her back. Violet smiled at the hopeful expression on her face as pieces of bread were passed along the table. She put a little bit of butter on one and handed it to the girl, who scooted closer when Myra pushed by with the clattering kitchen trolley.

'She'll take the dishes over to the house,' Violet said. 'Perhaps you should go back with her.'

But Marigold had put her bread down, her eyes fixed on something.

'What?' But then Violet saw it too. A faint tinge of red on Myra's fingers and wrists.

'You stay here,' she told Marigold fiercely.

She caught Myra just outside the door, navigating the trolley down the path.

'The sloes. It was you,' she hissed, stepping in front of her.

'I don't know what you're talking about.' Myra made as if to push the trolley again, but Violet thrust back at her, hitting her in her middle.

'What did we ever do to you? We didn't tell anyone about you-know-what, we always try to leave our table tidy, we never make things hard for you . . .'

Myra glared at her. 'You touched my things, the milk churn. I *told* you to stay away.'

'You left in a hurry,' Violet said defensively. 'I didn't want it to get wet, so I just closed it for you, I didn't see anything, I swear.'

But Myra gave a mirthless snort of laughter. 'I'm sure you didn't. I'm sure you didn't sit and mock me. Prying and spying on poor, pathetic Myra.'

'No one thinks you're poor and pathetic,' Violet stammered. 'We just felt a bit sorry that—'

'I don't need your pity,' Myra snarled. 'You with all your friends and your endless chatter, being paid – *paid!* – to be driven about and laugh and chat all day. Oh, I hear you, I hear *everything.*' She turned, saw the land girls crowding just inside the canteen, Marigold bobbing up and down anxiously next to Red. 'And now you have *her* from the big house to protect you, while I do all the dirty, disgusting work with nothing to show at the end of the day, and have to sneak off to the cemetery like a thief in the night.' The others were almost upon them, and Myra leaned in, so close that Violet could see right into her eyes, the dark ring around her pupils, the thick, glossy lashes. 'Do you know what happens after I lock you into the barn at night? When you're snug in your beds, feeling all ill-used about being cold and tired? I'm forced to kneel on the kitchen floor for hours. Praying for my sins, for my soul, my mother's soul. So yes,' she straightened abruptly and gripped the trolley, 'yes, I hate you, and yes, I did it, and I would do it again, and worse.'

Violet stared at her, open-mouthed, torn between loathing and pity. 'But can't you . . . I mean, you could . . .'

Leave, she'd been about to say, but at the very last moment, she swallowed it back, because leaving, she realised, was a luxury not afforded to all. Leaving needed people like Duffy to organise it, a place to run to, and a job to earn money for food. Violet was only here because she'd had all those things, had them, she flushed, through no real effort of her own either. Myra, with her sack-like dress, her chapped red hands, the overlarge kerchief covering her hair, had only Hardwick to fall back on.

The others were advancing, and Myra hissed at them like an

angry cat, hair escaping in staticky strands as the space in front of the canteen filled with the muttering of angry voices.

And then, suddenly, something else. The puckering of motors, a faint drone in the distance, ugly and discordant in the crisp, fragrant autumn air. A sound so agonisingly familiar and yet so completely and utterly unexpected that Violet's body reacted to it before she could even consciously form a thought. She froze, hands digging into the sides of her legs, head twitching up to search the sky. 'Planes!' she said hoarsely, then again, more loudly, 'Planes!'

As if through a haze, she saw others crane their necks, heard the swell of noise, saw the dark specks on the far horizon.

'Surely those must be ours? The Germans never come this far west,' Kit said, horrified, but as if in answer, a siren shrilled somewhere across the valley. Almost instantly, people started scurrying in all directions, confused and disorientated.

'The house, they'll have a shelter,' Joan said wildly but someone else shouted, 'No! We're supposed to go into the orchards, to the cold storage.'

All was noise and chaos, and someone was now hitting the large gong used to summon workers to the canteen, a clanking, clanging sound that wove into the steady rat-tat-tat above them. And still Violet stood, frozen in place. *From Darkness, Light.* Her eyes found the words below the sundial, traced them over and over again, desperate for something to anchor her and keep her here, but already she was back in London, in a doorway lit up by fire and filled with smoke, the skies rent with ear-splitting noise . . .

'Into the canteen,' Kit shouted. 'Under the tables, quickly.'

At the sound of her authoritative voice, knots of workers, grooms and land girls surged towards the canteen, Red pulling Marigold along with her. There was the sound of tables scraping across floorboards, and then Kit was shouting something, something Violet knew was important, just like she knew she had to move with them. But the planes' drone bounced around inside her head and made her heart beat faster and faster until she could barely breathe, and all she could see was blood spreading wetly across Romy's silver dress, so much of it, Duffy's horrified eyes white against his soot-smeared face . . .

She felt herself fold into a strange crouch, right there next to the abandoned trolley in the now-empty stable yard, a strange roaring in her ears as she let the noise of the planes fill her up and take her away, like they had taken Romy.

And then something ran right at her, hit her hard in the lower back. A hand pushed and dragged her until she was across the threshold of the canteen. She lay there, braced herself for the crashing impact of a bomb, the sharp cracks, the booming noises she knew so well. But none came, and when she looked up, she saw amber eyes flashing above her.

Thirty-Five

It couldn't have been for very long – after all the commotion down below, the planes turned out to be flying high and fast, clearly on their way elsewhere – but to Violet it seemed like for ever, the floor hard beneath her back, Myra's body swimming above hers. Not folded over, hands over her head, clutching her gas mask like the others under the canteen tables. No, Myra was kneeling with her face upturned to follow the sound, the underside of her jaw a smooth, graceful sweep as at last the planes faded into the distance. She looked down at Violet and jumped to her feet.

'Thank you,' Violet croaked. 'I'm sorry . . .'

But before she could finish, Myra was out the door, dragging the trolley so fast that the rattling of dirty plates and cutlery was almost louder than the planes had been.

'Lily!' Kit was white. 'What on earth was that? I said *hide*. And you were standing there out in the open, gawping. You could have got yourself killed. Her, too—'

'Get a hold of yourself, Kit,' Red cut in sharply. 'They weren't interested in us, apparently. Lily, say something. Are you all right? Are you going to be sick?' She held out an empty soup bowl encouragingly, but Marigold, who'd crawled out behind her, took Violet's hand and towed her towards the door.

'Good thinking,' Red said approvingly. 'Smells less that way.'

'They'll be going to Yeovil, I'm sure,' Lucy was saying anxiously as Violet collapsed on a small patch of grass outside, her arms wrapped around herself as her body twitched and trembled with the vivid memory of Romy's blood.

'There's a big aircraft factory there, Matthew was telling me . . .'

'Cook says to feed a shock,' Marigold murmured, and pressed something soft into Violet's hand. It was a piece of bread, balled up and squishy with butter.

Violet didn't think she could possibly open her mouth without all the things crowding her mind spilling out; she loosened her tie and unbuttoned the top of her shirt to ease the pressure. But Marigold was hovering and she forced the bread between her lips, trying to drown out the others' voices behind her, talking and talking, please God, could everyone just stop talking so Violet could hear herself *think* . . .

Someone loomed at the edge of her vision and she flinched, choked on the last bite.

'Oh come on, silly.' Kit held out her hand to help her up. 'I didn't mean to shout at you. Not quite so loudly, anyway. But you have to admit . . .'

Marigold frowned censoriously at her and Kit broke off, tugging gently at one of the little girl's braids. 'You're right,' she said with a wry smile. 'If you go to the trouble of apologising, which I'm not in the habit of, mind, then do it properly. Are you all right, Lily?'

'Here, I'll retie your bandage.' Lucy gathered the fraying ends of the gauze and started winding them back round Violet's hand, her touch cool on Violet's burning skin.

'Where were our boys, then?' She scanned the skies again. 'The planes must have found a loophole – goodness, I hope the people in Yeovil will be all right. Here, Lily, I think it's starting to look better already, and that salve smells heavenly. I wonder, would they give us the recipe if we asked?'

Violet worked hard at being Lily, nodding and trying to remember to say the right things at the right time. No one talked about the sloe berries any more; even Hardwick was momentarily distracted from punishing them, and it was difficult to care about the red smudges on Myra's hands when Violet's insides continued to churn with the memories the planes had brought back, that horrible feeling of being trapped in place and pushing to flee at the same time. She had taken the open sky for granted, she realised; somehow she had let herself be lulled into the security of being Lily. And not only the security, but the *joy* of it, of shedding her Violet-shaped skin and becoming one of them, one of the pack. But now she knew that inside, nothing had changed since the night Romy died, not a single thing. She found the scars on her arms and pushed in deep, waited for the pain to fill her up, because she was as weak, as useless as she'd ever been . . .

She finally escaped by saying she had to take Marigold back to the house. The little girl skipped lightly next to her, her hand warm in Violet's, her unassuming silence soothing. When they knocked on the door, there was an anxious exclamation and Marigold was pulled inside instantly, the door slammed shut before she was even fully across the threshold, as if the appearance of the planes had reminded everyone that even out here, war was close.

On the way back, Violet's steps became slower and slower until, at the corner of the stables, she finally stopped. At the other end, the bell tower arch and the canteen, which had seen so much frantic activity not long before, now sat in silence, the outline of the sundial's garish face muted in the dusky darkness. A thin stream of smoke curled up from Hardwick's office, and Violet shivered when she thought of his dark, malevolent presence behind the blacked-out windows.

She scanned the sky the way she'd been doing every few minutes since the planes had come over, but she found that even more than their potential return, she was dreading going back to the attic. It wasn't late yet, another hour or so to go before curfew, and the land girls would be grouped around the stove, by turns excited and scared, their chatter bouncing shrilly off the eaves.

On the other side of the wooden wall, she heard horses stamp and snuffle, and by the door, a groom was whistling. His lamp had been muted down to the smallest possible prick of light, and Violet pressed herself into the shadow of the wall as he walked across to the carriage house, the lamp dancing through the darkness like a firefly.

Quickly, before she could change her mind, she slipped in through the crack of the door he'd left open. Another lamp was hanging on a nail, its dim light just bright enough for her to walk down the row of boxes, pausing occasionally to stroke a neck or scratch a pair of ears, until, down at the end, she saw a familiar white streak across a brown nose.

'Hello, you,' she whispered. Merry blew hay breath across her face, then dipped down to search her pockets. She laughed shakily and stroked his neck and ears, using her fingers to brush out his mane. When they were little, she and Romy had sometimes imagined running a stable together, although not a racing stable, Romy had said every time. Violet had secretly admired the jockeys, who were wiry and aggressive and pounded along the course, but Romy had hated any kind of cruelty. Once, she'd rescued what she swore up and down was a small rabbit but Nanny had screeched was really a rat. She'd snatched it out of her hand and dashed it against the edge of the fireplace. Romy had cried for hours.

Merry's ears wavered in front of Violet's eyes as she remembered the time they'd found a newborn foal at the Hyde Park stables. They weren't supposed to go into the box, Violet had whispered, for once the sensible one when she saw the dam moving anxiously close by. But Romy was already touching the funny little creature swaying on its long legs, all bones and sinews and yet immeasurably soft, too. It had teetered and collapsed onto her, and Violet, hanging over the half-door of the box and laughing helplessly, had tried to disentangle her cousin from the flurry of tiny limbs before the enraged groom could bear down on them.

Automatically she braced herself for the sharp tinge that poisoned every good feeling now, the bitterness that turned any memory of Romy into self-loathing and guilt. But somehow here, inside this warm, hay-scented cocoon, she suddenly found that she was empty of the energy to hate herself, and when she closed her eyes, it was still there: Romy's face above the foal's back, her delighted giggling in the church, her warm fingers settling the necklace against Violet's skin at the Wentworth. Romy, bright and full of love, the way she had been before the air raid, before Violet had broken it all.

Merry's white stripe blurred in front of Violet's eyes again, and this time she didn't force it away but put her arms around his neck and cried. Not only because of the guilt she knew she would never shed, but because in this moment, she felt Romy's loss more acutely than her own part in it. Whatever shape her life took from here – whether her mother found her and forced her to marry Edward, or whether Violet ran away and lived in a cottage by the sea – it was a life that wouldn't have Romy in it. And that, above her shame and guilt, she didn't think she could possibly bear.

Merry stood, stoically putting up with Violet's grip on his neck, until down at the other end of the boxes, something clattered to the ground. Violet froze, heard two voices exchange a comment, then a halo of light brightened inside the door and started coming towards her.

She moved quickly and silently. Surely there had to be a back door down here, somewhere she could slip out and disappear before the light reached her. Her fingers caught a seam of something; an enclosure of some sort, maybe a tack room. It would have to do. But the bolt was infuriatingly uncooperative, as was the door, which clearly hadn't been opened in a while and groaned in protest when she pulled at it. She held her breath, her hand on the bolt.

'And what, if I may be so bold as to enquire, might *you* be doing back here?'

Thirty-Six

Lean and glorious in evening dress, hair unusually tidy, shirt glowing snowy-white between the lapels of a particularly well-fitting jacket, Guy Crowden lifted the lamp.

'I wasn't doing anything, I promise,' Violet said hurriedly. 'I just came in to see Merry.'

Guy Crowden nodded. 'Entirely reasonable to find a land girl checking on a prized horse in a stable where she has no business being at all.'

Silence fell. Beyond him, the corridor was lost in shadow, the room behind her a velvety black hole, and where the two met, the lamplight a pool of warm yellow.

'He missed you.' Guy looked over his shoulder at Merry, whose ears pricked up hopefully, his small rustling noises comforting and gentle. 'And if I'd known I'd run into you here, I wouldn't have gone to the trouble of summoning you for tea this afternoon.'

He threw her a quick glance to see if she'd got his meaning. She had.

'Although I won't say that I didn't enjoy being dressed down by you just a little bit,' he added. She should have said something brash and bold, something Lily would have thrown back at him. But she felt oddly defenceless and vulnerable, as if the German planes had peeled away the layers she'd built up around herself in the last few weeks, leaving her exposed and fragile. Tears welled, stupid, weak tears she couldn't bear him seeing. Groping behind her, she took a step back into the dark cocoon.

She should have known it would be a futile move, because a

moment later, Guy had ducked his head through the narrow doorway, pulling his leg across the threshold.

'What's wrong?' He snatched at her arm. 'Tell me.'

'I'm fine.' She pulled but he didn't let her go.

'You don't look fine. Is it your hand? Let me see.'

She hesitated, but he beckoned impatiently, and she finally held it out to him. He hung the lamp on a nail inside the door and slowly unpicked the bandage. Small ripples travelled up and down Violet's arm as he touched the back of her hand, and a small part of her marvelled that the contact didn't make her flinch like it always did, but felt natural, as if it was meant to be.

'Cold?' he asked when he saw goosebumps flare in the wake of his touch. His breath was on her cheek, his body warm next to hers. She was anything but cold. His mouth curved into a smile when she didn't answer, and one by one, he curled his fingers over hers. Part of her was casting around for something to say, something clever or grown-up that would cut through the charged air, but the other part of her was leaning in, because no words were necessary . . .

Abruptly she pulled back, slightly horrified to realise that her shirt was still unbuttoned at the top, her tie dangling, and she thought she saw something in his eyes that made her remember the things her mother had always said, about *fast girls* and *scarlet women*. She snatched her hand away, clumsily rewrapped the bandage and then fumbled for her shirt buttons.

'Leaving so soon?' he asked sardonically. She raised her eyebrows at him as she tightened her tie and he grinned. 'You know, for a land girl, you do that awfully well.'

'What do you mean, for a land girl?' Violet said haughtily. 'And what is "that", anyway?'

'Push your chin up to give me the snub. But fine, let's make things a little more decent.'

He reached for the lamp, and the light flared brightly, and

then Violet's hand dropped away from her tie, because for the first time, she saw the space they were in.

Platforms had been built against the walls, like cots or playing spaces; a ladder led up, a rope dangled down. Parked underneath was a small wagon, the kind children used to pull each other, and Violet thought she could make out books on a roughly hewn shelf, some blankets, a few cushions, a rocking horse. A sputter briefly dimmed the lamp, then it flared again and lit up the corners of the room, and Violet gasped. All over the walls and beams, someone had painted patches of bright colour: trees and clouds, the sun, the moon, stars scattered across the ceiling. On the wall opposite them, outlines of houses rose in bright, whimsical, slightly irregular shapes, the windows yellow splotches inside blue-grey rectangles. It was like being inside a cocoon of colour and wood and horsey smells.

'A little world all of its own.' She turned and smiled at Guy, a real smile now, because no one could stay haughty and proper surrounded by the joy, the sheer magic of this space. 'You could hide away here and no one would ever know.'

Guy stretched out his leg and sighed as he looked up at the walls.

'We were always underfoot in places we weren't meant to be, Olly and me. Not dissimilar to some other people I know.' He shot her a wry smile. 'So my father finally had this built. It was too narrow to do much else with, and that way at least we weren't going to end up under the wheels of a carriage.'

'There's even a tiny man in the moon.' Violet tipped her head back to study the ceiling. She thought back to the photographs in the drawing room. 'Did your brother paint this?'

'Yes.' He tapped the lamp and a beam of light swung across two boys waving from one of the painted windows, both fair-haired, both grinning. The movement made the lamplight flicker, but he didn't adjust it, allowing shadows to fill the room once more. The colours of the walls, the brightness of the

267

painted starry blue dimmed into a shadowland, with no contours, no beginning or end, where it was entirely natural for Violet to move towards that horrible bleakness she'd heard in Guy's voice until she felt his breath warm on her cheek, smelled the clean scent of his skin.

'He was a wonderful artist,' she said.

'He loved Winterbourne, the estate, the house, the orchards, more than any of us.'

Deep shadows smudged his eyes and the grooves around his mouth as he reached past her to touch an old globe on a shelf.

'We used to spin it, Olly and I. Used to close our eyes and tap a place on it and that was where we were going to go.' His finger left a line in the dusty surface of the globe. 'Mongolia, Panama, the Serengeti. I'd make up stories about it, would plot out how we'd travel. He loved the stories, but already back then, all he ever wanted was to be at Winterbourne, riding across the fields at dawn with his camera. He knew all the trees, knew the workers' names, he worked tirelessly, whether it was picking apples at harvest time or over in the distillery. He was part of it all in a way I have never been. He didn't want to go to war; in fact I can't think of a person less likely to be anywhere but here, checking on his apples and hedgerows and fields. There's always been a Crowden running Winterbourne Orchards, all the way back to the apple in the Garden of Eden, no doubt.'

He lifted his finger towards the globe again, but held it there without touching. 'I signed up to fight long before they started calling us up. I was dying to go *somewhere*; I was so bored being stuck here, trying to figure out how I could spend my life spinning that globe.' He turned away. 'He joined me, figured it was only right. So two Crowdens went to war together, and only one came back. And now I'm the one left, running the orchard. It makes me so angry all the time. Sad.'

'Devastated. And guilty,' she said softly.

'Hopeless and bitter.'

She nodded, then said haltingly, 'My cousin died in an air raid.' She didn't look at him, but at the perfect round shape of the globe. 'She didn't really want to go out, but I made her. There had already been a raid, I thought we were safe, but we weren't.'

Silence again, filling the shadowy darkness.

'It's not you who killed your cousin, you know that, don't you? Just like it's not me who killed my brother.'

'My head might understand that,' Violet said. 'But inside, I can't forget it.'

'But maybe you should forgive.' He said it matter-of-factly, as if that was all it would take, and for a moment, she believed that it might be possible. But then she shook her head. 'I can't,' she said. 'I can't seem to forgive myself.'

He looked at the globe. 'I can't either,' he said soberly. 'And I'm so ashamed. Because after all that's happened, I still want to spin that globe, I *still* want to run away.'

They stood for a long time without the need to say anything else. Then Violet touched the globe, spun it very gently.

'Me too,' she said, her eyes on the blur of oceans and countries, devoid of colour but strangely alive in the flickering lamplight. Yearning closed up her throat and she fought for breath. 'I want to walk and walk and never stop until I can live a new life, be a new person.'

'We could ride together,' he suggested. 'Merry has a lady friend, the prettiest little mare called Glory. You'd like her, I think. She reminds me of you. She's a bit stroppy, always ready for battle. But sweet too, underneath all that gumption.'

The globe spun slower, but still she followed it with her eyes, filled with a strange, breathless anticipation, as if the two of them were children again, ready for adventure, ready to believe that anything was possible. *Battle* and *sweet. Gumption. Pretty.* She could almost taste those words, see the horses carrying the two of them away across dew-sparkling meadows. It made her legs weak with longing, her skin prickle with the same delicious shivers as before, her chest open wide with the possibilities of such freedom, such *life*.

But then she reached out, stopped the globe with a sharp jab of her finger. It wasn't her, that pretty girl he was describing, with all that gumption. It was a role she was playing, a layer of Lily that hid the real her beneath, that weak and feeble society girl she could never let him see.

'I don't think so,' she said curtly, wiping the dust off her finger. A small, tense silence fell.

'Probably better that way.' His voice matched hers. 'What with the war and all. The planes earlier were a reminder that no one is safe anywhere.'

Violet swallowed with some effort, and his eyes softened again when he caught the movement of her throat.

'Don't worry, they don't really care about us down here. They sometimes get through the radar, depending on the weather and wherever the main action is; that's why the sirens were so late. They'll be after the ports and the munitions factory closer to the coast; they can't afford to be sidetracked by us. Their fuel only gets them a certain distance.'

She nodded. 'I . . . I don't really know what happens.' She spoke quickly. 'But when I hear them, my heart starts to beat so fast that I think I'll explode, and then I freeze. I freeze, but inside I'm still moving.'

'Shock.' He nodded.

'That's what Duffy said. It doesn't feel like shock, though, it feels like going mad.'

'Who is Duffy?' he asked.

'Will it go away?' she asked in lieu of an answer. 'The war's barely started. I can't be falling to pieces every time a plane flies anywhere within my hearing.'

He settled himself against the wall. 'Talking about it will help.'

She sagged back, exhaled. 'I couldn't possibly tell anyone else.'

'You told the indomitable-sounding Duffy.' He managed to make the name sound both ridiculous and childish, and Violet frowned at him.

'Duffy is very nice,' she said sternly. 'But I haven't heard anything from him; there hasn't been any post for us ever since I got here.'

'Then talk to me,' he suggested lightly. 'Tell me everything you saw and heard and felt, until you've got rid of it.'

For a long moment, she let the warmth in his eyes flood her. But it wouldn't feel right to talk any more about Romy with him, not when she was feeling all these things, when his eyes were so intent on hers and so full of something that made her pull her jacket tightly around herself, take a small step sideways and grope for the narrow opening.

'The others will wonder where I've gone,' she said. 'Curfew.'

This time he didn't try to dissuade her, just handed her the lamp. But when she emerged into the cooler air of the stable corridor, heard the horses moving and the groom still whistling out of sight, a small part of her, that secret, fizzy, treacherous part, wished they never had to leave.

'Well, goodbye then,' she said awkwardly, as Guy ducked through the doorway after her.

'Come back,' he said suddenly. 'Tomorrow.' He nodded at the playhouse door, which had blended back into the row of boxes.

'I can't,' she said quickly. 'Really, I shouldn't even have been here tonight, it's not . . .'

'Seemly?' He raised his eyebrows. 'I didn't think you cared quite so much about what things seem like. That's what I like about you. You're not like the girls I know, spoilt and protected, vapid. You're not afraid to say things, real things. To push back.'

'Me?' Violet stared at him, then smothered a laugh.

He grabbed her arm, held her back. 'If you happen to pass by with an apple for Merry at around eight tomorrow evening, I might just happen to be here to check on him,' he said quickly. 'Or the day after.'

He pushed his hand through his hair and made it stand up, and she looked away to suppress the sudden urge to trace the nape of his neck, where a few rebellious whorls of hair were daring to defy his otherwise sleek evening attire.

'Goodbye,' she whispered before she turned and started to run.

His voice floated down the corridor after her. 'I'll be waiting, land girl.'

Frankie

September 2004

Thirty-Seven

Over the years, the shopfront of Jools's Quality Vintage had changed colour more often than Frankie could count. Now, the facade was painted a bright yellow, the sashes picked out in red, with a striped awning that was – at 7 p.m. – rolled up neatly. The windows were so crammed with dresses and old-fashioned mannequins, signs and candy-coloured milkshake beakers set on an enormous old jukebox that it was hard to see into the shop beyond.

'Frankie!' Jools appeared in the door holding a pair of pinking shears. 'What are you doing here?'

'I . . .' Automatically Frankie braced herself for her stammer, but anger sometimes eased the words along. 'Could I stay with you for a couple of nights?'

Jools, whose biggest assets were her utter unflappability in the face of a crisis and an enormous, ancient samovar that was now spilling the smell of orange spice tea out onto the footpath, stood aside. 'Of course.'

Inside the overstuffed shop, the smell of leather and moth-balls instantly whizzed Frankie back to those long, peaceful afternoons untangling costume jewellery, winding up string and flattening paper bags. Jools refused to let anything go to waste, which was partly why she'd started a consignment shop in the first place. She couldn't bear the thought of all those beautiful clothes ending up in landfill.

'A hangover from the war,' she'd told Frankie more than once, 'when your clothes were falling off you. *Make do and mend*, ha! Not much to mend with, and little time to mend anyway when you were busy foraging for food.'

Jools had a lot of stories to tell, but she knew when to be quiet, too, watching Frankie drink three cups of tea and eat two slightly stale buns – 'nothing wrong with yesterday's pastry' – in quick succession until finally sagging back against the chair, fiddling with the last bun on the plate.

'I was waiting for you to call,' she said. 'I wanted to hear all about how the Jacqmar enjoyed the Gala last night, and then I picked *this* up on my way back from Violet's this afternoon.' She held up the *London Post*.

'I was just doing my job,' Frankie said wearily. 'Since when is that a cr—'

'What's this about her fainting?' Jools cut in sharply. 'She didn't mention anything at all to me.'

Frankie worried at the hard surface of the bun, then gouged out a raisin, thinking of Violet's request for discretion. 'Well,' she said belligerently, 'it's not like you two don't know each other well, right?'

Jools's mouth quirked up in a wry grin. 'Yes, I think you could say that.' She took the bun out of Frankie's hands. 'Talk.'

'She thinks that . . . that maybe she's . . .' Frankie started. She couldn't bring herself to say it, though, the word that neither she nor Violet had yet been able to speak out loud, that finite, un-take-back-able thing.

'She's not really . . . been herself,' she tried again. 'She's losing it, Jools.'

She told her everything, and when she came to a stop, she looked at the older woman pleadingly, as if she could somehow fix this, with her tea, her stories, her button box. But for the first time ever, Jools seemed completely lost for words.

'I knew it,' she said finally. 'God, I *knew* something was up. She's just so bloody stubborn; she always said everything was fine. Well it's a blessing that you're here now. Between you and me, we'll help her, we'll be there for her.' She got up and marched across to a sideboard, rummaged through the cupboard and came out with a bottle of whisky and two glasses. 'We *will*,' she repeated threateningly. But Frankie could see that her hands were shaking as she filled the glasses, and her lips almost disappeared, she was pressing them together so hard. 'Drink up,' she ordered.

Frankie coughed as the syrupy liquid scorched her mouth, already raw and scratchy from her shouting match with Violet just before. Without a word, she held out her glass for a refill.

'Anything else I should know?' Jools demanded angrily.

'Dad's going to be out of prison in a few weeks.' Frankie swirled the amber liquid around her glass. 'And I was going to move in with Violet.'

Even saying them out loud, those two things immediately bristled around each other, pushing and shoving with animosity, because one couldn't possibly be in the company of the other.

'I see.' Jools set her own glass down carefully. 'That sounds like . . .'

'Etherington dynamite? Yeah.' Frankie lifted her glass in a mock salute. 'Can I ask you something?' She didn't want to look at Jools. 'Did *you* think Dad was a no-hoper?'

'I don't have to ask where that came from.' Jools grimaced over the rim of her glass. 'Well, as it happens, no, I didn't. He had this hunger for life, your dad. And so chock-full of charisma, it was like a halo around him. You couldn't not like him.'

Frankie looked at her, her belly flooding with sudden, overwhelming gratitude. She remembered lying in a tent at the Clayton Festival, where the band was hoping to be spotted by one of the roving scouts. His band mates had gone off somewhere, and over by the stage, shouting and cheering indicated more intense revelry. But her dad had sat by the fire outside their tent, playing his guitar, laughing and chatting with people passing by. Many sat and listened for a bit, conversation easy and warm. It made Frankie drowsy with contentment, the way the fire crackled into her dad's soft murmurs, accompanied his laughter and crooned tunes, a beautiful melody keeping watch over her into the night.

'He was, wasn't he?' she said.

'I presume he still is,' Jools said drily. 'He's only in prison, not dead, you know.'

'He might as well have been,' Frankie said flatly. 'And it's all Vi—'

'No, love, I won't get into a slanging match over Violet. There was enough of that going on between the three of you when he was still around.'

Frankie sighed. 'Do you think he was bad for Mum, that she let him walk all over her?' she asked tentatively.

Jools hesitated, clearly choosing her words with some care. 'I think it bothered Violet that Stella became so much a part of him, was always content just to be by his side and go wherever he went.'

Frankie looked down at her empty glass. Her mum's gentle, unassuming presence had long become faded in her memory, reduced to fleeting snatches of remembered warmth, a few lines of a lullaby, a familiar scent. This image Jools had conjured up wasn't faded, though, but painfully familiar.

'I guess I was the s-s-same,' she said, stumbling slightly over the words. 'To be where he was, that was all I wanted. When Violet used to come to fetch me, leaving him was always so hard.'

'I'm sure it was for him too.' Jools took a sip of her whisky. 'But Violet wanted you to be your own person. Why do you think she was so insistent on fixing your stammer? Why did she encourage your writing? Why was she always trying to get you out there to stand up for yourself? She wanted you to be in charge of your own life, not following someone else's the way Stella had.'

'Judging by what she said tonight, I reckon she doesn't think I'm doing a terribly good job of it,' Frankie said wearily.

Jools put her hand on Frankie's. 'You're not your mother, Frankie, not that that wouldn't be a lovely thing to be. I think you were caught up between two people who loved you very much and you're still trying to love both of them back. But no one can please two people as different as your grandmother and your dad. Maybe it's time you took the best of them both and started being yourself. Which, if you ask me, is someone warm and clever and altogether different from either Harry or Violet.'

Frankie looked up at her. 'Is that why Violet hated Dad so much? Because she thought she had to save me?'

'Well . . .' Jools fidgeted with her glass. 'When Stella died, the world fell apart for Violet. And especially hard was the *way* she died . . .' She broke off, and Frankie leaned forward, tried to catch her eye.

'The accident, you mean, how sudden it was?'

But Jools seemed to have changed her mind. 'Actually, it's not really my conversation to have. You should talk to Violet—'

'Talk to Violet about what?' a voice suddenly cut in from behind them.

Frankie turned. Her grandmother stood in the doorway, framed by the colourful beaded strings that separated the shop floor from the back. She was still a bit flushed but seemed otherwise fine.

'That key is for emergencies only,' Jools said tartly, 'and certainly not for eavesdropping. But now that you're here . . .' She got up and wiped her cheeks, then went to envelop her friend in a tight hug.

Eventually Violet came and sat down opposite Frankie.

'I'm sorry,' she said.

'Yeah, f-f-fine, m-m-me too.' But Frankie didn't look at her, even when Jools raised her eyebrows meaningfully.

'I'm sorry for shouting at you and calling you a pushover doing a shabby hack job,' Violet specified.

Jools twitched and raised her eyebrows at Violet, much higher this time, Frankie was gratified to see.

'I'm sorry about Celeste.' Frankie gouged the last few raisins out of the bun and arranged them around the edge of her plate. 'And about the things they'll still p-p-publish. I'll tell them not to use your name from now on, but I can't stop them.'

'It's your name too,' Violet said impatiently. 'And you *can* stop them, you just . . .' She held up her hands and shook her head. 'Look, I don't want to fight with you, because I would love it more than anything if you came to live with me. But it is your choice completely. If you walk away, I will understand.'

For one terrible moment, that was exactly what Frankie wanted to do. How could she possibly move into Cavendish Place with all that anger still churning around inside her? How could she summon the things she'd need to get through this – compassion and generosity, patience and grace – when everything inside her still wanted to fly at Violet, fight with her to burn off the memory of her betrayal? Flying at Violet was no longer an option, though, and neither was walking away. Instead, Frankie would have to be right there, watching helplessly as her grandmother's life dimmed little by little, as her independence and grit – so infuriating but so *Violet* – seeped away and she became less each day, until she was gone. Violet, whom she'd once loved so much, who had been her mother, her guide, her childhood all rolled into one . . .

Tears made Frankie's throat swell up. She gave an angry cough to clear it and, with a massive effort, pushed past the moment of faltering. Then she threw her hands up in an air shrug, much like Violet had done only a moment before. Out of the corner of her eye she could see Jools smiling at the similarity.

'I'll st-st-st . . .' She heard the furious hiss of the 'st' and broke off, but Violet seemed to understand. She nodded, and abruptly Frankie reached for the plates and the lone bun, got up and disappeared into the tiny kitchen.

Looking over her shoulder, she saw Violet and Jools sitting with their heads close, talking again. She rinsed the dishes, put away the sugar bowl, found a bag for the bun. In a small pocket of silence, she could hear her grandmother's voice, low and anxious.

'I think I've brought it on myself, Jools,' she said. '*I* have made this happen.'

'Nonsense, you don't bring an illness like this on yourself,' Jools said impatiently. 'It doesn't work like that.'

'But maybe I opened a door somehow, because, well, you know . . .' She lowered her voice further, and Frankie leaned forward, holding her breath, but she couldn't hear what Violet was murmuring.

'For heaven's sake.' Jools crossed her arms in front of her chest. 'You're losing your mind but you can't somehow lose *that*?'

'It's not funny,' Violet said, her voice thin and anxious.

'No, it's not,' Jools agreed. 'But I wish you wouldn't waste another one of your sane thoughts on it. You've got enough to keep in your head as it is.'

'Stop talking about this so flippantly,' Violet hissed. 'It's . . .'

'. . . an illness that's not nearly as shameful as you make out,' Jools said. 'Happens to half the population. We'll get you the help you need, Vi, it'll be—'

'I don't need help, I need to get this out of my mind, Jools. It's constantly there, probing and burrowing; it's going to drive me mad. *Literally.*'

Violet had her back to Frankie, so she couldn't see what her grandmother took out of her purse. All she could see was the change in Jools's face, which was so abrupt and so dramatic that Frankie involuntarily shrank against the sink.

'No,' Jools said, ashen. 'We agreed not to talk about it. You hear me, Violet? Ever! It wasn't like that.'

'Yes it was,' Violet hissed.

'No it *wasn't.*' Jools swept her hand angrily across the table. There was the rustle of paper and then a clinking sound, a flash of something gold.

'What was and wasn't?' Frankie asked, stepping out of the kitchen.

'Ah, there you are.' Jools pushed her chair back. 'Ready?' She hustled them through the dark shop towards the door. 'Come back soon, I'll get some more buns. Bye. Stay safe.'

The bell tinkled cheerfully as the door closed, leaving them standing out on the street.

'Stay safe?' Frankie asked, confused. 'You live three streets away. And what was all that stuff you were arguing about when I was in the kitchen?'

'Just Jools being Jools.'

Violet seemed utterly exhausted all of a sudden, and barely made it through dinner, reviving only to refuse all help in getting ready for bed.

'I'm fine, Frankie. I promise.'

Frankie dragged a chair into the front hall and sat down just out of sight, guiltily grateful not to have to be in the bathroom undressing her grandmother again. Averting her eyes from Violet's signs, which she had put back up after they had eaten, she wrapped her arms around her knees and listened. Pipes gurgled, a cabinet door opened and shut. Footsteps, the bedroom window creaking, the ancient silver-backed hairbrushes clanking against the tarnished metal tray with the scalloped edges that Frankie had always thought so pretty . . .

She was drifting, her body growing heavy on the chair as the years faded. She was eleven, lying in bed with a hot-water bottle to ward off the damp, listening to her grandparents murmuring down the hallway.

When Frankie was with her dad, the days flowed into each other: warm, undulating, seemingly endless stretches of time filled with music and laughter over everything and nothing. When she was with Violet, life was ordered, the hours strung neatly along the day like beads: mealtimes and after-school activities, the dreaded public speaking sessions, homework rigorously checked, errands to be run, small jobs to do for Safe Haven or whatever project Violet was currently working on, bedtime strictly observed. *As predictable as weather,* Dad had often mockingly said. *Sounds utterly dull, darling.*

Sometimes, goaded by him, Frankie had joined in the mockery, had guiltily parodied the way Violet made her go to bed at eight on the dot, even with the sun still shining brightly through the curtains in summer; how her grandfather marked up the *Radio Times* for the entire week like a school timetable. But she'd felt hot with shame afterwards and hated herself for her disloyalty. Because deep down and in secret, she hadn't found it dull at all. It might not have been sitting up late into the night to play the guitar by a campfire, but Cavendish Place had a midnight melody all of its own: a voice burbling on the radio, the clink of a teacup. The snap as a newspaper was folded over, a murmured comment, a soft laugh. It was predictable, yes; the same, always. But it was also safe. It was a place to call home.

She wasn't sure how long she'd slept, or even how, without falling off the uncomfortable hard-backed chair, but when she jumped up, heart pumping with that nameless panic between deep sleep and sudden alertness, it was near midnight. She walked slowly down the narrow hallway towards her room and tried to blink the sleep from her eyes. God, she was tired. If only tomorrow was Saturday . . .

It took her sleep-addled brain a moment to hear it, and her body another moment to slow, become still. A voice, she thought. Or had she imagined it? She forced away the memory of Terry Wogan on the radio and someone laughing. Gramps was gone, Violet was asleep. No one was talking. Except . . .

There it was again, a low, hard voice. It came from Violet's bedroom; not a whisper, but not a daytime voice either. The last vestiges of sleep vanished as Frankie inched open the door and peered into the room, the curtains rustling slightly in the draught. Violet's sleigh bed was a mass of shadows, her grandmother's form clearly delineated on the left-hand side, lying perfectly straight, almost unnaturally still, hands clasped at her front.

The room was quiet, and Frankie waited a few moments before she turned to go. And then she heard it again. Three words, repeated over and over again, with hardly a breath in between.

It was murder.

Thirty-Eight

For most of the night, Frankie sat on her bed, wrapped in her blanket, and thought about the voice floating through the darkness. Disembodied, eerie, a monotone devoid of any human life.

It was murder.

It was murder.

Murder murder murder.

An endless, relentless repetition, scratched into the velvety darkness of the night like the tallies of wrongdoings onto the pages of the black book. Violent and jarring, it left too many questions open. Who was the perpetrator and who the victim, and what on earth did her grandmother have to do with it all? She remembered Violet and Jools's conversation earlier.

Yes it was.

No it wasn't.

She thought about the golden gleam, the clinking of metal on the table. Had they argued about it just after Violet had taken out the Land Army badge?

At first, Frankie had wanted to run right back to Jools, keep ringing the bell until she'd got an explanation. But she couldn't leave Violet alone in the flat, not with that word thrumming through the darkness, and besides, she knew from experience that pushing Jools on something she didn't want to do was like hitting a brick wall.

When dawn finally crept through the curtains, she went down to the kitchen to make a cup of tea. Absent-mindedly straightening the edges of the sign telling her to *Put milk back in fridge*, which were curling in the steam from the kettle, she wished that she was the kind of person who talked about things to people. But who? Con, nursing his spiky resentment? Bea, who'd probably be sharing Con's feelings? Max's face swam into her tired mind, with his unruffled half-grin and careless shrug. It was murder, he might say, hmm, let's see here. It *was* murder. It was *murder. It* was murder. He'd try out different inflections until the phrase had turned into mere words, to be broken down and analysed, not something that made Frankie shiver with dread whenever she thought about it. She looked at her mobile, pictured him answering, voice raspy with sleep, lying in bed with his hand behind his head as he listened.

She sighed, and found a piece of tape to fasten the milk-sign more securely to the cupboard door. Even if confessing came easy to her, it wasn't an option right now, not with Violet in the public eye the way she was, not with Hugo and his loaded questions, his interview schemes.

Instead, she sent Felicity a carefully worded email telling her that she was out doing an interview for the Guildhall piece, then rang Mrs Potter – a woman of few words and endless abilities – and asked her to return as soon as she was able to.

'It's unfair to keep her out of work a day longer,' she told Violet, who came down into the kitchen looking tired but otherwise seemingly untroubled by her nightmares. It was the right thing to have said. Horrified, Violet fell over herself apologising when Mrs Potter arrived a few hours later.

'Knew something was going on,' Mrs Potter said when Frankie followed her down to the kitchen, anxious to explain the state of things. 'Glad to come back. Being at home didn't suit me one bit, me and Hal on top of each other all day.' She patted Frankie on the back. 'It's so good to see you, Frankie. And don't worry, we'll have all this tackled in no time.'

But there didn't seem to be enough hours in the day to even scratch the surface of *all this. All this* was medical appointments and phone calls to Dr Morrissey; it was putting in place a rough schedule for Jools, Mrs Potter and Frankie to be with Violet around the clock while also extricating Violet further from her public life with the help of the inimitable Mia.

And *all this* was made infinitely more complicated by Violet's increasing obsession with absolute secrecy. She hated the thought of anyone knowing that things weren't 'quite right' with her, couldn't bear embarrassing herself in case she got 'a bit muddled', and in conversation with the few people whom she grudgingly accepted did now know, she never referred to the situation in any but the haziest terms. It was most likely part of the illness, Dr Morrissey thought, magnifying her already deep-seated aversion to exposure into a neurosis. After his initial visit, he had referred them to a specialist and an appointment for a brain scan, both of which they were currently waiting on.

'Come *on*, Vi, what is it with this cloak-and-dagger act?' Jools said exasperatedly when Violet was convinced someone had been following her down the street and rushed around closing the blinds in the front room, snapping the string so hard it came apart in her hands.

'Stop haranguing me.' Violet was trying to fasten the string back to the blind, her face red and upset. 'Do you think I want to read about myself in the paper tomorrow? All these people just out to get me.'

'Violet, no one's out to get you,' Jools said impatiently.

'Yes they are,' Violet insisted. '*You* know they are, and you know why.' Her fingers started fluttering against the seam of her shirt, her eyes huge and afraid as she backed away from Jools, looked at Frankie beseechingly. 'I just need to try harder,' she pleaded, her voice high and thin. 'I just need to think, I need space, I need to *remember*. Please don't say anything to anyone until I've sorted myself out. I just can't bear it.'

Stricken, Jools turned towards her, but Frankie was there

first, taking Violet's arm and gently turning her away from Jools, making her voice very calm and quiet.

'It will be all right, Violet. Don't worry. We won't say anything to anyone. Jools is just trying to help.'

'I don't need any help.' Violet reared up, looking mulish.

'I know,' Frankie soothed. 'But we're here nonetheless. Me and Jools, Mrs P and Mia.'

'Don't tell Mia, not all of it,' Violet rushed in, anxious again.

'I won't, I promise.'

Violet sagged back against the table, looking determinedly at the floor and clearly hoping for them to leave her alone. After a minute, Jools, her face unreadable, turned towards the door. Frankie followed her.

'Jools,' she said quietly. 'What is it that Violet is really afraid of people finding out about? It can't only be the illness. I know she tried to talk to you the other night at the shop, and you didn't want to. Maybe it would help if *I* did. Does it have to do with the Land Army and her time in Yorkshire?'

Startled surprise flickered across Jools's face and for a moment, her hand gripped the door handle tightly; then she pushed down her shoulders and let go of it.

'Isn't it obvious?' She looked back at Frankie. 'Violet thinks hiding her illness will make it less true. So if you want to help her, stop talking about "fixing it" or making it "all right". It's not all right, it never will be all bloody right again.' She scowled ferociously to keep the tears from spilling over and marched down the front steps before Frankie realised that she hadn't answered her question at all.

'Jools leave?' Violet appeared in the door. The anxious red flush across her cheeks had faded a little, but she still looked jittery.

'She did,' Frankie said carefully, hoping Violet hadn't heard Jools's parting words. 'But I wondered,' she strove for a casual tone, 'is there anything you want to talk about; you know, really *talk* about? It might help you feel less worried if you got it out.'

Violet was staring down the road, where Jools was rounding the corner. The wind had kicked up, stirring leaves into a moody, restless dance across the pavement.

'No.' Violet's voice was so quiet that Frankie had to lean in to hear her. 'No, Frankie, love. I wouldn't have you be part of this.'

'But I want to be,' Frankie said urgently. 'Please, Violet, let me be part of it if it helps.'

But Violet shook her head. 'I think I'll go and shut my eyes for a bit,' she said. 'I'm sorry I'm such a nuisance. I don't know I'm being a nuisance half the time, which maybe is a blessing, but I can tell it's difficult.'

'There's nothing to be sorry about,' Frankie said. 'Don't worry, Violet, you'll be all ri—' She broke off, flushed a little, then gritted her teeth. 'Have a lie-down. I'll bring you a cup of tea later.'

So what if she was trying to comfort Violet? she thought rebelliously as she waited for the soft squeak of Violet's mattress before padding down to the kitchen. What was so terrible about hanging on to a little bit of hope? And Jools was wrong. Clearly this darkness in Violet's past was bearing down on her mind; was perhaps even driving her illness forward. If Violet didn't want to talk and Jools didn't want to help, then Frankie would look into it herself. Research the Yorkshire Land Army in autumn 1940, see if she could find any crime or court case that seemed to fit with Violet's words; confront Violet, help her get past it. She was a journalist, for heaven's sake, a writer. Writing her way through confusion and uncertainty was what she did best.

Writing, however, was no longer a refuge but a hell of its own these days, in a newsroom thick with tension over staff evaluations and the impending lay-offs.

'Francesca, I swear, if you keep muscling in on my *Tatler* story . . .'

'Francesca, your phone's been ringing off the hook. Make it stop, for heaven's sake.'

'Francesca, could I possibly impress upon you that newspaper space is precious? Don't use five beautiful words when one pithy one will do.'

'Hey, Frankie, are you ever going to stand still long enough to go for a coffee?'

Max seemed to be the only one who remained calm amidst the frenzy, while the others – with June Seymour still not back in the office – fought tooth and nail for Hugo's attention. This, perversely, often landed on Frankie, and the more she tried to put her head down and get on with things, the more Hugo hovered over her. At first she had been flattered, until she realised that his focus on her was partly due to a new torment, provisionally entitled 'The First Ever Etherington Interview'. Hugo had quickly moved on from 'Think about it, will you?' to a slightly more threatening 'Let's discuss' and, most recently, 'When will I have something to read?' accompanied by him waving the evaluation folder in an ominous kind of way whenever they crossed paths, clearly hoping to chip away at her obvious resistance until she finally caved. Well, he could chip all he wanted, she thought, because there was no way that interview would ever come to pass.

Acutely aware of the others' hostility and resentful mutterings at Hugo's perceived favouritism, she tried to keep out of their way, and had barely exchanged a word with Con in days. Con, in turn, had befriended Victoria and Mallory and got on just fine without Frankie anyway. Bea had been out on a training course since the day after they'd arrived, leaving Frankie a frantic and somewhat bewildered voicemail asking her if everything was all right and could they please catch up when 'all this' was over.

Twice she was able to slip to the library between outside meetings to squint her way through microfiche copies of old newspaper issues, but pickings were slim. The Women's Land Army seemed to have got fairly little column space – unfairly so, Frankie thought, given how crucial its role was – and she couldn't find anything on a regional murder that fitted the dates. Although, she grimaced as she scrolled down the pages at lightning speed, with the major events that autumn – battles in the Atlantic, the horrors of the Blitz, the Germans raging across the Continent – anything local would have most likely taken a back seat. The regional papers would be a better bet, but she didn't have specific enough questions to ask over the phone, and going out of town to search herself simply wasn't an option at the moment.

During her lunch breaks, she conferred with Mia over requests for Violet's presence at events, or tore across Belgravia on her grandmother's ancient bicycle to check on things at Cavendish Place. Meanwhile, her dad's release date loomed closer. She had to find a cheap bedsit, set aside a small portion of her salary for him. Transition was difficult for ex-inmates – she'd read up on it – and she was desperate for him to establish a foothold in normal life again. She tried to picture him walking out of the prison door the way they did in the movies, his step buoyantly underscored with music as he returned to a life where they would finally not sit across a table bolted to the ground, with guards hovering, but somewhere small and cosy. He'd play the guitar and tell her stories and make her laugh about whatever poky daytime job he would have to take. The strained, tense look on his face would fade, and Frankie would be filled once again with that feeling of possibility, of lightness that had always surrounded him. But whenever she came to that point, she forced herself to stop, because she knew full well that things would get infinitely more difficult once she was responsible for Harry O'Brien as well as Violet.

It was hard to put into words what it was like to be back at Cavendish Place after all these years, feeling angry and desperate and helpless, privy to every tiny difference in Violet's demeanour. She could see the look in her grandmother's eyes change from one minute to the next, amused warmth turn distant and faraway; she could *feel* the fear, the anxiety eating away at her, even in her better moments, making her sharp and snappy.

There were times, many times, when Frankie wanted to run as fast as she could away from Violet and Hugo, Harry and Con, to a place where she could escape the weight of it all and just be Frankie, the girl who didn't celebrate her birthdays, who wrote more words than she spoke, who just wanted to make things work.

Every time she was close to breaking point, however, something made her go on. She would find Violet reading the paper and looking up to smile at her, patting the sofa and asking after her day before returning to the news with a caustic remark on the sorry state of the government, which put a hard lump in Frankie's throat because it was so like the old Violet that she thought she would die. At work, something would remind her of what it was all about. A rare nugget of praise from Hugo, dug out from beneath layers of dismissal. Listening to Xavier Merrell discuss his piece on the party leadership three desks over, then seeing it on the front page the next day and knowing she'd been there at its conception. Seeing her byline in the paper, not her own name and not necessarily next to pieces she was all that proud of, but surely paving the way to where she eventually wanted to be. All she had to do was stick it out. She was good at this, she would keep her job. She would be there for her dad when the time came, and, God willing, she might still help Violet get better.

Thirty-Nine

The following Wednesday, Hugo was out of the office for an unprecedented work trip to Edinburgh, and word had come in that his return train was delayed. Frankie speed-typed an article on a new nightclub rumoured to have been involved in money laundering, then nipped back to Cavendish Place for a late lunch break. The night before, while discreetly – and slightly guiltily – nosing around Violet's overstuffed bureau for any old photos or wartime mementos that might get her further in her WLA research, she had discovered a wad of unopened post. Among the bills, advertisements and greeting cards were a number of late payment reminders. This was puzzling, because the Violet Frankie remembered was fastidious about her account staying in credit.

Despite her ritzy Belgravia address, no one who had seen the inside of her well-worn, shabby flat could accuse Violet of extravagance. After her mother had passed away, she had converted the house into flats, selling the top two because they didn't need all that space. They had always lived within Gramps's salary, cared very little about life's finer things. Violet was gleeful when she could pass off one of Jools's finds as a designer dress at events; she drank the cheapest tea brand there was and rarely dined out. She didn't talk about it much, but neither was she embarrassed by the fact that she had little to contribute to her projects money-wise. Instead, she exploited her name and network shamelessly, able at any point to persuade an old crony to help out where it was needed most.

Now, however, maybe because she was keeping away from old cronies and felt the need to compensate, things had changed.

Large amounts had been transferred to Safe Haven, to Great Ormond Street Hospital and to an illiteracy project she'd organised, and any incoming money from pensions and such was immediately swallowed up by the outgoings.

Violet's bank account was glaringly empty.

'Come in, darling,' Violet said when Frankie poked her head around the door. 'Why aren't you at work? Or is this "Portrait of the Lady as an Old Woman"?'

Relief flared at Violet's clarity of mind, momentarily lifting the weight off Frankie's shoulders, even though the comment had been rather tartly delivered. They hadn't talked about Frankie's articles or Hugo again, but she knew that Violet felt she was wasting her talent; that she should be firmer with Hugo in requesting a transfer to a weightier beat.

'I'm on my lunch break.' She sat down on the little threadbare footstool.

'Lunch?' Violet frowned. Frankie's heart squeezed a bit.

'You had a sandwich, remember?' she said. 'And those crisps you like so much.'

Her grandmother turned her head and smiled at her. The sun hit her face, eyes tired and smudged with shadows, skin thin, like paper. 'That's all right then,' she said agreeably, and Frankie felt the weight settle back, heavier than before.

'Listen,' she began, 'I've put a call in to Mr Hopkins at the bank, because I found a few statements on your desk and your account seems to be somewhat overdrawn. Lots of money going to charity. Do you know what happened?'

Violet frowned and shook her head. 'I usually have enough every month,' she said. 'Lately, though, it's got a bit hard to count out the coins and bills; they all seem to look the same.'

'I understand,' Frankie said carefully. 'But it's way past counting coins and bills; we're talking about hundreds of pounds, transfers mostly.'

Violet shook her head. 'That doesn't sound like me at all,' she said firmly.

'I know.' Frankie swallowed. 'But do you know if there is any . . . well, if there's money elsewhere? Because right now, there's not all that much to pay for food, utilities, those kinds of things.'

Or for any extra treatment that might be necessary beyond what the NHS would provide, some of which could take a while to come through, according to Dr Morrissey. In the meantime, Violet would be dependent on Frankie's salary. And Frankie's salary would be dependent on her fate at the *London Post*.

'Oh, I know what to do, darling.' Violet's frown cleared. 'You know that nice Mr Hopkins at the bank? Give him a call, he's ever so helpful.'

Frankie opened her mouth, closed it again. 'I will,' she said with some difficulty. 'You'll be all right this afternoon with Mrs Potter . . . Wait, what are you looking at?' For the first time, she noticed the photo album on Violet's lap, felt a dart of excitement at the flash of black-and-white photos.

'Taking a trip down memory lane.' Violet grimaced wryly. 'Which is very much a place I wish they'd sell road maps for.'

She gave a comical, self-deprecating shrug, and even though Frankie knew she shouldn't indulge, hope reared its head again.

Violet felt for her glasses and settled them on her nose. 'Look, here's your mum. She was the most peaceful baby. It's probably good we never had any more, because to this day I'm convinced that all babies are as quiet and content as my Stella. She was such a joy to me, such a comfort.'

Frankie peered at a tiny bundle, all squashed face and no hair. *Yorkshire, 1941*, the caption said.

'Damp and chilly, even in late summer.' Violet traced the artfully jagged edge of the photo. 'That's why she was all bundled up.'

But Frankie's eyes were sliding towards the picture of her

young grandmother. Violet had half turned away to show the baby to the camera, so Frankie could only see her slim figure, the hair swept back from her face the way she'd seen recently in her wartime research.

'Do you have more pictures?' she asked carefully. 'From before, I mean – 1940, maybe.'

Violet's finger stopped in mid trace. 'No.' She gave a sharp flick to the next page, as if making it very clear that they were moving forward in time instead of back. 'I didn't really start taking photos until Stella was born. I couldn't get enough of her, you know, wanted to capture every moment. Here, we're back in London in this one; look, she's riding a horse. Sadly, she wasn't a natural, but she did give it a good try. She was so good-natured, just went along with things.'

Frankie wanted to ask questions, dig deeper, but Violet was turning the pages more quickly now and Frankie forgot about the Land Army altogether as she watched her mum's pretty, elfin face change through the pages, saw her dad occasionally crop up, so young, so happy . . .

'I wonder what your babies will be like,' Violet said, her eyes on the page.

'My babies? Do you know something I don't?' Frankie laughed shakily.

'Well, the way things are, it doesn't look like I'll be around to see them.' Violet was gazing at a photo of Stella holding a squirming Frankie up to the camera.

'You m-m-m-might.' Frankie's mouth was working painfully to form words. 'Although I have yet to c-c-come across some-one who'd be there.' She pointed at her father next to Stella, wearing a proud expression.

'There won't be enough time.' Violet was still looking down. 'There won't be nearly enough time for all the things I want to do with you, want to see you do. I'm greedy, I know, *I want I want I want*, like a spoilt child. I want to be around to see you married, to meet your husband, your family. But there won't be time now.'

'Violet, you'll be able to do so many things still. I'll help you, I promise . . .' Frankie's voice faltered and she blinked back tears.

'You're already helping,' Violet said quietly. 'By being back with me. I know it's not always easy. I'm sorry you're having to spend your lunch break here, all your evenings when you should be out there with people your own age, when you need to be working on your career. But mostly I'm sorry about not helping your dad when he needed it, when *you* needed it.'

For so many years Frankie had pictured the moment when Violet would finally concede that she'd been wrong. She had imagined it like a scale that would suddenly right itself, some poison that would be extracted, leaving her lighter, freer. But now, looking at her grandmother's drawn face, she felt no vindication whatsoever, no triumph if this was the price she had to pay to get it.

'Why did you dislike him so much?' she asked carefully. 'I never understood that. It was so easy to like him.'

Violet didn't immediately answer, then she said, 'We were just very different.'

'I don't think there's a word in the English language that describes what you two were,' Frankie said drily. 'But still . . .'

'Frankie, love, leave it.' Violet's voice brooked no argument. Slowly, mechanically, she leafed through the last few pages of the photo album, bare and white after her daughter had died.

'Leave what?' Frankie was getting a little tired of people telling her to leave things. 'I don't mean to start an argument or anything. I honestly want to know. It would . . . help. Maybe.'

'Their car was falling apart at the seams,' Violet said, her eyes on the last page of the album. 'I had offered to help Stella buy a new one; she was such a nervous driver, I was worried she didn't feel safe.'

Her voice was odd, her words so quick, the telling efficient, and Frankie had the feeling she had gone over this in her mind many times. Right then, she wanted to take back the question, wasn't sure if she really needed to know at all.

'Harry refused, of course, but he didn't fix that heap-of-trash car either. And then he sent her out for that curry.'

A car accident, that was what her dad had always said; another car going through a red light, a terrible turn of fate.

'Stella would have been going slow enough to stop even when the other car came through the junction – God knows, she always crawled along at a snail's pace . . .'

Frankie wanted to put her hands over her ears, wanted to close her eyes and not hear this last bit.

'. . . but the brakes finally gave up the ghost. She slid right into the path of the other car. It was going too fast. She had no chance.'

Everything inside Frankie squeezed tightly, so hard that she couldn't breathe.

'It w-w-wasn't his f-f-fault,' she finally stammered. 'He didn't mean to.'

But in her heart of hearts, she knew that if Harry O'Brien never meant for things to happen, he didn't take the time to make them right either. He never thought of what would happen afterwards, he just went for them.

Someone always has to pay, that was what Violet had said when they'd fought the other day, and Frankie closed her eyes, felt tears spill down her cheeks and wished with all her heart that it hadn't been her mother.

A moment later, she heard the chair springs creak, felt a hand on her cheek. Violet had never been much of a toucher; hers had been a furious, brisk kind of love. Even now, the movement was ever so slightly awkward, but gentle too, her fingers warm as she wiped away tears, smoothed back Frankie's hair.

'You're right, it wasn't his fault,' she said quietly. 'Stella could have taken the car to be repaired just as easily as he; she could have made him get the curry. I wouldn't have said anything if you hadn't asked, but, selfishly maybe, I wanted you to understand why I felt the way I did.'

She put her hand under Frankie's chin and forced her to look up.

'I wanted Stella back, I wanted her so desperately, and when I couldn't have her back, I wanted you. You were this warm, loving, lovely little girl, so much like your mother and yet so different, too. I just *wanted* you and he wasn't going to give you up, so I fought for you. It's all I know to do, fight for things, and maybe – hopefully – when I'm gone,' she grimaced, her own eyes bright with tears, 'that'll be the one thing I've taught you.'

'I'm sorry.' Frankie hung her head. 'I'm sorry that I never opened your letters. Returned your phone calls. I'm—'

'You have nothing to be sorry for. I did what I thought was right, but if I could go back in time, I'd give everything to do it differently.'

Her glance strayed to the photo album in her lap. 'I'd do so many things differently.' She looked at Frankie again, her face drawn, her eyes sombre. 'But I wanted you to know that I'm sorry now, because a point will come when it'll be too late. When I won't remember to say it.'

Forty

Frankie knew she had to go back to work, should have been there half an hour ago already. Instead, she quietly slipped into her bedroom, closed the door and sat down on the bed. Violet had never really altered the room from when Frankie's mum, and then Frankie herself, had lived here. It still held the narrow bed, the old wardrobe, the small desk by the window, the faded alphabet sampler on the wall.

It was just as spare now. Frankie always travelled light, a habit from shuttling back and forth between her two childhood homes, so there were just a few clothes in the wardrobe, a travel alarm clock on the bedside table and a photo in a small tarnished frame next to it. In it, her dad had his arm around her mum, beaming into the camera, her mum's fine fair hair wind-tousled around her sweetly smiling face.

In less than a month, he would be back in her life. *And then the good times will roll with a vengeance*, he had told her during their last conversation. With a small wrench, Frankie remembered how willingly she had entered into the spirit of things, had helped paint a picture of freedom and possibility when, in reality, he would now have a crime on his record for ever and his new life would be a modest set-up at best: a cheap bedsit, a run-of-the-mill job, nothing to match the story he wanted it to be. That was the problem, really. Harry O'Brien was all story; his entire life was about sniffing the air for revolution and change. He'd never once given her the exact details of the accident, had perhaps even convinced himself that it really had been a fateful confluence of events. Part of her wished Violet hadn't told her, that she could go on loving her dad in the same way as before, the bright, warm presence he'd always been. But Violet had, and it had shifted the perspective, made the same facts tell a different story altogether. One where it wasn't enough to fill the world with a sense of adventure, to have a wandering heart and let the good times roll, but where someone always had to do the dull things, like scheduling dentist's appointments and buying new shoes. And fixing the faulty brakes on a car.

'Excuse me, Frankie? Are you up here?'

Frankie quickly wiped her face and set the photo back on the table. She grabbed her bag and her jacket and stepped out into the hall, starting a little when she caught her own pale, hollow-eyed reflection in the mirror. Just that morning, Felicity had asked her loudly whether she had the flu, with the consequence that everyone now flinched back when she was near. This afternoon didn't look likely to improve, not least because Mrs Potter was looking uncharacteristically ill at ease.

'Could I have a word downstairs?'

Please don't say you can't stay, please don't say you have to leave, Frankie prayed as she followed her downstairs, through the kitchen, where a saucepan bubbled on the stove, and into the small warren of cellar rooms that had once been used for coal and ice storage.

'I thought you might want to see this.' Mrs Potter pointed to a small room on the right.

Frankie remembered it, a narrow, windowless tunnel, where Gramps had once trapped a mouse in a small cage. Seeing Frankie's distress, he'd taken the whole trap, nibbled-on piece of cheese and all, upstairs into the garden, where they watched the little creature scamper away. Back then, the cellar had held narrow racks for an assortment of ancient wine bottles and other random bits and pieces. Now, however, it resembled nothing so much as a small shop.

More shelving had been fitted against the walls – Frankie had a sudden mad image of Violet traipsing through the Wembley

Park IKEA, persuading a willing young man to load the car for her – and was stacked with plastic and wooden crates. There were piles of blankets, pillows and clothes, batteries and torches, large water containers. Whole shelves were filled with tins and boxes of non-perishable food, neatly stacked on top of each other. Dried milk, biscuits and chocolates, enough tea to last several years. There were haberdashery items and tights in their original packaging, and in the middle of the floor, two mattresses, still wrapped, sat on wooden pallets. Behind the shelving, the walls had been fortified with a criss-cross of metal strappings drilled into the stone.

'This definitely wasn't here when I left,' Mrs Potter remarked as Frankie stared open-mouthed at the narrow room. 'Looks like someone is preparing for a siege, if you ask me.'

There was a hiss and the sound of something splashing, and she disappeared back into the kitchen, leaving Frankie surveying the place where, she now knew, at least part of Violet's money had gone. Not a siege, she thought. This was a shelter, clear as day.

A million things were waiting for her at the office, but she couldn't remember a single one of them as she walked along the shelves, ran her hand over the scratchy wool, counted the Quality Street tins. She wondered absent-mindedly if Violet still loved the little green hazelnut triangles. They were Frankie's favourite too, and they'd always shared them evenly between the two of them.

Some of the shelves were clearly waiting to be finished – the one holding towels and bandages was only half full – and she pictured her grandmother coming back from one of her walks with a new item and squirrelling it away down here, in secret and alone. She shivered, wrapped her arms around herself. *Time is unravelling*, Violet had said. *The beginning of a thread starting to unspool all over again.*

Frankie looked at the shelter and imagined, strung along the thread like beads on a rosary, the things Violet was remembering. The Wentworth and the air raid. Romy's death. The Land Army. What would be next? she wondered, and shivered again.

The shelf at the back held a variety of cardboard boxes labelled *1900–1925, 1925–1939, 1940–1976, 1976–2004.* Inside, meticulously organised, file folders contained all manner of things: family photos and letters, pictures drawn by Frankie, old essays, a row of slim photo albums similar to the one Violet had been looking at upstairs, small mementos, every now and then a piece of clothing, carefully folded flat. The items were loosely packed, as if made for browsing. Large dividers labelled in thick red marker separated the sections: *Birth. Christening. Miss Poole. School. War. Wedding. Stella. Frankie birth. Friendships. Charity moments. Frankie school. Frankie work.*

Frankie blinked, and the letters swam in the dim light, became fuzzy haloes of brightness around the memory of a lunch box sitting on a car seat. Violet was doing it again, labelling things to assign them a place in time and space, to make them belong. Only now, she was labelling *herself*, her life, her memories.

Frankie let her fingers drift over the contents of the boxes, pictured her grandmother going around the house and choosing what to keep and what to let go. Why had she kept these three brightly coloured buttons in a plastic sleeve and those letters bundled together? Why did she save this particular photo, that newspaper cutting? How had she chosen what story these boxes would tell her once she could no longer remember?

Many times over the last few days, Frankie had cried, into a pillow, a balled-up towel. But to imagine Violet methodically, clinically almost, preparing for a journey into darkness and deciding what to bring with her, then stealing down to this secret, dark room in search of herself . . . it was beyond tears. It was bewildering and desolate and it was lonely, so lonely Frankie couldn't bear it. She stroked the embroidered edges of a thin folded handkerchief with the initials GWC, which was slotted into the pages of a book, then drew herself up. She was here now, she had seen this room, these boxes. She would help Violet remember her story; she was *part* of Violet's story. Come what may – and *that* didn't bear thinking about either – Violet wouldn't have to be alone with it. Maybe Jools didn't think talking about the past helped, but Frankie knew that it would. She was seeing it right here, how important it was for Violet to keep remembering.

She replaced the lids on the boxes, lining them up carefully the way she'd found them. *War. Wedding. Stella.* She flicked a quick look towards the kitchen, where she could hear humming and pots clanking. Looking through any of the boxes' contents would be wrong, obviously, like reading someone's diary or eavesdropping on a private conversation. But surely, if it helped in some way . . . Before she could change her mind, she reached into the box, brought out the folder marked *War* and slid it deep into her bag.

'Oh, and one last thing,' Mrs Potter said as Frankie emerged into the kitchen. She reached into her apron pocket and brought out two small pieces of paper. Frankie's heart sank as she saw the bank logo, her grandmother's handwriting, the big red stamp that told her the cheques had been returned due to insufficient funds.

'Mrs Potter, I'm so sorry. I'll get it sorted, I promise.'

Someone should ban the word 'sort', Frankie thought wearily as she sneaked up the back stairs. The brisk syllable, the confidence that problems could be ticked off just like that. No one who promised to sort things out had been washing their grandmother's soiled underwear, had discovered a war-like hoard in the cellar, was now peering around the corner to see if Victoria or Mallory were at their desks, or Con, staring stonily at his screen.

She braced herself. Blinked. Exhaled.

While up front the TV screens blared as usual and two politics editors were noisily debating something, the back end of the newsroom, where Frankie sat, was empty. Cautiously she approached her desk area, did a slow turn to survey the empty workspaces closest to her. Victoria's was neat as always, Mallory's awash with papers and cuttings, coffee cups and Post-its, a tidal wave that stopped exactly at the tape still dividing their desks.

'Excuse me,' she asked another journalist – Roland, she thought his name was, from Travel. 'Do you know where everyone is?'

'Well, Hugo's still stuck behind a failing train somewhere north of Leeds – surprised we can't hear him roar from here – and didn't they all have that drinks thing planned?' He gestured at the empty row of desks and grinned. 'Looks like they're making the most of the cat being away.'

'Drinks thing?' Frankie repeated faintly.

'Leave you behind, did they?' The sympathy in his tone made her cringe with humiliation.

'No, of course not.' She quickly forced a smile. 'I just forgot.'

He walked away and she scanned Con's desk for a clue, saw a scratchy fax. *Pick a main and either an appetiser or pudding, then pass it on,* Con had written in his loopy, beautiful handwriting, just below the logo of the Seven Bells, a neighbourhood pub. So *Con* had actually organised the drinks thing, she thought savagely. Without even checking on her. She bit the inside of her lip as she went over the past few days, most of which she'd spent rushing from pillar to post, trying to stay away from Hugo and the others as much as she could. Yes, so maybe she'd been a bit preoccupied. But not to invite her at all was a bit rich, wasn't it? Was Max among them, too, not part of the scheming, maybe, but not particularly bothered by her absence either? The thought of him sitting around the table with the others made her ball her fists. And Con, who'd been her friend first, now laughing with them, at her maybe, getting more elaborate the more there was to drink. She heard a shout of laughter from somewhere and flinched, then relaxed when she realised it wasn't about her. She pressed her lips together and sat down, still holding the menu.

A couple of hours later, neither her colleagues nor Hugo had returned. As dusk fell outside the tall windows and the newsroom slowly emptied, Frankie sat in her deserted corner and worked on autopilot, filing copy and sorting through her projects, clearing her desk all the way down to the folder marked *War* and her leather-bound notebook.

If Violet had her red pen to label things, then Frankie had her writing to instil order, and she had continued chronicling Violet's days, trying to detect a pattern, to find something that would help. She leafed past scribbled notes from a phone conversation with Mr Hopkins, who'd urgently suggested she obtain power of attorney for Violet's finances, then bullet points from a recent doctor's appointment, a list of questions for when Jools had calmed down a bit. She had asked Jools to come round and sit with Violet after Mrs Potter had left tonight, so she could have a chunk of undisturbed time at her desk to catch up with herself. Undisturbed, ha, she thought as she glanced round at the empty desks. At least it meant there was no one looking over her shoulder to see her inspecting the contents of the folder.

It wasn't a whole lot. Photos, mostly, of a young Violet in a white dress, other girls, similarly dressed, milling around in the background. *Me doing debutante things*, Violet had written on the back. There was a photo of Romy, pretty and slender, a copy of which had sat on the sideboard in the drawing room for as long as Frankie could remember. *My cousin Romy, 1939*, Violet had written on the back. *She died a year later.*

Frankie swallowed painfully at the way these notes were

phrased, as if present-day Violet had to explain each photo to future Violet. She picked up a newspaper cutting, yellowing and stiff with age, with a Post-it stuck to the front. *My father, died in Africa during the war.* She picked out a few words from the article – *Henry Etherington . . . died with honour . . . El Agheila . . . December 1940* – and bit her lip, increasingly uncomfortable at intruding on this unsettling conversation Violet was having with her future self. Especially because, so far, there was nothing here at all that looked like it could unravel the thread of the past any further towards the WLA and *It was murder.*

In the books and online accounts she'd read about the Land Army, there had been the occasional between-the-lines reference to the fact that the farming community hadn't always looked kindly on women doing men's work, especially in the early years of the war. There were also mentions of loneliness and homesickness if a girl was billeted alone in a remote area. But above all, there was a can-do spirit, a sense of community and having a bigger purpose that lent the land girls a patriotic patina, emblematic of the way Britain just got on with it and ended up winning the war. It was lovely, actually, seeing the way the comradeship united women from different walks of life, which made it especially hard to believe that there would be any kind of darkness here.

Frankie smoothed out the obituary, set it on top of the thin stack of photos, then reached for the last item, a bundle of letters between her grandparents during the later years of the war. She was just debating whether she could bring herself to read them when she noticed a different-looking envelope at the very back. Lined with crackly old paper, the back flap was embossed with the letter C among a ring of vines and an apple. Inside was a single black and white photo.

Grainy and a bit fuzzy, the rough edges soft with age, the picture showed four young women. Frankie's eyes immediately zeroed in on the girl in the middle. The slim figure and swept-back hair were unmistakable, even if she hadn't seen them only a few hours ago. She turned the photo over, gave a small noise of surprise.

Winterbourne Orchards, autumn 1940.

So Violet hadn't been in Yorkshire at all, safe and out of harm's way, waiting for the arrival of baby Stella. Violet had been in Somerset, a land girl with – she squinted at the row of names in her grandmother's handwriting – *Kit, Red, Joan, Lily.* She frowned in confusion, heart beating fast as she scanned the faces again. *Kit, Red, Joan, Lily.* Where was 'Violet'?

The women had bunched together, no doubt to fit them all into the frame, the curls of one in the face of another, someone's hat askew, arms tight around each other's shoulders. They were dressed identically, in the uniform she'd seen in the reference books, but there were no toothy grins, no sunny vitality here. Watchful eyes in thin faces, none of them smiling, except for one girl to the right of Violet, whose lips were quirking up, impish, with the faintest hint of rebellion.

Frankie snatched up her phone, punched in a number.

'Jools!' Her voice rang accusingly across the empty newsroom. 'Why on earth didn't you tell me that you were a land girl with Violet?'

Forty-One

'Well hello to you too,' Jools said belligerently. 'And it never really came up.'

'Yes it did,' Frankie said exasperatedly. 'In fact I asked you specifically about the WLA. I know about the black book and the Land Army badge, I heard you two that night at the shop; what were you talking about?' she persisted.

'Since you obviously hung on our every word,' Jools snapped, 'you'll have noticed that I didn't want to talk about it then and I certainly don't want to talk about it now.'

Frankie decided to change tack. 'I have a photo here; it says "Kit, Red, Joan, Lily"—'

'How did you get that?' Jools cut in sharply.

Frankie flushed. 'I found it.'

'Went snooping, did you?'

'No,' she said through gritted teeth. 'God, it's like pulling teeth with the two of you. Who are these women?'

'Red is what they used to call me.' Jools sounded almost proud. 'I was a communist.'

'And Violet?'

She sighed. 'Violet was Lily.'

'Lily? Why? Why did she change her name?'

On the other end of the phone, Jools made an impatient noise. 'She'd run away from home. Enlisted in the Land Army under a false name.'

'She did?' Frankie almost dropped the phone in astonishment.

'Yes, but before you get all excited, I'm not going to say any more. It's her story to share. I have a healthy respect for other people's privacy, unlike—'

'You were all good friends?' Frankie interrupted her impatiently.

'We were very close, yes. We had to look out for each other in those days.'

'But why have I never heard about these women? Are you still in touch? Are they still around?'

There was a long pause, then Jools sighed again, and for the first time she sounded sad rather than snappish. 'We send each other Christmas cards every year, that was the deal.'

'Why did you need a deal?' Frankie asked.

'What I need is for you to drop this. I mean it, Francesca. It was a long time ago.'

Jools only called her Francesca when she was getting mad, and Frankie paused, but only for a moment. 'Do you think if we call them, ask them to come and see Violet, it might help her with her anxiety?'

'No!'

Frankie sat up straight and stared at the phone. Had Jools just shouted at her?

'No,' Jools repeated, marginally quieter. 'Leave it be, Frankie, I'm serious. You will not help Violet by raking up her past. Please, just trust me on this.'

'Then tell me how to help her,' Frankie said desperately. 'We have to do *something*, Jools.'

'I told you, and I'm telling you again, what we need to do right now is be there for her. Get her through the medical process, make sure she has her tests, that we understand what it all means. We do not stir things up or make trouble. I've looked it up on the internet and she needs things to be predictable and calm. *Calm!*' Jools hissed. 'Now, I'm going over to Violet's to spend a very calm evening playing cards, and I suggest you take this opportunity to go out. Socialise with your peers. Get your head out of all this mess for a few hours and do something an ordinary twenty-eight-year-old would do.'

And before Frankie could say anything else, she'd hung up.

Slowly Frankie replaced the receiver on the cradle. Jools's voice hung in the air, brisk, snappy, irritated. And yet beneath it all, there was something else there. Something she'd heard in Violet's voice as well, dark and foreboding, something that, to Frankie, sounded a lot like fear.

It was like an adventure story, Frankie thought, pulling her desk lamp closer to study the picture again. Running away and enlisting in the Land Army. Something to be proud of and tell your grandchildren. But not only had Violet never mentioned it, she had actively lied about it, was afraid of it. Frankie felt surer than ever that these women were part of the mystery.

She reread the names, and it was then that she saw, right underneath, in tiny, crabbed letters, three words: *From Light, Darkness.*

It took her a moment to recall where she'd seen this before. The Winterbourne stamp inside the little black book. Only there it had been worded the other way around, making it marginally more reassuring. Here, the watchful eyes in the picture infused the inverted poetry with an unsettling rhythm, a jarring undercurrent that picked up the faint echo of fear in Jools's voice. Frankie suppressed a small shiver.

Suddenly she heard the newsroom door open. Craning her neck to squint through the half-gloom of the office, she realised how late it had become, how empty the floor was.

A shadow fell into the doorway, a long dark swash of legs. A phone rang on someone's desk, momentarily drowning out the sound of her heart thumping against the insides of her ribcage, then stopped abruptly. The shadow slid into the room, became smaller, until she saw a shock of white hair, a narrow face, dark suit impeccable even after hours on the train.

'Evening, dearie,' Hugo said. 'Holding the fort, are you?'

He wove through the desks, pausing occasionally to squint at something on someone's pile. She quickly nudged her notebook closed, set it on top of the WLA books, but realised only when he was next to her that she was still holding, of all things, the photograph.

'What are you working on?' he asked.

She could smell the sweet and bitter notes of wine as he leaned against her desk, imagined him sitting on the train, slim white fingers wrapped around a glass as he stared into the darkness rattling by. It seemed to have mellowed him, though, because he was calmer than she'd seen him so far, moving languidly almost as he crossed one leg over the other.

'Oh, this style guru interview.' She tried to roll the photo quietly but the thick paper wouldn't give, so she turned it inside the hollow of her palm as best as she could, curling her fingers around the edges. When she looked up to meet his gaze, he was watching her hand with bemused curiosity.

'Secrets?' He raised his eyebrows.

'Just . . . nothing really. How . . . how w-w-was Edinb-b-burgh?' She tried to breathe openness into her throat, but some of his calmness seemed to rub off on her, and when she spoke again, her tongue moved smoothly enough. 'I think getting the McLever interview was more insightful than getting the head of the Scottish National P-P-Party to comment.'

He nodded appreciatively and leaned back, his smile genuine, his manner easy as he chatted on about Scottish politics. Little by little, Frankie felt her jaw loosen and her fingers relax their sweaty, claw-like grip around the photo. God knew she'd lost some of her illusions about Hugo, with his fondness for public showdowns, but still, here she was, talking with him just like any other colleague.

'So, how've you settled in?' he asked. 'They're a bit of a rowdy bunch, aren't they?' He laughed easily, his hair glowing white in the dim light of the desk lamp. His collar was open at the neck, his cheeks tinged with a delicate flush.

'Yes,' Frankie said fervently, 'they certainly are.' Unguarded, she might have said more, about the drinks and the incessant needling, if she hadn't caught sight of his gaze fixed on her with an odd intensity. Her skin prickled warningly. 'But it's been very interesting . . .'

'Of course.' Hugo nodded, looking slightly disappointed, then picked up the fax and glanced at Con's message.

Even the usual murmur of voices from the floor below had now ceased, and suddenly Frankie wanted to be away from here, away from Hugo, who was even closer, the fax held delicately between two fingers.

'It's getting late.' She flicked back the cuff of her cardigan to ostentatiously check her watch.

'Felicity said you'd moved in with your grandmother?'

She cursed Con for his indiscretion.

'How's that going?' His voice was casual enough, but she wasn't going to slip up again. 'Oh, just f-f-fine.' She started to pointedly shuffle her papers together, slipping the photo underneath her notebook, screwed the cap on her fountain pen, bent to reach for her bag, straightened back up – and froze. Violet's photo was now in Hugo's hand, held as delicately between those long, pale fingers as the menu just a moment before.

'Lovely.' His eyes raked greedily across it. 'Women's Land Army, it looks like. When was this taken?'

He held it closer, his eyes burrowing into the image, and Frankie wanted to rip it out of his hands and run.

'It's just something I found.' *Please don't turn it over, please don't turn it over . . .*

Hugo turned it over. 'Ah, here we have it. "Winterbourne Orchards, autumn 1940",' he read out. '"Kit, Red, Joan, Lily." *From Light, Darkness*? My, my, how dramatic. Almost has a biblical ring to it, doesn't it, so darkly prophetic.'

Frankie held her breath, praying that he wouldn't pick up on the discrepancy of the names. But his eyes bored into hers the same way they had burrowed into the picture, unblinking, probing, and she realised he was already a step ahead of her. 'Is one of these her middle name? Or a nickname? Flowers, I'm guessing – is she Lily? Aha, I'm right,' he said when Frankie gave a tiny, involuntary twitch. 'Then the next question is, why? Why was she Lily and not Violet?'

'No reason,' Frankie snapped. 'I mean, nothing important,' she added more politely.

He raised his eyebrows. 'Little Francesca's claws are coming out. You should always ask why, though, Francesca, that's the mark of a great journalist.'

'May I have the photo, please?'

She thought he'd refuse, but he handed it back with a faintly martyred air of being misunderstood.

'Do they still believe that light begets darkness, Kit, Red, Joan, Lily?' He folded his lips lovingly around the last name.

'I have no idea,' she said, 'but if you'll excuse me, I really . . .'

He settled himself more securely against the edge of the desk, stretching out his legs so she would have to push across him to leave.

'Now, no doubt you've been working hard to persuade your grandmother to give us an interview. But this,' he gave a small, soundless whistle, 'this would make a truly magnificent story. *From Light, Darkness. Land girls, ladies and their secrets.*' He pursed his lips thoughtfully. 'You could track down the other three women, get them talking.'

'What? No!' It was so close to what Frankie had just been thinking about that she was a lot more emphatic than she'd meant to be. She forced herself to lower her voice. 'It's just an old photo, Hugo.'

'Never know until you look into it, though, right? Everyone's got something to hide. And Violet Etherington is such a curious breed – so visible, so outspoken, and yet so hesitant to share her private life. And now she's practically disappeared. Rumour has it she's retiring, although getting anything out of that icy assistant of hers is almost impossible. But before too long there'll be the usual round-ups to celebrate her many achievements. Arbiter of social change! Relentless campaigner for women's rights! Wouldn't it be nice if we were a step ahead of them all and told an unknown story from the days when it all began? She seems untouchable, your grandmother. *Lily*-white.' He nudged Frankie with an indulgent chuckle. 'Get it? It piques the public's interest in a special way, and I, for one, am paid to make sure that interest should be acknowledged.' There was a nasty inflection on the *I*, and his eyes pinned Frankie against the wall.

'Hugo, trust me, there's nothing th-th-there,' she managed, but her stammer made her sound anything but confident, because obviously there were way too many things there that she didn't want him to know about, not least of all Violet's fear of exactly what was happening this very minute.

Hugo considered her answer long enough for Frankie's shoulders to relax a fraction, then he set a fingertip on the pub menu. 'Should we ask Conrad to join in? It worked on the Celeste story, and he'd be keen as mustard, I'm sure, to prove his mettle. He looks like he's good with old ladies; I'm sure he could get the four of them to have a nice chat.'

'Violet wouldn't do it.' Frankie tried a different approach. 'You know that as well as I do.'

'Well, there's enough here for us to get started; a lot of this will be in the public record. And the more details we acquire, the more amenable she might be to sharing some of her own to set the record straight.'

'Blackmailing an old lady?' Frankie knew this wasn't the way to talk to your superior, but she absolutely had to nip this one in the bud. 'No. It's not an option.'

'Okay.' Hugo slid off her desk.

'What do you mean, "okay"?'

He looked at her coolly. 'I mean "okay" as in I don't like being told no and it's certainly not your place to do so. "Okay" as in I came back for those staff evaluation sheets because I have a meeting with the board next week to tell them who stays and who goes. "Okay" as in goodbye, Francesca, enjoy the rest of your evening.'

'Hugo, please,' she said desperately. 'Give me something else, *anything* else, I'll do it. But I don't want Violet bothered with this; she's . . . Well I just don't.'

'I understand.' He nodded, and Frankie was flooded with relief.

'Thank you, and I'm sorry if I sounded . . . if I overstepped the mark.' She laughed a little shakily. 'You know how keen I am to be here, obviously. I'll prove it to you, just try me—'

'Sure.' He cut through her babble. 'But just to be clear. Either you take on the land girl story, or I'll give it to Conrad.'

Forty-Two

She watched him weave his way back through the desks, heard his footsteps in the corridor, his office door squeak open and close. There was no way she could possibly write a story on Violet – on *Violet*; how absurd could things get? But equally, if she didn't, then Con – eager, ambitious Con – would be starting to nose around. She took a deep, steadying breath. Okay. Fine. It would be all right. She'd say she would look into it and then just sort of stonewall, wait it out . . .

'I'll put it on the ed meeting agenda for tomorrow.' Hugo stuck his head back in. 'Bring the photo.'

He disappeared again, and Frankie slid down until she was sitting on the ground next to her desk, then reached up to retrieve her notebook and the photo, because she clearly couldn't be trusted with them, and closed her eyes.

It was entirely possible that she'd drifted off – she hadn't averaged more than a couple of hours the last few nights – because when she next looked up, she was staring straight into the eyes of Max Sefton.

'On the floor again?'

Long legs in jeans soft and faded with age, old, clearly beloved trainers that carried the smell of rain and autumn air. His knees creaked as he lowered himself down next to her, and he rubbed his back against the wall like a dog comfortably scratching its fur. 'Goodness, it's chilly in here,' he remarked. 'Here.' Something was wrapped around her, then hands tucked it between the wall and her back. Warmth seeped through her body, delicious and comforting. His jacket, she realised when she saw him sitting cross-legged in just his flannel shirt.

317

'Anything in particular happen?' he enquired. 'Or has it been the usual around here?'

'The usual.' Frankie laid her head sideways on her knees.

'So, Hugo's making you do things you don't want to; everyone else is making you pay for whatever Hugo's making you do; and your friend has turned on you.'

Frankie had to laugh.

'Did you know I wasn't coming to the drinks?'

'I wish I had; I mightn't have bothered. They decided to make the most of Hugo's absence, although by the second bar they were convinced they were doing some very valuable team-building and were debating expensing it all. You didn't miss a thing.'

'That's what I thought.' She smiled and sank further into his jacket.

'So what's up?' he enquired.

Automatically Frankie opened her mouth to divert him, her usual route of 'it's a long story'. But then she stopped herself. Maybe it was her tiredness and the warmth of the jacket, or maybe, for once, someone actually seemed interested. 'Hugo wants me to write a story on this.' She handed him the picture. 'Dig up some secrets about her time with the Land Army, which I obviously can't, because it's my grandmother.' It came out in what seemed like a single breath, and it felt utterly amazing.

He studied the photo for a long time, turning it to catch the light and reading the inscription. But where Hugo's eyes had felt intrusive, Max was holding it almost reverently, and Frankie was filled with profound gratitude.

'It's very special,' he said finally. 'There are a lot of publicity shots of her, but all of them are staged, of course. Something like this – a young woman on the cusp of adulthood, still unformed, innocent – well, to be honest, I'm not surprised Hugo's keen. There's a hunger for these kinds of war stories, of bravery and spirit and getting on with it. Why would it be so bad?'

Because I don't know what exactly it'll throw up besides bravery and spirit, Frankie wanted to say. Because whatever it was was making both Violet and Jools – the two most formidable women she knew – afraid. Because even if there was some explanation, there was no way to keep Violet's recent . . . developments out of it either. Because it was exactly what Violet had become so neurotic about, being spied on and exposed – and now potentially by her own granddaughter.

'If I don't do it, Con will.'

Max whistled softly. 'Well played, Hugo,' he said, almost admiringly. 'Still, there's hardly any potential for it to be awful, is there? Readers love land girls. There's only upside.'

'You know, the funny thing is,' Frankie said thoughtfully, 'before he told me to do it, I was thinking it would be nice to get in touch with them, ask them to come and see her.'

She took the photo from him and laid it across her knees. Squashed between Jools and a tall, bosomy girl, the young Violet looked out at them soberly. Her face was so thin, her hair windswept, her frame slight inside the bulky jacket. But her eyes were the same, looking straight at the camera with a hint of defiance and restlessness.

'Because she's not well.' She exhaled all the words at the same time. 'She's been struggling with remembering and not remembering, and I don't want her pushed on this. It's been . . . well, it's not been easy, to be honest.'

The legs of her chair, the metal filing cabinet, even her feet in their scuffed black shoes wavered in front of her eyes, but with a monumental effort she kept herself from crying. He reached for her hand, a matter-of-fact gesture rather than a romantic one, and she was glad, because anything else would have complicated things.

'They had to carry my nan out of her house kicking and

screaming because she wouldn't accept that she couldn't live on her own any more.' He sighed. 'I went and saw her in her new home, and it was as if she'd known that the moment she left she was done for. Pretty devastating,' he added gruffly.

'Do you see her often?'

'She passed away last year. You're doing the right thing, Frankie, living with your grandmother.'

She nodded. 'You must be cold,' she said, and started shrugging out of his jacket. 'Here.'

'I grew up in a miner's cottage, three down from my nan.' He grimaced. 'I'm totally immune to the cold.'

She sank back. 'Thank you. For not asking too many questions, I mean.'

'We're both being very poor journalists, you know,' he remarked. 'Stories not being written, questions not being asked, things not being told.'

She laughed shakily. 'I'm beginning to doubt my career choice. All I ever wanted to do was write.'

He thought about this, then said, 'Just do it anyway. Find these girls, get them together. For your grandmother; not for Hugo necessarily. They say that reliving memories, looking back at your life, does help. It would be worth a try, don't you think? If you want, I could give you some pointers on tracking people down.'

'Oh no, you've done enough,' Frankie said quickly. 'Giving me your jacket and listening to me go on and on and everything.'

He gave a small growl of laughter. 'Your standards clearly aren't very high. I do this kind of thing all the time: look through online resources, military databases. It's scary how easy it is to find someone when you know where to look. Or,' he gave her a level look, 'are you worried I'm taking over your story?'

'Of course not,' she said quickly. 'Only that you . . . I d-d-don't really need . . .' The words and letters fell over each other, got twisted, and still he was looking at her, his eyebrows raised in question, until she rolled her eyes. 'I was going to say I don't really need any help, but actually, I do. If you could point me in the right direction, it'd be very kind.'

'See how easy that was. I'll send you a list of websites to get started.'

'Okay, thank you,' she said, suddenly breathless, because he was grinning again, his warm eyes making hers feel stormy and her insides confused. 'My grandmother will be waiting for me.' She broke their gaze with some effort and scrambled to her feet.

'What's it like living together?' Max stood up a lot more gracefully than she had, held out her coat. 'I mean, if you haven't spoken for ten years, as you said, that's a lot of intimacy all of a sudden.' He leaned against the edge of her desk, unhurried and relaxed, giving her the space to think as she threaded her arms into her jacket.

'It's making me remember all sorts of good things I'd forgotten,' she said finally. 'My dad was always on the move; he loved change. But Cavendish Place, it never changed. It's unthinkable that she . . . that everything is now changing after all; I guess it makes me appreciate that she was always there.'

'After your mother died, you mean?'

'You know about Mum?' Frankie looked up.

'Yes, and before you get all paranoid, it was a big story at the time. I didn't seek out the information specifically.'

'Sorry. I don't know why I'm perpetually surprised at how exposed we all are.'

'Not me,' Max said drily. 'I'm just a poor boy from Wales. But you can't fault Hugo for sniffing around someone like Violet Etherington. And,' he continued, 'there is something to be said for keeping ahead of a story rather than trying to wait it out. You'd retain some control over it, look at it that way. You can do it, Frankie. You'll find a way to keep everyone happy. Just think of those fires crackling away inside you.'

'Maybe,' she said, and then, impulsively, she reached and gave him a hug. It was meant to be perfunctory, the bodily equivalent of a peck on the cheek, but she lost her balance a little and fell sideways, and he caught her in a full embrace, the kind that was altogether more intimate. Before she'd even clocked that his shirt really was as soft as it looked, while his body was pleasingly hard beneath it, she had pulled back.

'See you,' she said breathlessly.

'I hope so,' he grinned.

Violet

October 1940

Forty-Three

War had come to Winterbourne.

Running back from the stables, praying she wasn't too late for curfew, Violet found the barn door unlocked and the girls huddled around the stove, talking excitedly.

'Can't lock us in any more,' Red informed her gleefully when Violet had climbed up the ladder. 'Too dangerous now that we're under fire. Who'd have thought it would be the Germans who'd give us back our freedom?'

'Hardly under fire.' Kit frowned at Violet. 'Where were you? We were worried.'

'Hmm,' Violet said vaguely, glad when almost immediately discussions picked back up, about where the planes had been going, what had happened there and whether they'd be back the following day.

'They clearly don't care about little old us down here,' Red said dismissively. 'Which is sad in a way, because there's less chance of one of them being shot down. Can you imagine? There we are, pulling up sugar beets and minding our own business, when – *kerpow!* – a plane gets shot out of the sky and lands right on top of Hardwick. We get to go and have a gawp at him – dead as a doornail, of course – and some Germans – wounded but not fatally, so it'd be entirely within our rights to give them a good, hard kick on the shin . . . it'd be like Christmas and Easter all rolled into one.'

'Oh Red, for heaven's sake,' Joan moaned.

Eventually, and with great reluctance, the girls removed to their beds, but Red didn't stop whispering about flying and killing

Germans, while Kit's glower had increased in direct proportion to her worrying about her mother, and Lucy's only thoughts were of news from Matthew.

'Please, Kit.' She hovered next to Kit's bed first thing the next morning, making the older girl yelp in alarm when she opened her eyes and saw Lucy's face mere inches from hers. 'Can you ask Hardwick about our letters? Or could we get permission to go into the village? Maybe they've just forgotten we're here.'

Seeing the deep shadows under Lucy's red eyes, Violet felt desperately sorry for her, and Kit obviously did too, because she patted Lucy's shoulder awkwardly.

'I'll talk to him. But only if he doesn't kill us about the sloes first.' She made a face and swung her legs out of bed. 'It won't be good, I can feel it.'

'Let's just stay in bed.' Red, who had slept in her uniform and coat, pulled the blanket over her head. 'People can make it for three weeks without food, you know.'

'You wouldn't last an hour,' Kit said scathingly.

Pushing her feet into her breeches, Violet wondered what Hardwick would do to them, thought about the faint tinge of purple on Myra's hands, tried to summon up the outrage and fear from the evening before. But it all seemed far away, like years had passed in between, years of closeness and warmth with Guy, of remembering Romy. She had dreamed of her last night. Not the usual nightmare, but a spinning, colourful carousel of memory shards that seemed to have been bottled up inside her since Romy's death and were now all pushing to the surface at the same time. Maybe this, finally, was proper grief, this bone-deep yearning, this sweet and painful sense of loss that had somehow been unlocked in the playhouse, that strange, magical space where it had been possible to talk. To Guy. Her cheeks grew warm when she remembered his parting words – *I'll be waiting* – and even more so when she realised just how much she wanted to go back, and how impossible it would be for her to do just that.

The moment they left the relative safety of the attic, however, reality asserted itself. Hardwick would be waiting, Violet knew, ready to punish them. The group walked slowly through the foggy dawn towards the canteen, the sky leaden with dark clouds that hung so low they seemed to touch the ground.

'It'll be fine,' Kit muttered every now and then to no one in particular, but her words rang hollow and the girls stayed close on the narrow path, jostling to walk in the middle of the pack rather than at the periphery. It reminded Violet of a picture Barker had shown her in one of his books, a huddle of Antarctic penguins constantly swapping the ones out at the edges with the core. *It's in their blood, see, they need everyone to survive or else none will keep alive, so they pass their warmth back and forth,* he had said. Here, in a strange inversion of nature's push for survival, it was fear that travelled through the group, feeding into an unsettling sense of foreboding.

'Hush,' Kit hissed sharply, and threw out her arm to hold them back. Down one of the narrow paths leading away from the stable yard, where Violet had seen chickens kept in coops, a figure, contours obscured by an overlarge sack-like dress, was hunched over a tub.

The land girls' steps had been muffled by the clucking, feathery blobs scratching at the ground, so Myra hadn't heard their approach. She was crouching in a furtive way that reminded Violet of the cemetery, back rounded protectively over something cradled against her.

'Revenge for the sloes, girls,' Red murmured threateningly, 'now that she's alone . . .'

But just then Myra moved, straightened, and there was a glint and the faint sloshing sound of water. She had folded her sleeve all the way up to her shoulder, and her arm gleamed, slender and white, as she pulled it out of the tub and gingerly set it along the rim. She scooped something from a bowl on the ground and smeared it across her arm, and then a sound travelled clearly down the path, a sharp, agonised hiss as her entire body tensed with pain.

'She's hurt,' Ellen breathed.

'Probably fell or something,' Red muttered dismissively.

'Or . . . I mean . . . he wouldn't, would he?' Kit made a face.

The land girls crowded closer together, faces grey and waxy in the flat light of dawn as the answer to her question jumped in little jolts from one to the other.

Over at the canteen, the breakfast gong rang, and Myra jumped up, awkwardly dragged her sleeve down. Without looking left or right, her arm pressed tightly against her, she melted around the corner of the shed, a flurry of furiously clucking chickens in her wake.

They filed past Myra silently, held out their bowls for porridge, each of them studiously averting their eyes from the large bruise on her arm, the edge of which was just visible below the cuff of her sleeve.

'She didn't fall,' Ellen muttered. 'How would you fall onto the *top* of your arm?'

'But do you really think he was the one who . . .' Lucy swallowed as they slid onto the bench, hunching over their bowls.

'That I believe in a heartbeat.' Red frowned. 'Maybe we should ask the Land Army to reassign us, Kit.'

'I don't know how much longer I can stay,' Lucy agreed. 'He's dangerous, that man.'

'We're here to bring in the harvest,' Kit said severely. 'This is exactly what the WLA frowns on, leaving when the going gets tough. And we talked with the lord only yesterday; let's see what happens.'

'Aristocrats never side with the masses,' Red said scathingly. 'They just want us quiet and functioning.'

'Hardwick will have to pay us eventually,' Joan pointed out.

'Yes, when he's done bullying us,' Lucy said bitterly.

Violet listened to them without saying anything, keeping her face carefully neutral to disguise her panic. She couldn't leave Winterbourne, Duffy had been very clear about that. Her paperwork had got her this far but would most likely not stand up to any further scrutiny, he'd said. And the thought of her masquerade falling apart and revealing her for who she really was was unbearable. Not just because she didn't want them to know that other part of her, so different from them, so much less than them, but also because she didn't want to give up the freedom of being Lily, not yet.

But the others disbanding and leaving her behind didn't bear thinking about either. Her heart felt heavy when she imagined having to say goodbye, and for the first time she realised just how much, despite Hardwick and the back-breaking work, despite the early mornings, the curfew, the isolation from the other workers, she didn't want this to end. Not when she was – she frowned down at her spoon, saw her fingers tighten around the handle – *happy*. She belonged with these girls, these friends, she wanted to keep being part of their world.

'It would be nice to stay together.' Joan seemed to echo her thoughts.

'Yeah,' Red said eagerly. 'We could use that as a selling point: seasoned work crew, ready for anything.'

'No one would take a whole group of us this late in the year.' Kit shook her head. 'If anyone wants to be reassigned, I can't keep you from asking. But if they need us here over the winter, we should count our blessings and stick it out like we're meant to do. And then, come spring, we could apply for a new posting, all of us together.'

A pause fell, then, one by one, the others nodded. Red's eyes strayed briefly to the bruise on Myra's arm, and she threw Violet a questioning look, but Violet only felt the overpowering giddiness of relief.

'I'm in,' she said firmly.

At first, Hardwick barely spared them a glance when they emerged from the canteen and joined the hastily assembled workforce under the bell tower. Instead, he proceeded to reel off the tightened regulations. Blackout was to be observed more strictly than ever. All staff were instructed to congregate in the apple sheds – centrally located, partially underground and considered the safest space away from the house – the moment the gong sounded for two minutes without stopping. Everyone was to keep an eye to the sky at all times, and bringing in the apples was of the highest priority now, above any other farming work across the estate, just in case the Germans decided to step up the level of attack on this part of England.

Listening to his rapid-fire staccato of orders, Violet tried to imagine what he'd done to Myra. Had he crept into her room at night? Had he lain in wait for her this morning? Had he cut or punched or twisted her arm, leaving hand-shaped bruises on his daughter's smooth, pale skin? The feeling of relief that they were all going to stay together slowly ebbed, and the porridge she'd just eaten churned in her stomach as her eyes found the sundial and tracked the three words running along the bottom, the way they always did, wondering if the person who had carved them into the facade had ever stood here waiting for a punishment. *From Light, Darkness* would be a better fit with Hardwick, she thought. She frowned at the exaggerated swirls of the sun, the two crumbling holes gouged out for its eyes, then forced herself to look away and concentrate on the overseer, who had dismissed the rest of the orchard workers and was now waving Kit forward.

'Ask him about the post,' Lucy hissed as Kit followed Hardwick's beckoning hand with extreme reluctance.

They watched them, Hardwick doing all the talking, Kit not saying very much at all, her shoulders sagging until she stood there, round-backed and miserable, nodding in time with his words. They couldn't hear what he said, could only assume it wasn't going to be good, until the end, when Kit asked a final question.

'Post?' he said incredulously. 'The Germans are upon us, the country is going to starve, and you're thinking about writing letters? There's a war on, you know.'

He had deliberately spoken so loudly that people stopped and turned. Face beet-red, Kit slunk back to where the rest of the land girls stood.

'Three demerits each and money docked from our pay,' she whispered miserably. 'And I'm sorry, Lucy, I'll try again about the letters next time.'

Forty-Four

A thin sun was valiantly trying to break through the fog, picking out dew drops and making wet leaves sparkle, and their spirits lifted as they followed the woman with the red-spotted scarf – Susan they had now found out she was called – through the gates and on into the orchards.

'I suppose it could have been worse.' Red's breath curled away in a small cloud. 'We could have been dismissed in disgrace, you know. Come on, let's just get through the day. Things are bound to improve.'

'By the next meal, you mean,' Kit said bitterly, obviously unable to forgive herself for not being able to do better by them.

Once out in the orchards, however, where the ground was padded by grass and the rows of trees made the air smell of wet greenery and ripening fruit, it was easier not to think about Hardwick, especially when Marigold came running down the path to join them, the little leather case she always carried bumping up and down on her back.

'Nanny chasing you again?' Violet smiled. Marigold nodded and giggled, a funny little sound that seemed to surprise her, because she immediately stifled it.

'Pick up the fallen fruit, then shake the boughs gently to see what's ripe to fall next.' Susan was rattling off instructions. 'The riper the better. Set rotten and buggy fruit aside, they'll find a use for it. God knows, at the rate Hitler's going, we'll need every last bit.'

'Any more news from London?' Kit was trying to keep pace, but Susan merely tossed her head and walked faster.

'I think Kit's met her match,' Red whispered to Violet.

'And the navy?' Lucy panted after them.

'Do I look like a newspaper?' Susan said tartly. 'Aren't you listening to the wireless up in your fancy hostel at night?'

Red gave a bark of laughter and some of the other girls smothered incredulous giggles, but Susan frowned at the long-handled picker in Red's hand. 'Hold that straight, or you'll bend the hook,' she snapped. 'He wants you over here, those rows down to the wall. And apparently it's my job to see that you finish, so I'll be back to check.'

'"Fancy hostel",' Red mouthed, wiping her eyes in exaggerated mirth as the red-spotted handkerchief bobbed away.

'They all seem to think we're having wild parties every night in our posh digs,' Ellen said. 'My sister asked was it true we had running hot water and got paid as much as the lord's footmen.'

'Makes you wonder what Hardwick's been saying about us across the valley.' Kit frowned. 'Well, never mind, we'll just have to . . .'

'Work hard,' Violet mouthed, and Red snorted.

Kit stared them down haughtily and then turned to follow Marigold, who had dragged Violet's bucket to the first tree and started picking up apples from the ground.

'We'll divvy up and work down these rows,' she said over her shoulder. 'And Red, if I see you eating more than one apple, I will personally report you to the Ministry of Agriculture. Don't put those in with the ones from the branches.' She turned to Marigold. 'They go in the buckets over there.'

'Kit, I'm betting she's done this before.' Red watched Marigold deftly hook the picker around a branch and shake it gently to check the apples' readiness. 'Why's the ladder padded at the top?' She pointed to the cloth wound around the upper edges.

'So it doesn't hurt the trees.' Marigold reached up and settled the ladder more carefully against the tree trunk. 'You don't want gashes in the bark, it'll let the bugs in. Then you need to paint the trunks, to keep them away.'

'Are we done with lesson time?' Kit put her hands on her hips.

'Oh Kit, she's so clever; do be kind,' Joan tsk-ed.

But Marigold loved being bossed around by Kit, clearly taking it as a sign of being a bona fide part of the group. She refused to laugh at any of Red's jokes and nodded solemnly all the way through Kit's list of instructions; then she followed Violet to their assigned patch and started picking up windfalls, the leather case on her back bobbing up and down above the grass.

'Like a pig rooting for mushrooms,' Red laughed. 'Let's just hope she doesn't pick up any more mangled creatures.'

But Marigold's buckets were among the fullest by midday, and when it became apparent that Hardwick wasn't going to send lunch their way, most likely as additional punishment, she disappeared in the direction of the house and returned dragging a basket. She beamed as a great cheer rang across the clearing.

Violet sat on some burlap sacks with her food, listening to the chat and laughter around her. The sun had become more confident and the breeze wasn't quite as chilly as it rustled through the leaves. Above, skylarks sang, and out of nowhere, Violet felt a sharp, fierce tug of hope. The orchards swallowed all sounds of the outside world, the sky was empty of threat, Hardwick seemed far away, here between the trees, and no one had mentioned leaving Winterbourne again. Her hand strayed to her scars and she rested her fingertips lightly on top of them. Maybe it would be all right. Maybe she'd never need to reveal her masquerade, and one day she'd wake up to find that Violet had simply become Lily for good.

She started a little as Marigold plopped down next to her, her hands full of long grass stems, late wild flowers and sprigs of heather. As around them talk turned once again to the German planes, she started to weave a thick braid.

'London's more or less ruined.' Ellen leaned forward. 'I heard two women talking about it after breakfast. It's only a matter of time until we break.'

'We will never break,' Kit said angrily. 'And any more of that unpatriotic talk and I'll personally find you another posting, far away and worse than here.'

'She didn't mean it, of course,' Joan said. 'I heard them too, though. It's frightening.'

Ellen swallowed. 'The Netherlands gone, France fallen, the Atlantic a mess—'

'Stop,' Violet said sharply as Lucy's face went ashen.

Ellen clapped her hands in front of her mouth, looking utterly horrified. 'I'm sorry, Luce, I'm such an idiot, I didn't think.'

The girls were scooting closer to Lucy and murmuring consolingly when Violet realised that Marigold's small, rustling presence next to her was gone.

'She popped up and ran off.' Red rooted through the basket and heroically handed Lucy the last cheese sandwich.

Violet found the little girl all the way at the end of the row. Sitting with her back against a wooden shed wall, she had opened the leather case she carried on her back and taken out its contents. A child's gas mask lay carelessly off to the side, but the main purpose of the bag was to hold a camera. Not one of the big old-fashioned ones that opened at the top, but a smaller, more compact model. Marigold was cradling it in her lap, winding the leather strap through her fingers.

Violet thought back to the glass display case in the drawing room and Oliver's beautiful black-and-white photos.

'You're a photographer too?' she asked lightly.

'It's not mine,' Marigold said in her small, soft voice. 'I'm just minding it.'

'Ah.' Violet sat down next to her, leaning against the wall.

'I do know how to use it, though.' She stroked the little knobs on the top. 'Oliver showed me. I was going to be his apprentice,' she spelled the word out carefully. 'But he's in France. He fell there. Falling, that's what you say when someone dies.'

'Yes,' Violet managed.

'They haven't brought him home yet. But I wonder if they will sometime?'

Violet, who had no idea what happened to the war dead, swallowed repeatedly. 'I . . . I don't know.'

'I should so like to see him again.' Marigold cradled the camera. 'So I know for sure, you see. Maybe they made a mistake, thought he was someone else. They all look the same, after all, in their uniform. What if he got lost and they just *thought* it was him?'

Violet looked down at Marigold's smudged face, hair framing her eyes like a feathery halo, and with every fibre of her being she wanted to say that there was still hope. She thought back to the mangled rabbit, to Myra's shrine, to the pitter-patter of soil on Romy's coffin, and took a deep breath.

'They won't have made a mistake, darling. They wouldn't put the family through terrible news like that if they weren't totally sure.' She put her arms around the little girl, felt the small ribcage shudder. 'I'm sorry.'

From somewhere close by came a shout.

'Kit, stop fussing.' Red could be heard, exasperated. 'They're here somewhere. That girl knows her way around the estate better than anyone.'

There was a rustle, and then Red, Joan and Kit came out from between the trees.

'Oh dear,' Joan said when she saw Marigold's tear-stained face.

'They're here,' Red called over her shoulder, and a moment later, Ellen, Lucy and the rest popped out from the trees.

'No more talking about France,' Violet said as Joan and Red

crouched low, murmuring something, and the others stood in a commiserating circle. Kit surveyed them, then pushed through and held out her hand. 'Come on, Marigold, let's get back to work, shall we?' Her voice was just brisk enough to get the girl's attention, but kind as well. Marigold nodded, slid the camera back into the case and slowly climbed to her feet.

'I think I need a lesson with that picker tool,' Red announced.

'You certainly do, you've been dropping more apples on the ground than in the bucket,' Ellen said, then hastened to add, 'No she hasn't Kit, honest, I was just saying it to cheer things up, it's not that bad really . . .'

'I've found some plushy grass for your braid.' Lucy patted Marigold's back and Kate gave her a handkerchief, pulling her into the middle of the group as they walked back to their row.

Later, as the light started to wane, the little kitchen maid appeared. Could Miss Marigold please come home? Marigold shook her head violently, the braid – now woven into a tight wreath – hanging off one arm.

'Darling, we would take you with us to eat, but it's all topsy-turvy with the blackout and everyone nervous, and we're still in such trouble about the sloes,' Violet said gently. 'You're better off at the house.'

Marigold looked at her pleadingly and Violet sighed. 'Please pass on the message that she'll be eating with us,' she said. 'I'll bring her back afterwards.' She made her voice firm and final, overriding any anguished spluttering from the maid about what 'Nanny' and 'Cook' would say. Red raised her eyebrows in admiration as Marigold skipped ahead to the canteen, clearly worried that they might change their minds.

'Poor little mite,' Joan said. '*Nanny. Cook.* What kind of family is that for her? I guess they're all taken up with their own sadness, but still, she seems . . . I don't know . . .'

'It's as if they've forgotten about her,' Violet said. 'She'll just have to be with us, and if you say one thing about her slowing us down . . .' she snapped at Kit, who'd just opened her mouth.

'I wasn't going to, honest.' Kit held up her hands and laughed. 'She's very good at farm work. But now we know what gets your goat, Lily. A little injustice and you start taking charge. How you sent that maid packing was impressive. Next thing we know you'll be taking on Lord Crowden himself.'

Forty-Five

Taking on Lord Crowden. Violet stared down at her soup. If only they knew, Kit and the others. About the playhouse, the charged air, Violet's constantly churned-up insides whenever she thought about it all. Would they be horrified but secretly thrilled? Would they disapprove or encourage her? Swinging wildly from one emotion to another herself, Violet was fairly certain they would frown on it. As they should. She shouldn't have been in the play-house. It was wrong, every which way you looked at it, and it would be wrong to go back and meet him again.

It hadn't *felt* wrong, though. It had felt lovely and wild and free. But no, she told herself sternly, picking up her spoon. She wouldn't go and see him again. Not just because it was improper but also because it was dangerous. She shouldn't be out on the estate at night. Hardwick hadn't stopped shouting and ordering people about all day, and everyone worried whether there would be more planes that evening. And yet . . .

'Where do you think you're going?' Hardwick barked when he saw Violet holding Marigold's wreath while she put her coat on.

'Taking her back to the big house, Mr Hardwick. Sir.' Violet stepped in front of Marigold, who, she'd noticed, always gave the overseer a careful berth.

Hardwick narrowed his eyes. He didn't like Marigold's pres-ence among them one bit but clearly couldn't do anything about it without openly slighting a member of the family.

'You go alone, no torch, and see that you don't dawdle,' he said coldly, clearly keeping himself from adding that if she broke her neck in the dark or was shot down by German planes, then good riddance to her.

They passed Myra on their way out. There was a small bulge beneath her sleeve to indicate that she'd wrapped a bandage around her arm. Violet hadn't spoken to her since the air raid, but she'd had a lot of time to think about her angry words and to wonder what it would be like to be Hardwick's drudge, to live with the humiliations, the indignity of being put down in front of everyone, and to be hurt by him. She couldn't quite put her finger on it, but it all seemed to come back to Silvia, the woman they'd glimpsed in the photo from the urn, with the same dark curls as Myra and the same provocative slant to her eyes. Little things began to make sense. Myra was always in the same sack-like dress and kerchief, as if Hardwick was deliberately trying to make her ugly and invisible, as if he couldn't bear the sight of her. Violet was no great people-reader, and she was reluctant to think about Hardwick in great detail at all, but it almost felt like he was punishing Myra every day for being her mother's daughter.

'Marigold, about your wreath,' she whispered. 'I wondered if you might like it to be a gift for someone?'

Marigold let the wreath slide down her arm, held it out to Violet. It was beautiful, the grasses and heather woven into a pattern, little bits sticking up artfully, here and there an empty acorn shell tucked between the folds.

'Not me,' Violet quickly said. 'Her.' She nodded at Myra, now sweeping the canteen floor with angry, jerky jabs of the broom.

Marigold frowned censoriously. 'She got you in trouble.'

'Yes, I know,' Violet said. 'But I think she needs cheering up. She'd love it, it's so pretty.'

She fished the small pot of Miss Cox's salve out of her pocket and carefully inserted it into one of the wreath's folds, then they hung it on the edge of the trolley where Myra wouldn't miss it before hurrying down the path and out of sight.

'Is that Marigold?' an impatient voice enquired sharply from inside the house the moment Hawkins opened the door.

'Bye, Marigold.' Violet hastily retreated.

Too late.

'Ah, the land girl.' Guy Crowden stood in the doorway, dressed in riding clothes and a warm jacket. 'Hawkins, accompany my sister upstairs and make sure,' he gave Marigold a withering stare, 'that you deliver her safely into Nanny's hands. And put that camera back in the drawing room where it belongs. You'll break it.'

He barely waited for Marigold to be across the threshold before he stepped outside and closed the door. 'You came,' he said, half disbelieving, half smugly delighted.

'To drop off your sister.' Violet backed away quickly. 'I'm expected back at the barn; curfew is very strict now.'

'Cloudy tonight,' he said. 'Highly unlikely we'll see any action. I'll walk you back.'

'I'm fine, really,' Violet said, but he had already started steering her down the path.

'I can't possibly have a land girl under my protection stumbling alone through the darkness.'

She tried to bristle at his high-handedness, but the smile in his voice and the thrill of those words, 'under my protection', made her fall in step with him. He must have felt her struggle, because he laughed softly and tucked her arm through his. 'Good girl. Now don't fight me any more; I don't want to waste our time together.'

They walked slowly, Violet matching his halting gait, scanning the dark, moody sky every now and then. But Guy had been right, and the only sounds were those of the trees moving above and the long grasses restlessly scratching in the wind.

'You would have stood me up tonight, wouldn't you?' he said accusingly as they turned a corner. 'That way, through the kitchen garden; it's the same direction, just nicer,' he added exasperatedly when she stopped in her tracks. 'It would have

341

been so cruel, you know. I would have had to pour my heart out to poor Merry again.'

Violet was glad she had to duck under the low-hanging branches of a tree. Guy said things you only ever read in novels, delivered with an air of entitlement that brooked no argument and was both thrilling and infuriating.

'I spent the day with your sister,' she said, deliberately not entering into the conversation he wanted to have.

He made an irritated noise. 'Just send her packing the moment she's a nuisance.'

'I won't do anything of the sort,' Violet said, shocked. 'She is absolutely starved of human company – and not Nanny's kind, let me tell you that.'

'She's just a little girl,' Guy said dismissively. 'Children should be—'

But Violet had stopped and pulled her arm from his so abruptly that he had to reach for a tree to steady himself.

'Children need someone to talk to too,' she said sharply. 'Marigold is grieving, just like everyone else, maybe more so because she doesn't really understand what happened and no one will take the time to explain things to her. She's carrying around that camera like a baby because she misses your brother, and all you do is shout at her.'

'She is well taken care of,' Guy said stiffly. 'She's got Nanny, she's forever underfoot in the kitchens, and now she's apparently got you, too.' He crossed his arms. 'Which is more than I can say for myself.'

'But it's you who is ultimately responsible for her,' Violet said angrily. 'You and your mother.' She remembered her own mother's coldness, the tirade of accusations after the air raid. 'That's what family should do, draw together.' Her voice was raw with sudden tears. 'Be loved, regardless of what has happened.'

'Here we go again, you giving me a lecture.' He scowled at her.

'She's so lost, Guy, so alone . . .'

He started when she said his name, and then exhaled, his shoulders stooped. He didn't look at her but down at the ground, barely visible in the darkness.

'She loved him best of all,' he said eventually. 'She doesn't remember anything about Father; he died just after she was born. It was always Oliver. They were so similar, too, both batty about animals and horses, both rooted here at Winterbourne, part of it all the way I never was. And Mother – she was so young when she married Father. She came over from Bath, never quite managed to feel at home here, and certainly not once he was gone.' He leaned against the broad trunk of the walnut tree. 'We were so far apart in age, the three of us, I never really took any notice of Marigold. Olly was more of a father to her, I suppose, than anything else.'

'She's just lovely,' Violet said softly. 'So bright and precious. She'll love you for ever, if you'll let her. I know you don't really want to be here, having to take charge, Guy, but she's here now, and so you have to be too.'

'And God knows, this is where I'll be until the day I die.' He thrust his hands through his hair, then unexpectedly he reached for her hand. 'I like it when you say my name. I'll talk to Mother about her, we'll find a solution. I promise.'

'She doesn't need a solution.' Violet frowned. 'She needs—'

'Hush now. I said I will see to it,' he said firmly.

She tried to pull away towards the path, but he held her back easily, even with his bad leg. 'Don't go yet; surely you won't be missed this quickly? And if you are, I can always have a word—'

'No!' Violet said, alarmed. 'There's no need for words, I don't want—'

'Then you have to stay. And you have to meet me again tomorrow night. Eight o'clock, at the stables.'

'Blackmail.' She glowered. 'Very nice.'

'Desperate times call for desperate measure.' He pulled at her again, gently but insistently, fixing her with his eyes until she acquiesced, felt his shoulders touch hers, his arms lift – and then, before she had any chance to stop things, he kissed her.

It was a real kiss, the kind that she and Romy had giggled about as girls, but it was nothing like she'd imagined then. *She* was nothing like who she thought she'd be. This daring woman whose arms came up around Guy's neck, who pressed her whole body against him hungrily the moment their lips connected. She could feel his warmth all the way through her coat, felt a trembling as he gathered her into him, one hand sliding up her back to curl around her head, almost as if he was afraid she would bolt otherwise. When they finally broke apart, he didn't let her go far, but kept his hands splayed across her shoulder blades and rested his forehead against hers, his mouth smiling. He kissed her again, more gently now, his hand travelling slowly across her cheek, his thumb tracing the curve of her lower lip until she was soft and fluid and would have done anything he asked of her.

'Lily,' he whispered, and she blinked, suddenly disorientated. Lily? Who was it really who was so bold as to run her hand across this man's shoulder and down his arm, lean in for another kiss? Who had stopped thinking about how to explain her absence to the other girls and was melting, helpless and eager? But time dissolved inside the tight circle of their arms, was borne away on the breeze, and little by little, who she was ceased to matter altogether.

Forty-Six

The kiss. That glorious, unstoppable, thrilling kiss that made Violet feverish with longing and cold with dread. Ironically, it was the very gloriousness of it that felt most wrong, because – she was hot with shame every time she thought about it, and she thought about it a *lot* – it had erased every ounce of self-control and turned her into a wild, wanton creature without a will of her own.

Not going back, she told herself as they got up the following day, assembled under the sundial, received their instructions and went out into the orchards. *Not going back*, she said, averting her eyes from Marigold's disappointment when she suggested she return with the kitchen maid that evening.

The weather stayed foggy and damp as land girls and orchard workers swarmed across the Winterbourne estate to pick apples, pears and the last of the plums. There was no more sight or sound of German planes, and little by little they felt safe again, stopped scanning the horizon and straining to listen. Myra didn't reference the appearance of the wreath, but Violet, who now made everyone put their dishes on the trolley and wipe down the tables, thought that the girl's shoulders weren't quite as tense, her scowl not nearly as angry when they left the canteen in the mornings.

Two days after Violet's clandestine meeting with Guy, dawn broke clear and cloudless. The grass was white with frost as they walked to their assigned patches, dew hung like pearls on leaves and branches and the air smelled smoky.

'Can you show me one more time?' Violet asked impatiently.

Marigold raised the long picker, plucked two selected apples from up high and rolled them into the fabric sleeve. Someone at the house must have had a word, because she was now officially allowed to join the land girls every morning, dressed for orchard work with proper boots, the camera still slung across her back. After their conversation about Oliver, she had reverted to her silent, watchful self, keeping close to Violet, listening in without much more than nods and shy half-smiles.

'I think this is broken,' Violet grumbled when she'd tried to imitate Marigold and twisted the cord for the fifth time. Marigold stifled a giggle and climbed up the ladder.

'You know,' Violet said as the little girl handed down apples, 'it's all right to laugh and be cheerful. Oliver would be so proud of you.'

Marigold kept her eyes on the nubbly red and yellow shapes passing through her hands.

'He loved the orchards, didn't he?' Violet unhooked the full pail off the top of the ladder. 'He'd be so pleased that you're out here with us, helping with the harvest, being so clever about the trees and how things are done. You know more about this than any of us, maybe even . . .' she gave an exaggerated grimace and lowered her voice to a comical conspiratorial hush, 'Mr *Hardwick*.'

Marigold's hands finally stilled. 'He's a good manager, Oliver always said.'

'Sure. But,' Violet raised her eyebrows, 'you could be running the estate with your brother one day.'

Marigold quickly shook her head and climbed higher. 'Mr Hardwick makes me afraid.'

'He's not in charge, though; *you* are, you and G— I mean, your brother.'

From somewhere down the line of trees, they heard Kit whistle for elevenses, and Marigold, who loved the times when they were all together, fished for the top of the ladder with her foot.

'Left,' Violet said, trying to catch her flailing foot, 'no, the other . . .'

There was a ripping sound and Marigold came sliding down fast, the camera clattering on her back, the strap catching on a branch.

'Jump,' Violet shouted. 'You'll get stuck on that bit . . . *Jump*, Marigold.'

She was already mentally preparing herself for having to tell Guy that his sister had been dismembered by the broken branch halfway down when Marigold suddenly launched herself off the tree, small body arched, the camera whirling as Violet ran to catch her. The impact sent them rolling through the long grass, where they finally came to rest in a tousled, muddy heap, laughing breathlessly.

'*And* you know how to fly!' Violet said. 'Clever girl. Although I hope we haven't broken that camera.'

But it was fine, and they lay in the grass for a moment, cold seeping into their shoulder blades as they looked up at the billowing clouds racing across the deep blue, the leaves above them tinged a delicate shade of pink and orange. Marigold scooted closer, rested her head on Violet's shoulder. 'It's so beautiful,' she whispered.

'Yes it is,' Violet said. 'I know it doesn't seem as though the future looks anything but bleak. But there will be a time where it feels good again to laugh and talk about it all, or to cry.'

She gently thumbed away the tears clinging to Marigold's lashes and rested her chin against her forehead, until Kit appeared and tartly enquired whether it was too much to ask for them to postpone their mid-morning nap in the face of national need, or if she should let Red eat all the sandwiches after all.

Checking on them a little later, Susan finally thawed enough to say, rather grudgingly, that the country might stand a chance after all if all of *them land girls* were as unfussy about things as they were.

'It's her.' Red jabbed her thumb at Kit, who was striding up and down the rows, inspecting progress. 'She's worse than Hardwick at times, honest.'

Susan blanched and took off at a trot, and Kit, worried that she'd tattle the comment to Hardwick, whipped them into such a picking frenzy that they had cleared their patch by mid afternoon.

They walked into the stable yard just in time to see a horse and cart pull up. But instead of picking equipment, apple crates or people, it was carrying . . .

'Bicycles!' Red screeched.

It was a rather motley collection of five bikes in all shapes and sizes, some more ancient than others, painted black with *WLA* spelled out in crooked letters. The girls surged forward and ringed the cart, making the horse shy in alarm, then fell on the bicycles the moment they were unloaded, touching handlebars, ringing rusty bells. More laughter as they started squabbling good-naturedly over who was going to ride first.

'The lord came good,' Joan said fervently. 'These could change *everything*.'

'They're not manna from heaven.' Kit rolled her eyes. 'If Hardwick doesn't let us leave the estate, it doesn't matter that we have transport.'

'But surely, if the lord has gone to the trouble to get these for us, Hardwick can't keep us from using them,' Ellen said.

'Could we please stop calling him *the lord*,' Violet asked waspishly. 'He's not God.'

'Don't be a spoilsport, Lily,' Red breathed. 'They're gorgeous.'

The hubbub had drawn more people into the yard, and a groom shouted encouragement as Red mounted the first bike and whizzed around the excited fray. Myra stopped, holding an armful of hay, her face almost painfully envious as she watched

Red aim straight for two girls wrangling over a bike and send them flying.

'Lily!' Red shouted. 'Come on! Marigold can go on your back.'

Violet pulled Marigold out of Red's way as she came flying by, Lucy now in hot pursuit. Joan, statuesque but surprisingly nimble, had claimed what looked like a delivery bike with heavy-duty baskets attached front and back.

'They've gone mad,' Kit said. But she laughed as she saw Red career in a figure of eight, almost lose her balance, right herself with her foot and shoot forward again – straight past Hardwick coming down the path with a pile of papers.

'What on earth is going on here?' His voice cut through the melee like a gunshot. 'Stop this at once.'

It took him a few minutes to restore order. Myra melted around the corner, although Violet could see her hovering, watching as her father sent the other workers scurrying back to their tasks and ordered the land girls to collect the bicycles scattered across the stable yard. 'Inning,' he barked in the groom's direction.

'Mr Hardwick.' Inning advanced nervously.

'Take this lot away.' Hardwick swept his hand at the bikes.

Throwing the land girls an apologetic glance, Inning picked one up, dusted it off and started wheeling it across the yard. 'Er, where would you like them, Mr Hardwick?'

Hardwick looked around, but before he could jab his hand impatiently at one of the sheds, a voice rang out from across the yard.

'Oh good, they've arrived.'

Forty-Seven

'It's the lord,' someone hissed. 'It's *him*.'

Violet's heart stopped, then thudded back into her chest, started beating again wildly, joyfully, as Guy Crowden walked into the yard, dressed in the dark jacket that fitted his shoulders so well, smiling that wry smile of his. *Not going back*, she thought despairingly, *not going back*.

'So, how are they?' he said in a friendly way. He was addressing Kit, but Violet noticed that his eyes were roving across the group, realised he was looking for her, and how absurdly thrilled she was by that fact.

Most of the land girls had lapsed into an awestruck silence at the presence of a real-life, genuine lord in their midst, one or two, Violet noticed, smoothing down their hair before freezing at a particularly vicious scowl from Hardwick.

'Your lordship.' His voice was polite but not servile. 'I'm sorry if you were disturbed, we were just about to—'

'I wasn't disturbed,' Guy Crowden cut in. 'I saw the bikes being delivered from the window and thought I'd come and see for myself.' His eyes were still combing the group, until finally – and Violet wasn't remotely surprised, because her face was as red as a beacon – alighting on her right at the back. His smile deepened.

'Like that, is it?' Red murmured to Violet. 'I did think there was a frisson.'

'You sure know some big words,' Violet muttered.

'A fairy tale.' Red clasped her hands together in mock rapture. 'The land girl and the lord.'

'There is no "and" in there anywhere,' Violet hissed, as

Hardwick, following Guy's gaze, frowned at her. 'Stop it, or I'll be in trouble.'

'I wondered if you could spare a few land girls,' Guy said amiably.

This Hardwick had clearly not expected. His polite countenance wavered for a second, but his tone when he answered was as firm and confident as before. 'I was about to send them back to work, your lordship.'

'Well, I need someone to run up to the village,' Guy said, a little impatiently.

Hardwick held himself straighter. 'The harvest . . .' he began.

'I know, I know, I wouldn't take all of them, but I have an urgent letter to be dropped off at the post office and—'

There was a loud gasp, and then Lucy pushed through the ranks. 'I'll do it,' she said, so quickly that the words ran together. 'Please may I? Please? We've finished picking and I can ride uphill very fast. I'd be back in no time.'

Guy looked a little startled at her eagerness and, caught off guard, Hardwick reared up, but before he could say anything, Guy answered, sounding bemused.

'Of course you may.'

'Oh thank you, *thank* you,' Lucy breathed. Studiously avoiding Hardwick's glare, she sidled the other way and picked up a bike.

'Four would do, Hardwick.' Guy turned to the overseer. 'The house staff are all working flat out. We need supplies picked up from the village shop and I have to get this letter off to London today. You wouldn't be put out at all; they could use the bicycles to carry the things back. After all, that's what they're there for, to relieve you.'

It seemed to take Hardwick an enormous effort now to keep his expression even.

'Very well, my lord,' he finally ground out. He was about to lift his hand to choose the messengers when Guy did it for him.

'You,' he said to Red, 'and you' – Joan – 'oh, and you.' He pointed at Violet.

Marigold urgently tugged on Violet's sleeve.

'Can Marigold please also come?' Violet asked, careful not to look at him directly but flushing nonetheless.

He grinned. 'Are you having fun?' he asked his sister, who nodded shyly and bobbed up and down on her toes.

'The rest are all yours, Hardwick. Oh,' he seemed to remember something, 'and it's pay day tomorrow, isn't it? I'm sure they're looking forward to receiving their wages.'

The land girls drew in a startled breath but didn't dare look at each other as, with a casual nod, Guy Crowden dismissed Hardwick, who had no choice but to round up the rest of the land girls and sweep them ahead of him along with the last of his dignity. 'Surely you cannot be finished already,' he could be heard barking at Kit, who stammered that they were and had delivered all their apples, before they were lost from sight.

'Run along to the kitchen,' Guy told Red. 'Mrs Dawson will provide you with baskets and the lists. You two can teach my sister the rudiments of bicycle riding. And you,' he smiled at Violet, 'come and get the letter.'

He walked quickly towards the house, and the moment they were out of sight of the others, he clamped a hand around her wrist. 'I don't think I've ever been stood up like this,' he said darkly.

'We all need new experiences every now and then.' Violet tugged at her wrist. 'Let me go.'

'I was waiting for you at the stables.'

His grip slackened but she didn't pull away. 'Look,' she said in a low voice. 'Sneaking around. Forbidden meetings. It's not how I imagine . . .' She groped for a word that wasn't *love*, precisely.

'Your life?' he suggested.

'Yes.' She narrowed her eyes at him. 'You can make fun of me all you want, but it's not how I want things to go.'

There was a pause as they both digested the deeper meaning of the word 'things'.

'Who are you really, Miss Burns?' he asked slowly. 'You're no land girl, I know that much.'

She exhaled slowly, carefully. 'I can be whatever I want. Why can't I be a land girl?'

He came closer, and she looked into his eyes, dark grey, lash-fringed and beautiful. For one mad second she thought he would kiss her, right here, and for an even madder second she leaned in, was desperate for him to do exactly that.

Instead, he pulled a thick envelope out of his coat, held it out to her.

'You'll tell me,' he said. 'Tonight, at the stables. Or I'll come and fetch you myself.'

'You what?' Red stared at Violet, momentarily lost for words.

'I can't ride a bicycle,' Violet said hotly. 'So what?'

'You should have said.' Joan shook her head. 'He could have sent someone else.'

'Well, he wasn't hanging about discussing things, was he?'

Violet flushed every time the letter crackled inside her coat and had to resist the impulse to slip her hand in and actually stroke it. Instead, she fumbled for Romy's necklace, ran her fingers along the chain and felt her heart slow a fraction.

'I'll show you.' Clearly anxious to go, Lucy leaned her bike against a shed. 'Put your foot up there.' She moved Violet's foot. 'And push forward.'

'Really lean into it,' Joan urged.

'And go fast, it's easier,' Red instructed. 'Marigold, you're with me.'

'You should probably stay,' Violet said to Marigold. 'This seems terribly unsafe.'

But Marigold had already climbed onto the back of Red's bike and Joan was pedalling down the lane.

It took Violet two tries and an almost-tumble, but eventually, dusty and more than a little sweaty, she was up, weaving and bumping over the packed dirt.

'You got it, Lily! Now go faster,' Lucy shouted.

Violet stood up, using her weight to push down the pedals. The bike obediently shot forward. She caught her balance just in time, pushed down again until she was closing on Red and Marigold.

'I'm riding a bicycle!' she shouted, pumping the pedals furiously to keep moving.

'You are!' Marigold called as Violet swerved around a big hole, teetering dangerously. God, if only her mother could see her now. Or Duffy, or Romy . . .

She pushed harder, passing Red, then Joan, the chapel a golden blur by the wayside as she shot past.

'Wait for us,' Red bellowed, but Violet had reached the top of the small incline from where she'd go straight down towards the village. She lifted her legs up and let the pedals whip around until it felt like she was flying. Guy and Hardwick, her mother, Duffy and Romy, they all faded in the rush of the wind whipping across her face, her hair streaming behind her, her heart bursting with hope.

'Brake, Lily, brake!' Marigold squeaked behind her, and Violet's heart lifted even further. Yes! Lily could ride a bicycle and stand up for herself, Lily could outrun them, outfly them all. She could finally be free.

'Slow down!' Red shrieked as the first houses came into view, and that was when it happened. Confused – how did one brake again? – Violet dropped her feet, got them caught in the flying pedals. The bike juddered and spun. With surprising presence of mind, she steered towards a field on the right, freshly ploughed and soft-looking, and let go of the handlebars.

'That was so worth it.' Violet brushed at the muddy patches on her trousers and grinned happily. 'I'm telling you, wherever I end up in the world, there'd better be a bicycle there.'

'Let's go to the shop first to drop off the list, then the post office,' Joan said as they dismounted in the village square. 'Although I wish Kit was here to scuttle us about. She always knows what to do.'

'It's the great curse of women everywhere, forced to be followers,' Red said, and barged into the first shop with a hearty 'Good afternoon.'

Having handed over the list and been told to pick up the groceries in half an hour, they chained their bicycles to a nearby fence post.

'Can't be too careful,' Red told Marigold. 'Never forget, the world's full of bad people.' Marigold nodded solemnly. 'Just look at our very own Mr Hardwick. If he could get away with it, he'd murder us in our beds.'

'For heaven's sake, Red,' Violet hissed when two women hovering at the stoop of the shop frowned in their direction. 'You can't go saying things like that. Hardwick is very well respected in the village.'

'Must be all that flower-arranging he does in church,' Red said dismissively. 'He's really a woman in disguise,' she added to wide-eyed Marigold. 'Or he's buying himself a place in heaven.'

The women stuck their heads together, whispered heatedly.

'You've done it now, Red.' Joan shooed them down the road towards the post office. 'That'll go straight back to Hardwick.'

'There it is,' Lucy said excitedly, and before they could move, she was across the street.

'Quickly.' Violet motioned the others to follow, which was just as well, because inside the small building housing the post office, Lucy was practically climbing across the counter.

'I can't just hand over the post for the house.' The woman was batting away her hands as Lucy scrabbled hysterically at the edge of the counter.

'But you must have *some* letters for us, surely,' she sobbed.

'Lucy!' Violet lifted her off the counter. 'Help me,' she panted, and Red dragged Lucy bodily backwards while Marigold darted around anxiously offering her a handkerchief and the other half of a sweetie she'd been given in the shop.

'Ask her,' Lucy howled, startling Marigold into abandoning all efforts at consolation and retreating into a corner.

'Good afternoon.' Violet's voice was cool and crisp. 'We're the land girls at Winterbourne.' The woman regarded her warily, but at least she'd lowered her arms. 'First, I have this for you.' She extracted Guy's letter from her coat. 'And then I wonder if you might be able to help us with something else. We seem not to receive any letters at all, haven't for several weeks. Under-standably, we're concerned.'

She felt Marigold's eyes on her and stood a little straighter. 'Now, I know your staff are pushed for time, so we're offering to make things easier for you and take the post back with us.'

'I'm not going to just hand over a sack of post to a stranger,' the woman muttered, although she sounded more conciliatory.

'Of course—' Violet began, but the woman interrupted her.

'And anyway, I've been sending down your letters every other day, along with the rest of the estate post.'

Forty-Eight

'This means war,' Red said grimly.

'Don't you think there's enough of that around here?' Kit snapped.

'We have to talk to him,' Lucy said wildly. 'Now.'

'Well . . .' Kit looked unsure. 'I suppose we've finished our chores and . . .'

'Of course.' Red rolled her eyes. 'Even if he'd just strangled your sister, you'd make sure you'd finished the day's assignment before you went to identify her body.'

'. . . we can ask him to hand over the letters,' Kit finished, pointedly turning her back on Red.

'I just can't believe it,' Lucy was saying over and over again. 'All this time, Matthew's letters have been right here, and I've been worrying myself sick, and he's too spiteful, too mean . . .'

There had been no whooping or shouting on their way back. The maid had been watching out for them and immediately shepherded Marigold inside for tea with her mother, leaving Lucy, Red, Violet and Joan to join the others in the canteen. No one had much of an appetite once they heard about the scene at the post office.

'Come on, let's get out of here,' Joan finally said, putting down her fork, and they deposited their dishes on the trolley and stepped outside into the stable yard, looking past the arch-way towards Hardwick's office.

'So what do we do?' Kit said uncertainly.

'Ask Hardwick to hand our letters over,' Lucy said promptly. 'And if he doesn't, we'll talk to the lord again. *I* will go and talk to him; he seemed nice.'

'We can't constantly run to a man to sort out our troubles,' Red said loftily. 'We're fully able to stand up to—'

'Oh, shut up, Red, shut the hell up,' Kit howled. 'I swear one of these days I'll forget myself and strangle you—'

'He's in,' Violet cut across them as someone settled the blackout curtains across the windows of the office.

'Okay, he always wants us to come in on our own, two at the most,' Kit said. 'So why don't I go, and Joan?'

But Joan shook her head in horror. 'Red can go, seeing as she's ever so keen.'

'Red is going nowhere.' Kit straightened her shoulders. 'Lily, you come with me.'

Violet was extremely reluctant. 'Why does he not want more than two?'

'I have no idea,' Kit said. 'But we're trying to butter him up into handing over those letters.'

'I hate that creep.' Lucy's voice was bitter. 'Why is he allowed to stay in England, being vile and horrid, while others are having to leave, possibly never to return?'

Violet squeezed her arm. 'Your Matthew is a hero,' she said firmly. 'Hardwick is and always will be a coward. That's what bullies are, they're cowards.'

She lifted her head just in time to see Joan's eyes widen in terror, then turned slowly to find Hardwick standing there. He had heard her, she thought, panicked, he *had* to have heard her. But only the tiniest flicker in his eyes gave a hint of what was going on behind his impassive, pale face.

'Mr Hardwick,' Kit said nervously. 'Ever so sorry to disturb. We've come to discuss something that's been on our minds.'

'Two at a time.' He disappeared into the shadowy interior of his office. Violet watched him go, and every fibre of her being refused to follow him, the thought of standing like sinners in front of that big desk unbearable.

'No,' she said suddenly. 'We'll all go in. Regardless of what he says. We'll all squeeze into the room, then he can't pick out individuals.'

There was a moment of stunned silence, then Joan said, 'Lily, I really don't think . . .'

But Kit nodded fervently. 'Best idea ever.'

'Ooh,' Red breathed, 'it'll be like those people all squeezing into a telephone box for a laugh; I saw a picture in the papers.'

One by one they pushed into the office. Hardwick, who had kept his eyes on the ledger he'd been reading, looked up and started slightly when he saw them all packed tightly in front of his desk. But before he could order them to leave, or say anything else at all, Lucy jostled her way to the front.

'We know you have our letters,' she said. 'And we'd like them right now.'

Violet might have phrased the request slightly differently, but she murmured her assent along with the rest of the group, which swayed and moved, crowding around the desk until they'd practically surrounded Hardwick.

'How dare you come in here demanding things?' he said coldly.

'Mr Hardwick. Sir,' Kit said. 'The postmistress told us you had them. Just hand them over and we'll be on our way. We won't say anything to anyone either, we'll just take them and leave.'

'Yes, we *would* say something, if we only knew to whom,' Red murmured angrily, but even she didn't dare be openly bold, not when Hardwick's face had lost all expression, his eyes glittering dangerously inside the dark, shadowy room.

'I'll hand out your post along with everyone else's at the end of the working day,' he said curtly. 'If there is something for you, you'll have it then.'

'It *is* the end of the day,' Lucy cut in angrily. 'And anyway, why didn't you give them to us before?'

'Sir,' Kit added faintly.

'We'd really like them now,' Violet said coolly.

'Yes,' Red chimed in, emboldened, 'now is good.'

'Meaning no disrespect, of course,' Joan threw in quickly.

They were too muddled in their delivery, Violet realised, running the gamut between apologetic and brusque. If he didn't want to give them the letters, there was very little they could do about it. His mind seemed to be running along similar lines.

'End of the day.' He turned back to his ledger in clear dismissal.

'You'll give them out now,' a voice said behind them. It was a small, light sound, a little uncertain perhaps, but so unexpected that the land girls drew apart and Hardwick looked up.

Marigold had changed out of her brown jacket and heavy boots, presumably for her tea with Lady Crowden. Now she was wearing a high-collared dress under a beautiful black coat shot through with silver thread. It threw her delicate pallor into stark relief, but the severity of the outfit gave her a sudden maturity. Her hair had been pinned back tightly and her face and hands were clean.

For a moment, Hardwick seemed utterly lost for words – and not only he but everyone else was gaping openly – then he said, clearly striving to sound paternal, 'This doesn't really concern you, Miss Marigold. You'd better run along home for your tea—'

'I've had my tea,' she interrupted him. She stepped across the threshold, her shiny button boots making a clacking sound on the hardwood floor, but remained just inside the door, waiting. It was a brilliant stroke, Violet thought admiringly, establishing her superiority by forcing him to get up and come out from behind the desk unless he wanted to continue the conversation by shouting at her. 'Now I'd like the land girls' letters.'

A flush crept slowly up Hardwick's neck. Marigold returned his look coolly, seemingly at ease, with her arms casually crossed behind her back. But, standing just behind her, Violet could see the girl's hands wrapped tightly around the belt of her coat.

When Hardwick pushed his way through, Marigold recoiled a little and Violet reached to steady her, even though she had trouble not flinching herself, because up close, Hardwick looked terrifying, his pale face mottled with red patches, his lips white and bloodless.

'Where are they?' Marigold's voice squeaked slightly. 'If you please.'

'I'm getting them now,' he snarled. The land girls looked from Marigold to Hardwick, then someone gasped loudly as he extracted a bulging jute bag from a wooden chest.

Violet felt herself starting to shake when she saw that bag, lumpy with parcels and letters, feeling such a white-hot rage that, given only the slightest opportunity, she would have killed him and gladly. He tossed the bag to Kit and the silence snapped. The girls muttered angrily, louder, until Red said, 'This isn't right. You shouldn't have hidden these here.'

'What if there was something urgent?' Kit was so shocked she didn't even tack on a *sir*. 'We're at *war*.'

She stepped into Hardwick's path as he shouldered his way back to his desk, and others did too, a hubbub of raised voices, questions and accusations ringing off the wall. Marigold looked at Violet, wide-eyed with fear, and Violet quickly motioned for her to slide along the wall towards the open door. As she followed, she felt something move behind her back. Hardwick's coat was hanging on a wooden peg, that respectable black churchgoing coat she'd first seen when she'd burst into Winterbourne chapel the day she arrived. The lining showed, shiny and worn, and there in the inside breast pocket was a small rectangular shape.

It was a matter of seconds. Her fingers scrabbled against the slippery fabric, closed around the black notebook and slipped it out, letting it drop into the voluminous pocket of her breeches before she pulled Marigold backwards through the door. On a swell of rage, the rest of the land girls burst out of the office behind her, Kit clutching the bulging sack of letters.

Forty-Nine

Marigold was the heroine of the hour. Steered down the path towards the barn amidst much cheering, she was hoisted up the ladder and deposited on a bed, where she sat, proudly smiling. Kit climbed up onto a box, ceremoniously reading out names before feeding letters and packages into the girls' eagerly reaching hands.

Lucy, after her restless anger, had gone very quiet, twisting her hands as she watched the letter dispensation. Kit caught Violet's eye for a second.

'I haven't got anything either yet,' Violet said quietly to Lucy. 'There's loads more coming . . .'

'Lily!' Red called across. 'Three letters from London, postmarked – ooh, look at that – Bel-grav-ia,' she spelled out slowly. 'Sounds fancy, doesn't it, girls? And it looks like a man's handwriting, too. An admirer?' She flapped the letters about, pretended to fan herself with them, then caught sight of Lucy and dropped her hands, tossing Violet her letters. 'Hurry up, Kit, will you?'

Trying to squash down a sudden reluctance at the sight of the three envelopes, Violet left Marigold sitting on her bed and retreated into the shadowy cavern of the attic. Slowly she shuffled them into order, starting with the first, which had been written a few days after she had left London.

Dear Lily, it said in surprisingly neat, careful handwriting, an ink blot transformed into a face with two dots for eyes and a smiling mouth below. *I hope this finds you very well and working hard. I'm sure you'll be anxious, given the news from London, and while we're forced to take it day by day – or night by night, I should say, because we can*

*barely clear up the mess of one night before another one is upon us – so far
I am fine and, you'll be pleased to hear, fully determined to remain so.
Thankfully, no one of our mutual acquaintance has yet suffered any losses,
although Lady Carmichael's house was hit badly the other night. They
thought they had saved the family silver by burying it in the garden, but
when the bomb fell it exploded everything, showering forks and knives
everywhere. The maids were clambering through the ruins digging for dessert
spoons with Lady C standing on a mound of soil shouting directions.*

Violet laughed shakily. God, she could almost see Duffy, rolling his eyes comically, fizzing with laughter. She wiped away
tears, then pushed her knuckles against her mouth to stop herself crying. Surely, *surely* she couldn't be homesick?

Which brings me to the next piece of news. Here, Duffy must have
paused, because when he put pen to paper again, the ink was
darker and the words were even more cautious. *Your mother has
taken your departure much to heart, more so than we could ever have
anticipated. She remains in London, no matter how much I beg her to
leave, because* my *mother won't go without Aunt Eleanor, who in turn is
convinced that t h i n g s* – he'd written the word so exaggeratedly
neatly that Violet knew she was supposed to read a special
meaning into it. But what? An investigation? The police? Her
mother roaming the streets looking for her? – *will slacken if she
isn't there to personally oversee them.* Another pause in the flow of
ink, more splotches. *I hope you're taking good care of yourself, as you
being out of harm's way is a great comfort to me. Equally, if I were you,
I would prepare myself for all eventualities. At least my mother is moving
into the Wentworth, but yours remains at home, from where she terrorises
those she feels are not putting enough effort into t h i n g s. Thankfully –
although I'm not sure if I should be offended that she clearly doesn't think
I'd have the courage to be involved – no one has come asking for any but
the most straightforward help from me. Still, I'm resolved to stay well
away from the hysteria. You know how I crumble under pressure, which
is in no way adequate enough a word to describe your mother's current
state of mind.*

Yours, affectionately as ever,
Duffy

Violet stared down at the page, not knowing whether to laugh or cry. Her mother had remained in London. In *London*! She was hysterical. Terrorising people. It defied everything Violet had assumed and hoped would happen after her flight, namely that her mother would simply accept her disappearance. She now realised that she had been not only stupid but unutterably naïve. And how could Eleanor sacrifice her sister-in-law's safety too? Why couldn't they just have gone to Yorkshire the way it was planned; why did she have to meddle and spoil it for everyone?

She reread the letter more slowly, shivering slightly at the word *t h i n g s* and trying hard not to imagine her mother suddenly driving into the stable yard, the stares and whispers of the other girls, the gulf that would open between them. The Land Army was the very last place Eleanor would look for her, she tried to reason with herself, and as long as Duffy stayed strong and Violet remained at Winterbourne, her disguise would hold.

With some trepidation, she picked up the next letter. It seemed more light-hearted, talking about the outrageousness of the emerging black market, friends who had enlisted – *Celestina Cooper-Wray rolled up at Café de Paris the other day showing off her uniform, which, between you and me, made her look a little bit like a postbox. Just blue, obviously* – but between the lines, Violet sensed a bleaker loneliness. *I go to Romy's grave every other day or so after work,* he wrote, *praying that even the Germans would have the decency not to bomb a cemetery. I left her a posy from you, too. I thought you'd have liked me to. It's quite peaceful there. I sometimes sit for half an hour just thinking of all the things we used to do together.* There was more cautious talk about Eleanor's *exploits*, which, mercifully, seemed to have come to a bit of an impasse, caught up in the bureaucracy of a city in the grip of war. *No one can be bullied into looking for a runaway when people are dying every night,* he wrote soberly. *Never, in one's wildest dreams, could we have foreseen the extent of the devastation. Stay where you are, at least you're safe there.*

It was the last letter, however, that cut her to the core. It had arrived only the previous day and was the shortest of them, written quickly and to the point. *If I understood my mother correctly, then Aunt is currently trying to get in touch with your father, to push him to make his way home. Communication with Africa is proving exceedingly difficult, but you know how your mother is when she's got the bit between her teeth. I can't imagine he'll get leave, but if she were to have her way, I can think of many reasons why this wouldn't be ideal at all, not least that the Atlantic is positively heaving with U-boats and any unnecessary travel is undertaken only by those truly desperate . . .*

'Lily.' Marigold materialised next to her and Violet started violently. 'Come.'

Up front, Kit was extracting the last few letters, moving slowly and with obvious reluctance, and amidst the girls now strewn across the room, busy with their post, Lucy still stood in the same place, her eyes fixed on the emptying bag.

'I'm so sorry, Luce,' Kit said miserably. Joan put a hand on Lucy's arm, but the other girl shook her off and turned to walk back to her bed, where she sat with her head slightly bowed, hands clasped.

Marigold ran across the room, climbed onto the bed next to her. 'I've asked Guy for a bicycle of my own,' she said in her soft voice, 'and then I'll ride up to the village every day to check on letters from Matthew for you. And when it's sunny again, shall we take a picture of you with the camera, and you could send it to him?'

Violet looked down at her own letters, her heart heavy. Crouching down, she folded them up small and slipped them into a pair of balled-up woollen socks that Duffy had bought her along with the red scarf. 'Feet and heads are the first to get cold,' he'd said. 'Consider these my leaving present.' For a moment, she missed him so much she didn't think she could move; Duffy and her father, who was – her heart felt like a stone in her chest – possibly embarking on a dangerous journey that she could under no circumstances allow. She stuffed the socks into her suitcase and went to sit next to Lucy. Joan followed, and Kit, too, until they were all sitting crowded round the narrow bed in silence.

Curfew came and went and the skies remained as quiet as they had been over the last few days. Lucy had finally cried herself to sleep, and, little by little, the rustling and whispering had settled down. Violet lay in the darkness feeling her old life snatching at her, that useless, vapid life that had grown so much more useless now that she'd seen it from afar. She had thought her mother would send her father a telegram – God, how naïve she'd been – had even thought her father might actually be proud of his daughter enlisting. Never in a million years had she pictured him possibly coming home on the assumption – fed by her mother – of Violet being in peril. She wasn't in bloody peril; she'd left a *note*. But between him coming home and Violet giving herself up . . . well, the choice was clear. It *had* to be clear.

She turned sideways and stared at the shadowy outline of the hatch a few feet away. It was happening after all, she thought bitterly. The group would be breaking apart; she'd lose them, lose Marigold, she'd not see Guy again – Guy, who would be waiting for her right now, stroking Merry's head. Although he wasn't waiting for her but for Lily, Lily who was gutsy and strong and who wouldn't just be lying here accepting her fate and ready to do as she was told.

Run, whispered a voice in her head. Away from the barn and the letters under the bed, away from the knowledge that she had no other choice but to be Violet for evermore – *just run*. And before she could think anything else, she was down the ladder and outside, half running, half stumbling towards the stable yard.

Frankie

October 2004

Fifty

Violet had good moments and bad moments. Sometimes she seemed exactly the same: funny, acerbic, impatient. Other times, her eyes would get restless and her fingers would find the shiny patch at the bottom of her cardigan. Often Frankie would find her standing by a window watching the rain running down the glass and the boughs of the apple tree shivering moodily in the wind. Bringing her a cup of tea and a couple of chocolates, she would ask a question or comment on the weather and it would take Violet a long time to come back from wherever her thoughts had strayed. Sometimes it was the old Violet who came back, asked Frankie about her day, broke her chocolate in half to share, made her sit down to chat. Other times she seemed edgy and argumentative, still occasionally managing to sneak out for her walks and once a drive that, mercifully, didn't take her far but ended with the Hillman Hunter backed into a rubbish bin. After that, Frankie had the car towed over to Jools's and hidden round the back of the shop, telling Violet it was being fixed in the garage.

And then there was the issue of Kit and Joan. As it turned out, Frankie didn't need Max's help in tracking them down after all because they were both listed in Violet's address book.

'Snooping again?' Jools snapped when she came upon Frankie flicking through Violet's enormous A4-sized book bulging with at least fifty years' worth of acquaintances and friends.

'Just looking,' Frankie said, guiltily slipping a piece of paper with two phone numbers into her back pocket.

'Sure,' Jools said, but beneath her bristling, Frankie noticed how exhausted and grey she looked. 'What is happening with Violet's brain scan? When are you seeing Doctor Morrissey again? And have you given any more thought to getting a statement out there before the baying press hounds start concocting stories of their own?'

Mia, too, had suggested more than once that they should get ahead of things.

'I've cancelled what I could without raising too much interest,' she'd told Frankie on the phone the day before. 'And I've withdrawn her from the Safe Haven fundraising presentation. Thing is, it's a bit tricky; they've offered wheelchairs and assistance and all sorts of things that I couldn't quite deflect satisfactorily enough. Truth be told, Frankie, the more we're cancelling under vague pretexts, the more questions people are asking. Might it not be advisable to at some point tell the truth?'

Yes, of course it would be advisable; Frankie was a journalist, she didn't need Mia or Max to tell her that. But any mention of that kind of publicity sent Violet into an emotional tailspin, ranging from angry to pleading, leaving her disorientated and afraid. And, privately, Frankie wasn't at all keen to get anything else out in the open that would further fan Hugo's interest in the land girl story and force her to make some very difficult decisions. Only this morning he had demanded a progress report, managing to imply that not only Frankie's future at the *London Post* but quite possibly any other jobs around town were riding on a speedy delivery of a story.

'Violet doesn't want to do a statement,' she said to Jools, who was buttoning her coat with impatient jabs. 'But I think if we could just . . . Kit and Joan, I mean, maybe . . .'

Maybe seeing them again would unravel the final piece of the thread, bringing her closer to its end and, perhaps, a sense of closure?

'Leave it be.' Jools slammed the door.

Frankie sighed. She listened in the direction of the bedroom, where Violet was having a lie-down, then smoothed out the paper and picked up the phone.

'Hello, is that Kit Hayes? I'm Violet Etherington's grand-daughter, maybe better known to you as Lily Burns.'

Kit and Joan were coming down the following Sunday. Knowing how mortified Violet would be if her condition was being discussed behind her back, Frankie didn't go into all the details with Kit, just said that Violet had been under the weather and that – she gave a defiant shrug in the mirror – Jools had suggested Frankie get in touch and invite them for tea.

The week was packed with interviews and 'chats' at the *Post*, where the evaluation process had intensified. Several people had already left, and a girl Frankie knew from her *Phoenix* days had been seen coming out of Hugo's office red-eyed and silent. June Seymour was still absent and a horrible rumour had started that she wasn't sick but being phased out, which made people panic even more, because she was much beloved. Frankie knew full well that she should be doing everything she possibly could to stay in Hugo's good books, especially given her and Violet's strained financial situation, just as urgently as she should be telling Violet about the land girl story before it took on a life of its own. Caught between two such diametrically opposed forces, however, she did what she had always done. She avoided both. Hedging and fibbing her way through meetings and confrontations with Hugo, she managed to keep things at an impasse for several days.

'It's like standing in the way of a hurricane,' Max said on Friday after Hugo had bawled Frankie out once again for not getting anywhere. 'Is it really that difficult to track the women down?'

'Well, no.' Frankie scanned the newsroom.

'He's off harassing Mallory,' Max said. 'What's up, then?'

'I found them already.' Frankie kept her voice low. 'They're coming to see Violet for tea on Sunday.'

'Really?' Max's voice was sharp with surprise, and Frankie

realised that not keeping him in the loop at all wasn't a terribly nice way to repay him for his offer of help. 'I was going to tell you,' she said quickly. 'I literally just arranged it and, well, there's just a lot going on.'

'You can say that again.' Max shook his head. 'So the women . . .' He waved his hand impatiently to get her to elaborate.

'They were a bit surprised, but Joan especially sounded lovely.' Frankie felt better even thinking about her phone conversations with them. She threw a cautious look over her shoulder, but Hugo was nowhere to be seen. 'I think it'll be great for Violet. Joan's a retired schoolteacher in Aylesbury and Kit lives in High Wycombe, ran a dairy farm up there. She said they all started at Winterbourne at different times and then left together in October 1940. But get this, she then sort of backtracked and I'm fairly sure she said they left not just their posting at Winterbourne Orchards but the Land Army altogether . . . What?'

A zing of citrus hit her nose.

'Sounds like you've suddenly got a whole lot further than just an hour ago, angel.' Hugo's voice was dangerously measured.

'Well, no,' Frankie stammered, face reddening. 'Max was just kind enough to—'

'We're all incredibly kind around here,' Hugo cut across her. 'Update, please.'

Con chose that moment to emerge from the meeting room. His eyes fell on Frankie and, perhaps a reflex born out of their long friendship, he grinned, so much like his old self that she forgot how awkward they were these days and smiled back.

'Ah. Come join the fun, Conrad,' Hugo said. 'Seeing as your workload obviously doesn't get your undivided attention, Francesca, let's find you a helpmeet. Conrad, you're on the land girl story now.'

Con stopped in his tracks. 'Of course, I'd be glad to, it'll be good to work with Frankie.' His voice was incredulous, fawning and hopeful all at the same time, but when he caught sight of Frankie's anguished expression, his face closed up immediately, became white, his eyes slits of resentment. 'Clearly Francesca would prefer me not to, however,' he said woodenly, looking at her with such dislike that she baulked.

'I didn't say that,' she protested, 'but you must have a lot on, and I really can do it on my own.'

'Well, we haven't seen much of that, have we?' Hugo barked. 'Instead, by the sounds of what you've just said, you've been stringing me along, dear heart. All right, here's how this is going to go down. *You*,' he pointed at Frankie exaggeratedly, 'bring *him*,' he pointed at Con, 'up to speed. I want a nice big reunion. I want secrets aired, confidences bestowed. *Land Girls, Ladies, Dark Secrets*,' he wrote into the air. 'And I want to be kept in the loop. No more shilly-shallying.'

'Conrad,' someone shouted from across the newsroom. Con looked anxiously at Hugo as if asking for permission to leave.

'Dear Lord, go,' Hugo hissed. 'But I swear, if you make me tell you how to do your jobs again, neither of you will *have* one by tomorrow.'

Say something, Frankie told herself. Tell him you can't possibly do that story, tell him, Frankie – do it *now*. But her mouth refused to form the words, and she stood next to the printer, watching him stomp away.

'I'm so sorry, Frankie.' Max exhaled slowly. 'Hugo is like something out of *Nineteen Eighty-Four*, honestly.'

She forced a smile. 'Don't worry. It was bound to come to a head at some point. I can't see how I can get out of it now.'

'Regardless of the story, it'll be great for your grandmother to see her friends. And as for the rest of it, you'll make it work, I have no doubt.' He smiled at her, and she remembered the hug-that-was-a-bit-more-than-a-hug, which neither of them had referenced again. Once again she was convinced that mind-reading was one of his qualities, because he quirked his eyebrows, walking backwards so he could keep his eyes on her. 'You sure have livened things up around here.'

She forced the hug out of her mind and looked across to where Con was talking to Felicity, looking a lot perkier than he had in the last few days. Felicity put her hand on his arm, and he nodded excitedly.

God, Frankie hated this. She hated Hugo and Felicity and Victoria, she hated everything about this story that wasn't supposed to *be* a story. But most of all, she hated who she was turning out to be. A weak, spineless pushover, someone who couldn't stand up to anyone, not to Hugo, not to Violet. Someone who took a circuitous route back to her desk, slid whatever she needed for the weekend into her bag and sneaked down the back stairs and out of the office.

Fifty-One

Never in her entire life would Frankie forget the look on her grandmother's face when she opened the door and saw Kit, Joan and a very grumpy Jools on the threshold on Sunday afternoon.

When Frankie had told Violet about the visit, she had braced herself for discussion or histrionics, certainly fear and anxiety about what they might or might not know. But she had simply stared at her, mouth working, and then breathed out a long, shuddery breath and sank down in her armchair. 'Yes please.'

All Saturday, Frankie had watched her grandmother chat and smile as they tidied the drawing room, took the signs down, prepared a tea tray and unpacked the cakes they'd bought, and more than once Frankie had to blink away tears because it was so lovely to see her like this.

She still hadn't told her about Hugo's story. Instead, coming home from the office on Friday night, she'd fixed herself a very large drink down in the kitchen and decided not to think about the issue at all until Monday morning. So she didn't tell Violet about her shameful escape from Con and how she'd determinedly ignored his calls all evening. How Joan had rung in anguish because a tree had fallen across the train tracks and she couldn't make it, and Frankie had decided to call Max for help. How Jools had shouted at Frankie for a good ten minutes when she learned about the visit, refusing to come, then suddenly appearing just as Joan had been helped out of Max's old Ford and throwing herself onto her and Kit with such force that they all threatened to topple over.

They walked up the steps without a backward glance at

Frankie and Max to where Violet stood in the doorway, her arms wide open.

'Look, Frankie,' Max said quietly. 'Just *look* at them.'

There was a moment's silence, then Kit made the first move and fell into Violet's embrace – Violet, the least physical person Frankie knew, was *embracing* them – closely followed by round, kind-faced Joan, and finally Jools, who draped her arms around everyone all at once. Excited murmurs and greetings came from the knot of limbs and heads, which slowly disentangled itself.

'I can't believe you're here,' Violet said faintly. 'I can't believe it.' She had her arm looped through Kit's, touching Joan's shoulder, as if they might disappear. 'It's been too long. But why are we standing here in the rain, come in, come in.'

They trooped into the front hall, all now talking at once, and a cheerful racket filled the flat that had been so tense with strain over the last few weeks.

'This was the best idea ever.' Frankie turned to Max, who stood on the step below her holding an umbrella over both of them.

'I told you.' He shook his head in wonder. 'It doesn't matter, all that Hugo business; *this* is what it's about.'

'She's been so happy, so *there* . . .'

And maybe all the emotion and happiness were somehow contagious, or maybe it was the rain dripping down the back of her neck, but Frankie, her face level with his, moved closer under the umbrella and her cheek touched his, and then she kissed him; right then and there, on the steps of her grandmother's house. The umbrella dislodged a small shower of raindrops, voices were still chattering inside the flat as they kissed on and on, and Frankie's heart was soaring, lighter than air, because it all finally seemed to be right. Violet happy, Violet well – or at least better, surely – and Max's body solid against hers, with the smell of mint and rain and a sneaky cigarette at the last rest stop.

'Ahem.'

They sprang apart to see Violet standing at the top of the steps.

'Francesca Etherington, carrying on with a stranger in the street,' she said in a mock-scandalised tone. 'Whatever will the neighbours think?' But her face was open and her smile warm.

'Violet, this is Max, he's a . . .' she felt rather than saw Max's eyebrow lift, 'a friend of mine.'

'The chauffeur, of course. They've been complimentary about your services.' Violet shook her head and laughed. 'Always ready to fall for a bit of charm, those hoydens.'

For the first time since Frankie had met him, Max seemed lost for words. He looked up at Violet transfixed, and Frankie felt a sudden swell of pride as she followed his gaze. Violet was wearing a skirt and cardigan in bright magenta. She'd set her hair in the elegant backward waves that Jools always said were so old-fashioned they had come around to being in vogue again. She stood straight, her face more relaxed than it had been in a while, her smile bright. It had become a little hard to remember lately that inside the panicked, anxious woman rushing around the flat and banging down the blinds, there was still this Violet too: formidable, beautiful, confident.

'Delighted,' Max stumbled slightly over the words. 'It's a pleasure, Mrs . . . I mean, ma'am.'

'It's so nice to meet a friend of Frankie's,' she said, 'and thank you again for bringing them. Now if you'll excuse me, I have to make sure they're not tearing the place apart in search of tea.' She disappeared through the door, leaving Frankie to fiddle with the edge of her sleeve and Max fastidiously straightening the umbrella above them.

'Well *that* was interesting.' He gave her a wry smile that told her he didn't only mean meeting her grandmother. 'You might have picked a better moment, you know.'

'Yeah.' She shrugged awkwardly, then grinned. 'It was nice either way.'

377

Max nodded, jabbing his chin at the door. 'Go on, you're missing it all.'

'Oh – but you should come in and have a cup of tea,' Frankie said, 'after being so kind and driving them and all.'

'You don't need a stranger in the room,' he said firmly. 'But I'm loaning you this.' He handed her a bulky object wrapped in newspaper. 'Looks a bit ancient but works perfectly, and I think it'd be fun. Used to belong to my nan, so it should fit right in.'

He was already backing down the steps, but Frankie held him back. 'Under all that gruff amusement, you're like some guardian angel, do you know that?'

'For when my current career goes down the toilet?' He winked at her. 'Now go and make some memories.'

'There she is,' Joan beamed as Frankie, bearing the tea tray, turned the corner into the reading nook. 'Lily, you can be proud of your granddaughter; she was such a lovely travel companion.'

'You came over from Aylesbury, Joan.' Kit raised her eyes upwards. 'Hardly considered "travel". But yes, she is lovely. And look, she's brought us tea,' she added approvingly as Frankie set the tray on the sideboard. 'You've trained her well, Lily.'

It startled Frankie, the way they called her Lily. It somehow brought a sixth person into the room, a young, anxious girl running away from home and falling in with these women – no, girls then, too, she had to keep reminding herself. Lily and Red, Kit and Joan. Faded, sepia-coloured ghosts of girls with thin faces and watchful eyes, who had once believed that light brought darkness and who were now present in every small pause and meaningful look running below the cheerful banter between these respectable-looking elderly ladies. Mentally she compared them to the photo, noticed that Kit still had that air of robustness, even though she walked with a cane now; that her face was animated and she spoke confidently. Joan's hair was sparse and her features had softened, but she had the same sweet expression as back then.

Frankie had switched on the little lamp to see better for pouring out the dark caramel-coloured liquid that Violet – and judging by Kit's happy hum of approval, the others too – preferred. The women had fallen silent, and Frankie, intent on the cups, suddenly thought she could feel their eyes on her. And yes, when she looked up, glanced at Kit, she caught her squinting at her face, bathed in the yellow glow from the lamp.

'What?' she asked, flushing slightly as she looked from Violet to Joan and Kit. 'Am I doing something wrong?' But she knew it wasn't about the tea; she had felt them looking before, when she'd first rung Joan's bell, and then when they'd picked up Kit from the station. Appraising, intent.

Joan shook her head quickly. 'Kit's just dying for a cuppa,' she said, rolling her eyes comically. 'Ever impatient.'

'The years haven't cured you of that?' Violet asked, smiling.

'How do you think I've kept this well in my old age?' Kit said archly. 'Your beau didn't want to come in, Frankie?'

'Oh, he's not my beau,' Frankie said quickly. 'And he knew you'd have lots to talk about.'

A small pause fell, and then Kit said easily, 'No doubt about that. Never did stop chattering, that lot, you know.'

'When we weren't falling asleep in our boots, that was.' Joan nodded. 'Proper hard work we did then. Not like now . . . What is it *you* do, Frankie?'

'Frankie's a journalist,' Jools said proudly. 'A high-flying one to boot, right, Violet?'

'Yes.' Violet's voice was neutral enough, but she allowed a small pause to bloom, which Joan clearly didn't understand but hastened to fill.

'I can't quite get used to hearing you called Violet. So devious she was, Frankie, kept us all in the dark – remember when we were so surprised you couldn't ride a bicycle? Poor Lucy was so

379

distraught about those letters. But did you hear that she and Matthew have *nine* grandchildren?' She shook her head. 'At least some good came out of it all, eh?'

Another small pause fell and Frankie saw that Joan had coloured a little, was groping for something else to say.

'I'm still green with envy that I didn't get to go on your village trip,' Kit jumped in.

'You were too busy bossing everyone around,' Jools said sanctimoniously.

'Well, what can else could I do with Red around?'

Frankie had made some noise about leaving them to chat, but they wouldn't hear of it, so, sitting on the small footstool next to Violet's chair, she listened to the conversation flowing above her head, lubricated by yet more tea. There was much cheerful ribbing (Jools) and patting of arms (Joan), and some good-natured argument between Kit and Violet. It wasn't just land girl memories, though; in fact those fell away quickly as talk turned to Kit's delinquent grandson and Joan's village choir, Jools's shop and Violet's life as a *grand dame*, as Joan put it, sounding awed.

'Why are you surprised?' Kit shook her head. 'Always on about changing the world, that one.'

They talked on, and little by little, Frankie forgot about the ghosts from the photo and Hugo and the land girl story, and settled back to watch her grandmother sitting among her friends, wondering if, in all these years, she'd ever seen her quite like this. Violet wasn't a solitary person, not when she knew half of London, was forever stopping to chat with acquaintances on the street, had a million and one social engagements over the years. But she'd always been ready to push back against any perceived intrusion, which perhaps came with the territory of who she was. Never this at ease, this loose. *Safe.* The word floated into Frankie's mind seemingly from nowhere, but once it was there, she realised that that was what this felt like: cradled as a small part of something bigger, letting go inside the confines of a group. The only other time she'd ever seen Violet truly relaxed was with Jools or Gramps, talking quietly at the end of a busy day, free from the faint aura of guardedness, which she hadn't fully grasped had even been there until she saw Violet now, among these women.

'You know, I reckon this was a good idea after all,' Jools murmured next to her, as if she'd read Frankie's thoughts. 'I didn't think it would be.' She shook her head ruefully and grimaced. 'I'm such an old know-it-all at times; emphasis on "old". I'm sorry, Frankie.'

'It's all right,' Frankie said gratefully. 'She's looking great, don't you think?'

Jools kept her eyes on Violet but didn't say anything.

'Hey, you haven't opened your package.' Kit pointed at the parcel.

'From your admirer.' Joan clasped her hands.

'Wrapped in newspaper,' Jools tsked. 'Hardly romantic.'

'But appropriate for a journalist.' Frankie felt small darts of warmth when she remembered the kiss – *she* had leaned in to *kiss* someone – and started peeling away the paper.

'He's a journalist?' Violet hadn't spoken sharply, but something in her face tightened as she leaned forward, her eyes narrowed at Frankie.

'Yes, from the *Post*,' Frankie said, surprised. 'Sorry, I thought I'd mentioned it. Why?'

Violet opened her mouth as if she wanted to say something, then shook her head, her eyes on the crumpled-up newspaper in Frankie's lap.

'Is it a love token?' Joan crowded in eagerly as Frankie looked down at the object and felt a smile tug at the corners of her mouth.

'Better.'

She held up a Polaroid camera.

*

At first, it was perfect. The women insisted on turning on all the lights and pulling the heavy drapes out of the way, and Frankie was flooded with longing for Max to see them all here, laughing and getting silly as the pictures spewed out of the camera, bending over the emerging contours, demanding retakes for closed eyes and goofy expressions, using up most of the two rolls of film until only a few pictures remained.

'A proper group shot,' Frankie said. 'One for each of you to take away. Kit, you could be over here; you stay where you are, Joan. Vi in the middle, next to Jools.'

But it was as this very moment – Frankie, flushed with laughing, pushing fine hair out of her face and peering into the viewfinder – that the afternoon suddenly, inexplicably turned.

She'd been so preoccupied with getting them all to fit into the frame, faces pushed tightly together, arms around each other, that she hadn't noticed that the nook had gone quiet all of a sudden. When she looked through the viewfinder, she saw that the four women weren't laughing or even smiling any longer, but staring right past the camera and straight at her.

'You're awfully serious,' she frowned as she clicked for the first picture, then the second. 'Can I have one smiling, please?'

But the mood had shifted, now laced with something that made Joan look anxious and fidgety and Kit sit rigidly upright, and when Frankie went to set the pictures on the windowsill, she felt their gazes following her.

'Goodness, Lily,' Joan whispered faintly. Kit muttered something in response and Frankie turned back just in time to see Jools squeeze her arm warningly.

'What?' Frankie said, confused. 'Why are you all looking like that?'

'There's one last picture.' Jools jumped in quickly. 'What'll it be, girls?'

But Frankie was still looking from one to the other, waiting.

'Years ago, we had our picture taken,' Kit finally said,

reluctantly. 'Much like this – in fact, almost exactly like this. It reminded us . . .' She broke off.

'Of Marigold,' Joan said very quietly.

Violet never moved, never looked up. *Time slides*, Frankie thought. *Something that happened in the past is suddenly right here, part of the present.* Marigold had taken the photo that Frankie had found.

'Marigold?'

'She was part of our group. At Winterbourne.' As Joan spoke, another sepia-coloured ghost slipped into the room, bringing something else with her, something that suddenly sat in Frankie's mind like a threatening hum. *It was murder.*

She swallowed with some effort, looked around the room. Joan gave a small, uncertain titter and got up to inspect the photos lined up on the windowsill, her back turned to the others with a determined air, Kit bent over the tea tray on the table. Frankie wanted to ask more, because here, finally, was something connected to the weight on Violet's mind. But her grandmother's eyes had started flicking restlessly between her three friends, she was flushed and her hand had started to worry at the edge of her cardigan, twisting the fabric until it bunched up. Frankie threw Jools a quick, anxious look.

'Right, the sun is most definitely over the yardarm.' Jools clapped her hands briskly. Violet started at the sound, and Frankie could see the curve of her jaw jut out. Jools pitched her voice more quietly as she went on. 'Just a small one and then we should probably make a move. Joan, there's a little tray of glasses over there.'

Things recovered somewhat as Jools produced a bottle of sherry out of her bag and splashed some in everyone's glass, and gradually there was a gentle swell of murmured conversation again; not like before, but enough to cover the lingering air of unease. Violet had settled back into her chair and her colour had calmed down a bit.

Frankie sat close to her, not really listening any more, not even bothering to ask about Marigold. Instead, she kept checking Violet's face in case the faraway look crept in, watched her hand for the telltale twitch against her leg, and her heart, so buoyant earlier, was heavy.

'We should go, I suppose,' Joan said after a while, reluctantly. 'But we'll be back tomorrow, bright and early, to spend the day together, yes, Lily?'

'Wait, there's still one last picture.' Jools held up the camera. 'One of all of us, shawled and hatted and gloved?'

Frankie looked at the row of pictures lined up on the windowsill. 'Actually,' she said, 'could you maybe take one of just Violet and me?'

Afterwards, the others rose from their chairs, preparing to walk the short distance to Jools's house, where Kit and Joan were staying the night.

'Lovely picture of the two of us.' Violet nodded at the Polaroid in Frankie's hand.

'Yeah,' Frankie said. But her heart felt like lead as she looked down at the photo. It wasn't silly and smiley the way the first ones had been, or even serious like the last four. Instead, Violet was looking straight at Frankie, her eyes intent on her face, as if she was trying to commit it to memory. Something immeasurably sad seemed to linger between them, something final and full of longing that made Frankie swallow hard and close her eyes so as not to see what was right there: the faint but unmistakable hint of farewell. As if Violet already knew it all to be fleeting: their closeness, the ease and happiness of an afternoon spent with friends.

How had Frankie been able to fight this for so long? Unravelling the thread of Violet's past, bringing the women here – it was lovely, but it wasn't going to help; none of it was. Time would continue to slide, inevitably, inexorably, until the end. And perhaps it had needed this afternoon of seeing Violet among her friends to understand – to really and truly *see* – just how irreversible the change in her was. Soon, the relaxed, vivacious Violet from this afternoon would be replaced once more by a woman pushed and pulled by a seesaw of confusion and fear. Soon her story would, little by little, cease to be inside a living, breathing person and would sit in cardboard boxes in the secret shelter beneath them.

Frankie didn't trust herself to look at Violet, not just now. She got up, her hands shaking as she started gathering the tea things, wishing the others would simply disappear, wishing Violet would go to bed and leave her alone to grapple with this new, sudden understanding: that no matter what she did, how much she grieved for and raged against or tried to understand what was happening to her grandmother, it would continue happening. That to fix Violet's darkness wasn't the point; had never been the point at all, because ultimately it wouldn't halt the illness, it wouldn't change a thing.

The others had trooped out to the hall to noisily locate coats and scarves, their chatter ringing from the walls. Frankie hung back with the tea tray to let them pass, and her eyes fell on one of Violet's signs, forgotten and half hidden behind the drapes.

Close blinds.

The cups on the tray clattered a little as her hands started shaking.

'Here, let me.'

Violet took the tea tray and set it on the bureau. She followed Frankie's gaze to the sign, but she didn't say anything, just put an arm around her and drew her close, murmuring things that Frankie couldn't make out but that were warm and safe and went straight to the place inside her where a small girl was sitting on a bed, snug in a towelling robe, watching her grandmother get ready for a night out.

Fifty-Two

'They didn't stop talking, and then this morning they picked right back up where they'd left off.'

Max had sent her a message asking if they wanted to meet at the café across the road before work, and he was such an attentive audience, asking questions in all the right places and smiling at Frankie so warmly, that the words were pouring out of her in a distinctly un-Frankie-like fashion. The only thing she didn't tell him was the way the afternoon had ended. The desolation she had felt when she broke away from Violet's embrace and helped her get ready for bed, then sat on the chair in the hallway and listened to her settling down to sleep, holding the last Polaroid and trying to imagine a life without her grandmother in it.

Getting up this morning, she had pushed the picture into the back of her notebook and resolved not to think about it again, and it wasn't hard to feel a little more optimistic when Violet had woken up looking rested and ready to bear her friends off for breakfast at her favourite café. And it certainly wasn't hard to be distracted, at least a little bit, when you were sitting across from someone as enthusiastic and smiley as Max.

'Sounds like it was pretty special for your grandmother. How did the camera work out?'

'It was perfect, thank you so much.' She handed him a bag containing the wrapped-up camera. 'I'm afraid I used up both the rolls of film, though. I know they're a bit expensive, just let me know how much . . .'

'They were a gift,' he said firmly.

'But I can totally repay you.'

He put his hand on hers. 'Repeat after me. "Thank you, Max, for this thoughtful gift between friends."'

'But . . . Oh, okay, yes, thank you.' She hid her confusion by getting out one of the pictures. After the weird reaction to the group shot, Violet hadn't looked at hers again and Frankie hadn't felt too bad borrowing it. 'Here they are.'

Max leaned in, his shoulder touching Frankie's in a disconcerting way, his fingers inadvertently grazing hers.

'Clever you, posing them exactly like the previous photo,' he said, his eyes on the picture.

Frankie frowned, then realised that it was indeed the same line-up as the land girl photo. 'What do you mean, "clever"?' she said slowly.

He looked across at her and smiled. 'I can't call you clever?'

'But what about the photo is clever?'

'Well,' he shrugged, 'if you do decide to run with the story, it would look amazing. You could put the two photos right on top of each other in the middle, text running around it . . . What?'

'But I don't want to do that story.' Frankie leaned back in her chair and crossed her arms.

'You'll have to do *something*, though. Hugo'll want an update and Conrad's probably up there, waiting and livid.' Max got to his feet.

'I can't.' Frankie stayed where she was, though she bent to pick her jacket up from the floor. 'I think I'm going to ring in sick today.'

'Coward. Here.' Max handed her her notebook. 'Time to take a stand.'

'I'm not made for stand-taking,' Frankie muttered.

'Rubbish. And John's seen you in here already; he'll tell Hugo you're not sick.' He pulled her up from the chair, gallantly helped her into her jacket. 'But one of these days, should we ever find ourselves in a place where we're not chasing stories or avoiding Hugo, we should talk about yesterday afternoon.'

He reached for her hand, threaded his fingers through hers

and pulled, not hard, just enough to make Frankie stumble against him. His shirt was soft, his cheek rough with stubble.

'That would be nice,' she whispered, 'and maybe somewhere a bit quieter . . .' She felt laughter rumble in his chest as he moved her out of the way of two men coming into the café, narrowly avoiding a collision with the waitress behind them.

'Definitely,' he agreed.

Somehow, floating on a rush of warmth and dread at the same time, Frankie managed to lie her way through the editorial meeting. 'It's all in hand,' she said, determinedly ignoring Con's incredulous look. 'We've called the women and are bringing them in . . . No, I don't know the exact time, I'm waiting for them to juggle their schedules.'

She was the first to leave the conference room, snatching up her mobile and slipping through the back door. Hidden behind a concrete pillar, she closed her eyes and avoided all thoughts of the mess she was making of everything here while Violet was out with her friends, blithely oblivious to the land girl story brewing, with Frankie at its epicentre. Instead, she focused on the one good thing in her life right now, the moment when Max had held open the door of the café, smiled down at her and squeezed her hand in secret promise.

'You were always rubbish at hiding.'

Reluctantly she opened her eyes.

'I'm not hiding,' she said. 'I'm taking a break.'

'Whatever.' Con surveyed her contemptuously. 'You know, I always thought you were one of the rock-solid people, someone you could depend on no matter what. Why the hell have you been avoiding me for sixty-five hours?'

'You counted.' Frankie pushed her hand through her hair defiantly.

'Are you that afraid of sharing the glory? I don't even know why I haven't ratted you out to Hugo. Have you even written anything for that stupid story, or are you too busy canoodling with Max Sefton?'

'I'm not canoodling,' Frankie hissed back. 'We're friends.'

'How sweet,' he said scathingly. 'Well, I didn't come to fight, just to let you know that I'm quitting my job here. So there, you can rest easy. I'm going back to Reigate to stay with a mate . . .'

There was the sound of a door opening at the far end of the corridor, and Con broke off at the sound of a crisp, snappy voice.

'You still don't have any more than I've seen already,' it said.

'Not so brave now, eh?' Frankie whispered venomously. 'Have you actually quit or are you just trying to make me feel—'

'Shut up,' he mouthed angrily.

Frankie had as little desire to be seen by Hugo as Con did, though, so she grudgingly made room for him behind the concrete pillar, then started when a familiar gruff voice rose in reply.

'I'm close, I promise. Here, look.'

There was a rustle of paper, then Hugo whistled softly through his teeth. 'All right, so what's the plan? You've been grooming that situation for a while now without a solid point of connection, Max.'

'I'll have to go down and talk to her again, but I'm pretty sure my hunch was right.'

'*My* hunch, you mean.' Hugo's voice became fainter as they moved away, washing over Frankie, who was straining to hear Max's soft growl again, so familiar, so lovely . . .

'. . . Winterbourne.'

Snatches of conversation floated back to them, but Frankie was no longer listening, because that single word had cut through everything, straight to the bottom of her belly. Then a strange, warbly buzzing started up in her ears. Surely not. Surely, *surely* not?

Winterbourne. Max. Hugo.

'Frankie!' She heard Con hiss through the woolly layer that was trying to shield her mind from the thing she couldn't quite wrap her head around: that Max, who had helped her, had said all those things to her, whom she had kissed on her grandmother's front step – *kissed!* – had all along been working an angle; was Hugo's sidekick . . .

Words chased each other: *grooming that situation . . . Why would it be so bad? . . . Clever you.* Clever you. Oh my God.

She sat down on the ground, very suddenly, as the woolly buzzing stopped and a strange calm descended on her. She knew she shouldn't have let her guard down, she *knew*. People always turned on you, they *always* did. She'd gone and stupidly, naïvely fallen for someone who had seemed so easy to fall for, who she thought had been on her side in this godforsaken place, who had made it all bearable . . .

'Frankie, I swear, if you don't say anything now, I'm calling an ambulance and you'll have the very undignified pleasure of being carried out on a stretcher in front of Felicity and Hugo.'

'He's after that story,' Frankie whispered hoarsely. 'Max – that's why he's been helping me, that's why he was always there . . . and all along he was working on Hugo's orders. He was so nice . . . I thought . . .'

I thought he liked me. But she couldn't say it out loud, that for the first time in a long time, someone had really *got* her, with all the promise of lovely, zingy things to come. It had been an act, a means to an end. All along, it had been about Violet.

'Oh my God.' She looked at Con, suddenly even more horror-stricken. 'I told him about the darkness, about Violet's *condition*. I asked him to pick up Joan . . . Oh Con, what have I *done*?'

'I don't know until you tell me,' he hissed.

She searched his expression for a subtext, a secret ambition. She'd known Con for six years. Six years of sharing an office, of having each other's backs, of sparring and fighting and good-natured competition, and after all that time, she'd chosen to confide in a stranger, dropped a friend, just like that.

So she told him. Not about *It was murder*, but everything else, from the day she picked Violet up from the police station; she told him about the land girls and Violet's fear, the picture, the motto, meeting the women.

'I was trying to help her, Con. She's ill, her mind's going, and she refuses, absolutely refuses, to have it made public. I thought she might get better if I just tried ... I didn't *want* to write a story, that's why I've been so off. I'm sorry, Con, you seemed so keen to get ahead, and Max said to stay in control, but I just stuck my head in the sand, and I'm so worried about Violet, so so worried, and I don't know what to do ...'

To Con's enormous credit, he didn't say anything along the lines of *I told you so* or *how could you*. He just sat there thinking.

'He's not talked to your grandmother yet, has he?'

'No, and she wasn't keen on him at all once she knew he was a journalist. And she was right. I was so stupid, so infernally—'

'But he said "I'll have to talk to her *again*", so he has already talked to someone. Did he mean one of the other land girls during their car ride?'

'No.' Frankie shook her head as if she could clear her mind. 'He ...' She broke off, thought back to the conversation they'd just overheard. 'He was showing Hugo something,' she said slowly. 'He was ...'

She looked at the notebook in her hand, remembering that glorious moment when she'd unwrapped it at the café, this properly grown-up notebook to mark her leap into times of revolution and change. She opened it reluctantly, because she didn't think she'd be able to bear this last treachery, riffled through the pages.

'He took the picture,' she said slowly. 'I picked up my jacket and he handed me my notebook. He must have taken it then.'

A small *drring* from her mobile made both of them jump.

'A text from Violet,' Frankie said urgently. 'She never sends me texts, she usually forgets ...' Her head whipped up. 'She says they're going out of town for the day, to Somerset. Con, they're going to *Winterbourne*.'

Fifty-Three

'Jeez, it really is all happening there.' Con shook his head.

'I wish they weren't going,' Frankie said worriedly. 'It's a long drive and Jools better be taking good care of Violet. And how are they even getting there? I hid Violet's car. God, this is all my fault. Violet got so suspicious when she heard that Max works here; that's probably why she didn't tell me this morning that she was planning to go.'

Violet must have known that Frankie wouldn't defend her when push came to shove, that her granddaughter, who was so good at letting everyone walk all over her, would cave in the end. Shame crawled up her spine and she blinked furiously. Then she drew in a sharp breath. 'Wait, Con, do you think that's where Max is going too? "I'll have to go *down* and talk to her", weren't those his words?'

'Somerset isn't really "down", but yeah, I guess.' Con opened the back door and peered into the newsroom. 'I can't see him, but that doesn't necessarily mean . . .'

'He's got to assume that I'm cracking on with things, with Hugo breathing down my neck,' Frankie said angrily. 'He'll want to get ahead. And to think I liked him – and Hugo, too; I genuinely admired him, I looked *up* to him.'

'Far be it from me to defend Max Sefton,' Con said thoughtfully, 'but my guess would be that Hugo probably put quite a bit of pressure on him, what with the whole job evaluation thing. He gets Sefton to supply all the dirty stuff he knows you won't want anything to do with, then puts both of you in the byline for credibility. Maybe Max really did like y—'

'Don't say it,' Frankie said furiously. 'He didn't. You heard him. He was just grooming me, digging for dirt on Violet. I was his shovel, basically.'

'Well, is there dirt to be found?' Con asked.

Frankie pursed her lips and didn't meet his eyes.

'There is?' he said incredulously. 'What? An illicit affair? Embezzled money?'

She chewed her lip, trying to sort through the pieces in her head. Violet running away from home. *From Light, Darkness. It was murder.* And now, a fifth girl, Marigold.

'I don't know. But whatever there is, I'll be damned if I let Hugo find it. And since the entire world is, apparently, paying Winterbourne a visit today, I'm going too.' She squared her shoulders. 'I'll tell Hugo I have flu; that way he won't foist Max on me under some pretext, if he's even still here. Then I'll train it down there and—'

'Under no circumstances am I going to miss all the fun,' Con said. 'I'm driving. And Frankie,' he held her back, 'I'm really sorry about your grandmother. I wish . . . I'm sorry. It sounds awful.'

'All right.' Hugo glowered at Frankie, who must have looked shell-shocked enough for him to buy into her illness. 'Don't come back until you're well. I don't need half the newsroom felled by your lurgy.'

'Of course,' she said, hoping that the distance between them and the hoarseness in her voice went some way to disguise her confusion and rage. 'Con is on top of the land girl story; he's going to the library to do some research.'

'Oh, how wonderful,' Hugo said sarcastically. 'Someone around here doing what they're supposed to.' He raised his eyebrows, perhaps hoping for her to stammer her apologies or reassure him of her ceaseless devotion. But Frankie didn't trust herself to speak again. She nodded and turned towards the door.

'Hope you're feeling better soon,' he said grudgingly from behind her.

'Yeah,' she muttered.

'Oh, I've missed this,' Con sighed as they passed a flock of sheep milling about in a field.

'What, your usual run of clandestine rescue missions?'

'No, the country,' Con said just as Frankie craned her head.

'Wait, turn left here.'

They drove through an enormous and beautifully ornate gate and she wound down the window, stuck her head outside. Trees lined the drive, which was covered in leaves, and when she took several deep breaths, she could smell wet smoke from bonfires and chimneys. For a moment, she was back in Violet's bedroom, the trees scenting the darkness as her grandmother lay in her bed and remembered . . . well, *this*, Frankie realised with a small shock. She blinked, tried to picture land girls in the trees they passed, tried to picture Violet *up a ladder, young and strong*.

'Do you think Violet actually knows the people who live here?' she asked.

'There's a sign for parking down there.' Con veered left as the lane split. 'Horses and deliveries. All quite upstairs-downstairs, isn't it? But wow, now that's what I call a mansion.'

They had passed under a sweeping archway in gold stone and driven onto a wide expanse of packed dirt and sand lined by wooden stable buildings. Two horses were being brushed down by a cheerful-looking girl; a white horse watched interestedly and nipped her hand every so often for a treat. A gaggle of them were led towards a gate, presumably to a paddock beyond, and a class was going on in one of the indoor schools. And behind it all, Winterbourne House rose gracefully, its facade glowing in the afternoon sun.

'It's like something out of a movie,' Con said, deeply

impressed. 'Although there are a few too many horses around for my taste.'

'Parking is over there.' Frankie nudged him. 'And there's a London cab. But,' she scanned the cars parked in two rows, 'it doesn't look like Max is here yet.'

'I guess rich people don't need doorbells,' Con said a little while later. They were looking around the huge double doors for a way to make themselves heard after repeated knocking hadn't brought anyone to greet them. 'We'll have to wait and . . . Frankie, what on earth are you doing?'

'Well, it was unlocked,' Frankie said defiantly as she peered through the now open door into the front hall. 'Hello?'

'But we can't just go in,' Con said, aghast. 'We'd be trespassing and . . . Oh, okay then.'

Frankie was beginning to think Winterbourne House might not be occupied at all as they walked through the long entrance hall, their footsteps silent on the straw matting. A pair of muddy boots and some wellies were sitting below a coat rack, which held . . .

'That's Jools's,' Frankie hissed excitedly, pointing to a camel-coloured swing coat with wide arms. 'Come on, I think I hear someone's voice down there.'

Con waved his hand theatrically. 'After you, then.'

Ahead of them, an enormous staircase swept upwards and out of sight, and the late-afternoon sun streamed in through back doors that led to what looked like a lawn. There was a bench with an elaborately carved back, and right at the end, from behind a set of double doors, came the clink of metal against china and the bark of Jools's laughter.

But now that she was standing in front of the doors, Frankie felt distinctly awkward at being here at all, and judging by the pained expression on his face, so did Con. She squared her shoulders. She'd say she was concerned by Violet's text, had decided to follow them; that the door had been open. But she still didn't move, looking around at the heavy wooden furniture instead, the enormous gilded frames covering the walls, beautiful black-and-white photographs . . .

'Goodness!' She turned so suddenly that she made Con walk into the hallway table. There was a loud rattling noise.

'Frankie!' he hissed.

Inside the drawing room, conversation had abruptly ceased and there was the sound of a chair moving. But Frankie didn't pay any attention, nor did she acknowledge Con, who was rubbing his elbow.

She was staring at a portrait on the wall. It was enormous, perhaps to accommodate the horse, a large, haughty-looking creature, because the young woman holding its reins certainly didn't warrant the size of the vast ornate frame. In her late twenties, early thirties perhaps, she was small and slight, blonde hair like a halo around an elfin face, and her expression, although not sombre necessarily, was reserved. Wary.

'Jesus Christ on wheels.' Con's voice was awed. 'Frankie, it's . . . is it?' He turned to Frankie, who was mouthing wordlessly. 'It's *you*.'

Violet

October 1940

Fifty-Four

Sometimes, in the mad, whirlwind days that followed, it felt to Violet as if she'd jumped off a cliff the moment she eased open the stable door and saw Guy standing there. A great, thrilling leap into the unknown, away from the decision about Duffy's letter and giving herself up, which she had to make soon, today, tomorrow at the latest – or maybe she'd wait out the end of the harvest, just a little bit longer . . .

By day, she had wild plans to race up to the village and cable her mother, but by night, she barely waited for the last irregular snuffling to turn before she was out the door, ready to throw herself over that cliff again and again. She knew, she *knew* that what she was doing with Guy was reckless and wrong and that it kept her here when she should go. She knew she should tell him who she really was. But she couldn't bring herself to say the words out loud, just like she couldn't possibly tell the other girls. Guy wanted Lily, who wasn't spoilt and protected, vapid, like all the girls he knew. *She* wanted Lily. She couldn't give her up, not now.

So in the secret hidey-hole of the playhouse, where the world outside ceased to exist, she just kept on being Lily, a wild midnight girl who went further and further until at last there was no going back.

It wasn't necessarily the best time to be wild. While Red and Kit occasionally muttered something about people rustling in their sleep, the harvest kept them busier than ever and the girls fell into their beds so exhausted at night that no one paid too much attention to Violet's movements. Hardwick, however, was another matter entirely.

Where before he had ignored them most of the time, had seemed largely in control of himself, the flat, cold mask of indifference firmly in place, the humiliating defeat over their letters and wages seemed to have unravelled something inside him. More than once, Violet thought she glimpsed the real Hardwick beneath the surface, a dark, brooding, malign presence, and seeing his sweaty face, hair uncustomarily dishevelled, his black suit missing a button, she wondered uneasily what would happen when it finally broke through.

Marigold was their good-luck charm, Kit often said, because with her there he had to keep himself in check, a fact he was clearly aware of and obviously loathed. But it wasn't until a few days after the incident with the letters that Violet began to be truly frightened.

Kit had roused them a little earlier because it took them longer to get up these days, bodily tired as they were, limbs aching and slow with cold. She was arguing in an undertone with Red, who was refusing to get up, threatening to upend a bucket of water over her, when suddenly a different noise cut through the early-morning yawns and rustles emanating from the beds. The barn door had scraped open.

Violet, crouching next to her bed and fishing for her suitcase, looked up. 'Kit,' she hissed as footsteps came towards the ladder; not Myra's light tread, but heavy-footed and brisk. Frowning, Kit turned to count the girls moving about, but before she had reached the end, Hardwick had come up the ladder, his muscles standing out sharply as he pulled himself up into the attic.

It was wrong, was Violet's first conscious thought; everything about this felt *wrong*. How could he invade their private space, this feminine, messy early morning, with girls still curled under blankets, knickers pinned to a makeshift laundry line behind the stove and photos of family and lovers stuck to the underside of the eaves. Kit was opening her mouth, perhaps to say something similar, when Hardwick turned and they saw that his hands were shaking slightly, his fingers uncurling and curling into fists, something deeply unpleasant in his eyes.

Dread creeping up her spine, Violet stayed in a crouch, only her head visible above the mattress. Others were not so fortunate. Ellen had been caught hovering over a bucket of water in her underclothes; Lucy by the mirror, brush in hand, one side of her hair already pinned up, the other curling away from her head in messy whorls. Red, eyes wide open in shock, was lying below Kit, who was still clutching her blanket.

'Mr Hardwick,' Kit finally managed.

'Not quite as bold without your minder, are you?' Hardwick said, and whatever had been moving behind his eyes was now also in his voice, which was hoarse and splintery with loathing.

He walked down the line of beds, turning his head to look at each and every girl. His lips moved as if mentally cataloguing them, and Violet suppressed the strange feeling that he was somehow looking right inside them, where their secrets were hidden and their fears lay naked and exposed: Kit's anxiety for her mother and Lucy's for Matthew, Joan's motherly softness, Red's blustery defiance. And then he came to Violet. Pinning her in place against the side of the bed, his eyes travelled over her nightshirt, lingered on Romy's necklace visible against her collarbone, reached her face.

'Up here, you're all alone,' he said softly, 'and you never know what might happen.'

'Er, Mr Hardwick, can we help you with something?' Kit tried again, but he ignored her, his eyes probing into Violet's, scrabbling around inside her mind. She tried to move, or even just to swallow, but her mouth had gone dry, her chest was so tight she couldn't breathe. When he finally turned to look back at Kit, Violet gulped in air, small bursts of brightness fizzing up in front of her eyes. Breathing hard, she watched him prowl back along the bedsteads, poking at the end of a mattress here, lifting a blanket there, kicking a girl's bag and peering inside.

By the hatch, he turned and faced them again. 'I'll be watching you.' He paused. 'When you think you're on your own and you can talk freely, I'll know; when you laugh amongst each other, I'll hear of it. You won't be able to do anything, say anything, *feel* anything without me being there.'

Kit threw Violet an uncertain look. Was this what he'd come to say to them? This mad, deranged raving?

But Violet moved her tongue around her dry mouth in another vain effort to swallow, because she suddenly knew why he was here and what it was he wanted. The black book.

She had regretted stealing it from his jacket almost instantly; even touching it revolted her, the way the black linen was worn away at the sides by his fingers, the letters flashing by when she accidentally let it fall open, the tallies marching angrily down the page. She should have burnt it or ripped it apart and buried it. Instead, she'd wrapped it up in an old piece of sacking that looked a bit like the underside of the mattress and tried to forget about it. But he clearly hadn't, because the same day as his visit to the attic, Violet ran to drop off her red scarf before Hardwick could object, and found Myra sitting on her bed, holding the book in her hand.

'What are you doing here?' she hissed, one foot still on the top rung of the ladder.

Myra slid slowly off the bed, and then did something that didn't make any sense to Violet at all. She knelt and lifted the corner of the mattress, slid the book back beneath it, tucked the sheet carefully back the way it had been.

'He thinks you took it. Sent me here to look.'

Violet came closer. 'Well then?' She knew she sounded rude, but she didn't care.

Myra's hand stroked the edge of the sheet, her reddened,

chapped hands rough against the worn fabric. 'When his mind is on you, it's not on me.' Her eyes followed her hand along the sheet. 'I can hear him at night, you know. Moving, pacing, talking to himself. Something is eating away at him. I can feel it in there, waiting. Growing.'

Her hand abruptly stopped and she got to her feet, dusted off her dress carefully, as if it wasn't the same ugly brown one she wore day in and day out. Violet stepped in her way.

'But what about you, in that house? What about your . . .' She flicked a glance at Myra's arm. 'I noticed you'd hurt yourself.'

Myra lifted her arm and bent it experimentally at the elbow, then twisted her mouth into a mocking scowl. 'I was careless. It won't happen again, not if I can help it.'

With a quick, light movement, she flicked her apron aside and Violet saw a bunch of keys hanging off her belt. 'By day, he doesn't want me in his sight, and I'm good at locking doors at night, after all. But you . . .' She looked at Violet, all trace of mocking gone. 'You'll want to be careful.'

Thinking of her nightly run to the barn to meet Guy, Violet swallowed. She should keep away, she knew, but she hadn't been able to. 'I don't know why I took it.' She gestured to the mattress. 'It was just an impulse, I suppose, doing *something* when you're feeling helpless.'

Myra's amber eyes gleamed briefly in understanding. 'Thank you for the wreath and the salve,' she said.

Fifty-Five

And then the apples were in.

Just after midday, workers had started drifting out from between the trees, some still shouldering baskets or pulling the last carts piled high with crates towards the sheds.

'Girls!' Susan was waving impatiently from behind the orchard gate. 'Everyone'll be in the orchards, come . . .'

'We've always had a feast at the end of harvest,' Marigold said, skipping to keep up with Violet. 'On the lawns, with a band and tables and dancing. Mother didn't want to do it this year, with Oliver gone.'

'Nothing's been quite the same since Mr Oliver passed,' Susan agreed. 'But it's all right to sit together, mark the end of the harvest, be thankful for a good crop. There'll be food from the kitchens and maybe even a bit of fiddling if we can persuade Inning to play. He's ever so good.'

Kit looked nervously over her shoulder. 'I'm not sure we're allowed,' she started, but Susan shooed them down the lane to where they could see people milling, fires lit. 'It's tradition,' she said firmly. 'And I told him, too, how industrious you've been. What with all the men gone, we wouldn't have done it without you.'

It was the first time anyone had praised them, and for a moment, no one said anything at all. Then Red laughed.

'I bet he didn't like that very much.'

Susan rolled her eyes. 'Well, I told him anyhow.'

'Ah, the land girls!' A woman doling out food from the back of a cart put her hands on her considerable hips and smiled at them. Her voice cut through the clearing, and the girls flushed, feeling uncomfortably exposed. But almost immediately the chatter and laughing resumed, and a number of people even gave them a wave.

'Miss Marigold, how on earth are you still looking peaky when you're running around with them girls all day long?' The woman pushed a slice of bread into Marigold's hand. 'Now you four I know; the rest of you, I'm Mrs Dawson, and this is Molly.' She nodded towards the little maid, who beamed behind her mistress's broad back.

'Delighted, to be sure,' she whispered. 'Can I have a go on your bicycles one day?'

There was stew and bread and cheese, apple compote and cream, a seemingly never-ending supply of tea from two enormous urns, augmented by cold spring water, apple juice and cider. Fires crackled and burnt on the edges of the clearing, making the air feel warm and smell of smoke. Slightly overcome by so much bounty, the girls took their food, smiled their thanks at Molly and settled themselves at the edge of the clearing. Mrs Dawson passed by several times to refill their bowls, telling Marigold off for refusing a third helping then standing over her to watch her eat another piece of buttered bread.

'Well, I didn't think you would last the week, let alone the month!' Kit grinned and held up a mug in Violet's direction. 'Here's to surprises.'

Violet held up her own mug and drank. Joan eyed her sceptically. 'Have you ever had cider before?'

'No, why?' Violet took another swallow of the sweet, fizzing beverage. 'It's delicious, isn't it?'

'I'll say.' Joan snatched the mug out of her hand and tipped its contents into her own, then handed her a beaker of water. 'Easy does it,' she said sternly.

'Speaking of lasting the week, I wonder where Hardwick is,' Kit said suddenly.

'Ooh, maybe he got rip-roaring drunk and is sleeping it off in a discreet corner somewhere,' Red offered. 'Lying in a puddle of his own vomit, splattered in sick—'

'Red!' Lucy said, revolted.

'He's in his office.' Molly passed by with a jug of cider. 'I could see him through the window; he was just sitting there, glowering to himself.' She shivered, spilling some of the cider across her hands.

'He must be well respected around here,' Joan said diplomatically. 'Running an estate like this is no small feat.'

Discordant strumming broke into their conversation and they saw that a makeshift band had assembled on a grassy knoll. Inning, the groom, was picking out the notes of a familiar song while conferring with a woman manhandling an accordion almost as wide as she was tall.

'He's well feared.' Molly tipped generous helpings of cider into their mugs. 'He turned a bit funny when his wife passed away some years ago.'

Red and Violet exchanged a quick look.

'But I'm not supposed to be gossiping,' the girl added regretfully, with a look in Mrs Dawson's direction.

'Oh, go on,' Red said cosily. 'Just us girls here, right?'

'They say she was pregnant,' Molly whispered eagerly, 'but she didn't want the babe. Went to a local woman,' she widened her eyes dramatically, 'but something went wrong. Hardwick found her, and then Mr Manson – you know him, fat, moustache – well, he was called to the scene, said he'd never seen anything like it, blood and screaming—'

'Molly!' Mrs Dawson called sharply from across the clearing. 'I think those girls have had plenty of cider by now. Miss Marigold, come and fetch some cake for your friends.'

'Don't tell anyone I said anything,' Molly begged. She bobbed a small curtsey and splashed another sneaky helping of cider into their mugs before following Marigold back to the cart.

'What was that all about?' Violet said, confused.

'Going to a local woman means she got rid of the babe,' Red told her.

'Like falling down the stairs,' Kit said when Violet still looked blank. 'Taking hot baths and drinking gin.'

'People do that?' Violet said, aghast.

'Maybe there's a different way in London.' Kit grimaced. 'But yes, although not openly, obviously. It's a crime, you know.'

'Silvia didn't want the baby,' Violet repeated, 'because . . . of Hardwick?'

'Can't have been Hardwick's,' Red said knowingly. 'She gets knocked up elsewhere, tries to get rid of the evidence, Hardwick bursts in, Silvia dies, Manson shows up . . .'

'Good Lord in heaven.' Joan shuddered.

'Well, we know how much Hardwick loves being upstanding and unblemished. Not so unblemished after all, eh? At least it explains why he's always at church, and so slavish around Manson,' Red said. 'Wants him quiet. And Manson, the pig, makes him sweat. Not that I feel sorry for either of them, mind.'

But despite her flippant tone, she looked troubled and Joan furtively scanned the clearing. 'All the more reason to keep well out of Hardwick's way,' she said.

Hardwick really had been making Myra pay, then, this girl who looked so much like his errant wife, who reminded him every day of the shame Silvia had brought. And more, Violet thought. He was making *any* woman pay. Had he hated women before Silvia, or did he hate them now because of what she had done? Either way, she resolved to find Myra at the first opportunity, talk to her about . . . well, about what? Running away? The luxury that was freedom?

Abruptly she got up and walked over to where Molly was cutting slices of sheet cake. 'You know Hardwick's daughter Myra?'

'Don't I just,' Molly said darkly. 'Face like a wet weekend.'

'Where was she when all this happened?'

'Well,' Molly said reluctantly, 'I just know what I heard said.'

Violet raised her eyebrows.

'Well, I have ears, I listen. Life can get a bit dull around here. Although this,' she looked down at her knife, 'actually sounded rather sad. The daughter was right there, in the room. Saw the whole thing.'

Violet couldn't stop thinking about Myra and Hardwick and what she'd just heard, and when up on the knoll at the edge of the clearing the accordion flung a scatter of bright chords into the air, it felt jarring and strange. But around them people cheered and clapped, Hardwick was nowhere to be seen and neither was Myra, and, little by little Violet let herself be swept up by the buoyant feeling again. There was a dancing mood in the air, you could tell, but people hadn't quite dared step out into the open space between the bonfires, milling around the edges instead, warming hands or humming in time with the music. There were not nearly enough men to go around, but a pimply youth approached Ellen, and Violet laughed as he swung her up high, causing her to shriek with glee.

'Come on, Marigold, let's you and I dance.'

The bonfires crackled and sparked as Marigold turned at the end of Violet's hand, graceful and sprite-like. Kit wove in and out of the others with Joan, Red energetically twirled Lucy. They danced for a long while until finally drifting back to the edge of the clearing. Kit found her drink behind a tree trunk; Red was ribbing Ellen about the pimply youth. Marigold's hand was looped through the crook of Violet's arm, and they stood catching their breath, shoulders touching, heads together, as Inning started a song they all knew well.

Oh, Danny Boy,
The pipes, the pipes are calling . . .

Pearls of sound wove around the clearing, haunting and

beautiful, and all around, people pushed the familiar words through throats suddenly choked with tears.

The land girls were a swaying, humming knot of beige and green, flushed faces turned towards the music. Lucy's eyes were bright with tears and Joan was patting her back. Violet pulled Marigold's arm more closely through hers and melted into the limbs and the warmth of the song. How could she possibly leave this, she thought as the flames wavered and oscillated in front of her eyes; how could she possibly go back to where she'd been before?

Red nudged her from behind. 'Don't go all sentimental on us now,' she whispered. ' "Danny Boy" is a weepy, everyone knows that.'

'It should be forbidden,' Violet said in a choked voice.

And all my grave will warmer, sweeter be
For you will bend and tell me that you love me . . .

The last few notes drifted across the firelit space until Inning finally stopped, the fiddle poised against his cheek, and took a quick, shy bow as the clearing rang with clapping and cheers. Then they started up again, a merrier tune, which had people turning to their partners in relief, wiping their eyes and hitching smiles back onto their faces.

'Marigold,' Lucy said suddenly. 'I was wondering, would you take a picture of us? It's such a beautiful afternoon and I'd so like to share it with Matthew.'

Marigold's eyes lit up, and she scrambled eagerly for her camera, which she'd hung on a nearby tree during the dancing.

'You need light,' she explained, and Violet smiled at the seriousness in her voice, 'so by the fire would be best.'

'Don't waste your film on us,' Joan said, but Marigold shook her head. 'It's not a waste. You have to capture the moment, that's what Oliver always said.'

Not quite trusting herself to speak, Violet watched the girl solemnly turn the dials at the top of the camera, mouthing numbers and words to herself as she peered through the view-finder. There was a bit of laughing and smoothing-down of hair among the girls, two workers threw in good-natured comments from the sidelines and Molly ran over on the off chance she might be included.

'Oh, I wish we were in fancy frocks,' Joan said. 'Not *these*.' She pulled out the balloony sides of her breeches.

'We're working women.' Red put her hands on her hips. 'What's more attractive than that?'

'Pretty dresses and lipstick.' Ellen fluffed up her hair and tilted her chin down, smiling into the camera.

But the haunting melody lingered, and with it a faint under-current of longing, which even the chatter over the pictures couldn't dispel. It was in Lucy's thin and anxious face, eyes suspiciously bright as she tried to smile for her Matthew, and in the serious way Marigold composed the photos as if there would be no chance of a retake. It was in the slow tendrils of dusk that had started creeping beneath trees, pooling in hollows and nooks. The sense of something coming to an end, the almost unbearable nostalgia for an afternoon, an evening slipping away with no assurance of what the morning would bring.

'Lily, Red, Kit and Joan.' Marigold beckoned them forward. 'That's the last one.'

She made them move close together, arms linked behind each other's backs, then carefully smoothed down their hair, straightened their uniforms. Violet felt the lump in her throat harden when the girl's fingers brushed across her cheek, fine fair eyebrows drawn in concentration, and she suddenly wanted to grab her and hold on, hold all of them and clutch them tight . . .

'Well, girls, this is it.' As if she'd read Violet's thoughts, Kit's voice was rough with emotion. 'Apples are done. Leaves'll be gone. Winter's coming.'

'For heaven's sake, we're trying to smile here, Kit,' Red said exasperatedly.

From light, darkness, Violet thought.

And Marigold clicked the shutter.

A little later, Violet and Marigold were watching the dancing.

'Come on, Lily,' Marigold begged, half shivering, half skipping on her toes in time with the music. 'Let's dance again before the blackout.'

Violet unwound her red scarf and wrapped it around the little girl's neck, tucked it beneath her jacket and buttoned it up all the way. 'I'm fine for the moment, but you go with Red, darling; look, she's waving at you.' She gave her a gentle push.

'What about you?'

'I'll watch.'

As Marigold scampered into the fray, Violet caught a movement among the trees. *Hardwick* was her first thought, and her heart jumped into her throat. But then she made out the lean figure, the fair hair and dark woollen jacket, and her heart slowly slid back into her chest, tight with sudden longing. Looking around, she quietly backed into the bushes behind her, then slipped around the clearing, taking care to keep out of the light from the bonfires. It was darker now, and a chilly dusk had settled like a dome around the brightness of the fires. It had to be almost time for the blackout, but the mood was so charged with relief and post-harvest exhilaration that, clearly, no one had had the heart to call an end to the festivities yet.

She caught up with Guy by the apple sheds, and the moment he saw her, he gripped her arms hard, pulled her close so she fell against him.

'I thought we were going to meet later?' she whispered.

'I heard the music and knew it was time for the feast. I wanted to see you.' His eyes were glittering strangely in the firelight.

411

'Are you upset because people are celebrating?' she asked anxiously. 'Here, let's get away from it for a bit.'

She pulled him further down the path, the music and voices growing fainter as they slipped behind one of the sheds.

'They don't mean to be so cheerful,' she said. 'It's just been a long few days.'

Just at that moment, Inning launched into something bracing and hearty about England and never giving up, and a great cheer went up, accompanied by singing and clapping.

Guy grimaced. 'The feast was a fixed point in our year; the whole harvest was. Olly . . .' He pushed his hand through his hair and rubbed his face. 'Let's go to the playhouse, Lily, come on.' He seemed angry and impatient and upset, his limp more pronounced as he clamped his hand around her elbow and pulled her in the direction of the stable yard.

'I can't just leave now,' she pleaded. 'Not when they're all there. They'd notice and ask questions. It wouldn't be . . .'

'Seemly? It's a bit past that, don't you think?'

She flinched at his mocking laugh and stepped back, and he held up his hands, instantly contrite. 'I'm sorry, Lily. I'm sorry. That came out . . . I suppose you're having too good a time over there; don't let me keep you.'

'Don't be like that,' she said quietly. 'I'll try to get away as soon as I can. There's . . .' she hesitated, 'there's something I have to talk to you about, actually, that I should have told you . . . but I have to go before they miss me.'

He glowered at her, then gave a last sharp tug on her arm that brought her close to him again.

'I'm sorry,' he murmured, and tilted her face up to his. 'I just . . . I want us to be together.'

'Me too,' she said, running her hand across his cheek, smoothing down his hair. 'Wait for me in the playhouse. I'll come, I promise.'

Fifty-Six

Guy was swallowed up by the growing darkness. Shivering a little, Violet looked back towards the clearing framed by bonfires and knew that their conversation had just sped up what the song – and Duffy's letter before that – had already set in motion: the beginning of something ending. The harvest was done; she would talk to him. Tonight. She would tell him the truth: that she belonged to the same world as he did. Finally she would tell him that she wasn't Lily but Violet. She would tell them all. It was time.

And yet she stood by the shed and found she couldn't move. Maybe she didn't have to do it; maybe she could talk to her mother, could persuade her to let her stay, cable her father; maybe she could find a way—

It came out of nowhere. A body slammed into her, a hand clamped itself over her mouth, smothering whatever noise she might have managed and pinning her, writhing and jerking, against the shed wall.

'There's no use calling for help.' Hardwick's voice was soft. 'Meeting your lover, are you? Acting all pious and innocent during the day, but I've watched you, oh I have . . .'

Terrified, Violet bucked against his grip, but he dragged her along the wall, easily avoiding her kicking feet and lashing fists. She smelled something medicinal and sharp, like the distillery when they'd dropped off the remaining sloes, but then all rational thought ceased when a door opened with a soft creak and she was thrust inside.

A small torch flared, then fell with a metallic clank, and for a split second, Hardwick let go of her. She opened her mouth, tried to scream, but he had already whipped out a piece of fabric, slung it around her face and pulled hard. She gagged, struggled to keep it away from her nose. *Air*, she thought desperately, *breathe* . . . She finally succeeded in shifting the fabric down a fraction. Hardwick was a mass of bulging shadows, and when the torch flashed across his face, Violet saw his sweaty forehead, the manic glint in his eyes, the rictus-grin slash of his mouth. *Drunk*. The thought darted into her head, although she'd never seen someone drunk like this, a violent, furious loss of inhibition, an incoherent swell of words and insults, spittle flecking her face.

'. . . teach you,' she made out. 'Whores, all of you. I saw you going into the stables, grinning like the Cheshire Cat when you came out, all lit up. Doing it, you were, I know it, and you won't keep it from me either . . .'

He scrabbled at the front of her jacket, intrusive fingers burrowing between the buttons of her blouse. Behind her gag she keened in terror, bucked and strained, but that only seemed to excite him further. 'Make all the noise in the world. They're too busy drinking and carrying on. No one will hear you.'

They wouldn't, Violet thought, horrified, not with the music, and the way the other girls had come to respect her occasional need for solitude.

'Go on, groan some more.' He was goading her now. 'Is this exciting, like the stables? Were you sighing and moaning like a slut?'

He burrowed at her front again; she felt fingers scraping her flesh as her uniform shirt tore. She threw herself back and forth, her only hope to keep moving and never stop, until morning had broken or he had passed out or—

'Let her go.'

Hardwick jerked back. In the torchlight, his eyes swivelled to the door.

'Oh look, the more the merrier,' he sneered mockingly as Kit, Red and Joan pushed in.

'Let her go,' Red said again, loudly, and she brandished a sharp metal pick in his face. A hoof scraper, Violet thought absurdly, remembering Romy's Desdemona daintily presenting her hooves to have them cleaned. As she shook her head to fight the disorientation that made her fade in and out of the scene, something silver flashed in Hardwick's hand, sang through the air right next to her cheek. She stilled instantly, hung motionless against the wall, and the three girls fell back.

'You're hurting her, please, Mr Hardwick,' Kit said breathlessly.

'And what will you do about it, eh?' Hardwick sneered. 'The harvest is in and I'm going to let you all go tomorrow. I'll make sure you never terrorise another farmer again. No one will believe anything you say anyway; everyone knows what girls like you are like.'

Holding the knife out to keep them at bay, he reached for Violet and very deliberately dragged his hand across her front, cupping her breasts. Behind her gag, she screamed and bucked, and then it all happened very fast. Red lunged and drove the metal pick forward, straight at Hardwick's chest. She had put everything she'd got into it, Violet could see it in her face: every single moment they'd been picked on, singled out, made to feel small. She meant it; she was going to kill him.

Hardwick threw himself sideways, but Red was wiry and scrappy; she turned with him and the scraper pierced his palm, skewering through skin and flesh, glancing off a bone and pinning his hand to the wall beyond. They screamed, all of them, because it was terrible, Hardwick's head was thrown back as he howled, his hand pinned up next to him like some grotesque trophy.

Kit turned to Violet. 'Please tell me he . . . did he . . .' Her hand trembling, she touched Violet's ripped blouse, the torn jumper, the claw-like red marks on her shoulder.

'No,' Violet said hoarsely. She fumbled for the buttons with shaking hands, then froze. The space between her collarbones was empty.

'My cousin's necklace,' she croaked in anguish. 'I think he tore it off me.'

Hardwick was groaning, kicking the wall as Violet snatched up the torch and shone it across the floor, crouched to feel for Romy's necklace in the dirt. The lapels of her shirt flapped across her naked breasts, her fingers were covered in splinters, her face was grimy with dust and tears.

'Lily, please, take this.' There were tears on Red's face too; she pulled her jumper off and tugged it over Violet's head as if she were a child. It smelled of carbolic soap and the green herby things Red was always foraging for in the orchards, and it took Violet straight back to that first morning at Winterbourne, when Red had helped her up onto the wagon. Crouched on the floor, she breathed hard to fight the spots dancing in front of her vision.

'We need to go,' Kit said urgently, 'right now.'

But at that moment, with an almighty roar, Hardwick managed to wrench his hand free. Droplets of blood flew as he came towards them, eyes glassy with pain and drink, and yet even now he was tossing his head back, his expression both triumphant and taunting.

Violet's breath caught in her throat. Myra and Silvia flashed through her head, Kit's cigarette pack ground into the dirt, Lucy's ripped blouse, the letters sitting in his office. His mocking disdain, his arrogance, his sneering contempt. This would never be over; people like Hardwick would always terrorise girls like them and get away with it. She would come out of the shed with her clothes torn and her face bruised and they would whisper and stare at *her*, while he would walk free. It was happening right now, he was making for the door . . .

'No!' She wasn't soft and weak any more. Her muscles were hard under her skin now from working. She roared again, galvanising the others. There was a surge of bodies, a flurry of footsteps, and they had ringed him.

'What are you going to do, eh?' he taunted them. 'What—'

But his voice broke off when Violet, surprising even herself, reared up and slapped him hard on the side of the jaw, slapped him again before he could react, and when he tried to grasp her hand, his was too slippery with blood to get traction, allowing Joan to drive an unexpected fist into the fleshy part under his arm.

He grunted as Red kicked out at him again and again. 'You deserve everything you get,' she shouted. 'You dirty, cruel bastard . . .' But he managed to shove her back so she fell against Kit, and then, unbelievably, he started laughing, a horrible, mocking laugh that rang off the walls, shrill, discordant, too loud.

Violet lunged, pushing off the floor with all her might, just as Kit came at him from the side. Red had rolled herself into his way to knock his legs out from underneath him, and Joan's hands were flying as she moved in for a last punch. Eyes bulging in surprise, he grunted at the combined impact and fell backwards, into the darkness beyond the torchlight. There was a sickening crunch, and then all was still.

The four girls breathed heavily, pushing hair out of their eyes.

'Oh God,' Kit said in a trembling voice. 'Oh God. Oh God. Oh God.' She raised her clasped hands in supplication. 'Please . . .'

'Kit, stop.' Violet felt blood trickle down her temple as she shone the torch into the corner. Her hand was shaking so hard it was difficult to make him out clearly, but she groaned with relief when his uninjured hand came up slowly to shield his eyes from the glare of the beam.

'He's all right,' she said shrilly.

'We need to go, we need to go,' Joan was babbling. 'Girls, we need to go *now*.'

'We'll say we were never here.' Red wiped her hands frantically on her breeches. 'We'll rejoin the party, we'll pretend we were there all along.'

'But *he* will tell tomorrow, and they'll believe him when he says it was us.' Kit's voice was choked. 'He's said so many things about us already, they won't trust us . . .'

'Quiet,' Violet hissed. She lifted her head like an animal scenting danger, felt her heart beat faster. Kit frowned, looked at Red, but then they all heard it.

A faint puckering sound in the sky.

They must have been like a bullseye in the night, Violet sometimes thought afterwards. The bonfires, the smoke. Maybe the planes had come back from somewhere else and needed to shed the rest of their weight; bombers often did that, she had heard, to be able to make it home. Or maybe the pilot had felt all that life down below, the love and friendship and joy and music, all of it thriving in spite of their attempts to snuff them out.

They don't care about us, it'll be fine, it'll be fine, it'll be . . . but it was different, and she blinked hard to understand why. They were flying closer, lower, the sound swelling and ebbing as if they were circling . . .

'The gong,' Joan said hysterically. 'Why is no one sounding the *gong*?'

Her words sounded woolly inside Violet's head, where the twitchy, trembly need to hide warred with the urge to run. *Fight or flight.* She started shaking, harder and harder.

'No one's *there* to sound the gong, they're all over by the clearing!' Kit shouted.

The clearing. Violet's mind was suddenly sharp; the twitching, the shaking, the woolliness had disappeared.

'The others,' she shouted. 'Marigold!'

Across the valley, a siren was wailing as they ran, following the torch's wildly jerking beam towards the clearing. The sound of the motors was no longer gently puckering but an insistent drone that wanted to fill Violet up, make her burrow into the undergrowth. But she pushed her legs down and sprinted faster through the trees, tossing the flashlight into the grass when the bulb dimmed and died. It was easier to see now because smoke, white and wet, was billowing into the night sky.

'They've doused the fires,' she shouted as noise swelled above. People came running towards them, some veering towards the house as if it was going to offer shelter, others to the apple sheds as instructed.

'Marigold!' Violet screamed through the chaos. 'Ellen! Lucy!'

And then a discordant, ear-splitting boom split the fragrant autumn evening and the ground shook, throwing up soil and rocks and parts of trees. People were swarming in all directions now, headless with panic. Frantically Violet squinted through the dust and smoke for a small figure. The clearing hadn't been hit directly, she thought wildly; the bombers had been confused, perhaps by the white smoke from the wetly smouldering fires.

Suddenly a small shape came hurtling out of the trees and collided so hard with her that she was sent toppling backwards into the long wet grass.

'Marigold!' She clasped the girl's shaking body against her and rolled them all the way underneath the trees. 'We have to get away,' she rasped. 'Where are the others?' But already Lucy's lanky frame was looming out of the smoke, Ellen and the others behind her.

'Kit!' Lucy shrieked. 'Where have you *been*?'

She pulled Violet and Marigold up, and they all started running, ducking low beneath the trees although Violet knew they wouldn't offer any protection.

'They're turning.' Kit materialised by her side, Red's face a mask of horror next to her. 'They're coming back! We have to go, *now*—'

Another ear-splitting explosion rocked the ground just ahead.

'Stop, *stop*,' Violet screamed, because there was nowhere *to* go, there was nowhere safe. She gave a cry of horror when she saw that the east wing of the house had been grazed, taking out the kitchen garden, and another bomb had . . . Oh God, the archway, the canteen, the *stable yard* – and that was when her heart stopped altogether.

'The stables.' She let go of Marigold and thrust her at Kit.

The planes dipped one last time and Violet ran like she had never run in her life, even though she knew she'd never be able to get there in time, would never reach him. There was the agonised screaming of humans and horses, and Violet heard her own screams weave into the melee of terror, louder and louder until she was convinced that even Guy, waiting for her in the playhouse, would hear her. But then the trees thinned and she saw flames lick high, and by the time she reached the stable yard, fire was everywhere.

Fifty-Seven

The morning came all too soon, and it was a particularly glorious kind, the icy blue sky especially beautiful, the sunrise such a poignant explosion of colours that it seemed to mock the devastation below even more harshly.

Winterbourne House glowed golden as the early-morning sun caressed the enormous gash at the edge of the east wing where the outer wall had been neatly cut away, showing a cross-section of the rooms stacked one on top of the other: dark wooden furniture and beds, curtains ballooning out the side, picture frames on the remaining walls. Elsewhere, uprooted trees had fallen across trenches of upturned soil, root balls sticking up in the air; sheds had been hit by falling trees or damaged by flying debris.

It was the stable yard, however, the heart of Winterbourne, that had suffered the most. The archway still stood, as did the tower, with the sundial smudged in black. But the wooden stable buildings had continued to burn through the night, and frantic efforts to control the fire had only succeeded in keeping it from spreading to the rest of the estate buildings and the distillery. Even now, the stables were still smouldering, tendrils of grey smoke drifting up into the crisp air, curling lazily around the soot-blackened remnants. A few wooden posts were still standing, with the occasional cross-beam jutting out, and here and there, hanging forlornly on a nail, a saddle or a piece of tack had miraculously survived.

It was Violet who'd told the firemen that there was a good chance Guy Crowden had been caught in the stables. At the sight of her face and the sound of her dead, lifeless voice, they didn't waste time asking more questions, and, since he was nowhere else to be found, began the long, horrifying task of cooling down the ruins enough to start looking for a body.

Violet stood and watched, as close as she was allowed, before some official barked at her to *get back, please, miss, it's not safe*. Obediently she moved, before, inch by inch, creeping back to her original place. At first the other girls had tried to pull her away, without even really knowing what was keeping her there. But eventually they let her be, only periodically coming back to check on her.

'Marigold?' she asked, eyes fixed on the wreckage.

'With her mother,' Kit said, and Violet nodded.

Shouts and conversation flew back and forth behind her, occasionally managing to rouse her from her fog of despair and help her piece together what had happened. As soon as he had heard the second impact, Guy must have let loose as many of the horses as he could, because people running away from the clearing had met the animals tearing into the orchards. Two had perished in the fire, though, and it was thought that Guy had wasted precious time coaxing them towards the door.

Violet imagined him dragging his leg along, face set in a furious scowl of pain and rage at not being able to move faster. She pressed cold fingers to her mouth to stop her teeth from chattering, but her hands were shaking so much they were tearing at her lips, nails rasping across her cheeks. Every now and then, her body convulsed, making her wrap her arms around herself, fighting the temptation to fall into the same black void that had opened up in the days after Romy's death. She couldn't do that now, though, she *had* to keep looking at that narrow enclosure behind the last horse box, where the ceiling would be scattered with brightly coloured stars and the man in the moon had smiled down at her and Guy wrapped in each other's arms on a narrow cot, spinning the globe and dreaming of freedom. She couldn't look away, because as long as she looked, it wasn't true, it wasn't final. Guy would appear, perhaps any moment now, smiling that slow, secret smile he'd smiled just for her, pushing sooty hands through his hair. *There you are! You've been keeping me waiting . . .*

I'm here, she answered in her mind. *I'll always be here.*

When they finally retrieved what was left of Guy's body, Violet couldn't see the remains – heaven had granted her that at least – but she watched them bring out a shroud, carrying it solemnly between them and confirming the news with a quick nod that spread like wildfire around the stable yard.

'Lord Crowden is dead,' one whisper passed on to the next. 'He was killed in the fire.'

They parted when Lady Crowden, distraught beyond recognition, appeared briefly, supported by Marigold, whose face was set in a tear-stained scowl.

When Lady Crowden collapsed and had to be carried back to the house, the feeling of chaos and disorder intensified. Confused, disorientated, devastated, people spilled in and out of the orchards, where horses still roamed beneath the trees. Most had been up all night and were still randomly sifting through the wreckage; others were tending to the injured, but overall no one seemed to know quite what to do.

'Excuse me.' Kit stopped an official-looking man who was trying to corral a group into clearing rubble. 'Shouldn't we have a single area for the wounded, where the doctor can check on them more easily? Maybe in the canteen? I know there's a stack of spare cot beds for the migrant workers; we could set them up in rows.'

Looking harassed and very tired, the man was about to snap something dismissive when he caught sight of the land girls' uniforms, their black and dirty hands and grim expressions.

'Go find the doctor and help organise it,' he said. 'But I wish to God someone would come and tell us who all these people are and who's missing. Where on earth is Mr Hardwick?'

The name, finally, cut through the swirling fog in Violet's head. She turned in time to see Kit and Joan exchange a look of horror.

'He's not here?' Red's voice sounded thin and horrified. 'I thought I saw him earlier, over by the office.'

'Not been seen since last night,' the man said distractedly. Someone shouted for him and he was gone.

'Lucy,' Kit said shrilly, quite visibly gathering her wits about her. 'Take Ellen and the others and go find the doctor. We,' she gestured with a shaking hand at herself, Violet, Joan and Red, 'will round up the cots. Be quick,' she snapped when Lucy hung back, looking worriedly at Red, who was breathing so hard through her nose she looked like she was about to faint.

'He wasn't . . . I mean, he . . .' Under the thick layer of soot and grime, Joan's face was ashen.

'Maybe he's confused,' Red hissed. 'Maybe he got hit on the head and isn't himself and is now wandering around somewhere. We just need to find him.'

'Or he got caught in the raid,' Kit said. 'Staggering back to the bonfires, just like us, and was hit by something.'

'We'll go and look.' Violet shrank back from the sound of her own voice, unemotional and not at all like herself. 'We need to go back to the shed and make sure he's not still there, or if he is, then we have to tell someone – the police – that it was an accident.'

'Are you mad?' Kit said, aghast. 'We're not telling anyone anything.'

'And we need to stay as far away from that shed as possible,' Red agreed urgently. 'No one knew we were there, and no one will remember that we left the clearing just before the air raid. The chaos is on our side, it's our only chance.'

'No,' Violet said. 'We *cannot* keep this quiet.'

There was sudden movement and shouting from the gates leading into the orchards. Word spread fast in situations like these, travelling like wildfire from mouth to mouth, gaining momentum.

'It's Mr Hardwick,' someone shouted. 'Found in one of the apple sheds. He's dead.'

Violet was never quite sure what her very first emotion was after she heard. Shock or regret? Guilt or relief? She didn't probe too far for an answer, though, because deep down she was afraid of what she might find. The others groaned and whispered and looked ashen, all the things you did when someone died, but was there a hint of relief on Kit's face? A flitter of triumph on Red's? And what on earth were they going to do now?

They tried to come to a decision for most of the day, furious hissed debates snatched whenever the other girls were preoccupied with the makeshift hospital, but they couldn't agree on a way forward. Several times Violet slipped away to try and find Myra, tell her how sorry she was, ask if she could help. But Hardwick's living quarters were silent and dark and no one answered the door when she knocked.

'Probably staying with a relative,' Kit said distractedly.

'I'm not sure she's all that sad, though, to be honest,' Red muttered. 'Would you be?'

'Bite your tongue!' Joan said, unusually sharply.

'But what if she has no one?' Violet asked.

'She'll fall on her feet.' Anxiety made Kit even more snappish than usual. 'Okay, let's think one more time . . .'

'Ah, terrible day, terrible day,' Mr Manson greeted the hastily assembled crowd – orchard workers, house staff and those villagers present at the harvest feast – below the sundial next morning. 'We're full of sadness about the death of the esteemed Mr Hardwick.'

Violet felt nausea flood her and tried to breathe it away. Dimly she saw something move, then Marigold was there. Her face was pale and she looked very tired, but oddly composed, too, her eyes fixed on Mr Manson. She didn't slip her hand into Violet's the way she usually did, or melt against her side. She just stood close enough so Violet felt her warmth and the scratchy wool of her black and silver coat.

Manson droned on, although his audience wasn't fully attentive, with people whispering in twos and threes, Inning walking past holding armfuls of ropes and leather for the last few horses running wild.

'While we mourn those who were lost in this senseless tragedy,' Manson raised his voice like a whip, and Inning froze in his tracks, 'there is a more serious matter to contend with. There are some questions surrounding Mr Hardwick's death, and I would like the owner of this item to step forward, please.'

And then Violet's insides gave a final, devastating heave as Manson held up something small and shiny dangling from a chain. She didn't have to squint like the rest of the crowd, shifting and moving closer to see, then muttering to each other, wondering whose it might be. She had touched it all the hours of the day, that small disc ringed with diamonds that had been her lifeline to Romy over the last few weeks and which Hardwick had ripped off in the shed. As if in a trance, she detached herself from the land girls, started to move. Kit's hand shot out and pushed her back into Marigold's arms.

'Let me go,' Violet whispered furiously, but Marigold wrapped her arms all the way around her middle, held on while Kit and Red shielded her from view.

'You don't understand,' Violet hissed.

'You'll never get out of this, Lily, never,' Red muttered. 'Hush up.'

But it was too late. Mr Manson's head had already turned in their direction. He narrowed his eyes in assessment, then, nodding to a man in a dark suit to follow him, approached the land girls.

'We meet again,' he said, delighted. 'I only wish it was in more favourable circumstances. I take it this has caught someone's eye, eh?'

The chain had been broken, and dirt had been trodden into the grooves of the diamonds during the struggle with Hardwick. It gleamed dully in Manson's milky palm, his smooth white fingers playing with the chain almost suggestively, the dirt on the back of the disc scraped away to reveal Romy's name. Violet couldn't help herself. She reached for it, reconsidered halfway through, tried to turn it into a shrug.

'Aha! I think we have our culprit.' Manson raised an eyebrow. But the land girls drew together, closing all the way around Violet, and a hush fell over the stable yard as all eyes fixed on the stand-off between Manson's soft pale hand stretched out in Violet's direction and the green and beige pack of land girls, grim and impassive, staring back at him.

Alas, as if the last twenty-four hours hadn't brought enough, fate intervened once more. The sound of tyres crunching on the ground had become so familiar over the last day that no one paid any attention at first, and it wasn't until the black-suited man nudged Manson that heads began to turn, watching a large, shiny car pull slowly into the stable yard.

Fifty-Eight

'Who on earth is that?' Manson snapped as workers and staff ebbed and flowed in a wide circle around the car, talking excitedly.

'That,' Violet said quietly, 'is my mother.'

She gave a small, shuddery sigh. In a strange way, after the weeks of imagining her mother here, after her horror at the prospect of having her true self revealed, she suddenly felt an odd sense of release. As if, with a great wrench, Guy's death had ripped everything wide open, her London past, her land girl present and the wild seesaw between the two, and the final, inevitable discovery by her mother would be forcing them to re-form into something entirely new.

Joan had whirled around and was gaping at her.

'You're royalty?' Red breathed, looking so incredulous that Kit had to laugh, despite everything.

'How did a communist end up with a lady for a best friend, eh? I always knew there was something that didn't quite add up about you,' she told Violet.

'No you didn't,' said Red heatedly. 'Don't mind her, Lily, she's just jealous.'

'Excuse me!' Manson had finally gathered his wits and was just about to reassert his authority when the car's passenger door opened.

Eleanor Etherington had always known how to make an entrance. She emerged from the vehicle and took a moment to settle her coat, then straightened haughtily. But when she came closer, Violet saw that her hair was shot through with grey strands that hadn't been there before, deep grooves criss-crossing a face that seemed white and old.

Eleanor silently took in the land girls' appearance, identically tousled and dirty and heavy-booted, then looked at Marigold, who was watching the scenario unfold with a little frown, and finally settled on her daughter. They regarded each other warily. Violet held her breath, waiting – for what? A furious embrace? A public dressing-down? An outburst of anger?

Her mother, of course, did none of these things; instead, after an interminable moment, she leaned forward slightly stiffly, put both her hands on Violet's arms and pulled her close for a second, then released her again.

The land girls sighed in awe at such regal behaviour, while Manson seemed to be grasping for something to say. Just at that moment, however, a second figure came trotting around the car. A familiar face, good-natured and round, a shock of blond hair pushing up at the back.

'Duffy!' Violet broke the silence, and before anyone could stop her, she threw her arms around his neck. 'I can't believe you're here,' she said into his hair. 'I'm so glad.'

Duffy looked a bit embarrassed but also pleased as he patted her back awkwardly. 'As you can see, I crumbled under the pressure. But I had to, Vi, it was getting a little absurd. She was so upset, and I hadn't heard from you in so long. I was worried about your father, too—'

'Excuse me.' A strident voice came from behind them. 'We're in the middle of a criminal investigation, sir, so if you'd kindly step aside, please. We've had a harrowing few days, not to mention an unlawful death, in which this pretty lady—'

'I beg your pardon?' It was the first time Eleanor Etherington had spoken, and as she drew herself up, even Manson baulked slightly. 'Of all the ridiculous things that seem to have been going on in this godforsaken place, this really is the limit.

This is my daughter, and I'm taking her back to London with me.' She snatched up Violet's arm and jerked at it.

'Her necklace was found next to a dead man,' Manson said loudly, motioning for an official to take Violet's other arm. 'I beg you, ma'am, don't cross me.'

'I very much hope you're not saying what I think you're saying,' Eleanor said coldly. 'Who is in charge around here? I want his name, and then, my good man, you'll be sorry.'

A whisper and not a few giggles rose from the crowd. Manson went puce and started sweeping the land girls towards Hardwick's office.

'Where are you going?' Eleanor snapped. 'We're not finished.'

'We will discuss this in private,' Manson said imperiously. He motioned for one official to shoo the girls into Hardwick's office, then instructed the other to start taking down details among the crowd.

Afterwards, Violet wondered whether Manson had chosen Hardwick's office deliberately to wrong-foot them, or maybe it was her own memory of the last few times they were in here, but the moment she stepped across the threshold, she felt small and defenceless. Manson wisely opted to stand, but not before offering Eleanor Etherington the uncomfortable wooden chair with a flick of his hand, clearly so he could then turn his back on her in pointed indifference.

'Line up, please,' he said sharply as the land girls muttered. 'Quietly. No one speaks unless spoken to.'

'Do not address my daughter like that.' Eleanor got up from the chair. 'We are seeking legal counsel immediately.'

'Leave it, Mother,' Violet said quietly. 'I'll deal with this.'

It was the first time she'd spoken to her mother since she had arrived, and certainly the first time she'd ever addressed her like that, which seemed to take Eleanor by such surprise that she sat abruptly back down.

'Now, Miss Burns,' Manson spoke silkily.

'Etherington,' Eleanor barked from her chair.

'An impostor,' Manson clarified. 'Write that down, Constable.'

'Nothing more than a silly little runaway,' Eleanor said dismissively.

Violet turned and looked at her mother for a long moment without saying anything, without even moving. Eleanor was the first to break away, muttering something under her breath.

'What's the question again, Mr Manson?' Violet said evenly.

'The question is, do you recognise this necklace?' Manson once more held out the little pile of broken chain and muddy silver.

'Yes, it's mine,' Violet said.

'Then would you explain how it came to be trodden into the ground next to Mr Hardwick's body?'

'I – I don't know. I lost it during harvest last week,' Violet stammered when she felt Red's fingers dig into her back.

'And the other things in the shed?' Manson demanded. 'Blood, and a hook of some kind, and—'

But at this moment, the other official popped his head round the door. 'A word, Mr Manson,' he said shyly.

'You're not to say another thing,' Kit hissed out of the corner of her mouth. 'I mean it, Lily. We can sort this out.'

Violet sighed and looked at her, at all of them, Joan chewing her lip worriedly, Red uncharacteristically quiet, Marigold deathly pale and red-eyed, Lucy, who looked like she hadn't slept in weeks, Ellen and Kate and the rest of them.

'My name is Violet,' she said. 'And I'm sorry about not telling you, about any of this. I was ashamed of who I was. I just wanted to work. Forget about my cousin's death. Do something that would make a difference. But most of all, I loved being here with you.'

The girls nodded; someone patted her arm.

'Violet's pretty,' Red said. 'I think we can live with that.'

She gave her a little nudge, and Violet felt winded with relief that they didn't think less of her.

'It doesn't look like I'll be with you much longer, though,' she said hollowly.

Behind them, Manson was talking in a low, urgent voice, and Violet turned to Marigold.

'I'm so sorry,' she whispered. 'First Oliver, now Guy. I'm heartbroken for you. But I know you're strong. Remember fighting for the letters, riding a bicycle, flying from the tree. You can fly, darling, you really can.'

For just a moment, Marigold shrank against her, small and pale the way she'd been when Violet first met her, as if she was trying to make herself invisible. But Violet put her hand under her chin and brought her face close to hers. 'Guy once told me that a Crowden has always run the Winterbourne Orchards. That'll have to be you now, do you hear me? You can do it, better than anyone.' Her throat was tight with tears when Marigold gave a small head bob, put her hand on Violet's sleeve.

'Two flowers,' she whispered. 'Even with your new name, we're still two flowers.'

Violet blinked and tears fell on Marigold's hand. 'Exactly,' she whispered.

'Well,' Manson stepped back in front of them, 'it looks like there's a new twist. Two workers . . . esteemed village women, very well respected,' he added, clearly to nip any objection from Lady Etherington in the bud, '. . . claim to have seen you leave the festivities. Four of you, to be precise. The tall one,' he pointed at Kit, 'the red-haired one – that'll be you, will it, young lady?' He flicked an appreciative look at Red. 'And a plump, dark-haired one.' He raked his eyes down the line and Joan squared her shoulders.

'Me,' she said coldly.

'And you,' he looked at Violet, practically quivering with ill-concealed excitement, 'obviously.'

So this was it. This was the end of the line. Violet wasn't going back to London, she was going to prison, they all were . . .

'They were with me,' Marigold said suddenly. 'Lily . . . Violet . . .' her lips quirked a little, 'had offered to find me something warm to wear because it was getting so cold. It took her a little while and I asked the others to come with me – it was ever so dark – to search for her.'

'Miss Marigold,' Manson said with a show of concern, 'I'm so sorry that you feel compelled to be a part of this. You shouldn't be here, you should be supporting your poor mother – what on earth both of you must be going through at the moment doesn't bear thinking about. Constable, fetch someone to take her back to the house.'

'Thank you for your concern,' Marigold neatly plucked the constable's hand from her arm. 'But I'll stay right here. As I said, we went in search of her, the four of us.'

'And you found her at the apple storage shed,' Manson said, after a brief pause. 'We know this—'

'Of course not,' Marigold said coldly. 'Why would anyone go to the apple storage shed at night?'

Duffy made a small, indeterminate noise of mirth.

'She'd gone all the way back to the barn and we met her there.'

'The barn?'

'Where they sleep,' Marigold clarified, and Violet's mother bit back a groan.

'And she brought you a coat? This one? It looks too new.'

'Why would I wear my good coat to the last day of harvest?' she said dismissively. 'And what would it be doing in the land girls' barn? No, she brought me one of her scarves.'

'A scarf.' Manson seemed nonplussed, and Violet couldn't blame him, not when Marigold was looking at him with such derision.

'Yes.' The girl opened her coat a little and pulled apart the lapels to reveal Violet's red woollen scarf.

'Oh, I knew it would come in handy, Vi.' Duffy sounded pleased. 'It was a gift from me,' he told Manson proudly, before remembering his aunt's presence and lapsing into silence.

'It's very nice,' Marigold told Duffy, who solemnly accepted the praise. 'And very warm,' she said to Manson. 'And then,' her voice faltered a little, 'on our way back, we heard the planes.' She swallowed, and her eyes shone with tears. 'We ran back towards the clearing, because we had to help everyone there douse the fires and get away. We got separated in our haste; it was . . . it was terrible,' she finished, and there was so much fear and grief and desperation in those last few words that no one could speak.

'That it was,' Lucy finally said. She looked straight at Violet, then at Kit, Joan and Red, her face expressionless as she caught Marigold's eyes for the briefest of seconds. Marigold nodded, dabbing her cheeks with the large white handkerchief that Duffy handed her, and the nod travelled across the group, a vibration of silent assent that was passed from one to another as they drew together, a pack of identical beige and green, standing close for the last time.

Frankie

September 2004

Fifty-Nine

'How can this possibly be?' Frankie was still staring up at the portrait. It wasn't her, obviously; the young woman's face was less heart-shaped than Frankie's, her eyes set a little wider apart, her mouth more generous. But the likeness was unmissable, as if someone had taken Frankie's clear grey eyes and fair brow, the cut of her cheekbones, her fine blonde hair that insisted on feathering up when she was agitated, and reassembled them in a different but unmistakably similar way.

'I'd quite like to know the same,' a voice came from behind her.

Frankie twitched around, and next to her, Con gulped. 'We're so sorry,' he said hurriedly. 'We didn't mean to break . . . I mean, we heard Mrs Etherington was here, that's why . . .' He broke off and turned to Frankie, but Frankie was gazing at the woman.

She was a good few decades older than the one in the painting. Her hair had gone entirely white, and her face was lined and leathery, like someone who had spent a lot of time outdoors, presumably on the back of the horse still surveying them haughtily from the painting. But the likeness was the same, and for a moment Frankie had the disorientating feeling that she'd just strayed into her own future.

'I'm Marigold Fairweather.' The woman moved with a lightness that belied her age, raking her eyes across Frankie's face.

Frankie backed away, dragging Con with her, until the backs of her legs hit the wooden bench. She reached out and held onto its curved back. 'You're Marigold? I thought that maybe you were . . .' She'd been about to say *dead*, but it sounded ludicrously melodramatic. Con was still staring, his eyes flicking back and forth between the woman, the painting and Frankie.

'You and I *have* to be . . .' Marigold had slowed, was speaking more quietly, as if not to spook Frankie further.

'Related, yes.' Violet stepped out from behind her, flanked by Jools, Kit and Joan. 'Great-niece and great-aunt. Frankie, what on earth are you doing here?'

Marigold had clapped a hand over her mouth. 'You don't mean to say, surely . . . All these years . . . *Guy*?' she said from behind her knuckles.

'Who is Guy?' Frankie could feel herself fraying at the edges, and dug her nails into the wood. 'Violet, what's going on?'

'It's why I'm here, partly.' Violet swallowed as she looked between Marigold and Frankie. 'I wanted to tell you, Marigold. So many times I wanted to get in touch, you have no idea. But I couldn't come back. We had agreed, remember? But now . . . Stella was Guy's daughter.'

She broke off, and her fingers strayed towards the shiny patch on her cardigan. Frankie, whose head was spinning with a million questions, shook it hard to clear it, then reached for Violet's hand to pull it away, but Violet seemed to catch herself, relaxed her fingers.

'I'll explain all of it, Frankie. But first I have to speak to Marigold. And you,' she rounded on the land girls, 'we all have to finally . . .'

'. . . talk,' Jools muttered resignedly.

'Yes,' Violet said fiercely. 'About everything, before it's too late, before it drives me completely mad.'

'It was this time sixty-four years ago,' Joan whispered.

Marigold let out a long breath, suddenly looking as old as she probably was. 'So much death on that day.'

'What happened?' Frankie couldn't stand not knowing any longer. 'You didn't . . . You're not . . . Did you *kill* someone?'

'Of course they didn't,' Con said quickly. 'Er, did you?' He looked nervously at Violet and Marigold.

A second passed, then another, and Violet's mouth was

moving but no sound emerged. She was trembling; Frankie could see small shivers running up and down her body.

'We . . . I mean, there was an air raid,' Kit said in a rush, as if she couldn't bear the silence a minute longer, 'and he—'

'No.' A sheen of sweat glinted across Violet's forehead. 'It wasn't the air raid. It was me. It was my fault. I shoved him, so hard I can still feel it.'

'Don't be stupid, Lily.' Kit's voice was firmer now. 'It was all of us. *I* hit him, too. Red kicked his legs out from under him, or he would never have gone down. Joan punched him in the side and sent him right into your last shove. His name was Hardwick,' she told Frankie. 'And he wasn't a good man. He was a terrible bully. He would have *raped* Lily that night.'

'It didn't give us the right to just leave him there,' Violet said roughly.

'We weren't *going* to, though,' Joan threw in quickly. 'It all happened at the same time, the air raid, the other girls and Marigold out there. Hardwick was alive, we *saw* him move. We wouldn't have just left him there if we hadn't assumed he'd be able to get away.'

'Yes, get away and tell everyone some sick tainted story about us being whores and criminals, until no one would touch us,' Jools said savagely. 'He died because he wanted to hurt us, because he was attacking us and got a dose of his own medicine back. At the very least, it was self-defence.'

'It was *murder*.' And Violet sat down on the hallway bench, covered her face and started to cry. Sobs racked her frame, a torrent of words, indistinguishable and horrible, poured out from behind her hands. Abandoning all questions, her sense of horror, her confusion, Frankie fell onto the bench next to her. 'Please, Violet, don't cry. It'll be fine.' She patted her heaving back and looked up at the women pleadingly.

'"Fine" wouldn't really be the word I'd use,' Jools muttered, but she sat down on Violet's other side, motioning for an

439

alarmed-looking Con to produce a handkerchief. 'Come on, Violet, easy now.'

'Something sweet is what she needs,' Joan said anxiously. 'I'll fetch her some tea. Kit, don't just stand there, do something.'

'I'm fine,' Violet said hoarsely. She accepted the pack of tissues from Con's hand, wiped her face, took several deep breaths, pushed shaking palms into her legs to stop them from trembling.

'Whatever it was, it wasn't just you,' Kit said firmly. 'It was all of us.'

'And Myra,' Marigold said quietly.

'Myra?' Violet wiped her eyes. 'What do you mean?'

Marigold sighed. 'I'm not usually in the habit of making men run errands for me, but would you be so kind as to fetch me a chair, that one there?' she asked Con.

He hurried to bring not only the chair but a small stool for Joan as well, then quickly sat down on the floor next to Frankie's legs, his face upturned as if this was a particularly good story hour at the library.

'Myra turned up for the funeral,' Marigold said. 'We had to go; obviously it would have looked strange if we hadn't. But then she disappeared and I . . . Well, my mother wasn't in any state to run things, so we found a new overseer, although I would have much preferred for you to take things over.' She gave Kit a wry grimace. 'Anyhow, that meant I wasn't able to keep track of Myra. I heard that she'd become a gunner girl or something, and then I lost sight of her for many years, until Mrs Dawson received a letter from her. I hadn't quite realised that Mrs Dawson was probably the only person Myra felt close to, close enough to let on how truly awful things had been with her father. Being there when her mother died, Hardwick refusing to bury Silvia properly because she'd cheated on him, the baby, the shame, punishing Myra for it all. It got a little better when he was distracted – by the land girls – but she realised that something about you was making him unhinged. She was waiting for it to come to a head, for something to happen, and at the harvest celebration, it did. He'd forbidden her to go but she'd seen him leave the office, and when he didn't return, she went looking for him.'

Marigold paused and swallowed. From the yard Frankie could hear the distant sound of voices, the sputtering of an engine, but in here the silence was absolute.

'When she found him, he had hit his head, was in a bad way. She saw him lying there, begging her to help him, but what with the air raid, she . . .' Marigold broke off, regrouped, but she didn't need to say anything else.

'She left him there?' Joan's voice was hoarse with horror. 'Her own father?'

'*We* left him there.' Violet's face was ashen as she stared at Marigold.

'Because there was an air raid,' Jools said through gritted teeth. 'The world was literally exploding, Violet. It was a bloody accident, when will you get that into your head?'

'She didn't just leave him.' Marigold looked around the group. 'She dragged a great big tree branch in front of the door and jammed it against the frame so he couldn't get out. And then she ran. By the time someone finally found him the following day, he was dead.'

Sixty

'Poor girl,' Joan whispered. 'Poor, poor girl.'

Kit exhaled noisily. 'And why did that pig Manson not investigate the door?'

'Parts of the orchard near there were hit afterwards, so it probably looked like the branch had fallen randomly. Also, he thought he could pin it on you.' Marigold jabbed her chin at the four women.

Silence fell again.

'It doesn't absolve us,' Violet said finally, her voice shaking a little. 'It just adds another person to carry the burden. God, haven't you felt it, all your lives? That ugliness, like a poison? I know I have. First Romy's death, then his. No matter how hard I worked, how respectable I was, how *good* I tried to be, I could never get rid of it.'

'You've helped so many women and children,' Jools said angrily. 'You've made people strong, got them back on their feet; you've saved lives in small ways a hundred times over.'

'I don't think any of us are free of him, are we?' Violet said as if Jools hadn't spoken. 'Joan has her faith; you, Kit, you have your farm; Jools, well, your *opinions*. But you can't tell me, none of you,' she swept her hand around the group, 'that he hasn't always been there with you.' She took a deep breath. 'You can't tell me that you weren't afraid that one day someone would come knocking on your door to ask questions, to dig something up and make you pay.'

'I had a close call once,' Jools said unexpectedly. 'They came to interview me for some centennial celebrations. Had got my name from some old records, wanted me to share my experiences. Experiences, ha!' She barked a sarcastic laugh.

442

'You never told me,' Violet said.

'Well, you and I had made a pact not to talk about it. Which you broke, by the way.'

'I was asked to be interviewed, too.' Kit twisted her fingers in her lap. 'They were doing a parade, old land girls in their uniform, that sort of thing, for a VE Day celebration in the nineties. A local journalist dropped by.' She made a face, 'I remember thinking how nice it would have been to talk about the happy times. There were good things too, you know, not just . . . *that*.'

'You didn't say anything, though, did you?' Jools asked, the fearful note in her voice unmistakable.

'Now will you look at that.' Kit gave Jools a pointed glance. 'The indomitable Red, afraid of *something* after all.'

'Just because I don't want to go to prison doesn't mean I'm afraid.'

'They wouldn't send old women to prison,' Joan said, shocked. 'Would they?'

'There's no statute of limitations on murder in Britain.' Jools raised her eyebrows.

Kit sighed. 'You know, I do feel like we paid for it, at least a little bit. With us. Our friendship. Having to leave the Land Army and keep apart to protect each other. I missed you all.' She flushed as she mumbled the last bit, but the others nodded.

There was a pause, then Joan said to Marigold, 'You covered for us. You lied to Manson to protect us even though you must have known . . . thought,' she amended, 'that we had . . .' She cleared her throat.

Marigold sighed and looked up at the painting. 'My life changed when you came to Winterbourne. Oliver dead, my mother effectively gone. And Guy – well, he was dying to go, too. I'm sure they loved me as best as they could given the circumstances, but it was like I wasn't even there. And then I met you. You were so alive, you talked, you were put upon and stood up for yourselves. And you,' she looked at Violet, 'you taught me how to laugh. You taught me how to *fly*, remember?' She smiled. 'There's always been a Crowden to run Winterbourne, that's what you said. I would never have imagined in my wildest dreams that it might one day be me, not until you told me. You set me on my path that day. And so I set you on yours. I know the kind of person Hardwick was; I know you didn't kill him in cold blood. You would never have done that. I was eight years old; it was simple.'

Something swelled through the group, then. A sigh of release. Someone blew their nose and Jools got up and made noises about finding a drink. But Marigold was still looking at Violet.

And then she nodded, a tiny up-and-down flick of her chin and Violet's eyes turned bright with tears, not the angry, noisy crying from before, but something softer that trembled across her face, her shoulders, made her lips press together until she leaned into Frankie and closed her eyes. She ran her fingers across the faint silver scars on her arms, slowly, gently, and when she sighed, the air was warm on Frankie's cheek.

'There's still time for us to be together,' Marigold said softly. 'To talk about it. There's no danger any more. Myra has passed away, no one else is around. No one will ever know about that night.'

Frankie's insides froze. There was a small movement below her and she caught Con's eyes, stricken with alarm. He gave a small jerk of his head and she knew she had to speak. Carefully she disentangled herself from Violet, sat up. 'The thing is—'

'Excuse me, is anyone home?'

It was a polite drawl with a hint of gruffness, and the tall, slim figure of Max Sefton stood in the open doorway.

He came towards them in the way he always moved, with that long-legged, confident stride, a big, open smile on his face. If he had caught Frankie a few hours ago, back at the *London Post*, on territory that belonged to him and Hugo, she might have hesitated, tried to make it work, been everything to all people, the way she had always done. But it was different here. Maybe because all these weeks she'd been trying to wade through a morass of things on her own, and now she was no longer alone. Maybe it was seeing her dad for what he was for the first time. Maybe it was seeing her grandmother for what *she* was for the first time. Or maybe Violet had finally set Frankie on her path, the way she'd set Marigold on hers so many years ago.

Behind her, she caught the words *looking for trouble* and *scandal* as Con muttered a hasty explanation, but then she was up and advancing on Max.

'How dare you show up here, after everything, how *dare* you.'

Max had blinked into the hallway, clearly momentarily blinded by the sunlight falling in through the back doors. When he heard Frankie's voice, he twitched and the colour drained from his face.

'Frankie?' She could see him trying to get his bearings, perhaps searching for yet another string of lies designed to manipulate her.

'Get out,' she said furiously. 'You have no right to be here. Leave Violet the hell alone.'

As Max groped for words, his eyes flicked from her to the wall behind her. She whirled around, glanced at the portrait, turned back to see him studying her intently. Intently, but not surprised, she realised. He had seen this before.

'You came here after I showed you the photo that night, didn't you?' she said in a choked voice. 'Didn't you?' she shouted, so loudly that everyone, not just Max, flinched.

'He was here last week,' Marigold said. 'Said he was doing a piece for a series on country houses; he showed me what they'd already published. I thought he was going to write about my business, my horses.' She fixed him with a calm but direct gaze.

'It was Hugo's idea,' Max said urgently. 'And at first it didn't seem so terrible. He was only after an interview with your grandmother because she'd been so . . . well, so reclusive.' He gave a strange little bow in Violet's direction, which was met with a stony expression. 'He asked me to ease you into things. I figured you could use a friend, and—'

'I don't need easing into anything,' Frankie bellowed, 'least of all into a piece on my own grandmother, under a byline that isn't even mine.'

'I think he would have given up,' Max said quickly, 'if he hadn't seen that photo. You *showed* him the photo. He rang me right away, made me come over to the office that very night and talk to you. He can sniff things a mile off, you know that as well as I do. And then he was like a man possessed; it took on a life of its own. He wanted that story, and the more details surfaced, the more he wanted it. But it had to come from you, at least partly, because – well, the byline.' He flushed a deep red. 'So I was supposed to coax it out of you and supply the rest, but then it ended up being so different to what I thought . . . *you* ended up being so different, us . . .'

'There *is* no us.' Frankie was no longer shouting, and she hated the catch in her voice. 'God, I fell right into your trap, didn't I? And to think I was lapping it all up, every little bit of praise, was devastated at every criticism, when it never had anything to do with me or my writing at all. For Hugo, it was all about Violet from the very beginning, and for you, it was about saving your ass at that paper. No wonder you were always so calm when things around us got more fraught every day. I thought you were amazing, how you were still able to laugh and joke around; I *envied* you. And all along it was because you knew that *your* job was secure.'

The group around her muttered and moved. Anyone else might have backed away in the face of such dislike, but Max looked straight at Frankie, not apologetically, not desperately.

'And what would *you* have done in my place?' he asked evenly.

'I found the overseer's murky death buried in the local papers, the land girls leaving the Land Army all at the same time. Your grandmother happening to be here, under a false name, when she said she'd been in Yorkshire. Your mother born less than a year later, actually *in* Yorkshire. And then this portrait that looked like you. Frankie, you're a journalist, tell me, what would *you* have done?'

She stared at him, then shook her head, dragged a hand hard across her eyes. 'I'd like to think I'd have done the right thing,' she said.

'You pitted against Hugo?' Max infused the words with such pointed meaning that Frankie flushed with shame, because if she was being brutally honest with herself, she didn't have a clue what she'd have done.

'I did try to stop it.' He leaned forward to force her to look at him. 'I tried to redirect him.'

'When? When you encouraged me to set up the reunion and drove Joan down? *Reliving memories does help*,' she mimicked him. 'When you loaned me the Polaroid camera, oh-so-bloody-thoughtful, and then stole the photo when I wasn't looking? And now, to top it all off, you're *here*, come to gather up the final debris?'

Silence fell across the hallway. From the stable yard, a whinny and a clop floated across, and behind them, the sun moved a fraction, dimming the light in the hall.

'I think you should leave.' Marigold drew herself up when it was clear that Frankie was done. 'I'm withdrawing any and all material, and I will sue you from here to the ends of the earth if you so much as mention Winterbourne in that paper of yours.'

'And you obviously know that if you hint at my name or those of these ladies in conjunction with any of this, or in any other way, so will I.' Violet's voice was hoarse but steady.

'Give me back the picture.' Frankie held out her hand, for a wild minute still hoping he could explain it all, would reveal a whole other story, a story where he was triple-crossing someone else, where he had befriended her because he liked her for herself, where he had kissed her because they had a future.

Slowly he leafed through the file in his bag, extracted the Polaroid photo.

'I wish it could have been different.' He held it out to her, then he turned and left.

Sixty-One

'Child, you don't need to sit with me,' Violet said tiredly. 'I just want to be alone for a bit, close my eyes.'

'I won't leave you. And I'm so sorry about Max and the paper, about not telling you. I tried to make it go away, but I should have stood up to Hugo more. It's just all been . . .' Frankie scanned Violet's face, alarmed at how drained her grandmother seemed, how small and frail she looked lying on a bed in one of the upstairs bedrooms. After Max had left, she had slumped down on the bench, not fainting precisely, but deflating, as if whatever had propped her up and kept her going all these weeks had vanished, leaving a shell behind.

'Go, be with Marigold,' Violet looked up at Frankie. 'You two have a lot to talk about.'

Frankie hesitated. 'Did, I mean, what did Gramps know about all this?' she then asked, quickly, before she could change her mind.

Violet didn't answer immediately. 'Duffy was a very special man,' she finally said. 'And he was right for me in the way that Guy never would have been. What Guy and I had, it was like a fire, intense and overwhelming. I was young and reckless, I threw myself into it. But I was always Lily then, Guy never truly knew *me*. Duffy did. He was there when Romy died, he was there when my mother dragged me to Yorkshire and my father died that same winter. I couldn't have done it without Duffy. He ended up being the love of my life, all the more because he took Stella, too.'

Frankie thought back to her indulgent, good-humoured grandfather.

'Don't let it change your memory of him,' Violet said quietly when she saw Frankie's face. 'He never had any regrets, there was no drama. We were part of the same world, we grew up together, and when I went back to London with Stella, we were married.'

Marigold was waiting just outside the door. 'How is she?'

Frankie marvelled how, after all that had happened in the last few hours, Marigold could still be so calm. The others had filled Frankie and Con in on more of the story surrounding Hardwick – clearly not all of it, but enough for Frankie's insides to twist with sadness and rage.

'She's not been well, you know,' she said. She found it a little difficult, actually, to look at Marigold. Her great-aunt, she kept reminding herself, but also a stranger.

'She told us.' Marigold nodded as they walked down the stairs.

'She did?' Frankie stopped, her hand on the banister. 'Everything?'

'Her illness.' Marigold nodded. 'That she doesn't think she has all that much time. That she needs help.'

'She *said* all that?' Frankie was flooded by a surge of relief that made her knees go weak. For the first time in weeks, she realised how much Violet's insistence on secrecy had isolated both of them, how Violet's refusal to acknowledge the reality of things had fuelled Frankie's own denial.

'I've tried to help her,' she mumbled, 'but . . .'

Marigold squeezed her hand and nodded. 'Let's walk a little. The girls took your friend Conrad to see the horses.' She smiled. 'Their idea, not his. I've asked Molly to stay upstairs. She'll hear Violet if she calls out. Nothing can happen to her here.'

They walked slowly through the gardens, the breeze warm on their backs.

'You know,' the older woman said conversationally, 'I wonder if he really is all bad, your Mr Sefton.'

'He's not my Mr Sefton,' Frankie said darkly.

'Maybe give him a chance to explain,' Marigold suggested. 'Properly. Not with all of us standing there, arms crossed, staring him down.' She laughed softly. 'Not much has changed, I can tell you that. Those girls are as feisty as they were back then. A good troop to have in your corner, but perhaps not the ideal setting for an honest conversation – or forgiveness.'

'If I never see him again, it'll be too soon,' Frankie said stonily.

Marigold stepped aside to let her go through a small gate. They didn't speak again for a bit, and Frankie was glad.

'The stables were rebuilt.' Marigold eventually broke the silence. 'But the orchards were sold off once I decided to step back. My husband is an ex-showjumper; he was keen to develop a yard.'

'Your husband?' Frankie asked.

'We have two sons, Olly and Benjamin. That's Ben over there.' She pointed at a tall man walking into the stable building. 'Do you want to meet him? After all, he's your cousin. Or is he your uncle? I never know what the right terminology is.'

Frankie hesitated. 'Would it be all right if I met him another time?'

'All a bit much, isn't it?' Marigold nodded. 'For me, too.'

'I sometimes wonder how much we can take in one go, before we . . .' Frankie broke off abruptly and stared up at the bell tower rising above the archway they had driven through earlier. The face of a sun was brightly if somewhat garishly painted, the pointer, glowing golden, threw a perfectly straight shadow across the clock face. And below it . . .

'*From Darkness, Light*,' she said softly.

'We recently had it restored,' Marigold told her. 'It's the family motto. Quite an apt one, don't you think? That after all the sadness and the loss, this . . .' she swept her hand around the stable yard, bright and cheerful in the sun, the sound of voices and laughter, 'is still here; we're here.'

Her face was serene, her step unhurried. But in her voice, Frankie heard all the things that were also there, the memories, the grief, the darkness thrown up by Violet and the others, the personal loss.

'Come, there's something I want to show you.' Marigold waved her on.

Frankie didn't think she'd ever seen a lovelier cemetery. The gentle incline was lush and green, the trees aflame in a riot of oranges and yellows, the breeze making leaves skip around the weathered old stones. The chapel looked serenely down at Winterbourne House, nestled amidst trees and parkland.

'This way.' Marigold walked up a small path towards a family plot sitting in pride of place below the chapel.

In loving memory of
Guy Winston Crowden
born 1919, died 1940

It was unexpected, the sharp pain Frankie felt as she crouched down, touched the slab of golden stone, blinked away tears. So young, she thought. Such a short but vital part of Violet's life, so much part of what her mind had been trying to unravel over the last few weeks.

Marigold had retreated, was busy assembling the things she'd gathered on their walk up: a few late wild flowers, sprigs of heather, some brightly coloured leaves and tall grasses.

'Pretty,' Frankie said, when she held out several small arrangements.

'A decorative but ultimately rather useless talent. Other people knit, I make posies for these . . .' She swept her hand across the plot, and Frankie's eyes travelled from Guy's stone further down the row.

Charles Aldrich Crowden
Margaret Seraphina Crowden, née Phillmore
Oliver Jonas Crowden

'For a long time, it was just me, surviving the war years here,' Marigold said softly. 'If I hadn't had Winterbourne, I don't think I could have borne it. Then I had my own family. And now you. And the girls – well,' she grinned at Frankie, 'women. Such a blessing.'

She tucked the posies along the row one by one, leaving Frankie to wonder how to count one's blessings in the face of so much death. But if anyone could do it, it was Marigold, she thought as the woman knelt at Oliver's grave, gently sweeping away some stray pebbles.

'Is he here too?' she suddenly asked.

Marigold didn't turn around, but her hand stilled in mid sweep. 'Yes,' she said.

Hardwick's grave was on the other side of the cemetery. A small plot, covered in grass.

'Myra isn't buried here?' Frankie asked.

'She never came back here, as far as I know.'

Marigold was already turning away, but Frankie lingered. The headstone was small. No *Beloved father* or even *Rest in peace*; just his name and two dates. Frankie shivered a little. No, Guy hadn't been the beginning of all that had happened; *this* was the beginning. And maybe not even this, but further back still, with Silvia Hardwick.

'The shrine they were talking about earlier, is it still here?' she asked.

Marigold shook her head. 'It was so long ago.'

They prowled across the lower part of the cemetery for a while, no longer the undergrowth Jools had described, but now filled with graves.

'I guess we should go,' Frankie finally sighed. 'Violet will be awake soon.'

Just then, she saw something. Not a grave, or a pretty, swirling pattern of pebbles, but a tree, stubbornly perched on a little overhang, its roots partly exposed. In the last sixty years, it must have leaned backwards to anchor itself, and right there, grown all the way into the roots, almost completely rusted away, was the neck of an old milk churn. There was nothing else, obviously, and even this would be gone before long, but it too belonged to the story, and Frankie was glad she had seen it.

'I wonder when Max's piece is going to break,' Frankie said as they weaved back through the orchards towards the house.

'Surely they can't run it when we're against it?' Marigold said, aghast.

'Course they can,' Frankie snorted. 'Not your quotes and things, but he can connect the dots with what's in the public domain. He's good at that, he and Hugo.'

She thought about Hugo, wondered whether Max had already rung him to say that she wasn't sick at all but intent on sabotaging things, was choosing Violet over her job. She imagined all of them at the editorial meeting, Victoria and Mallory, Hugo's fifteen-second pitches, Felicity striding about as if she owned the place.

'Will you go back there?' Marigold asked. 'It doesn't sound like the healthiest working environment, if you ask me.'

'To put it mildly.' Frankie grimaced. 'But I think nothing will ever change if you just retreat and let them get away with things.' She thought about the job evaluations and sighed. 'It might be a moot issue anyway. But I have financial commitments. I'll need to take care of my dad for a bit. And Violet doesn't have much money . . .'

'You could stay here with us, at least for a while.' Marigold was striving to sound casual, but Frankie could hear how much she wanted them to do that. It made her both happy and sad.

'We couldn't,' she said gently. 'Not that it's not the nicest offer anyone's made me in a while. We'll stay tonight if that's all right with you, but then we'll have to sort things out in London. Violet needs her home around her, familiarity, calm; I need to check in with Dr Morrissey and see where we are with our NHS appointments. I've stuck my head in the sand for too long already; it's time to get proper help. But we will come and see you as often as we can. After all, it's just a car ride away.'

She imagined herself and Violet in the Hillman Hunter, driving across the valley towards Winterbourne House, and the thought filled her with a surge of joy.

They were on the final stretch back towards the terrace doors, still open in the sun, when Marigold paused.

'I'm going to walk for a little while longer, but you go on, check on Violet and the others. I'm sure Molly will have some tea ready.' She fished for something in her pocket. 'And would you give this to Violet before I forget?'

A silver chain dangled from her fingers, a flat silver disc ringed with diamonds.

'I got it back after they closed the investigation into Hardwick's death,' she explained. 'Manson was always suspicious – he was so horrid anyway – but without a witness, they didn't have enough evidence. Afterwards, I wanted to send it to her – I had sent that photo of them all – but it seemed too precious to just put in the post. And,' she smiled ruefully, 'maybe I was hoping that one day I'd get the opportunity to give it back to her in person.'

Sixty-Two

For a week, they waited for the land girl story to break.

'Anything?' Marigold asked when Frankie rang her, as she now did every other evening. Marigold was so unflustered, so calm, just hearing her voice made Frankie's heart beat more slowly.

'Anything?' Joan asked when she called to chat with Violet, and Frankie answered the phone.

'Surely, it's got to be any day now?' Kit grumbled when she came for a visit.

'This must be their new form of torture.' Jools brought Frankie a cup of tea, set it down on the table in the drawing room. 'They're waiting for us to storm the building, fling ourselves at their feet and beg for the story to be published, just to get it over with.'

'I have no idea what's going on.' Frankie chewed her lip. 'Con said there's not been any mention of it around the newsroom at all; it's as if it just died all of a sudden.'

'Is he really leaving London?' Jools wanted to know. 'I liked that young man. Such good taste in clothes.'

'He says he'll stay if I will.' Frankie looked down at the papers and photos she had spread out on the table. 'And I think I will. I'll try, at least.'

'Oh, Frankie love, I don't think that's a good idea,' Jools said. 'Bad people will be bad people.'

'How can you still say that after all that happened at Winterbourne?' Frankie said impatiently. 'Being bullied and pushed around like that? You didn't take it lying down, did you?'

'Yes, and look how *that* turned out,' Jools said soberly. 'You don't have to stay there, Violet knows so many people, I'm sure she can help you get a new . . . All right, all right.' She held up her hands when she saw Frankie's face. 'Forget I mentioned it.'

'I'm going back even if Hugo makes me turn right around and queue up for unemployment. It's the only way I can square it with myself.'

There were quite a few things she needed to square with herself, actually, which was why she was still out with 'the flu'.

First and foremost, there was Violet. She had been up and down, sometimes alert down to the tiniest detail, other times vague and withdrawn. And while overall there was a sense of relief at finally being free from the sole responsibility for Hardwick's death, it seemed to have taken an inordinate toll on her. She seemed perpetually exhausted, and Frankie didn't want to leave her much.

And then there was her dad's return. He'd sounded more nervous, less deliriously excited about *freedom's golden wings* when she'd last talked to him, pressing her on what part she would play in his *journey back to life*, which she took to mean would she live with him for a bit.

'I've found you a room to rent and I'll visit as much as I can, but I have to be with Violet now,' she said, resolutely refusing to acknowledge the faint note of hurt that crept into his voice when he said goodbye. It was taking a bit of practice to be firm, just as it was taking a bit of practice not to care whether she was doing right by him. But if the last couple of weeks had shown her anything, it was the impossibility of doing right by everyone, not when everyone and everything was constantly at war with each other. How could she stand up to people and try to please them; how could she keep Violet's secrets and service Hugo's demands for full exposure; know about Violet's illness and refuse to acknowledge it at the same time? She didn't have a chance in hell of ever making all that work, and after twenty-eight years of trying to do exactly that, she was exhausted.

So she was going to stop, she had decided. It was time to be not in the middle of things, but to find her own place, and she'd come up with an idea of how to get started.

Two days later, Frankie stepped out of the lift and walked towards the newsroom. It was early, just gone eight, but Hugo was always in the office ahead of everyone else and she preferred not to have an audience.

He'd been absorbed in reading something on his desk. His shirt collar was open, his sharp face relaxed in concentration. For a moment, she stood there, remembering her first day here, seeing Hugo across the crowded conference room, her whole body quivering with anticipation and admiration, her stammer slamming into her throat when he first pointed his finger at her.

She moved her tongue experimentally now, breathed out long and slow, smiling at the memory of her grandmother's fierce face as she chanted:

When ye fight with a Wolf of the Pack, ye must fight him
alone and afar,
Lest others take part in the quarrel, and the Pack be diminished
by war.

'An early bird, just like myself.' His voice cut through the fading echo of the ballad.

'G-g-good morning.' Frankie forced herself to sound as steady as she could. She might not, strictly speaking, be unafraid of this conversation, but she certainly wasn't quivering. 'I wanted to talk to you.'

'You're all better, then?' He smiled blandly, but out of the corner of her eye she caught a flicker as his nails dug into the blotter. So not quite bland, she thought, and drew herself up.

'Yes, much better, thank you.' Uninvited, she entered, sat down. 'I have a proposition for you.'

'Do you really think you're in a position to make a proposition?' he enquired. He held up the paper he'd been working on. It was a list of names, some crossed out, others heavily annotated. 'Events have slightly overtaken your return to the fold, dear heart. You might find yourself out—'

'I have a p-proposition for you,' she repeated. She took a deep breath and let the rest of the letters out slowly. 'You can take it or leave it, it's your choice.'

She opened her bag, took out a thin stack of pages stapled together inside a clear plastic sleeve, with a few photos on top.

His eyes narrowed on the sleeve, saw the Polaroid images, the text.

'Go on,' he said grudgingly.

Frankie took a deep breath. 'Violet is in the early stages of dementia.'

He made a small movement, perhaps surprise, perhaps dismay, but she didn't wait for him to say anything that would be potentially hurtful.

'That's why she's been withdrawing from things. She's going to be retiring from all her projects and will no longer be out and about. She'll be releasing a more detailed statement imminently. I, however,' she paused, 'am offering you an opportunity to publish a first and last personal interview with her. If – and only if – you agree to all my terms.'

She didn't think she could go any redder, her face flaming and sweaty, because it was one thing to decide to stand up to people, another entirely to actually do it.

'Terms?' he repeated incredulously.

'It's your ch-choice.' She quickly slid the article out of the sleeve, holding it just out of his reach and fanning through the pages. 'Personal photos, not seen so far. And it'll be an exclusive. I'll need final approval, and your word – in writing – that this is the only thing about Violet that will ever appear in your paper, including in particular the land girl story. You may edit the interview; in fact,' she grimaced, 'I'd appreciate it if you would. It's not been easy to write. But I have final say, and no wrangling until I'm too exhausted to argue any more. And if you violate any of my terms, well, my grandmother may be losing her mind, but she still knows anyone and everyone in this city. It's only been with some difficulty that I've kept her from rolling up here looking for your blood.'

He studied her, his face unreadable. Then he suddenly gave a thin-lipped, displeased smile.

'Between you and Sefton, it's getting rather difficult to do my job these days.'

Frankie narrowed her eyes. 'Why?'

'Practically threatened me over that stupid story. Said all sorts of rude things about unethical behaviour. Ha. I'm all ethics, angel, until they stand in my way. But as it turned out, without your cooperation, it was a tad difficult for it all to hang together.'

He gave her a level look across the desk and she looked back at him, took in his narrow, pale face, the shock of white hair, the irritated set of his lips.

'Well then I guess we're done here,' she said quietly. 'I'll see myself out, shall I?'

She got up and turned. Behind her, he let out an exasperated sigh.

'All right, then, let's see the story.'

'Your word first. In writing.' She fished for the agreement Violet's lawyer had emailed her through just this morning. Hugo muttered something very rude.

'Why don't we call Legal now,' Frankie said. 'It's very straightforward.'

He picked up the phone with an irritated huff, and she sat back down.

'This is not how things are going to be in the future,' he said icily as they waited for someone called Michael to come down. 'Maybe we should put *that* into writing while we're at it.'

'The future?' She was so taken aback that she forgot to be aloof. 'What do you mean?'

'Well, before you came barging in here with your outrageous demands,' he swept his hand impatiently across the agreement, 'I was just lingering over your name. And I'm not sure why, because you brought all sorts of chaos into the newsroom and you go red any time anyone so much as looks at you and your public speaking skills are abysmal, but somehow my pen refuses to cross you out.'

'Yeah?' she said in a choked voice. 'And . . . ?'

'And I'm not liking *this*' – he waggled his hand back and forth between her and him – 'one bit. If you were to be lucky enough to stay on at the *Post* – which I'm not saying you are, because I might still change my mind – then let me assure you, dear one, that these demands and blackmail – and yes, that's exactly what it is, Miss Journalistic Ethics – is never happening again. I'm not having my writers barge in here and tell me what to do.'

He broke off and eyed her resentfully. 'Well?' he prompted.

Frankie blinked, tried to process what exactly Hugo, in his usual roundabout way, was saying, and what it was, deep down, that she really wanted herself. There was a knock on the door and a man stuck his head around it. 'You wanted a word?'

'Not really,' Hugo said darkly. 'But it looks like I'll have to. And I will call *you* back in a minute,' he told her. 'I suppose you'll want to get on with things. We need someone to cover the song contest finals next week.'

Frankie fought the hysterical urge to giggle, then she said, quickly, before she could lose courage, 'I haven't said I'm staying.'

For the first time since she'd known him, Hugo actually seemed at a loss for words. Then, to her great surprise, he leaned back in his chair, crossed his hands behind his head and nodded appreciatively.

'It looks like I've taught you well, Miss O'Brien.'

'No,' she said. 'It wasn't you who taught me that.'

*

Outside, she sagged against the wall, exhausted by this whole business of standing up for herself. Behind her, the indistinct murmuring rose and fell, and she walked down the corridor, towards the back door and into the newsroom. It had filled up since she had arrived, and she had to brace herself before walking purposefully towards a desk in the middle.

'Can I talk to you?'

Max's head snapped up.

'Of course,' he said once he'd recovered. 'Sit. Or how about a dishwater coffee in the canteen? Okay, too soon for jokes, I'm sorry. The back door?'

'Right here is fine,' Frankie said icily, and sat down in Victoria's as yet unoccupied chair, crossing her arms.

'So, the story is off,' Max offered. 'At least my part in it is off. Who knows what Hugo will do, but I'm really hop—'

'It's off,' she said forbiddingly. 'I've just spoken to him.'

He stared at her, went a little red. 'Okay,' he said uncertainly. 'I tried to ring you, you know, many times.'

'Hmm,' Frankie said. 'Harassing me, more like.'

'Yeah. Can't fault a guy for trying, though. And you did give me your number, don't forget; practically forced it on me.'

She narrowed her eyes at him and he stopped grinning immediately. 'And are you back for good, or—'

'None of your business,' she snapped.

He sighed and sank back against his chair just as Hugo appeared in the newsroom door, beckoning her over impatiently. She got up and would have managed to sweep away imperiously if Max hadn't grabbed her arm.

'I really am very sorry, Frankie,' he said. 'We never did get that drink and, well, the offer stands. You just let me know, okay?'

Epilogue

Frankie slotted her key into the door at Cavendish Place and let herself into the hall. It was midday, and this would be her last surreptitious lunchtime run, she had decided, if she was to have any chance of keeping her head above water at the *Post*. But when she'd seen the paper that morning, she hadn't been able to resist coming back and showing Violet right away.

She could hear Mrs Potter moving about, singing to herself, and she stood in the hallway savouring the quiet as she looked down at the folded-over newspaper in her hand.

From Darkness, Light

Frankie O'Brien in conversation
with Violet Etherington

There are moments in our lives when we are forced to take stock, the big crossroads of marriages, career changes, babies, deaths; when we look back at where we've come from to figure out where we might be headed. The older we get, the more we have behind us, until there comes a time when the end is in sight.

'I didn't want to see it. No one does, because it's much easier to pretend it couldn't possibly be happening. Not because I want to live for ever; no one can be so hubristic as to assume they might get that privilege. But because there's still so much I want to do and see and so much I'd like to remember. It is, perhaps, a blessing that dementia has so many forms, because there is no one recipe, no one path. You just have to take every day as it comes.'

Violet Philomena Etherington was born in 1923 as an only child, 'with some of the privileges, all of the societal demands and none of the money to go with it. I was barely seventeen when I was going to be married off to a very worthy – and wealthy – young man. Hard to believe it now, but back then, if your mother was determined, and mine certainly was, a daughter had little chance to stand up to her.'

The Blitz and her cousin's tragic death during an air raid put an abrupt stop to her mother's plans. 'I didn't think I could go on. It's trite to say, perhaps, but that's what it felt like. Like being imprisoned in yourself: in your own grief, the inevitability of an empty life stretching ahead, a love-less marriage looming. So I did the only thing available to a young woman at that time. I ran away and joined the Women's Land Army. Later, when my own beloved daughter died and I didn't think I could go on, I didn't have that luxury, because she'd left someone behind for me to take care of. A beloved granddaughter.'

The piece went on to talk about how Stella's accident had ripped apart her family, but how Frankie had lived with them and given them such joy. It highlighted Violet's many achievements, her determination to change what needed changing, her empathy, her compassion for the disenfranchised, the legacy she was going to leave behind. There was no mention of Hardwick or what had happened at Winterbourne; she didn't say anything about Guy or Myra. Instead, she talked about what was happening to her now and, guided by Frankie's questions, about what it felt like for your life to slowly disintegrate under a debilitating disease for which there was, ultimately, no cure and no future.

There were photos, too. A small one of Violet as a debutante, which she had grumbled about including but Hugo had insisted on; another one that Marigold had unearthed for them, taken on the night of the harvest feast and showing Jools and Violet in their Land Army uniforms. There was a picture of Violet, Stella and baby Frankie, and one of Violet opening a fundraiser for Safe Haven. And finally, the Polaroid of Frankie and Violet.

Frankie had retrieved the original photo as soon as they were done, had found a frame for it and placed it next to the picture of her parents. The pain when she looked at it had muted a little, the fear that something was slipping through her fingers wasn't quite as panicked any more. Because it was also a reminder that Violet was back in her life, that the past was the past but this was the here and now.

She looked up when she heard Mrs Potter come through from the back. 'Oh Frankie, didn't hear you come in. Your grandmother is downstairs.' She gave Frankie a pat and a smile as she passed, and Frankie clattered down the kitchen stairs.

When she didn't find Violet in the kitchen, she poked her head into the shelter. Violet was leaning against one of the shelves, eating chocolates.

'You're just in time.' She looked up. 'I'm not sure how much longer I could have held out. It's every woman for herself once you get to the bottom of a tin of Quality Street.'

She held out the tin and Frankie chuckled when she saw that it was mostly empty, except for all the Strawberry Delights, which they both hated, and two Green Triangles.

'What have you got there?' Violet nodded at the newspaper in Frankie's hand.

'It's the interview.' Frankie held it out to her. 'It looks wonderful.'

Violet didn't open the paper; she just held it in her hand as if weighing it, then gently set it on top of the closest memory box on the shelf opposite.

'You don't want to read it?' Frankie frowned. From here, the photo of the four land girls was just visible around the fold.

'It was very good, and thankfully, I still remember it from last week,' Violet said. 'That is, I remember now.' She sighed and offered Frankie the last Green Triangle. 'One day I'll look at all these,' she jabbed her thumb at the boxes, 'and I'll have no clue who that person actually is.'

There were any number of things Frankie could have said, any number of things she could have told herself, too: that there was still hope, that it might be ages, that they would make the most of it. Instead, she leaned back against the mound of blankets behind her and split the chocolate triangle in two, held half out to Violet.

'Let's just take each day as it comes.'

Author's Note

For centuries, war has broken apart traditional structures among men and women, and it was no different during the Second World War. With men called to the front, many women leapt at the chance to leave the confines of typically female jobs. They manned searchlights to track enemy planes, plotted air raid formations and worked in factories producing Spitfires. They flew aircraft between airbases, drove ambulances, supply lorries, messenger motorcycles – and they drove tractors. When Britain was threatened by the German blockade and desperately needed to increase its food production, posters of smiling girls holding hay rakes or feeding lambs called women from all walks of life to replenish the diminishing agricultural workforce and join the Women's Land Army.

'Readers love land girls,' Max tells Frankie, and it's never been truer than today, when, among the Second World War icons, Land Girls are as instantly recognisable as Spitfire pilots or Dad's Army. With their cheerful grins, green and beige uniforms, can-do attitude and wartime grit, they've become emblematic of a nation that pulled together against a common enemy and prevailed.

It's a lovely image of a national treasure, but once I started to research its history, I realised that it wasn't necessarily always bracing spirits, sunny skies and kindly farmers' wives.

Farming in England in the late 1930s and 1940s was undeniably the domain of men. In most places, farmers still lived and worked the way they'd done for centuries: hard physical labour from dawn to dusk. Women in breeches, especially ones demanding a salary, weren't always welcome here, regardless of what the Ministry of Agriculture and Fisheries suggested or what wartime circumstances demanded. Farmers' wives and daughters often resented the land girls' relative independence and autonomy, not to mention the fact that they were being paid for the kind of work (and often drudgery) they themselves had to do for free. Especially at the beginning of the war, rural communities suspicious of outsiders and driven by misogynistic prejudice saw land girls as spoilt city madams with potentially rather loose morals, who would ensnare their men with big-city wiles and who couldn't be relied upon to do proper work but would give up when the going got tough.

The land girls' reception on the job echoes some of the difficulties the WLA had from its very beginning. It was a voluntary organisation rather than a military one, so land girls were employed directly by the farmers, and often worked twice as hard with less remuneration and fewer perks than the armed forces. It was a one-rank force, and with the exception of becoming a forewoman or being rewarded for length of service, there was no opportunity for advancement.

All in all, personal experiences of being a land girl seemed to have differed as widely as the farmers they worked for. But for every memory of cheerful friendships, village socials and the easier aspects of farming life, there were also tales of bullying, disillusionment and homesickness. And when the war was over, most land girls went back to their lives without a fraction of the public recognition that the rest of the services received and that the land girls would have deserved in spades.

Because what made them so extraordinary, at least in my view, is that through it all, they just got on with it. Doggedly, cheerfully, stubbornly, the land girls worked to feed England while quietly fighting one of the first battles in the war of the sexes. They were so good at sticking things out that by 1942–3, the deeply held prejudices against them started to change into grudging realisation that they often worked harder and were more conscientious and adaptable than male workers – even if they did wear breeches.

I hadn't planned to write a book about the Women's Land Army. To the contrary, when I first started out, I wanted to write a story about freedom: the freedom to leave your world behind versus the freedom to grow into what you are meant to be, and whether it's possible to run away from either one. But at some point, the land girls cheerfully muscled in and took over, turning it into a story about friendship, too: about belonging, being a small part of something big and ultimately being lifted up by it to find your way.

If you'd like to read more about the WLA, there are many interesting accounts of what life was like as a land girl: Nicola Tyrer's *They Fought in the Fields* (The History Press); Virginia Nicholson's *Millions Like Us* (Penguin); Joan Mant's *All Muck, No Medals* (Amberley), to name just a few. On debutantes and society girls, you'll enjoy Anne de Courcy's *Debs at War* (Weidenfeld & Nicolson) and *1939: The Last Season* (Phoenix). Of books on the Battle of Britain and the London Blitz, my favourites are Juliet Gardiner's *Wartime Britain* (Headline Review) and *The Blitz* (Harper Press), as well as Patrick Bishop's *Battle of Britain* (Quercus).

Acknowledgements

Writing a book is an intensely solitary experience and yet impossible to do without the help of many hands. I'd very much like to thank

– my wonderful agent Caroline at Hardman & Swainson, for plot help and bracing talks

– the brilliant team at Headline, especially my editors Marion, Jess, Claire and Jane for making all the magic happen.

– Jenny and my mum, for being my very first readers; my dad for all-round support

– my husband and boys, for always respecting the sign on my door that says *Do Not Disturb* and for offering many a creative solution to knotty plot problems.

But most of all, I'm grateful to you, my lovely readers. Many of you have written to me after my first books to ask questions or say hello, and seeing an email ping into my inbox always puts a smile on my face. So please get in touch if you fancy a chat, I can be reached at nikola@nikolascott.com.

Once a month, I send out a newsletter, talking about what I'm currently reading, watching and working on. There are behind-the-scenes peeks at my desk, signed book giveaways, the occasional short story freebie and lots of pictures! Please sign up and be a part of it all, I'd love to have you.

Nikola

Sign up for my monthly newsletter:
www.nikolascott.com

And don't miss Nikola Scott's unforgettable
Summer of Secrets...

'Beautifully written' *Daily Mail*

August, 1939

At peaceful Summerhill, orphaned Maddy hides from the world and the rumours of war. Then her adored sister Georgina returns from a long trip with a new friend, the handsome Victor. Maddy fears that Victor is not all he seems, but she has no idea just what kind of danger has come into their lives ...

Today

Chloe is newly pregnant. This should be a joyful time, but she is fearful for the future, despite her husband's devotion. When chance takes her to Summerhill, she's drawn into the mystery of what happened there decades before. And the past reaches out to touch her in ways that could change everything ...

Available to buy now in paperback and ebook

REVIEW